Cowgirl Witness & Her Bodyguard

A Western Romance

Mark E Scott

Contents

Cowgirl Witness & Her Bodyguard: A Western Romance

Book Formatting and Cover Work by Trisha Fuentes

PUBLISHER'S NOTE

This is a work of fiction. Names, characters, places, and incidents either are the product of the author's imagination or are used fictitiously, and any resemblance to actual persons, living or dead, business establishments, events, or locales is entirely coincidental.

The author does not have any control over and does not assume any responsibility for author or third-party Web sites or their content.

If you purchased this book without a cover you should be aware that this is stolen property. It was reported as "unsold and destroyed" to the publisher and neither the author nor the publisher has received any payment for this "stripped book."

ISBN: 979-8-986752853 (Paperback)

Created with Vellum

Praise for Mark E. Scott

Cowboy Takes Flight

Very well written, well thought out romance/action story. It held my interest throughout! Great Book!!

— Thomas N. Duncan

I really enjoyed the book. You certainly have a gift for bringing your characters to life. Throughout the book, I assumed you either had to do a great deal of research and/or have had a huge range of experiences.

— Cindy Anne

(Sometimes), I have a difficult time grasping the plot and each of the characters. That has not been the case with *Cowboy Takes Flight*. By the end of the second chapter, I knew that I would really enjoy the characters and the pace. Since I have little, if any imagination, I am fascinated by the plot that you created. You certainly are gifted. Unbelievable!!!

— Cindy Anne

I really enjoyed *Cowboy Takes Flight*, read it twice. Your writing is everybit as good as the bestselling authors, except for Steinbeck. The Black Hawk scenes were fun, but I wondered why Montana's furlough lasted so long?

— Duane Arthur

Obsessed with A Rodeo Cowboy

Interesting story and fun to read.

— Thomas N. Duncan

The Felinius Healer

An outstanding first book-combining intrigue, new concepts about future worlds and a compelling storyline, the author kept my interest! I look forward to the next (Felinius) adventure!!

— Bryan Hutchinson

Lone Rock Cowboy

The steer roping scenes in *Lone Rock Cowboy* brought back vivid memories of summer camp. I taught horseback riding, saddled horses, and led them through Michigan trails. Western tales and horsemanship stories interest me, and this is one of them.

— Duane Arthur

Stunt Action Cowboy

Very good story, kept my interest throughout.

— Thomas N. Duncan

Dragon Cowgirl

This was the first of two fantasy novels I purchased of books written by Mark Scott. He has made a excellent story intertwine in the old west. My Dad was a Western Book dealer, and so I enjoy Mark's books intensely. Very fun reading with a bit of mystical fantasy! Well done Mark!

— Thomas N. Duncan

Victorian Cowgirl and Latent Dragon

This is a very good, fun packed fantasy novel with never ending twists. It is a must read indeed!

— Thomas N. Duncan

Praise for *Lady Warrior and the Billionaire*

Screaming Wuss indeed! Eden Beauregard lives in his bubble world of re-enactments and antiquities. His easy, safe life with his aging grandfather makes him happy.

Blaze & Angel are shapeshifters who share one body, but are two completely different women that want to be freed from the deadly life of espionage and killing. With the promise of that freedom, they must collect four mystic weapons.

Love at first sight... As soon as Blaze walks into the Antiquity Shop, she does the one thing that most women have been unable to do; catch the attention of Eden Beauregard.

From that point on, Eden's life gets thrown and turned upside down with each historic weapon He and his Lady Spy acquires.

With the Relics and the help of Eden's Grandfather, Henri, will Blaze & Angel be free? Will Eden be able to love two women equally? And why is he called The Screaming Wuss?

Mark E. Scott has done it again! What an excellent read!

Set in the southern historic states of Virginia & The Carolina Outer Banks, you will be transported to a world of spies and mayhem wrapped up with magic and love.

With an Adult Anime feel, this Antebellum Novel has everything to keep you reading till the end.

Enjoy the Magical & Realistic World of Beauty, Romance, Cars, Guns and so much more!

I Loved Reading 'Lady Warrior And The Billionaire'!

Brenda-Marie Whitehead,
Author, Actress, Co-owner of BrenRock Productions LLC,
Film Festival Director and Screenwriter

Praise for *Arizona Cowgirl*

A Whirlwind Romance Between Two Soulmates, Brought Together By The Grace Of God!

God has a plan for us all...you just have to listen.

Ryder Prescott is a rodeo cowboy who talks to God. On his wedding day, he asked God to bring forth his bride. The heavens opened, and God showed him a vision of a different woman.

Tragedy hit Ryder right in the heart. He blames God and turns his back. The Badman's alter ego takes over, but his heart turns to stone. Never again will he be broken. From now on, the stud cowboy concentrates on nothing but rodeo.

Ava O'Conner is about to graduate from college. One night, she rappels off a mountain, and fear seizes her. She receives God's calling while hanging off a cliff.... Three years later, Ava graduates with honors from seminary.

Ava asks God for a sign, unsure of her future or where to begin. While sleeping, Ava is given a vision. She follows her family to the Arizona high country and meets the man in her dreams...

When Ryder meets Ava, there is no doubt their connection runs deep. Will Ava, who has no knowledge of Western life, be able to serve as the new lady shepherd? Will she succeed in winning Ryder's stone-cold heart? And the greatest challenge, can she bring him into God's light?

Mark E. Scott has true talent. I loved reading *Arizona Cowgirl and the Badman!* I relished each page to see what came next!

Brenda-Marie Whitehead,
Author, Actress, Co-Owner of BrenRock Production LLC,
Film Festival Director, and Screenwriter

Praise for *Victorian Cowgirl and Latent Dragon*

If you are a fan of Science Fiction, Fantasy, Steampunk, Western World, or Hot Steamy Love Stories, this Book is for you! You will not only fall in love with the characters but with the world in which it is set. MARK E. SCOTT masterfully transforms you back in time with a stunning 5 Star adventure into two parallel worlds.

I Highly Recommend 'Victorian Cowgirl and Latent Dragon: A Western Fantasy'!!!

ONCE YOU BEGIN, YOU CAN'T STOP TILL IT ENDS!!!

Meet Chance, an orphaned cowboy with a passion for ranching. Raised by Jackson and Lyndsey Cordell, Chance wants nothing more than to make them proud. Jackson and Lyndsey are heading to Colorado Springs to join up with their adoptive daughter, Missy. The Cordells want to start a new life while Chance stays behind and sells off the ranch. He will leave Canada and meet them in the Rockies.

Meet Charity and Cheyenne; two personalities, one woman. A lady seer has spent 400 years training young lords to become warriors. She prepares them for future battles against the dark fae. But with each shapeshifting soldier they have trained, she has yet to find her lifemate. Now, she is tasked to protect Chance, bring out his latent dragon, and teach him to become the warrior he is meant to be.

At first, Chance wants nothing of it. But once it happens, Chance realizes that no matter how much he fears change, he has no choice but to accept it. For he knows it is the right thing. Along the way, Chance falls in love with Charity and, later, Cheyenne. Both women prove they can work a farm and raise cattle as well as any man. Months later, the cattle are sold, and the money is wired. It is time to travel to Colorado and join the family. Chance's biggest fear is what his family will think of Charity and Chey. After arriving, Chance finds that his worries are for nothing. His family accepts Chance's wingmate as one of their own. And even Missy comes to love Cheyenne like a sister.

Chance learns that his family has been keeping secrets and must accept that even with magic, there is more out there than he ever thought possible.

Can Chance make a life as a shapeshifter and a rancher and still make his father proud? Can he settle down and make both Charity and Cheyenne his wife? With love and family understanding, anything can happen.

Brenda-Marie Whitehead,
Author, Actress, Co-Owner of BrenRock Productions LLC,
Film Festival director, and screenwriter

Mark E. Scott

Film Festival Awards

The Wild Bunch Film Festival in Willcox, Arizona

TWBFF 2021 Best Western Sci-fi/Fantasy Manuscript:
Dragon Cowgirl: A Western Fantasy

TWBFF 2021 Best Western Romance Manuscript-2nd Place
Stunt Action Cowboy: A Salt Fork Novel

TWBFF 2022 Best Fantasy Romance Western Manuscript
Lady Warrior and the Billionaire

The Cowpoke International Film Festival in Electra, Texas

CIFF 2022 Best Western Fantasy Manuscript
Victorian Cowgirl and Latent Dragon: A Western Fantasy

CIFF 2022 Best Romance Manuscript
Savant Cowgirl and Her Lumberjack: A Colorado Novel

The Sunny Side Up Film Festival in Miami, Oklahoma

SSUFF 2023 Best Modern Western Sci-Fi Fantasy Action Romance Manuscript

Hawaiian Warrior and the Sea Dragon

SSUFF 2023 Third Place Movie Poster

Hawaiian Warrior and the Sea Dragon

The Wild Bunch Film Festival in Tucson, Arizona

TWBFF 2023 Best Sci-Fi Romance Manuscript

Dark Walker and Hidden Dragon: Dragon Fantasy Romance

TWBFF 2023 Best Modern Western Romance Manuscript

Arizona Cowgirl and the Badman: A Western Romance

DEDICATION

Jennifer Castillo loves strong, leading women, high-powered action, and steamy love scenes. And my leading lady, Desiree DeNiro, won't disappoint. Jennifer permitted me to hit the power scenes at full throttle, and that's precisely what I did.

Acknowledgments

This novel is dedicated to my loving wife, Jeanie Somerville Scott, who has supported me emotionally and physically after my spinal cord injury. The author is getting around a lot better with continued therapy and healing. Jeanie has enjoyed all of my cowboy romance and dragon fantasies. She has spent countless weekends performing the final edit. She has inspired my Western series with *Western Horseman* and *Cowboys and Indians*. I don't know where I would be without her. Jeanie has had my back and been two steps ahead of me. She is much loved and cherished.

This novel is also dedicated to the life of Nancy Scott, my mother, who participated in reading my grade school papers. She encouraged me to compose critiques and to do my homework faithfully. She proofread my essays and bought one of my first typewriters. May she be blessed in the afterlife.

Acknowledgment goes to my father, Duane Scott, who enjoyed all of my stories. He had an active imagination and excellent visualization skills. In former novels, the scenes of horsemanship reminded him of summer camp. He tutored young horsemen to ride the wilds of Northern Michigan. In our conversations, he wished he had continued riding. It was a hobby he truly enjoyed. After a forty-seven-day battle with Covid-19, the Lord took him home to be with his bride. I will cherish our conversations and always remember that he loved my westerns and fantasies.

Prologue and Disclaimer

The Western Romance story of *Cowgirl Witness & Her Bodyguard* is situated in Pine Whisper, Oregon. Lieutenant Desiree DeNiro makes a remarkable journey from a PTSD combat pilot to a Cutting Horse Champion.

However, her journey from terrifying nightmares to emotional stability didn't occur overnight. It all started out in Desert Sage, California. The bronze beauty landed her LifeNet helo and witnessed the execution of Tinder Williams.

Antonio Gonzalez gunned down a handsome, bronze athlete; and Desiree had to make sure that justice prevailed. She met with the local police, identified the murderer, and vowed to testify.

While spending her first night in a safe house, the syndicate hostiles took over the building. She was sequestered in a bedroom when hitmen assaulted her and tried to rape her.

Seconds away from the worst form of violation, Dayo Cazador blew through the outside wall. The Marine headhunter gunned down her assailants, and her rapist was terminated instantly.

From then on, Lieutenant DeNiro was focused on retaliation and survival. She teamed up with the fearless Marine, and they blew the safe house to bits. They took down the syndicate hostiles, blew up the convoy, and made a run for it.

This is an exciting survival story where Desiree and Dayo flee California and seek out a remote horse ranch. More than seven hundred miles away, she learns to pursue the important things. And through her struggle, the valiant pilot is presented with a once-in-a-lifetime opportunity.

Cowgirl Witness & Her Bodyguard touches on a number of Western and military themes. One theme of particular interest is the role that therapy dogs play.

In the case of epilepsy, a seizure-alert dog can anticipate the onset of an episode. There's a change in chemical scents, which alert the canine that a seizure is at hand. In the same vein, Desiree DeNiro suffered from post-traumatic nightmares.

Typically, horrifying flashbacks last between six months to a year. When the Lieutenant met a Belgian Malinois named Molly, her pupper was already accustomed to helping others.

Molls leaped into action, noted the lingering scent, and knew exactly how to proceed. Whenever Desiree reeled from a terrifying episode, her Malinois barked furiously and bathed her in doggie kisses. The onslaught of a good facial bath woke Desi up. And bit by bit, she learned to sleep the entire night.

In this story, the author chose a veteran Malinois. Molly had a strong work ethic and was continually on the alert. Achtung!

Not only did her dog's sense of loyalty and intelligence make her a great military dog, but Molls enabled her to face her deepest anxieties. And to top it off, her pupper knew the Schutzhund commands, so training was a piece of cake.

Real PTSD wounded warriors constitute as much as twenty percent of those veterans who served in the Middle East. Donations can be sent to the Wounded Warrior Project at woundedwarriorproject.org. The author makes contributions during the holidays. So, let's never forget these brave men and women who served our country.

In the story, *Cowgirl Witness & Her Bodyguard*, the author makes reference to Captain Cazador. He's a member of the Marine Raiders, a special force unit that terminates hostile leaders.

Even though the Marines have been named, the primary reason is that the word "Marine" fits easily into my literary style. The author has equal respect for all six military branches: Army, Navy, Marines, Airforce, Coast Guard, and Space Force.

Among the disclaimers is that a Longbow pilot cannot take an attack helicopter on a vigilante mission. The Marine unit mans a fully armed hawk, and together, they terminate a cartel kingpin and level his mansion.

This is a literary embellishment at its finest, and it makes for a delightful tale. Naturally, the combat choppers were wiped clean and returned to the military base, and no one was the wiser.

The author would like to transition to the ranching aspects of this story. When Desiree and Dayo reach the Pettigrew Ranch, they are faced with a team roping test.

To better appreciate team roping, the reader should watch a YouTube PRCA event, and discover the way cattlemen rope a steer. The NFR finals showcase a number of amazing team-roping finalists, and you'll be amazed at how fast the competition unfolds.

The team is divided into a header, who catches the horns, and a heeler, who scoops the heels. This two-man event allows men and women to compete, and it all comes down to the fastest time.

In this story, Cobb Pettigrew is a master horseman. And even though he participated in rodeo competitions, his real love was Reined Cow Horse (RCH) events.

Unlike rodeo action, Western riding entails superlative horsemanship, subtle rein signals, and great cow sense. The ultimate goal is to show off your Quarter Horse and demonstrate how fluidly your stud can read a steer, take control, and maneuver a cow.

Once again, YouTube offers Senior RCH events. Simply spending five minutes will explain boxing, fence work, and cow work. And it's impressive to see what these eighteen-year-old studs can do. They are commanding, intuitive, and fast as lightning.

As this prologue comes to a close, I'd like to comment on the cover design. Shutterstock models were selected, and even though they are captivating, my leading characters are slightly different.

Desiree DeNiro sported a mane of glistening ringlets, charming dimples, and a radiant smile. She was a shapely hourglass beauty, and the Commodores would have called her a Brick House. In spite of her traffic-stopping beauty, Desi was never vain, but always personable and outgoing.

Dayo Cazador flaunted an impressive physique, but the Marine also had an uncanny resemblance to Harry Belafonte.

His Caribbean charm was necessary at the RCH finals, and it enabled him to sidestep prejudice and exhibit his full skill set. Thinking more about Belafonte than the powerlifter will give you a deeper insight into Dayo's personality.

In conclusion, The famous author, Isaac Asimov, preferred to classify himself as a storyteller. Storytelling is one of the oldest crafts, whether by neolithic campfire or modern eBook. Electronic storytelling has changed.

Once, the point-of-view changes were designated by two spaced lines, but a scroll symbol replaced the spacing method. That designation has been used for both scene and POV changes.

I hope you, the reader, enjoy *Cowgirl Witness & Her Bodyguard.* It was a pleasure to tell the story, and I hope it finds a place in your heart.

Mark E. Scott

Chapter One

Lieutenant Desiree DeNiro leaped into her medevac helo and performed the triple checks. The due diligence for the aviation industry required multiple reviews. And her "Flight for Life" missions adhered to the strictest protocol.

The bronze beauty made sure all operating systems were a go. She glanced at her reflection in the aerodynamic bubble. The twinkling-eyed beauty had a mane of black ringlets, luminous bronze skin, and adorable dimples. Her Arabian eyeliner made her eyes pop and brought out her effervescent beauty.

She dumped a handful of post-traumatic pills into her palm and tossed them down. The medication wasn't doing the trick, and she still suffered from horrifying nightmares, body tremors, and sweat-soaked pajamas.

Every night, Dez was back in Afghanistan and no matter how much she tried to escape the terrifying memories, her subconscious played the scene over and over.

After a successful mission, her fully armed Black Hawk picked up a special op team and flew them to an American base camp. She remembered it like it was just yesterday.

The Sikorsky UH-60 shot over the Afghanistan desert with an

Army Ranger Unit seated in the cargo bay. It felt good winging over this god-forsaken terrain at a cruise speed of one-hundred-seventy mph.

Her combat helo carried Hydra bomb-clusters and Hellfire missiles. From the nose, a fully armed black hawk was a wicked thing of beauty. With a 36-foot rotator diameter and stub wings, it was one badass chopper.

Desiree jetted over the arid mountain range, and her base camp came into view. There was a Hercules C-130 prowling down the runway, and an array of helos were parked in a row.

Beyond the runways, a lively military base teemed with soldiers. There were rows of desert tan tents, and Quonset-style dormitories.

The bronze beauty landed her fully armed Black Hawk. The flagman gave the all clear, and the Army Rangers hit the ground, ducked, and ran for the debriefing tent.

She cut the engine and waited for the flagmen to block her helo. She was due for a glass of chilled water, and the shapely pilot entered the shadows of a hydration unit.

Suddenly, she heard the scream of a FIM Stinger missile and ducked for cover. To her utter horror, she watched the explosive detonate the debriefing tent.

An ugly red fireball shredded the tent and billowed into the sky. Never in her life had she felt more helpless. But to her astonishment, a second Stinger missile destroyed her hawk.

It happened in slow motion, and there was nothing she could do to stop it. Her hawk exploded into a million pieces, and an ugly fireball engulfed the shell.

It was like watching the death of a loved one; Desi really loved that chopper. It had been responsible for a string of victories, and now, it had been reduced to a burned-out shell.

Her subconscious played the scene repeatedly. It was bad enough she suffered from survivor's guilt, but the nightmare had reduced her to zero.

She was an incompetent pilot who abandoned her men, and the ambush was entirely her fault. Earlier this morning, she awakened to the same dream, soaked in sweat, and screamed into the night.

Desiree returned to the moment. The pretty pilot took inventory of the present. She had just landed in an urgent care facility and was preparing for an airlift. This wasn't the stinkin' Middle East, this was the California desert, and they were well outside LA.

The bronze bombshell tucked her glistening ringlets beneath her aviation helmet. For good luck she kissed the tip of her finger and touched her koala toy.

Kay Bear wrapped his little arms around the tilt stick and radiated pure happiness. She loved the way his large round ears listened to her profound thoughts. And his brown-button eyes reassured her everything was going to work out.

Of course, his oblong black nose and pink-lipped smile were as cute as the dickens. Desi stroked his backswept grey hair for good luck. Ever since Kay-Bear joined the team, there were nothing but successful missions.

She took him everywhere, and in her make-believe mind, he was actually a living, breathing little person. Can you believe it?

Her military shrink asked her if she had any superstitions? Dez answered in a negative. Kay Bear wasn't a talisman by a long shot. Since kissing her koala brought success, then it made him real. And that was all she needed to know.

Captain Thaddeus Montane rapped on her portal window and opened the door. Thad stood six feet, and his well-built frame filled out his LifeNet uniform.

He held his white aviation helmet and flashed a warm smile. "Desi, you've got an injured mountain climber, and medic Jim Barron will keep the patient oxygenated."

"All you've got to do is fly him to the Desert Sage hospital and make the delivery."

Desi curled her lips in amusement. These Flight for Life runs were a piece of cake. Flying over a sparsely populated cityscape had high power lines and windmill farms, but nothing as dangerous as ground-to-air missiles.

The Captain knew her history, but it was best to stay on his best side. "Captain, I'll peek through the bulkhead door, reassure our patient, and get him safely to the hospital. I've done this thousands of times, and you know that Kay Bear and I are great pilots."

Thaddeus stroked his grey circle beard and leaned closer. "Between you and me, I know Kay Bear loves desert flights, and the little guy expresses your feelings. But when you hit Desert Sage, it might be better if you keep the koala's feelings on the down low."

Desiree swept a hand over the dashboard. "You got it, Chief. Anything else I should know?"

Thaddeus tugged on his blue LifeNet cap, "When you arrive at the helipad, your helo is scheduled for a maintenance check. You're not due for a full overhaul for another two months."

"So, while you're at the hangar, just chat with the mechanics, and catch up on the latest upgrades."

She caressed Kay Bear's hairy little head, but Desi could tell something was wrong.

Captain Thaddeus flashed the warmest smile he could muster and punched her softly in her bicep.

"Lt. DeNiro, you're a first-rate pilot. I've reviewed your missions, and they're flawless. But I've got to ask a question: it's just procedural."

"Are you having any post-traumatic episodes during the day?"

Desiree stuffed a few ringlets into her helmet. She was somewhat relieved by the question.

"Actually, all my episodes occur at night. Whenever I slow down and my subconscious mind takes over, then all hell breaks loose."

The combat pilot lowered her long lashes, somewhat ashamed of her medical condition. But doggone it! She served her country, and she was totally functional.

"Thad, I assure you. I've never had an episode during the day. And when the first rays of sunshine shoot through my French doors, I'm ready to face the world."

She hooked a bronze thumb, "I'm hitting on all pistons from sunup to sundown. So, there's nothing to worry about, Cappie Bear."

Thad waggled his head, "Desi, you're a trip."

"Girl, keep up the good work, and if there's the least sign of a dizzy spell, you let me know."

The Flight for Life commander clapped her shoulder and closed the cockpit door. Little did the Captain realize how essential Kay Bear was.

K-Man helped her process her feeling. She managed to bring the inner darkness to the light, and afterward, the world was a friendlier place.

Desiree unbuckled her strap and whirled past the bulkhead. The mountain climber was loaded through the rear clamshell, so she had yet to meet the patient.

Desi pushed open the aluminum door and peered into the ambulance bay. Medic Jim Barron had the mountain climber hooked up. The green digital monitor fed the stats while the patient lay quietly beneath a mask.

Jim touched the patient's shoulder, "Marcus, this is Lt. DeNiro, our LifeNet pilot. She'll take you directly to a fully staffed hospital where you can receive the best treatment."

Marcus was a young athlete who appeared to be in severe pain. Jim wore a teal flight suit, an aviation helmet, and a communicator.

She met the dedicated medic back in Afghanistan. On a few occasions, she flew Middle Eastern missions, and they worked well together. They weren't close friends, but between the two of them, they were all about the mission.

Desiree spoke softly, "Marcus, you're not to worry. This is a routine flight, and we'll arrive in less than a half hour."

She touched the man's shoulder to see if he was coherent. "What actually happened to you?"

Marcus shrugged beneath the blanket. "Dumb luck, I suppose."

"I climbed up a two-hundred-foot escarpment, moved like a cat from one handhold to the next without a problem. But on the way down, I rappelled too fast, hit my climbing pad, and bounced sideways."

"It was uneven terrain, and I careened laterally, and I smashed my head."

The medic secured his left arm, "Not to mention that your wing is badly fractured, and you have a full-blown concussion."

"That's nothing to mess with. Closed-head injuries can come back to haunt you."

"I'm well aware of that, sir. Let's just get this helo going and pretend this never happened."

Desiree loved her patients. They were real people, and they deserved the best.

She touched the mountain climber, "Marcus, you're in good hands. We've got this! And before you know it, you'll be scramblin' up rock faces and enjoying all that natural beauty."

Weakly, her patient saluted, and they were on their way.

Desiree fired up the rotators and airlifted. The red, white, and blue helo hovered over the helipad, and she rapidly hit cruise speed.

It wasn't a Black Hawk by a long shot, but the Flight for Life helo had a Sikorsky body, a bullet nose, and triple tail fins. And the medevac work suited her just fine.

They cruised over the California desert. Immediately, she approached a windmill farm, and Desi banked around the whirling white blades and sailed above a stretch of Joshua trees. The cactus forest dotted a sagebrush desert, and it was an otherworldly sight.

She punched the turbo engines and quickly accelerated to maximum speed. Hitting one-hundred- sixty mph, highway traffic appeared to move at a crawl. She spotted the four-story hospital, the Red Cross marked helipad, and a nearby blue warehouse.

Desi reduced her engine speed, hovered above the landing pad, and gently touched down. The twin runners alighted upon the rubber tarmac, and an emergency crew shot toward the rear.

Within seconds, the bifold doors opened, and Marcus was lowered onto the ground. Thanks to the stretcher and its portable oxygen system, the patient remained in a sound condition.

The pretty combat pilot cut the engine and allowed the giant propellers to gradually come to a stop. The pit crew rushed over to her helo, and four men were all over it.

Desiree removed Kay Bear from the tilt stick and wrapped him around her wrist. "There ya go, buddy. It was a simple mission, and we saw a beautiful desert full of Joshua trees."

"I know how much you love the peaceful countryside. That's what I like about you, Kay Bear. You see the good in everything."

Desiree touched his adorable nose, "Remember what the Captain said!"

"Our LifeNet chopper gets a field check, and we're supposed to brush up on the latest upgrades."

She removed her aviation helmet and tossed her glorious mane. Ringlets cascaded over her shoulders as her flight shoes hit the ground.

Desi walked around the nose cone, and a pit mechanic yelled out.

"Why if it isn't Desiree DeNiro? You've got a bangin' body, and all I want to know is: when are we going on a date?"

The flirtatious mechanic continued, "Girl, you've got to take off that flight suit, it just doesn't do you justice. When you dine with me, you can wear a figure-hugging sheath. I'll lavish you with praise and gaze into your pretty eyes."

Desiree flipped her shiny ringlets. "Actually, Harrison, there won't be a first date, and I have no intention of dining al fresco."

"Kay Bear thinks you've got one thing on your mind. And he believes that I have a great personality, and I'm very intelligent. But the problem is, you're not interested in any of my attributes."

A second pit mechanic wore a tan tee and camo pants.

He turned from the uptilted nose cone, "Desi, don't let Harrison get to you. You gotta take it easy and stick to men you trust. And when you're good and ready, I'm sure you'll let us know."

She was caught off guard, but then again, Jeremiah was a dark-haired mechanic who served in the Middle East. He probably saw the signs of post trauma, and he went easy. If anything, the lead mechanic was more of a friend, and had no designs on her.

Desi touched his shoulder, "I appreciate it. And when I finally decide to date, I'd like to go out with a man like you. You seem like a man who is more interested in a woman's personality, and not just her body."

Jeremiah clarified, "I'm an all-American male, and Harrison is right about one thing. You do have a stunning hourglass."

He coughed into his fist, "But setting that aside, Captain Thaddeus, tells me you want to look at the upgrade tutorial. It's right inside the hangar."

"The place is empty, but in about thirty minutes, I'll see if you have any questions." The lead mechanic tipped his cap, and she felt validated as a beautiful person.

Desiree sashayed across the tarmac. A baby blue steel warehouse stood before her, and a huge sliding door was wide open. Inside the garage doors, an array of medevac helos were parked over a painted floor.

There were diagnostic toolboxes stationed around every Sikorsky. The bullet noses were flipped open, and yellow scaffolding led to the overhead engines.

Above the immaculate grey floors, hanging lights illuminated the bays like a surgical room. LifeNet took maintenance seriously, but the odd thing was that the hangar was completely empty.

The bronze beauty strolled over to a wheeled diagnostic station. She entered the password, and the upgrade tutorial came to life.

Suddenly, she heard loud voices and a flurry of footfalls. The sounds echoed off the warehouse walls. The evil was so thick, you could cut it with a knife.

Desi whispered to Kay Bear, "Be quiet, and keep your head down." She drew her 9 mm fluidly, held the muzzle down, and peered around the box.

There was a smug, heavy-faced Latino who came to a dramatic stop. He wore a pressed Italian suit, and his broad shoulders filled out his jacket. There was something about him that emanated pure evil.

His narrow lips were cocky and cruel. He was a crime boss, and the man was accustomed to getting his way.

Three armed bodyguards flanked the kingpin. And across the bay, a black man came to a stop. The bronze athlete had a cut physique, a purple tee, and a handsome beard.

He spread his arms wide and smiled in a friendly way. "Hey, you guys, what's this all about? You followed me out of the hospital, and now you're chasing me through a hangar. Is there anything I can do for you?"

The kingpin removed his sunglasses and pursed his lips, "Are you Tinder Williams?"

The bronze athlete froze in place, and his smile vanished. "Yes, my name is Tinder. What business do I have with you?"

The crime boss ordered his men to surround the man. Instantly, two bodyguards seized Tinder beneath his arms and dragged him forward.

"I think you know what concerns me. I run a clean operation, and I take care of loose ends. It just so happens that you saw me commit a crime."

"And I can't allow you to report the incident."

Tinder raised his hands innocently. "Hey, man, I left the hood years ago. And I'm not about to testify against you."

"What I saw doesn't really matter; it happens all the time. So how about you let me go? Then, we go our separate ways."

Desiree could feel an ominous vibe, and she knew there was about to be a murder. She calculated her odds to take down three guards and a pompous ass.

With a twelve-round chamber, she had better hit her mark every time. Desi slid the barrel forward and readied herself.

Just then, three additional guards joined the meeting. Her chances for success took a nose dive.

Dammit all! If she had her communicator, she could call for back-up. It was seven against one, and all she could do was wait it out.

Fear seized her throat, and she could barely breathe. Her hands trembled, and she was about to lose her bowels. It was like Afghanistan all over again.

She stood by helplessly, and there wasn't a dang thing she could do. Desiree waited for what seemed like an eternity, but it was only a matter of seconds.

She peered around the toolbox and watched the crime boss pull the trigger. In cold blood, the kingpin zipped a bullet-cluster into Tinder's chest.

The silencer spewed forth and there was barely a sound. The deadly silence made the execution eerie and unholy. *It was all wrong.*

An innocent man shouldn't be gunned down. Desiree covered her mouth, and her soul screamed. It was an atrocity, especially when the man was blameless and innocent.

Tinder Williams collapsed and dropped to the floor. He died instantly. The kingpin motioned to his bodyguards, and they moved with cold efficiency.

Quickly, they dragged Williams out a service door and threw his body into a trunk. *Good lord, she had to do something, but what?*

Desiree heard the squeal of car tires, and the sedan was gone. There was a deathly silence in the hangar.

Finally, she whispered to Kay Bear, "It's all right, little buddy. We saw a murder, and Momma Bear will make it right."

"You can't go killing a person in broad daylight, it's just not done! We'll report the crime to the authorities, and the bad guys will go to jail. Right?"

Kay Bear beamed his perpetual smile. She combed his light grey fur, "It's a good thing we held it together. I know you were scared spitless, but we kept our cool, and calculated the odds."

Desiree was about to have a traumatic episode, but the only way to keep going was to keep talking. She spoke to Kay Bear just like she did during the war.

If Desi kept spilling her feelings, then eventually, she'd level out. Kay Bear flashed his brown-button eyes and listened to every word.

After a half hour, she was all talked out. When she rose to her feet, Jeremiah appeared.

Calmly, the dark-haired mechanic inquired, "Am I interrupting anything?"

"No, I'm fine. I was just getting current with Kay Bear. We had a lot to discuss, but I've vented all my feelings."

Jeremiah pursed his lips, "Desi, I know you're going through a lot. And there's no way I can say that I understand. I've never experienced live combat, or seen men lose their lives. But if I may be so bold, I'd like to give you a hug."

Desiree fell into his arms and hugged the big lug. It was a friendship hug all the way. When she felt his arms engulf her, and he held her close, she experienced the beauty of human touch.

It was healing. Finally, she broke from his embrace. "Thanks, man. I really needed that. Kay Bear and I are done for the day. I'll punch out and catch the tutorial next time."

"Is there anything more I can do?"

"No, I'm good. My Jeep Wrangler is in the parking lot, and a bit of fresh air will work wonders."

Desiree eyed her Jeep Wrangler as she crossed the lot. The black hardtop, the red doors, and four-wheel drive brought her endless hours of pleasure.

The beauty of California were the four wheelin' trails and gorgeous natural terrain. The red Jeep could ford arroyos, climb rock fields, and go straight up a mountainside.

But it wasn't a Humvee, and it wasn't loaded with an arsenal. She carried a 9 mm and that was all she had to her civilian name.

But after seeing a drug lord gun down a civilian, she was having second thoughts. With an assault rifle, she could have made short work of those evil bastards.

Desi kept up the inner dialogue, but she didn't want Kay Bear to hear her wicked thoughts. She leaped into the Wrangler and attached her toy friend to the phone prop.

She knew the way, but under the circumstances, GPS directions to the Desert Sage Police Department would be helpful.

Moments later, her red Jeep hauled into a wide parking lot. There was a variable tan brick-building, which flew two flags. The red, white and blue, and the Bear State announced their sovereignty.

Her flight boots hit the pavement as she trotted up the precast stairs. An assortment of police cruisers and black SUVs lined the front lot.

Behind the cruisers, there were tinted windows with a large, cantilevered soffit. The overhanging eaves sported timber lookouts, which complimented the desert tan architecture.

If she were taking a tour, she might have found the Western veneer more interesting. But Desi was on a mission, and she hoped they wouldn't blow her off.

As a military veteran, she knew proper protocol, and she expected the Desert Sage homies to follow it.

The bronze beauty entered the front lobby and approached a blue octagonal desk.

A robust female wheeled from her chair, "Is there anything I can do for you?"

"Yes, I'd like to report a murder. I witnessed a drug dealer, probably a crime boss, execute an innocent man. I'd like to identify the perpetrator and the victim."

The buxom clerk gestured to an empty lobby. "If you take a seat, I'll inform the chief. We have a lot of cases underway, and this may take a while."

The chubby clerk gestured to a magazine rack. "We have an assortment of magazines, so make yourself comfortable."

Desiree straightened up, "Excuse me, you use the Flight for Life services, don't you? My name is Lieutenant Desiree DeNiro, and I don't appreciate the brush off."

"If you'd care to speak to my commanding officer, Captain Thaddeus Montane, perhaps, I could receive better treatment."

Right then, the police chief walked into the lobby. He was a full-chested man, wearing a tan button-down, breast pockets, and a crisp black tie.

He grinned beneath a shoe brush mustache. "Why hello, you're the LifeNet pilot who makes runs night and day. Captain Thaddeus told me all about you."

Desi glanced at his lapel, Chief Dwight Oberon. "It's a pleasure to meet you. I've flown medevac flights from the station, and I thought you'd be sympathetic to my report."

He huffed into his stache, "If I overheard you correctly, you witnessed a murder. For the sedate neighborhoods around here, that's a rare event, I must say."

"I agree, and when I saw it take place, it caught me totally by surprise."

The Police Chief touched her shoulder, "Phyllis, hold all my calls, and call Emerson and Kelly into the conference room."

Dwight continued, "Make sure they bring the FBI mug shots, and the latest forensics."

The buxom bureaucrat finally got the memo. She reached for the phone and whipped her team into gear.

Phyllis spoke forcefully, "Emerson, the Chief wants you and Kelly in the conference room on the double. We've got a hot one, and you may need the sketch artist as well."

Desi felt a moment of triumph. If she weren't among strangers, she'd tell Kay Bear how she maintained her cool and demanded respect. And what's more, she got results.

The bronze beauty walked into a glaring white conference room. A huge Formica table dominated the room, and there was a case board hammered to the back wall.

Even though Desert Sage was a small community, they had plenty of local projects. And by the looks of it, none of them were murderers.

Emerson carried a white laptop and set it on the desk. The man wore an FBI crime jacket, and he was flanked by Kelly, who wore a white blouse and a smart pencil skirt. They sat next to one another and waited for Chief Oberon to lead the meeting.

The Chief sat down with a cup of coffee. "Before you rehearse the crime scene, I'd like you to meet David Somerville."

"He's a local painter, but also our Forensic artist. Just describe the perpetrator as best you can, and he'll do a rough sketch. As you fill in the details, Emerson and Kelly will rifle through our files."

Desiree took a deep breath and began. "I was in the LifeNet hangar when a thick chested, well-dressed man ordered Tinder Williams to stop."

"The crime boss had a large square head, menacing eyes, and a South American complexion. His lips were narrow and arrogant, and his nose spread over his face like it had been broken several times."

She paused to watch the artist create a portrait. He created a square head, and rapidly added narrow hateful eyes, and a partially flattened nose, and a pair of thin lips.

Desi wanted to tell Kay Bear how good the rendering was. Her koala loved artwork, and they spent endless hours strolling through art galleries.

"That's a good start, but his ears are larger, more like Dumbo ears, and he had wavy black hair with streaks of grey."

"What about his build?"

"The crime lord had a thick chest and a bit of a paunch and large brown hands."

David finished his charcoal strokes and whirled around the image.

Desiree exclaimed, "That's him."

Everyone in the room stopped cold. They knew exactly who he was, but no one was disclosing the truth.

She turned to Chief Oberon, "Sir, do you know who that is? I'm pretty sensitive, and I can tell you know who I'm describing."

The Chief pounded his shoe brush stache thoughtfully. "Desiree, honey, there's a police procedure, we must follow. And I don't want to prejudice the identification process."

"So, I'll withhold the perpetrator's name for now, but when you make a positive identification, I'll let you know."

"All right, that sounds fair."

Emerson summoned a mug shot and tilted the screen. "Kell, I sent a mugshot of the perp, but it was taken twenty-years ago. We'll need an age progression, and once we're confident, we can show it to our witness."

Just then, the coroner called in. "Dwight, we've just recovered the body of an African American male, around thirty-five years of age. He's five-foot eight with a heavy beard and high sidewalls and a curly thatch of black hair. Does this sound like your man?"

Dwight left the table, but Desiree had keen hearing. The Chief walked over to a large vista window overlooking a cactus garden.

He lowered his voice, "Can you send me a photo? Be sure to dress up the victim and make his death look pleasant."

"We've got a very sensitive eyewitness, and I don't want to traumatize the girl."

"You got it, chief. I'll make the adjustments, take a postmortem photo, and send it directly. No one else is privy to the photograph, you're the only recipient."

"Thanks, Morty, I owe you one."

Desiree processed the incoming message. She witnessed Tinder William's death, and it was a triple shot to the chest. His face was unmarked, and his execution went fast.

Tinder was an enthusiastic soul, and he had so much to live for. The thought of seeing him in a postmortem state was going to decimate her.

It made her feel small and insecure and uncertain. Chief Oberon was right, maybe she wasn't ready to do this.

Right as she was about to excuse herself, Phyllis walked in.

"Hello, Desiree, I'm sorry we got off on the wrong foot. You must be traumatized over this horrible event. I whipped up a mango smoothie and made you a plate of snickerdoodles."

Desi touched the woman's plump hands, "Thank you, I really appreciate it."

The pretty pilot lifted the smoothie and strolled over to the picture window. She opened a glass door and strolled over a path of sandstone flags.

There was a cultivated xeric garden with blooming cactus, orange banner ocotillos, and yellow flowered cholla.

She held up her wrist and eyed Kay Bear closely. She whispered, "Little buddy, when we go back in there, I'm going to identify a crime lord. And by the looks of it, he's a badass mother."

Desiree paused, "Are you sure you want to do this?"

The combat pilot sipped her mango smoothie and gazed into the California sky. She stood on the precipice of a life-changing decision.

But an innocent man lost his life, and she had to do the right thing. She was compelled by a sense of duty. And more than the image of the crime lord, was the face of Tinder Williams.

He looked like a great guy. He was full of overflowing warmth, and his life was cut short. No one deserved that.

She made her decision. For the sake of Tinder and all bronze men, she had to put this criminal behind bars.

Desiree whispered to Kay Bear, "Little Buddy, things may get rough. But when this is all over, the bad guys will be put away. Okay?"

Her grey koala smiled at her with his brown-button eyes, and he was in complete agreement.

The pretty combat pilot entered the white conference room. She sat down and braced herself. Emerson displayed a photo of a young Antonio Gonzalez.

His mug shot was similar to the man she saw, but not identical. Kelly twirled her laptop with the age progression.

"This is Antonio Gonzalez today. I performed the aging process. Well, what do you think?"

Desiree stared at the aged image, "That's definitely him."

Emerson summoned a series of FBI photos and pointed to them. "Is this the man who killed Tinder Williams?"

"Without a doubt, that's the man. He did it."

Chief Oberon settled next to the investigation team. "And here's a photo you probably don't want to see. But the coroner sent over a postmortem of a thirty-five-year-old African American male. Is this Tinder Williams?"

Desiree took the cell phone and enlarged the photo. She beheld the tranquil image of Tinder resting on a slab table. The overflowing joy had been removed, and his enthusiasm was gone.

The finality of his death stared back at her. Desi felt the tears gather, and she got all choked up. The combat pilot wiped her nose as tears streaked over her bronze cheeks.

She struggled to process it all. Finally, she handed the phone back.

"Yes, that's Tinder Williams, the man I saw murdered this afternoon. The world lost a great guy, and his killer should be brought to justice."

No sooner did she perform the crucial identifications, than the door swung open.

Dwight rose to his feet, "Desiree, I'd like you to meet Pietro Sanchez, the Director of the Witness Program."

She eyed a mature man wearing a herringbone plaid suit and large framed glasses. Director Sanchez looked more like a realtor than a witness coordinator.

But he extended a meaty hand, "Miss DeNiro, Dwight informed me of the situation, and I hear you'll testify against Antonio Gonzalez."

"We've been after him for a long time, but he cleans his tracks pretty well. You'll change your name and receive a new identity."

"Our safe house is one of the best in North America. The trial date won't be for another three months, so you'll be in the program for the whole summer."

"Come fall, your testimony will put Gonzalez away for good. We want this guy bad, but in all fairness to you. Are you ready to enter the witness program?"

Pietro continued, "It's a life-changing decision, and I won't minimize the consequences."

The full impact of her decision hit her like a gut punch. She'd change her name and become someone else. Desiree barely had a grasp of her current identity.

Becoming a new person was life shattering. She wasn't sure she could do this. The waiting period spanned an entire summer. What was she going to do in the meantime? There was a lot of reading she could catch up on, but three freakin' months was ridiculous.

She twirled a long ringlet and thought about the consequences.

"Can I give you an answer in the morning? I've had a long day, and somehow, I thought this would be simpler."

"I came to the department to file a report, and I thought you'd put out an all-points bulletin, and arrest the killer."

"I had no idea I'd be drafted into the witness program. It's like I'm the only one standing in the gap."

She remembered Tinder's love for life and his joyful enthusiasm. The bronze beauty clenched her fists, "I'll get back to you tomorrow."

Desiree flew out the front doors like a bat outta hell. She inhaled the desert air and felt rejuvenated. The air conditioning was soothing, but the stuffy conference room, and a curtain of fear were more than she could handle.

She seized the iron cap rail and trotted down the concrete steps. Her eyes fell upon a handsome bronze Adonis. He carried himself like a jungle predator, and his every move was calculated.

She glanced at his open Caribbean shirt and the dusting of chest hair. The guy's cavalier manner made him look mouthwatering and sexy as hell. He was a vision of masculine beauty.

For a moment, she didn't recognize him, but finally, she made eye contact. She gazed into the dark brown eyes of Declan Cazador.

His heavy brows, flawless bronze complexion, and shadow stubble were gorgeous. It had been a long time since she'd been with a man.

And suddenly, her hormones came to life, and her arousal went on high alert. But a second thought hit her like a ton of bricks.

This wasn't the charming rodeo guy from high school, this was Captain Cazador, the leader of the famed headhunters. The Marine Raiders were notorious hitmen and damn proud of it. They targeted Islamic hostiles and hunted them down.

Desi clutched her purse and squeezed Kay Bear for moral support.

Declan cast her a charming smile, "Lieutenant DeNiro, I'm surprised to see you. Was there a LifeNet flight for one of the officers?"

She tried to process the question, but nothing registered. Then, she finally got it. "No, I came here to report a crime, and I'm not sure what my next move is."

Declan paused and eyed her carefully. The man's psychic feelers went out.

The Marine extended his hand and palmed her cheek. "Desi, are you all-right? You appear to be badly shaken?"

She peered beneath her lashes, and Dec seemed truly concerned. More than concerned, the guy looked like he was prepared to go into action.

He had a 9 mm slung around his hip, but looking at his black

Camaro, she figured this guy was armed to the teeth. Old habits die hard, and a headhunter doesn't come to the party ill-prepared.

Desiree laid her cheek into his palm and enjoyed his affectionate touch.

If the Caribbean stud had been at the hangar today, he could have taken out all seven. She was a combat pilot, not a tight-quarters fighter.

But if Cazador went into action with a single Beretta, there would have been four headshots and a pile of bodies.

Strategically, he would have worked his way around the hangar. He would have dispatched the guy with the assault rifle and taken out the others. There was no point in sharing her moment of terror, Declan would never understand.

Desiree stammered, "I'd rather not talk about it, right now. I've had a long day."

"Hey, I get it."

Cazador gazed into her soul. "Desiree, I'm on your side. If something happened out there, and your life has been threatened, I want to know about it."

Declan lowered his handsome brows, "We protect our own, and no one will lay a hand on you. I promise you."

His concern was touching and also terrifying. Out of sheer nerves, she giggled, "What would you do if there was a malicious threat?"

He curled his kissable lips, "I'd take them out, clean as day."

She listened to his words, and realized the commander wasn't given to bravado. What he said, he would do in a heartbeat.

If she wanted frontier justice, all she had to do was point Cazador toward Gonzalez. And all her problems would disappear. It was tempting, but she wanted to give justice a shot.

She wasn't about to tell him the truth. "I've been flying first response helos, what's up with you?"

"I just finished a SWAT team assignment. It appears my marksmanship and quick solutions didn't meet the commander's expectations."

"I had the bank robbers in my sights and used an enhanced sniper rifle. With quick bolt action, I ended the stand-off."

Declan shrugged his shoulders, "I guess they just wanted to keep talking."

Desiree wanted to burst out laughing. The guy spoke in a calm voice, and she had no doubt he was telling the truth. Not only was he a headhunter, but he was also one of their designated marksmen.

Declan slid his hands to her waist and gazed deeply into her eyes.

"Desi, there's something you're not telling me. For me to be effective, I need to know the details. And since you're part of the team, we function best when we share our feelings."

The Big Cat moved closer, and his muscular frame towered over her. He lowered his face and inhaled her perfume. His hand slid behind her luxuriant mane of shiny ringlets.

"Honey, I can feel your anxiety, and you're in desperate need of a hug. Would you like to share some body heat?"

The Captain didn't mean to crowd her, but her fears called to him. For some inexplicable reason, his heart went out, and he had to protect her.

Desi was trapped, and she placed a hand on his chest. She peered through her lashes, "Dayo, all you want to do is to feel me up!"

The commander burst into a glorious laugh. She must have realized how silly she was and joined his laughter.

"Actually, sweetheart, the girls are mighty enticing, but my motives are nothing but honorable. All I want to do is help."

She tilted her head in defiance and tried to give him the stare down. It didn't work, Dayo slipped his arms around the small of her back and hauled her into a heat-sharing body hug.

He could feel her defiance melt into acceptance. Desi wrapped her arms around his neck and crushed her breasts into his plane.

Declan brushed his chin across her ringlets, and his resolve became stronger. He vowed to find out what was going on and take swift and merciless action. If someone harmed this sweet combat pilot, they'd pay dearly.

When Dec released her, his bronze features broke into a carefree smile.

"Ya know, I'll never live down that day I sang the 'Banana Boat Song.'"

"I remember it like it was yesterday. I stood on the high school stage and did the best imitation of Harry Belafonte I could."

Desiree giggled, "It wasn't just the Calypso song, it's your uncanny resemblance to the Caribbean actor."

She paused to evaluate him and broke into a radiant smile. "Even though you're older, you still have that same magnetism."

Declan lowered his brow, "I'm used to it. The nickname followed me into the Marines, and the whole unit called me Captain Dayo. It's a term of affection and respect, so I really don't mind."

He finger-combed his dense black hair, "Just to set the record straight. I tried to get on first base more than eight years ago. And despite your Brick House figure, I'm not after the girls. I'm interested in your safety."

Desi held up her wrist, "Kay Bear thinks you're a very dangerous man."

Dayo curled his lips, "You can tell K-Man, I am a dangerous hunter. And what's more, you can tell your little friend that I eliminated the terrorists who took out your unit."

Her enormous eyes enlarged, "Do you mean the special ops unit that was hit by a Stinger missile?"

Declan curled his handsome lips with menace. "The Rangers were avenged, and we tracked down your assailants. Justice was served." The man spoke with finality and simplicity. He took matters into his own hands, and the legendary headhunter got things done.

Dayo studied her face, "Honey, do you rest easy at night?"

She deflected quickly, "Kay Bear wants to know if you rest easy?"

He shifted his weight. "As a matter of fact, I do. I have no regrets from the war, with the one exception that it ended. The unit came home, and we went our separate ways."

Declan gazed at the nearby desert. He continued, "To tell the truth, I'm a bit restless. And I'm trying to figure out where I fit in."

Desiree had to repay his thoughtfulness. "I appreciate what you did back in Afghanistan. My special op team was avenged, and it makes me feel a lot better. Of course, it won't bring back their lives, but it does help considerably."

For a horrible day, she found a small measure of peace.

Desiree realized a gorgeous Marine hunk stood between her and her Jeep. The days' events wore her out, and her nerves were frayed.

So much had happened in one day, it was hard to believe. And when she drove home to her Spanish Med, she had to make a huge decision.

But it was comforting to know that Declan was in the Witness Program. His presence was powerful, and a bit overwhelming. She was fiercely attracted to the guy, but she had to take things slow.

She pointed a delicate finger to her red Wrangler, "Dayo, my ride is right over there."

"Can you walk me to my vehicle?"

Ironically, his black Camaro and her red Jeep were parked side by side. The bronze warrior moved fluidly down the steps. His feline prowess and psychic awareness were amazing. The guy was never off duty, and for him, the war never ended.

Declan opened her steel door, and the commander intercepted her iPhone.

He punched in his phone number. "Darlin', if the midnight terrors descend, just give me a call. I'll talk you down, and we'll get through this together."

She wanted to tell him flat out, there was no "we." There was just Kay Bear. The thought she might run into him in the Witness Program thrilled her to pieces. It also terrified her.

Desiree had to set him on his heels. "Dayo, I think we should go our separate ways, and if I run into you, let's just keep it purely professional."

He palmed her cheek, "Desi, we're way past that. Remember what I said earlier. If there's anything you need, just give me a ring."

This man had such an effect. He broke all the rules and was a law unto himself. And from his alpha presence, she knew he was relentless, and he'd get to the bottom of her problems.

It felt good to know how much he cared, and terrifying to have such a mouthwatering stud in her life.

Desi popped her hip, "Hey Dayo, it was good running into you. Just try not to kill someone before the day is out!"

The bronze warrior curled his handsome lips, "The day is young, who knows what the future holds."

Desiree closed the door and fired up her Wrangler.

She turned to Kay Bear, "That stud Marine is a one-man wrecking ball. Don't worry about Antonio Gonzalez, we just met the most dangerous man in the world."

Chapter Two

Declan's black beauty purred into a slate covered driveway. He glanced through the tinted glass at his Spanish Med single story. Large terra cotta tiles covered a hipped roof, and down below, stucco trim surrounded every casement window.

He threw open the winged door, and his leather sandals hit the ground. After six years of combat boots, it felt good to occasionally cut loose.

He clicked the craft garage door, and the rustic portal opened slowly. The commander walked briskly across the immaculate floor and leaped into the mudroom changer.

He ripped off his Caribbean casual clothes, and donned a waterproof, triathlon body suit. Dressed in all black, he'd cut through the night in complete invisibility. He debated about the swimming cap, but the neon goggles were sufficient.

Dayo entered the garage and performed a few stretches, pumped out a hundred push-ups, and two hundred sit-ups, and he was ready to go.

The veteran cruised through the Spanish Mission neighborhood and cut through the open space. He shot past four stucco homes and appreciated the sunset glow.

In the fading light, the sunset illuminated orange poppies, cactus flowers, and tropical palm trees. He was back in California, and the evening glow cast its light on the distant Sierras.

The bronze warrior burst into another gear and broke into a fast-paced run. He was trained to keep this pace for hours, and the hill country was a sight easier than his former assignment.

Dec remembered that the triathlon was scheduled for three events: the running, the swimming, and the bicycling courses. Naturally, it wouldn't take place on level terrain, so a good workout meant hitting the hills.

He wasn't running from his problems, he just wanted to get today's haphazard events out of his head. The bronze warrior spotted the first incline and dug in his heels.

Each stride carried him over boulders, creosote roots, and sandstone rubble. Even in the twilight hours, he loved a good workout.

After he crested the first poppy laden summit, his thoughts turned to Desiree DeNiro. He enjoyed her shapely figure and her glorious smile and those adorably cute dimples. But what bothered him most was how deeply disturbed she was.

The Captain had to turn it off. His goal was to engage in a body-racking workout and put all nagging issues aside.

He skipped down the descent, hit the valley floor, and took off like a bullet. There's nothing like a hot desert sprint to cleanse the mind. He pumped his arms furiously, found a good rhythm, and shot through the evening landscape.

But his brain caught up with him. *"Why was he doing a psych eval on the combat pilot?"*

He churned his legs harder, and high stepped his way up a steep incline.

His brain answered him, *"You're doing this because Desi is one of you. She's a military warrior trying to integrate, and she's not doing a very good job of it."*

"Geezus, he could relate. But was that the only reason he was worried about her?"

"No, there were deeper underlying issues. The sweet thing was post-

traumatic and she wasn't hitting on all pistons." He was one to talk, but then again, he'd been off his rocker for more than a decade.

Declan battled with his mind. And his attempt to turn off his thinking had painfully backfired.

"Oh well, I give up. Let's analyze the situation and see what I can do. For starters, the girl went to the Desert Sage Police Station for reasons unknown."

She wasn't there for a Flight for Life mission, which puzzled him to no end.

But his psychic tinglers went off. Dayo pounded over the sandy alluvium and headed for a starlit reservoir. He was about to take a refreshing dip, and his brain just wouldn't turn off.

"Why the hell did he care? Now, there was a sensible question."

Because his damnable mind wanted to pull her into the unit. And Desi had to come under his shield, or he'd never find a moment of peace.

Dayo reflected on Desiree's life. Flight for Life pilots didn't really understand veterans. In fact, there hadn't been a civilian yet, who had the vaguest idea what happened over there.

And the poor girl's best friend was a koala toy.

Dec spoke out loud, "Hey man, that's harsh! She's doing the best she can, and the bronze beauty is definitely struggling. You shouldn't judge, and it's time to show a little compassion."

Declan spotted a moonlit lake with an inviting pier. The red deck extended into a twilight blue lake and the moon hung on the horizon like a glowing white ball.

The bronze warrior slipped on his swimming goggles and barely broke stride. He accelerated down the wooden dock as his feet hammered down the straightaway.

He reached the end and leaped into a racing dive. No sooner did he surface; the veteran warrior broke into a freestyle sprint. Thank god for cool water and a slap to his sweaty brow.

Declan sprinted for the buoy, banked around the orange tower, and headed for the far shore. Off in the distance, he caught sight of a bougainvillea tree and his mountain bike.

The athletic fighter concentrated, kicked his feet, and arched his arms in knife cutting strokes. He cruised into the shallows, and his feet hit the sandy bottom, and he powered himself to shore.

The commander sprinted up the embankment and raced toward the pink flowering tree. He twirled the combination and unlocked his ten speed and leaped onto the seat.

In one last attempt to clear his mind, the mountain biker roared over the terrain, and hit the toughest hills with fierce determination.

He pedaled until his thighs felt rock hard, and his lungs burned, but it felt fantastic. He pumped out ten miles, and before he knew it, he wheeled into his immaculate, lonely garage.

Declan dismounted in a deft move and whirled his ten-speed overhead. He hung his mountain bike in an inverted bicycle rack and dusted his hands.

He walked briskly to his work bench and brushed aside a pair of wire cutters. He was grateful for the garage organizer as he placed his cell phone on the bench.

His iPhone lit up like a Christmas tree. The old unit was checking in and getting their frustrations off their chest.

The commander leafed through the calls. His compassion for the unit hit him like a right cross to the jaw. And so far, he hadn't come up with a solution.

Declan played Heavy Duty's message. HD was a designated marksman and master of the M 2010 Enhanced Sniper Rifle.

Dayo clicked the message. "Life in the States sucks. If I have to excavate one more mansion, I'm going to hurl. Dammit, Captain, find us something we can do or I'm gonna pop someone."

Declan had been racking his brains, trying to come up with something. He went to the Coast Guard and suggested an interdiction land based, assault unit.

While the Coast Guard arrested cartel hostiles in boundary waters, his new unit would work their way down the Baja Peninsula and cut off land support. Hell, it looked good on paper.

The Baja Peninsula would be cleansed of criminal activity from

Diego all the way to Cabo San Lucas. In a not-so-subtle way, it would free up a ton of Mexican resorts, and Americans could move freely.

Returning back to reality, the Coastie brass loved the idea, but keeping a lid on a land-based interdiction team was tricky.

Unfortunately, Dec's great idea was bogged down in military committees and the Pentagon didn't even know where to begin.

The intrepid Marine entered his exercise room and threw his sweat-soaked body armor over a rocking chair. He padded into the sunroom, which was arrayed with machines, sandbags, and heavy balls.

Declan glanced through his open-aired NanaWall and beheld the California desert. He didn't have any neighbors behind him, so he enjoyed the desert landscape for as long as he could.

More exercise didn't seem quite so appealing. It was time to investigate the Witness Program and get more details.

He placed a padded cushion over his shoulder and clicked his tongue. A gorgeous blue and yellow macaw sailed through the weight room and landed on his shoulder.

"Hey Big Blue, What's happenin'?"

"Snafu, Snafu, It's all phucked up!"

"You got that right, buddy."

Declan placed a Brazilian nut on the macaw's black tongue. With an amazing dexterity, Blue cracked the nut and rolled the fleshy seed into his mouth.

Blue eyed him from zebra-striped markings, "Find any righteous babes?"

The large parrot had a curious intelligence. It was debatable if Blue said things out of reflex, or if he was truly intelligent. A few studies indicated that macaws were as smart as a chimpanzees and actually had an extensive vocabulary.

Declan scratched Blue's crown, "Actually, buddy, I did run into a righteous babe. And I can't stop thinking about her."

Blue eyed him curiously, "Are you gonna tap her sweet ass?"

"I wish it was as simple as that. I furious tupping might do us both some good. But this girl is a special case, and her feelings should be handled with the utmost care."

"Utmost care! Utmost care!"

Declan filled the feeding cup and hung a few tropical fruits on his perch. "Buddy, I need to talk with my unit, so I'd like a moment alone."

"You got it. You big and ugly dickhead."

Declan chuckled and fired up his cell phone. His second in command, Trick Johnson's image materialized.

Trick wore an open-chested chambray shirt with a black cattleman's hat. His alert blue eyes pierced Dayo's soul.

"Damn it, Trick. I wish we were back in the saddle, going after Islamic leaders. We were damn good at what we did, and you my friend, were one of the best."

He played the message, "Whip and I are working in Oklahoma. With the exception of rodeos and roping steers, we're bored stiff."

The message ended abruptly, but the implication was clear. Whip and Trick wanted him to pull a rabbit out of the hat.

There was always the Ukraine, but no one had a dog in the fight, so it really didn't make sense. Eugene Merriweather, their team hacker, had a few insane ideas.

Eugene figured he could locate a hacker nest within three strikes. It wasn't a very clean approach, and the surgical strikes would create tons of collateral damage. But there was big money in tracking down propaganda mills.

It wasn't very realistic. So, it was back to the drawing board.

Years ago, Declan participated in steer roping, tie downs, and team roping. In his former life, he loved ranching, and he and his brother Jovani made quite a team.

But the Cazador Ranch couldn't provide a future. So, here he was, a talented headhunter, entering his late twenties, and reinventing himself.

He clicked on the next message. To his surprise, an image of Tanya Williams appeared. The streetwise cutie wore her hair in a fluffy auburn perm."

"Hey Dayo, I miss the old unit. I want us to get together and have a weekend of camping and barbecuing."

Declan realized it wasn't a bad idea, but after a few brews, they were left with a glaring reality. Stateside, the adrenaline rush was nil and life moved at a monotonous pace.

Things were too slow and there was too much time for reflection. Dark memories tended to surface, and a man started doubting himself. Talk about hell on earth!

Rather than speak to the whole unit, he decided to give Eugene a call. The hacker extraordinaire was known as Wild Man, and on more than one occasion, his intel saved their bacon.

Dayo knew he was going to regret this, but conversations with Eugene went to the extreme.

"Well, Big Blue, here goes nothing."

The blue and yellow macaw bobbed his head, "Here goes nothing! Here goes nothing!"

The webcam revealed a stunning bronze dude with a circle beard and piercing blue eyes. Wild Man flashed a bright smile and shot across his blue command center.

The swivel chair raced across the rubber flooring until he came to another desk. There were huge screens lining the walls, and to add to the bizarre image, Eugene wore an Elvis Presley, high-collared white jacket.

"Hey, Captain, I wondered when you would call." The vertically challenged hacker leaped to his feet and crooned one of Elvis' greatest hits, "In the Ghetto."

The Wild Man finished his solo, and truth to tell, the handsome short guy had an exceptional voice.

"Well, Dayo, what do you think?"

"I'm speechless, Eugene. What's with the Elvis impersonation?"

"Hey dude, you got it made. You're a babe magnet, and you look like a masculine version of Belafonte."

"But short guys like me, we've got to attract attention."

"Yeah, I sort of see your point, but do you think this is the way to go about it?"

"Hell yeah, everyone loves the King. And to overcome my extraterrestrial appearance, there's nothing like a flashy outfit."

Declan tried to keep a straight face. The commander coughed into his fist.

"Eugene, you're a good-looking dude. Your stylish circle beard and piercing blue eyes could put you on the cover of GQ. So, I don't think the Elvis jacket is really necessary."

Eugene wheeled his swivel chair and came to a sudden stop. "I beg to differ, but let's get down to brass tacks. First of all, I've resumed my role as Robin Hood. Ya know, stealin' from the rich and giving to the poor, which is namely me."

Dayo wagged his head, "All right, I'll bite. What have you been doing?"

Eugene gripped his bullet-studded jacket, "There are so many requests for Dark Web intel and insider trading, it's unbelievable."

"Geezus, Wild Man! You better be careful."

The crazy impersonator leaped to his feet and performed a double-handed finger point.

"I'd say the same thing to you. The SWAT thing went well, and you got to eliminate three bank robbers with a long-range rifle. But the rest of us are going nuts. And to make matters worse, your idea to babysit key witnesses is laden with land mines."

Declan strolled into his laminar-tiled shower. A tall glass enclosure sparkled with green filtered light.

Dayo parked his iPhone in a cradle and hooked up the audio. The bronze warrior stepped over the shower curb and entered a world of watery bliss.

There were mood lights, a shower wand, and a flower-shaped spray head. He turned on the water and let the wall jets massage his weary physique. After a few seconds, Declan called out.

"What do you mean the witness program is laden with land mines?"

Dayo used his fingers to massage his scalp and work in the herbal shampoo.

He heard Wild Man begin his report. "Man, you're assigned to a benign case with Becca Whitfield. She witnessed an embezzlement and wishes to testify against a major firm."

"She goes by the alias of Tasha Sheridan, and she has the proof on a flash drive. It's a corporate case and no sign of piranhas."

"All right, I get it. I'll just prowl the premises, keep an eye on enemy raiders, and make Becca comfortable."

Wild Man flew across the floor, and Declan heard the wheels squeak. "But I'm tellin' ya, the Witness Program is filled with dirty cops and syndicate spies. Better watch your back."

Dec stepped over the green-tiled curb and toweled himself dry. He was a well-toned machine, and he treated his body like a temple.

He slung a pair of butt-hugging shorts into place. "Do you know anything about Desiree DeNiro?"

"I ran into her at the police station, and she wouldn't tell me what she was up to."

"But I'm tellin' ya, Wild Man. I got a real bad vibe from the girl."

Dayo turned the webcam back on, and Eugene burst into a curious smile.

"She's an interesting case. The FBI earmarked her testimony, and the girl is stacked and has a gorgeous ass."

"Man alive, I checked out her Miss Rodeo photos, and her sweet bottom rises above the saddle, and she's a thing of beauty."

"And it's not just her derrière. When she performs horse jumps, her chocolate ta-tas form the most delicious cleavage. But damn, that woman is built!"

"Hey, Wild Man, you apparently don't know much about women. Pretty girls don't like to be reduced to demeaning descriptions. They want to be appreciated for their unique personalities."

"Wait a minute, you dated Desiree back in high school. I can see why you're a bit defensive. So, I'll get back to the basics."

"Yeah, let's focus on the basics. But for your information, I was an underclassman, and only dated Desiree one time."

"Got it, Chief. No offense intended."

Wild Man rocked back in his hinged, swivel chair. "Dez is in the Witness Program."

"She goes by the name of Maggie Cunningham, and she's the key witness against the drug lord, Antonio Gonzalez. She saw the kingpin execute Tinder Williams, and she's willing to testify."

Declan received the news, and he felt for the girl. No wonder Desi was on pins and needles and wouldn't confide in him.

Eugene continued, "It appears that the Witness Director, Pietro Sanchez, has removed his protection officers, and a whole new cast has been installed."

The headhunter felt his fingers tingle, and his sixth sense went on high alert. Red flags went off when he met the girl, and now, he knew why.

Dayo walked into an adjacent closet and opened a double-door gun locker. His tactical arsenal was neatly assembled against a black beadboard wall.

An M 2010 Enhanced Sniper rifle, an M4 assault rifle, and boxes of ammo stood at the ready.

Declan removed the necessary artillery and stacked the weaponry inside several duffle bags. After the primary weapons were removed, he added flash bangs, and magnetic explosives.

In his mind, he visualized a corrupt safe house, and how he'd take down the syndicate hostiles.

He removed a Sig Sauer 9 mm and shifted the sliding barrel. His sixth sense reached into the future, and there were shifting shadows, but a thick pallor of death loomed large.

The Captain knew what he was up against, and a sense of peace and well-being came over him. Another mission was about to begin, and from the great beyond, the Universe informed him that a whole new era was about to begin. With the adrenaline, it was going to be a restless night of waiting.

Eugene asked, "What's wrong, dude?"

"Syndicate hostiles aren't taking down one of our own. I'll demolish that safe house and rescue the pretty pilot. It's that simple."

Wild Man folded his arms in annoyance, "Man, you're holding out on me. What's going on with you and Desiree?"

"There's nothing much happening. Desi suffers from post-traumatic episodes, and she processes her feelings through Kay Bear, a koala wrist toy."

"She flies Flight for Life missions and leads a pretty sedate life. The girl has been through hell, and I can't allow anything to happen."

"The fact is we dated once, eight years ago. And apparently, I tried to feel her up."

Eugene flashed a bright smile "Now, that's the type of intel I want to hear about. How was she?"

"Ya know, dude, it's been so long ago, I don't even remember that night. I mean Desi always looks great, and I remember she wore a figure-hugging sheath. But for the life of me, I can't remember palming her breasts."

"Hmmm, that's strange. With a girl built like that, I'd remember that hallowed moment forever."

Dayo chuckled, "Maybe nothing happened. Now, let's get back to Desi's safe house."

"Do you have blueprints and layouts?"

"I'll get to that later and forward you the info. But I just tripped across a bounty hunter Dark Web. There's a million-dollar bounty on Desiree's head."

Declan cursed, "Fook those bastards."

"I hear ya. The sharks are in the water, and half her protection team could be double agents. The day team are regular cops, but by nightfall, things are going to get dicey."

Eugene roared, "Whooeee! Have we got a hornet's nest on our hands."

Declan saw the ante rise, and the number of insurgents was increasing. He reached into a drawer and extracted his night camos, his communicator, and his bulletproof vest.

He tossed a pair of night goggles on top and considered the incendiary situation. With that many bounty hunters, he retrieved more explosives.

While the insurgents entered the safe house, he could plant explosives on every vehicle. Lastly, Dayo brought out a box of remote detonators.

He planned to light up a city block and with his scopes, he'd take 'em all down. Nothing was going to stop him from rescuing his target.

He had to keep his head on straight and avoid emotional entanglements.

Wild Man watched him expand his arsenal, "Hey Boss, here's the lay of the land. Desi's safe house is set on a normal suburban street."

"There are several homes in each direction, and here's her Spanish Med safe house."

"Nice digs with a swimming pool and lovely grounds."

A set of blueprints flashed over the screen. Eugene added, "There are several bedrooms, but I imagine the pretty package will settle into the master suite."

The plans materialized on Declan's laptop.

Wild Man rocked back, "After you blow up half the neighborhood, then what?"

"I take down the safe house and make a run for it. I'll lose my Camaro somewhere along the way, and you need to line up a getaway vehicle."

"Furthermore, we need a place to hole up for three months. I'm considering a remote ranch a thousand miles from here, in some godforsaken backwater. You got it?"

"Got it, boss. I'll tap into satellites, coordinate thermal read outs, and every available surveillance camera."

"I'll be your eyes and ears, and I'll be fifty steps ahead of you. And what's more, I'll plow an escape route, and you'll be ranchin' in the middle of nowhere."

Declan carried three duffle bags into his Spanish Colonial bedroom. A king-sized bed sat opposite a heavy mantled fireplace, and the vaulted ceiling featured stained beams.

It was a shame he was about to say farewell to his quaint custom home. It was never a real home and after his mission, there was no way he could return. Declan set his iPhone in an uptilted stand, so Eugene could make eye contact,

"Hey, Wild Man, I just want to thank you for this Spanish custom. I never deserved it in the first place, and by the looks of it, I'm about to say farewell."

"No problem, Chief. I purchased it from a Wall Street executive. He bought the property sight unseen and didn't realize it was in the California desert. So, I passed it onto you."

Eugene yelled, "Hey, Captain, I've got a great idea. Why don't we make this into a team effort. I'll assemble the unit, and they'll cover your tracks."

"Wait a minute, this is a solo mission. In-and-out, and then we disappear."

"Bad news, boss. The Vegas betting line and the Dark Web are going crazy. The bounty just went up, and our sexy package is one popular girl."

Eugene continued, "I'd chat with you more, but it looks like a long night ahead of me. And Captain, you're going to love what I have planned."

Before Declan could respond, his untraceable phone went dead. He never used his department phone, only the lines that Eugene supplied. When the hacker clicked off, the stillness was deafening.

While he stood in his Spanish bedroom, admiring the faux finish walls and arched studio room, he wondered why he didn't appreciate his lavish surroundings more?

But he wasn't like other people. The commander was restless, and dammit to hell, this was never going to be his real home.

The bronze warrior rolled back the sheets and folded his hands behind his head. He gazed out at the Milky Way. The heavens displayed a majestic, cosmic light show.

He mused on his combat life. Did he seek out enemies, or did life simply happen that way?

And why in the blazes couldn't he get into civilian life? He hurled his musings into the great beyond.

Before falling asleep, he uttered the words, "Show me the Way, Big Guy!"

And strangely, the future opened. He wasn't sure about all the twists and turns, but the Almighty planned to open a path, and his life would never be the same.

Chapter Three

Desiree wheeled her Jeep Wrangler into the flagstone driveway. She glanced at her cute Spanish Mission, and realized she was about to leave her refuge. The oversized red tiles contrasted well against a tan stucco façade. Her outer court featured an archway, which led to her turret-shaped foyer.

Desi seized her purse and spoke soothingly to Kay Bear, "Don't worry little buddy. We'll enjoy one last night here, and before you know it, we'll be back home."

"I've decided to testify against Antonio. It's simply not right for a drug dealer to gun down such a wonderful human being."

"Tinder Williams deserves to be honored, and his family will rest, knowing the murderer was put behind bars."

Kay Bear grinned and his perpetual happiness confirmed it. She was doing the right thing. After the bronze beauty notified Director Sanchez, she pushed open the Jeep door and entered her courtyard.

She glanced over the adobe stucco walls and surveyed her beautiful cactus garden. The barrel cactus was in bloom, and the orange ocotillo flags waved in the breeze.

Desiree marveled that the landscaper planted so many century plants, agave, and yucca. Her garden projected an air of tranquility, but she would have preferred more flowers.

She lifted her wrist, "Kay Bear, when we return from the Witness Program, I want to plant a border of zinnias, pansies, and rose bushes. Our home will look spectacular."

Kay Bear's button eyes beamed at her. The lovely pilot was doing her best to stay positive, but inwardly, she was terrified. And she really didn't like change.

But Sanchez assured her, the safe house would be like going to a summer resort, complete with a swimming pool, and all the novels she could read.

She strolled through her cozy little home and entered her bedroom. There was a slanted ceiling covered in square beams and natural latillas.

To add to the ambiance, the plaster walls were painted in aqua, and there were Spanish cross designs over the French doors.

Geezus, she loved this room. And it had been her sanctuary for the past year. It was a shame to leave the home she loved. But duty called, and she wasn't one to shirk her responsibilities.

Her eyes fell on an extensive teddy bear collection. There were teddy bears of every imaginable color and shape. An assortment of white pandas, happy grizzlies, and little track stars smiled back at her.

She turned to Kay Bear, "I'd like to take all of your friends, but only a few can fit."

Since she was partial to koalas, she placed a full-sized marsupial inside her grip. Within minutes, she packed her safe house clothing and two more teddies.

The medevac pilot was emotionally exhausted, and now she faced the night terrors. She would have preferred a dreamless sleep, but it never worked out that way.

She took the last of her post-traumatic pills and gathered her teddies. As she fell asleep, she remembered Declan's handsome face, and the way he palmed her cheek, and the look of deep concern. It was nice to fall asleep, dreaming about such a gorgeous Marine.

Desiree tossed and turned, but she couldn't escape the nightmare. She landed her fully armed Black Hawk, and the military team deployed.

She cut the engine and strolled over to the hydration tent. To her horror, she wheeled around, and watched a Stinger missile detonate her unit.

There was nothing she could do to stop the explosion. A terrifying feeling of helplessness overwhelmed her. The tension rose and her heart hammered, and finally, she bolted upright.

Desiree clutched her teddies and screamed into the morning light. She panted for air, and finally found her bearings. She clicked on the lamp, quaffed down a glass of water, and took a few pills.

Her hands were shaking, and she had to get moving. Only movement reassured her that things would be all right. She entered her closet and put on a cheery red dress with puffy shoulders, a trim waist belt, and a pair of elevated red sandals.

Desi posed in front of a full-length mirror, "Girl, you look sensational, and you're ready for a holiday."

An hour later, Desiree arrived at the assignment facility. She wheeled her Jeep Wrangler into the parking lot and beheld the classic architecture.

The Witness Program wanted to project a sense of law and order. The civic design resembled a courthouse with the grand hope that justice would be served.

The bronze beauty carried her suitcase up the steps and through a colonnade. To her amazement, there were security men gathered near the front door. They were dressed in blue blazers and carried an assortment of Uzis, shotguns, and communicators.

If they were striving for an undercover look, they totally blew it. Even with sunglasses, these guys were highly visible.

Just then a key witness emerged, and they escorted the individual to an armored car.

Good lord! They weren't taking any chances. She could only

imagine what the guy had seen, and why so much protection was needed.

She kept a vigilant eye and found herself comparing the Witness Program to a sound military unit. The problem was the lack of back-up.

There should have been snipers at the perimeter, waiting to take down the hostiles. These guys had an over-simplified view of the enemy.

Desiree took a wide berth around the guards and entered a contemporary facility. Her high-heeled sandals clicked across the marble floors as she entered the assignment room.

The moment she entered; every head turned her way. If she had been wearing a red sheath and a scandalous dress, the attention would have been warranted.

But she sensed a huge problem, and a descending spirit of personal invasion tore at her nerves.

Desi should have been anonymous, and only a few people should know her identity. But it appeared that she was the center of attention, and every employee recognized her.

She lifted her wrist, "Kay Bear, I think we have a problem."

A Witness Protection officer walked over to her. He wore a short-sleeve button-down, a heavy handgun, and black slacks. His sandy hair was slicked back, and his circle beard wasn't the least bit attractive.

"Ma'am, if you'd put your suitcase on the table, I'll check your belongings."

She complied with his request as a female officer patted her down. She was starting to wonder who was under house protection? They treated her like she was the suspect and not the star witness.

Desiree knew the drill: keep your eyes open, observe everyone, and formulate a plan.

Shite! She was back in Afghanistan, and instead of a protective program, she got a bad vibe. There were a mixture of honest detectives, but others with a clandestine agenda. She considered calling a halt to this whole idea.

The suitcase officer used blue surgical gloves to examine her intimate apparel and thumb through her beach clothes.

He extended a hand, "Ma'am, may I see your koala bear?"

Desi felt the dolt had invaded her privacy. And no one messed with Kay Bear. Reluctantly, she unwrapped his wiry little arms and handed him over.

The man chuckled, "What an interesting wrist cuff! Does your koala go everywhere with you?"

She placed a defiant hand to her hip, "Yes, he does. And he's more than piece of furry jewelry, he's a good luck charm. I received him in the war."

The inspection officer smiled, and then turned his back on her. *What the eff?*

She watched him do something to Kay Bear, but immediately her happy little talisman was returned.

Desi considered reporting the incident. There was no reason for this treatment.

Just then, she saw the familiar face of Dwight Oberon. The Police Chief approached her with a friendly smile.

He huffed into his shoe brush mustache, "Desi, you look wonderful today."

"Why, thank you."

"I came over here to make sure your witness program was going smoothly, and to reassure you that Pietro Sanchez runs a great operation."

The bronze beauty rocked her hip and darted a finger at a few plain clothesman.

"How about those guys? Are they privy to my profile?"

"When I walked into the inspection room, I felt like the center of attention, not an anonymous witness."

Dwight glanced casually at the detectives, and they didn't look out of the ordinary.

"Miss DeNiro, your profile has been shared only with a few select individuals. Other than Emerson, Kelly, and the sketch artist, no one in my department knows anything about your case."

"And as for the Witness Program, the director and his immediate team are the only ones who know your true identity."

Dwight squeezed her shoulder, "Desiree, you're in good hands. Any second, the protection team will escort you to your new home, and none of them know the details."

He tried reassuring her. "They're hired security guards, and they'll post the premises. And you'll be as snug as a bug in a rug."

Desi touched Kay Bear for moral support. And as much as she wanted Dwight's words to console her, she still had doubts.

"Was she being paranoid?" Possibly, but then again, paranoid animals live to a ripe old age, and she was all for that.

An SUV team escorted her to the safe house. From the backseat, she admired a classic, upscale California neighborhood.

The black sedan pulled into a brick driveway with a turnaround, and the security men went into action. They entered the Spanish Colonial, and men dispersed in every direction.

When the coast was clear, a security guard opened the door, and another carried her suitcase.

Beneath the arched colonnade, Pietro Sanchez stood beside two spiral columns. His hang jowl expression was so mundane, he didn't look like a director of anything. He looked more like an overworked realtor, who had seen it all.

Desi smoothed her dress and assessed her new home. It was a Spanish tri-level with a clay tiled roof, ivory colored stucco, and an impressive garage door. Flowers lined the walkway, and it seemed like a lovely place.

The cautious pilot met Sanchez at the front porch.

He extended a warm greeting with a hearty handshake, "Welcome, Miss Cunningham, this will be your new home. Care to step inside? I'll will give you the grand tour."

The Director seemed anxious to get her off the street. His eyes darted along the boulevard, but this early in the morning, even the commuters were still getting ready.

He opened the heavy wooden door as she entered an elevated landing. Gazing over the living room, she appreciated the light and airy ambiance.

There was a long living room with grooved wooden floors, ice blue furniture, and an overhead vaulted ceiling. Between the iron chandelier and the honey-stained timbers, the place had a lot of charm.

And way across the room was an airy white kitchen with a dining nook, arched cubbies, and exquisite cabinetry. Her safe house was fairly spacious, and even though three months was a long time, she could see herself living here.

Pietro led her down the steps into the lower living room. "How do you like the accommodations?"

"It's a splendid Spanish Colonial, and I love the modern elements which integrate well with the historical style."

She pointed through the French doors, "You mentioned an outdoor pool; I'd like to see where I'll spend time reading and relaxing."

They walked past a security officer, and she snapped her head back to reality. *"Soldier, keep your eyes alert. Never let down your guard, you may live to regret it."*

The words of her basic training came back to her. And quickly, she evaluated the guard stations. The security men touched their communicators and seemed dead set on doing their jobs.

They were aware of her presence, but they took little interest. And that's the reaction she wanted. Casually, she made eye contact with every one of them and slammed her will into their souls.

If there was a traitor among them, she'd ask for his dismissal immediately. The men seemed to know what she was doing, and each man gave a quick finger salute.

There didn't appear to be a Judas among them, but then again, looks can be deceiving.

She whispered to Kay Bear, "We better keep an eye on these guys. So, don't get too comfortable." Her koala smiled reassuringly. At least for the present, the coast was clear.

Sanchez tipped his finger to the stationed guards, and the men nodded. Desiree proceeded out an arched French door onto a lovely cement patio.

A mosaic of blue tiles beckoned the weary travelers, and she figured on spending hours, lounging around the water feature, and studying the local bird life.

Due to a backyard fountain, teems of songbirds feasted at the feeders. There were even hummingbirds sipping nectar from red bottles.

Desi picked an Audubon Bird book off a table, "This book will come in handy."

Pietro stroked his heavy jowls. "There's a limited number of species here. But by the end of summer, the migration comes through, and you'll witness a whole new group of migratory fowl."

There it was, the ominous word, "Witness." Despite the resort feel, this was really a heavily protected facility, and not her home.

She was here for one reason, and there was a long waiting period. Antonio's lawyers tried to postpone the trial as long as possible. And the fact his attorneys succeeded in pushing back the trial date concerned her.

She turned to Pietro, "I love the pool and the palm trees and the romantic back porch."

Desi eyed the perimeter guards, "Is there any problem if I hang out here most of the time?"

"It makes me feel like I'm not under lock and key."

Sanchez delivered a lame smile, "No, Miss Cunningham. You may lounge outdoors as much as you like. Simply notify security as to your whereabouts."

He pointed indoors, "Shall I show you to your bedroom?"

They strolled down a long hallway with decorative arches. There were iron lanterns hanging from a colonial beamed ceiling, and each step echoed as they walked over red herringbone brickwork.

The hallway was exposed by a series of arched doors, and there were security men posted at both ends.

Pietro punched in a code to open her bedroom door. It was a glorious Old-World boudoir with more charm than a Spanish castle.

A gilded four poster dominated the floor plan, and the saffron bedspread was to die for. And somehow the flagstone backwall played well against a crimson-colored sidewall.

Desi opened her suitcase and brought out her teddy bear collection. She removed the scarlet red pillows from a foot bench and placed her favorites in plain view.

Pietro dropped his voice in a hush, "I hope the amenities will suit your needs. The bureau appreciates your cooperation, and without your testimony, we don't have much of a case."

"And most of all, I realize what a huge sacrifice you're making. This isn't an Airbnb, but the lavish surroundings should take your mind off the inconveniences."

Pietro bowed curtly, "So, Miss Cunningham, I'll see you later this week. In the meantime, I have another safe house to visit and a trial to attend."

She wanted to discuss the witness headquarters and the unwarranted attention. But the director turned on a dime and disappeared.

Desiree turned to Kay Bear, "Well, little buddy, we're here. I'll change into a cute bikini, and we can take a dip."

Declan arose in the middle of the night and loaded his artillery. His black beauty shot through the darkness, and he drove a half hour to his destination.

He was on the outskirts of Los Angeles, sequestered in a desert community. The neighborhood looked peaceful enough, and the residents were sound asleep.

The charming bronze warrior entered Becca's safe house. The house wasn't stirring yet, and he had time to investigate the premises.

He wore a blazer and shades, and the Marine blended in with the agents. He slipped outdoors and surveyed the perimeter.

There was a light contingent, and security was posted at the boundaries. Dayo slipped beneath a palmetto, where he was cast in shadows.

For some odd reason, he checked the Vegas betting line. A long odds favorite was highlighted in red letters, Peter Sanchez and Desiree DeNiro. There was a morbid bet on her life expectancy.

The fearless Marine clenched his fists, "Not on my watch, mother effer."

"The girl will survive, and then I'm going after Antonio." He was pissed, but he reined in his emotions, and returned to his strategic plans.

He knew Wild Man was monitoring the situation, and none of this was a surprise. Declan braced himself, he had to go through a lot of bodies to free this woman, and she was damn well worth it. Desiree was one of their own, and you never leave a man behind.

Dayo assumed a casual position near the kitchen nook. The key embezzlement witness, Becca Whitfield, carried a clipboard and wore a beige pencil skirt.

As an office manager, she toured the safe house like it was a corporate office. The undercover witness, Tasha Sheridan, came to a curt stop.

"Sir, for the noon delivery, would you like a pepperoni or a supreme pizza?"

Declan broke from his covert behavior.

"A supreme sounds fine, put me down for three slices, and a sparkling soda."

Becca's features were pleasant. "I wish all the men could make up their mind as fast as you. They enjoy my managerial skills, and I think they're starting to take advantage of my kindness."

"If I had anything else to do, I'd put down my foot."

The covert Marine tipped his head, "Men are like that, miss. Give 'em an inch and the bastards take a mile."

"You said it buddy. I'll be sure to give you a special dessert. I can see you're on my side, and you'll be easy to work with."

To keep up his attention span, the security men rotated every hour and took up a new post. It didn't take long to figure out the system, but what interested him most was the night shift.

These guys bled red, white, and blue. There wasn't a syndicate hostile among them. But he wasn't naïve, the betting line said it all. And with the long odds going through the roof, the hit was going down tonight.

The hours went by, and thank god, he cruised past Desiree's safe house earlier this morning. By the dead of night, he took in every detail and calculated his line of attack.

The fearless Marine was getting anxious, but he kept himself alert with visualization skills. From memory, he broke down every weapon and reassembled it.

And from the lay of Desi's Spanish Colonial, he figured out his best move. He knew the bedroom layout, and he figured the lieutenant was in the master suite.

Once darkness fell, he had mere minutes to plant the explosives, locate the package, and perform a quick offensive.

Finally, the Western sunset fell over the sleepy hood. The distant Sierras were cast in an orange glow, and it was time to go into action.

He peered through the curtains and spotted the arrival of the night shift. Just as he expected, this shift was loaded with undercover hostiles.

They moved in a predatorial fashion, and a pallor of evil descended. Even though the hit wasn't scheduled for Becca's safe house, he feared the worst.

Dayo slipped into a garage and switched into his night camos. He wore dark fatigues, a Kevlar jacket, M4 grenade launcher, flash bangs, and host of explosives. The Captain arranged his combat helmet, voice communicator, and night goggles.

He emerged from the dank storage room, and no one took notice. Keeping to the shadows, he made it to his Camaro. His ride was parked a short distance from Becca's safe house.

Declan didn't use his headlights, and by cover of darkness, he cruised down the street, shot over ten blocks, and arrived three homes from Desi's safe house.

He popped open the trunk and programmed a tiny robot to toddle up Desiree's driveway. The white domed robot stood a foot tall, and looked like a child's play toy, but it was a high-powered explosive unit.

Dayo donned his assault gear, complete with an M4 grenade launcher, flash bangs, and several rounds of ammo.

He stuffed magnetic explosives in a shoulder sling and crept stealthily down the dark street. He slapped the magnetic bombs beneath five SUVs and double checked the remote detonator. The bombs were wired, and now, it was time for phase two.

The covert Marine left the shadowed street and headed for the backyards. He worked his way behind a hibiscus hedge and came to several hostiles. He moved with the silence of a great cat and dispatched them one at a time.

He glanced at the far perimeter, and the insurgents remained in position. There were no alerts, and his position was unknown.

Declan crouched low and ran toward the master suite. Wild Man was in his head, giving him a play by play concerning the heat images. He moved invisibly and arrived at the master bedroom.

He placed a sound cone to the wall and listened. Dayo located Desiree, who was talking to Kay Bear.

Wild Man came over his communicator, "I have a satellite read out, and by the looks of it, the hostiles are planning an execution."

"But there seems to be an argument, and a divergent group wants to rape her. There's a line up outside her door, and men are crowding into the hallway."

"The package is on the bed, and she's rocking back and forth. I'd say the girl is having a major meltdown."

A few hours earlier, Desiree finished a leisurely nap and enjoyed the last rays of sunshine. She fell asleep while reading her Good Housekeeping mag.

She stood to her feet and wrapped a blanket around her bathing suit. The bronze beauty adjusted her koala bracelet and entered the Spanish Colonial.

A new shift had arrived, and these guys were different. They made hand gestures, and eye signals, and a whole lot of covert communication was taking place.

Desi's stomach was doing flip flops; this was all wrong.

She spoke to the lead security officer, who wore shades, a thick beard, and an athletic suit.

Desiree asked, "Has the night shift come on duty?"

She tried to be as casual and calm as possible. But inwardly, her heart was hammering a mile a minute.

"Ma'am, there's nothing to be alarmed by. The night unit is staffed with trained professionals, and we have your best interest at heart."

"If you'll be so kind as to return to your bedroom, we'll alert you when dinner is ready."

Desiree sashayed down the colonnade hallway, and her movements gained considerable attention. When she punched in her bedroom code, a security guard approached her.

Standing outside her room, she used her cell phone and speed dialed Pietro Sanchez. Just as she heard him answer, the guard caught her wrist and smashed the phone to pieces.

"Hey, what the hell are you doing? I demand to speak to the director, and you can't stop me."

The big man belted her across the face, "Look bitch, you'll do no such thing."

Out of nowhere, two security guards leaped out of the darkness and hauled her into the bedroom. She tried to scream, but another slap to her cheekbone sent her flying.

Desi tried to crawl to the other side of the bed, but two men seized her ankles. Suddenly, the big man leaped on her chest.

The combat pilot fought with fury; she kicked him in the nuts and stabbed her fingers into his eyes. The son of bitch weighed a ton, and she had moments to break free.

The ugly bastard growled, "Pasquale, we've got a feisty one on our hands, lock the door, and we'll take the first round."

"You got it, buddy."

No sooner did the door click shut, the big man belted her a few times and ripped off her blouse.

"Whooeee! This chick is stacked, and there's plenty to go around."

Desiree kicked like hell, but she couldn't free herself. His accomplices tied her feet to the iron posts, and she was about to be raped. The big man stood above her, unbuckled his pants, and lowered his drawers.

This couldn't be happening. She felt darkness start to descend. And she was about to black out. It was Afghanistan all over, and this time she didn't have her Longbow.

In her fading awareness, she pictured her chain guns ripping this son of a bitch to pieces.

The hostile bastard pulled his erection out of his shorts and started to stroke himself. He nudged her thighs open and lowered his mass.

Declan stood back and aimed the grenade launcher. He blew a massive hole in a stucco wall, and furniture went flying. He tossed a flash bang into the room, and the suite lit up like fireworks.

The hostiles were blinded by the explosives, and he instantly assessed their positions. He drilled two insurgents at the foot of the bed and fired a cluster into the rapist's back.

The big guy collapsed on top of Desiree, and she screamed and savagely bit his shoulder. In a swift martial arts move, Dayo slit the restraints, and kicked the big man to the ground.

Desi leaped from the bed, spotted a survival knife, and leaped on top of her assailant. Her delicate hands performed a double-handed grip, and she plunged the Ka-Bar in a rapid series of impalements. She stabbed the shit out of the guy.

Time was of the essence, Declan caught her wrist, "Lieutenant, he's dead. We've got to take down this safe house and do it fast."

Desiree held her wrist high and stared into his eyes.

Dayo realized the shock of seeing a black-faced warrior standing over her. He already cut the power, so the room was cast in partial darkness.

He whispered, "Desi, it's me, Dayo. Put on your uniform, and let's get crackin'."

Her eyes were wild with fear, and suddenly, she recognized him. She removed what was left of her torn clothing and pulled on her night camos.

She positioned the bullet proof vest, slung her shirt over the top, and climbed into her combat pants. Within seconds, she had her artillery belt, her communicator, and night vision goggles.

The moment she seized her M4 with an undermount grenade launcher, a look of insane satisfaction crossed the girl's face. Kay Bear clung to her wrist, and his button eyes glistened.

Declan gave hand signals toward the far side wall, "We're going to blast our way into the living room and eliminate them."

Desi fell into formation and got ready.

Just then a voice yelled from the other side of the door. "Hey Pasquale, have you slapped the bitch into submission? I love sloppy seconds, and there are ten guys waiting."

Before he could stop her, the Lieutenant crossed the room, and fired the grenade launcher through the door. The portal went cartwheeling down the corridor. The combat pilot wasn't a tight quarters fighter, and he had to act quick.

No sooner did the door sail down the colonnade, Desi leaped beneath the archway, and sprayed a non-stop volley down the hallway.

The woman was enraged, and Declan couldn't stop her. She screamed bloody murder and kept firing. Thank god, she had some basic training.

In her rage, she used her night vision, focused on a target, and fired an automatic round. She didn't stop firing until every son of a bitch was dead.

Declan leaped to her side, used another grenade, and collapsed a stone archway. With rubble falling, he gunned down six lanterns, and turned his aim on the assailants.

By that time, Desiree dusted ten hostiles. There were heaps of humanity laying beneath steel and glass. He scanned out the backyard, and apparently, the gang bang brought in the perimeter. One problem had been solved, but they lost the element of surprise.

Dayo made a hand signal, and they rushed back into the suite. With so many syndicate dogs still alive, a getaway would be impossible.

He raced to the inner wall, "Back to my plan, Lieutenant. There's a chain of command here, and you've got to follow orders."

"Sorry, Captain. But those pieces of shit tried to violate Kay Bear. And I couldn't allow it."

She arched a volumized brow, "You understand, right?"

My god, the woman was nearly raped, and she processed everything through a hand puppet. This was no time to do a psych eval.

"Desi, we're going through that wall, and then we'll gun 'em down. Wait for the garage explosion, then we go in. Got it?"

"Roger that!"

Declan fired the launcher and whipped two flash bangs into the room. He pushed a button on his belt, and the garage robot bot exploded.

The entire living room collapsed, and hostiles scrambled for cover. They leaped onto a high landing, and they had the enemy pinned down.

Dayo worked at a furious speed taking the middle and far side. His M4 chattered bullet fire in steady bursts, and the Captain was an excellent shot.

Desi filled in the gaps. And anywhere he wasn't firing, she eliminated the insurgents. In a matter of seconds, the room went deathly silent.

Declan motioned for her to follow, and they descended the steps. He fired a round into the bathroom, and Desi blasted projectiles through the kitchen island. Two more bodies dropped, and the safe house had been secured.

Desiree watched the garage burst into flames, and they didn't have long. For Dayo's purposes, it was a perfect distraction. He pointed toward the front facing, picture windows.

"Lieutenant, get into position and ready your scope. There's going to be some fireworks, and then we can secure the front."

She wasn't about to question his orders. Desi worked alongside a famed headhunter, and the guy knew what he was doing. She glanced over at Declan, and he pressed a remote-control switch.

The driveway erupted into five massive explosions. One after another, fireballs billowed into the sky, and SUVs were hurled into the air like toy trucks. The vehicles crashed back to earth, and flames burst from the fuel tanks, and bonfires melted the tires.

"Lieutenant, look for hostiles. Aim, shoot, and destroy."

Declan used the explosions to maximum advantage. When the vehicles went airborne, he tapped the glass, scanned for security guards, and started dropping them in rapid succession. He took the street and Desi scoped the driveway, and within seconds, the perimeter hostiles were dead.

Dayo turned toward the kitchen and blasted the gas stove. It erupted into another fireball, and the house was a goner.

The Captain pulled out of position, and they leaped through a ragged portal and raced into the darkness. Down the way, streetlights flicked on. And way off in the distance, she could hear the wail of sirens.

She stayed in formation as they raced toward a black Camaro. Dayo leaped into the driver seat, and she piled into the passenger side.

He set a Stinger missile launcher in her lap, "Ya know how to operate one of these?"

"Hell Yes! Kay Bear and I do it all the time."

It wasn't the truth, but she was wild with excitement. Desi was sick of being a victim, and going after the enemy was a satisfying experience.

Dayo didn't bother with the headlights. Using his night vision, the Camaro squealed its wheels, and he blasted down the street.

The commander punched the onboard computer, and a blue-eyed short guy came across the screen. "Hey, Captain, that was some demolition job."

"I've dispatched conflicting messages to the police and the fire fighters. And Desi's safe house will burn to the ground. The less evidence the better."

"I agree, Wild Man, so what's our escape route?"

"I have you on my GPS tracker, and this is going to be tricky."

"Take Elmhurst two streets down, and whirl into a one-hundred eighty. You can take out two hostile pursuers."

Desi released the safety switch to the missile launcher and got ready. She peered at the dashboard, "Who the hell are these people? They just keep coming."

Declan said, "I'll explain later, but there's a huge bounty on your head, and we have incoming."

Dayo ran the Elmhurst stop sign and whirled the Camaro into a car spinning one-eighty. The doors flew open, right as two hostile SUVs hit the intersection.

Desiree aimed the rocket launcher and lit up one SUV. The Captain stood behind the door, aimed his M16 and took out the driver and the passenger.

As a hit team poured out of the vehicle, he took 'em down in rapid succession. And lastly, he fired low, and hit the fuel tank, and the car erupted into a fireball.

The commander was fast and efficient, and she couldn't match him unless she was inside the cockpit of her Longbow.

Dayo gunned the engine, shot out of the burbs, and hit the on ramp. He rifled through the gears and by the time he hit third, he accelerated to more than a hundred. They shot through the night.

Wild Man came over the screen, "Hey Captain, we have incoming in your review."

"State trooper?"

"No, I'd say there's a high-speed hostile on your trail, which makes me think the package has a bug."

"I'm not a package! You creep."

"My name is Desiree, and I'm getting mighty pissed."

Declan glanced at her, "Eugene, she's not carrying much. All she's got are black camos, and a new set of clothing."

Wild Man eyed her, "I think your teddy bear bracelet is hot, toss it out the window."

"No way, he's my good luck charm."

Declan produced a switch blade, "Sweetheart, check his stuffing, and make it fast."

Desiree opened Kay Bear's bottom and removed the stuffing. She discovered a hideous tracking device.

She screamed, "That son of a bitch violated my little guy. If I meet him in a dark alley, that sucker is going to die. Nobody messes with my sweet koala bear."

"All right, Desi. Button him back up and hang on."

Declan accelerated and overtook an Uber vehicle. He made a rolling hand signal and honked his horn.

The Uber driver rolled down the window. "Nice set of wheels, what's up, dude?"

"Here's a pack of M&Ms for your airport trip."

"That's exactly where we're headed."

Dayo tossed the sensor into the Uber's backseat, "Thanks, dude, I'll catch you later."

Wild Man came over the screen, "Nice work, Captain. The Uber driver circled around the overpass and the hostile is following him."

"Hang tight while I intercept the hotline and send the hunters to the airport. Your slick move bought us some time. Now head for the Sierra foothills."

"Where are we headed?"

"I've got a dump yard selected, and it's not going to be pretty."

"Hey, Eugene, I don't like the sound of that. What are you going to do?"

"Look commander, you wanted me to plan an escape route, and the salvage yard is the rendezvous point. Your next vehicle is parked in the lot."

Declan cruised through the Joshua Tree forest. By starlight, Desiree could barely make out the cactus trees, but off in the distance, the Sierra foothills came into view.

Wild Man called out, "Your turn is coming up in a quarter of a mile."

The commander turned into the salvage yard and cruised past rows of rusted vehicles. There were every make and model, and no discernable arrangement.

"I hate to see the Camaro breathe it's last, but it's the right decision."

He drove beneath a giant claw and came to a halt. "Desi, grab the M16s and the sniper rifle, and we're headed for the rendezvous point."

She leaped from the vehicle and secured the long-barreled assault rifle. Whatever Declan had planned, it involved long-range marksmanship. She checked the scope, and it was in fine working order.

Declan whirled two rifles over his shoulder and spoke to the onboard computer.

"Wild Man, where's our next ride?"

The lights of a black Humvee flashed on.

"See the Hummer? It's a beauty. I picked it out myself, and the muffler extension is cool as hell, isn't it?"

"If we plan to drive through a river, it may come in handy."

"Precisely, what I was thinking."

Suddenly, the claw reached down, seized his black beauty, and crushed the exterior. The wicked crane whirled in an arc and dropped his beloved car into a hydraulic crusher.

The engines fired up, and the hydraulic cylinders lowered, and an unearthly screeching sound occurred.

Desiree touched his hand, "Dayo, I'm really sorry. I bet you loved that car, and losing a classic sportscar must hurt like hell."

She pointed to Kay Bear, "He says he's really sorry for all the trouble we've caused, but K-Man plans to make it up to you."

The fearless Marine shook it off. In one night, he'd lost his home and his favorite car. He blew up a city block, and he was headed for parts unknown.

The life of a wandering warrior was in full swing. He glanced at Desiree, and his "leave no man behind" motto was taking a big hit.

But she was a living, breathing human being. Desiree was far more valuable than his Spanish Med and his Camaro. Someday, he would replace those things, but a human life was irreplaceable.

It was a selfish moment, but Cazador pushed aside his regrets. Desi was a breathtaking beauty who had lost her way. He jumped into the black Humvee and eyed the snorkel extension.

"Wild Man, where are we headed?"

"Ever cruise a river before? This baby will keep jugging, and when you four-wheel up the embankment, no one can possibly follow."

Eugene chuckled, "There isn't a bridge for miles."

Cazador rolled out of the salvage yard and headed toward the Sierras. He took a dirt road and spotted the river.

He turned to Desi, "Honey, hang on. We're going down the bank and into the stream. Make sure Kay Bear is high and dry and be prepared for a few sinkholes."

Desiree seized the hand grip as the Hummer tilted and slid down the bank. They entered a small river, and Declan cruised downstream. She removed her night goggles, and the early morning light was starting to dawn.

The creek was quite pretty. There were does drinking from the banks, and boulders scattered amongst the black currents. She glanced at the shoreline, and it was covered in water hyacinth, reeds, and cattails.

Declan engaged the four-wheel drive. And on one occasion, the Hummer dropped into a plunge pool. Water filled the footwells, but she managed to keep Kay Bear elevated. In a crazy way, the swill of water around her combat boots was refreshing.

After a mile of downstream cruising, sloshing through shallows, and dodging boulders, Declan spotted a dirt ramp exit.

"Eugene, am I taking that muddy ramp out of this streambed?"

"Yes, you are. No one in their right mind will follow. And what's more, you're about to go horseback riding."

"I've selected a mountaineer stable five miles away, and these mountain climbers are incredible. You're going up and over the high Sierras, and then you'll catch a train."

Desiree felt the adrenaline start to wear off. She was uncertain about her future and didn't even know where she was headed.

"Wild Man, I know you're a master hacker, but where in god's name are we going?"

"The Captain requested a remote ranch a thousand miles from L.A."

"I'm in the process of locating a rundown cattle ranch that is in dire need. You're not just a pretty rodeo queen. You do know how to herd cattle and rope steer, don't you?"

Desi felt like he was testing her. "As a matter of fact, I can herd cattle and even barrel race. But why are we running away like we're fugitives?"

"Why don't we head back to Desert Sage and find a way to work this thing out."

Declan turned to her. "The safe house was compromised, and that means both the syndicate and the police are after us."

He palmed her cheek, "Desi, there's no way we can return. There are bounty hunters, syndicate hostiles, and trigger-happy officers looking to kill you. You're worth millions dead or alive."

Wild Man chimed in, "Now, that you blew up the safe house, she's worth a half billion. The bounty hunter switchboard is going crazy."

"And the Dark Web is recruiting assassins from everywhere. Gonzalez is livid that his enemy witness lived out the night, and he's getting nervous."

Desiree was exhausted. She fought through the entire night, and escaped death countless times. Thanks to Dayo, she was still alive. Her nerves were shot.

She moaned, "Kay Bear needs a break, he just can't go on!"

Declan hauled into a horse ranch and parked the Hummer. He pointed to the top of a mountain. "When we reach the summit, you and Kay Bear can take a break."

She looked at Declan like he was insane. "Do you take psycho pills or something? Where in the hell do you get the energy?"

"It's a matter of necessity. If we remain in the lowlands, the enemy has a chance. If we can make it into the high country, we can rest and regroup."

Desiree watched the early morning light shatter above the horse barn. Way above the valley, she spotted the Sierra summit. The high peaks were a pathway to freedom, and she was all out of options.

Declan cut the engine, undid her seat belt, and hauled her into his lap.

"Lady warrior, you're all I've got. You and I make a two-man team. And I have a standing vow to take care of my men."

She watched his athletic hands reach for a first aid kit. He opened the red cover, extracted antiseptic wipes, and ministered to her swollen eyebrow.

With an unusual tenderness, the commander tended to her split lip and checked her vision. "Can you follow my fingers?"

"Are you kidding me? I scoped a half dozen hostiles, my vision is fine."

"Just routine procedure, sweetheart." His terms of endearment were touching. And beyond her combat abilities, Declan still regarded her as a lovely woman.

"I applied fast healing ointments. I don't want anyone to think I'd ever lay a hand to such a pretty face." She received his tenderness, and her eyes twinkled, and her lips curled into a radiant smile.

"It was touch and go there for a while. The ugly bastard had me pinned to the bed, but I kept kicking his balls and fighting."

"Poor Kay Bear witnessed it all, and I fear for his sanity. He was almost violated, and a little koala takes those things personally."

Declan had to agree, "Looks like K-Man overcame his fears, and he came out fighting like a wild banshee." The man's charming, Caribbean features broke into adoration.

"Desi, I know you've lost a lot in one day. Your former life is shot to hell, and your Flight for Life missions won't resume for a while. But I want to get you back in the air as fast as we can."

He continued, "Medevac flights are part of who you are, and I won't allow it to end."

The fearless Marine leaned closer. Sitting in his lap, there wasn't much space between them, and now the commander closed the distance.

His handsome mouth was barely a hair's breadth away.

He whispered into her lips, "Desi, you're one courageous woman, and I'm damn proud of you."

She flashed a happy, closed mouth smile, and he descended into a dreamy, slow-motion kiss.

She wrapped her arms around his neck and melted into his embrace. Time stood still as she parted her lips and allowed him to enter.

In a delicious French kiss, their tongues tangled in a beautiful way. For a moment, the distant Sierras, and the dark horse barn melted away.

It was just the two of them. All she had in this world was one amazing Marine and a happy little Kay Bear.

Finally, their lips separated, and Desiree lingered. Her rosy gold eyelids remained pressed to her cheeks.

Suddenly, her eyes opened, and they were back in reality. It was an abrupt re-entry, but the surrounding landscape was gorgeous beyond words.

Desi peered beneath her lashes, and hoped Declan noticed her Arabian eyeliner. The accent brought out her incredibly dark eyes.

The bronze beauty broke the silence, "Are you sure we can do this?"

Declan curled his lips, "Pretty sure. I've never ridden a mountain climber before, but it sure looks fun."

The commander was a fearless Marine. Of course, he could do it. Desiree hoped her nerves would hold out, and she wouldn't fall off a cliff.

Reluctantly, she said, "I'm all in, commander. But if I fall off a mountain, it's your fault."

Dayo palmed her cheek, "Babe, you've got this!"

She arched her S-curved brows, "Really?"

"Really?"

The man was totally insane, and the crazy part was, she was right behind him.

Chapter Four

Declan fired up the Hummer and relinquished his observation point. The moment the horse barn came into view, he wanted to make sure Desiree was onboard. The girl had gone through hell, and she wasn't firing on all pistons.

Typically, when he manned his unit, he didn't go around kissing his team. But to keep this soldier going, he pulled out all the stops.

Besides, she was a radiant beauty, and her mild neurosis was sort of charming. At least he knew what she was feeling. Kay Bear channeled her emotions, and it took the guesswork out of the equation.

Dayo cruised closer to a steep roofed, dark stained horse barn. The white clapboard homestead was buried in a nearby forest, and his eyes landed on a quaint, miniature log home.

He tapped the onboard computer, "Wild Man, how are we going to do this? Shall we enter the stalls by stealth and select a pair of hill climbers?"

"Boss, do I look like a rookie?"

Eugene's face grinned from a stunning circle beard. His silvery blue eyes blazed with merriment.

"You're lovin' this aren't you? But I remind you, Desi and I live in real time, and our ass is on the line."

"Got it, Chief! Your Ronald and Nancy Reagan masks are in the back seat, and there's a voice modifier, along with a blank credit card."

"Inside the log shack, there's a country cowboy. And he'll flip head over heels when we make him an offer. If he agrees to our plan, I'll load the credit card, and the kid will drive the Humvee to Salt Lake. In three months, the all-terrain Hummer is his."

"Remember to put on your riding gloves, use the voice modulator, and select a pair of fantastic mountain climbers. I suggest you go straight up the mountain and save time."

Eugene waved, "By the way, I notified the Unit, and they're on the way. They're going to clean your tracks, and they're as excited as hell."

The screen went blank. "Hey Wild Man, come back here!"

"You're going overboard. This was a quick in-and-out mission, not a full-blown op."

Desiree pulled on her Nancy Reagan mask, slipped on her riding gloves, and seized the voice modulator.

She spoke out loud, "This is the First Lady, and I'd like to select my favorite charitable campaign. I feel the sad ass witness programs are in dire need of renovation."

They both listened to Nancy's voice, and it was incredible. Desiree sounded just like the former first lady. It was hilarious. She handed the modulator to Declan.

"As your President, I plan to launch my Reaganomics programs and get our great nation back on its feet."

Dayo set the button to a male voice, and his timbre sounded identical to the fortieth president.

They slung their automatics over their shoulders and headed for the office. There was no reason to pretend they were ordinary mountaineers.

Declan and Desi entered the horse-riding office. The red stained timbers carried inside the interior. The moment they entered; a tiny cowbell announced their presence.

For lodge-styled decor, there were snowshoes, an Eastern saddle, and photos of ambitious riders. Dressed as Reagan, Declan approached the front desk.

A wiry cowboy ambled to the front and stopped cold.

In Ronald's voice, Declan spoke. "There's no need to be alarmed. We want to rent a pair of hill climbers and take the fastest route to the summit."

Desiree placed the blank credit card on the desk. She took the voice modulator.

In Nancy's sing-song voice, she said, "We'll need Eastern saddles, elastic breast collars, riding boots, and lightweight backpacks."

The kid hesitated. She intoned softly, "Is there a problem? You'll be compensated fairly, and there's even a bonus involved."

The young man pushed his sweat-stained cowboy hat. "Are you guys on the run?"

She read the name plate, "Johnny, the less you know the better. We came, we left, and your horses will be dropped off at the rendezvous point. Understand?"

"Yeah, clear as a bell. Hey, you guys aren't going to kill me, are you?"

She giggled in Nancy's breathy California accent, "Why would we go to the trouble? If we scrubbed you, who would run the horse ranch?"

Nervously, Johnny laughed, "I didn't think about that."

Declan walked over to a waterfall boot rack. He selected high-calf footwear, a lightweight hunter's pack, and two days of rations.

Desi followed suit, and they were all set. Dayo left the credit card on the table, "Johnny, it's time to see the mountain climbers and saddle up."

"Yes, sir, Mr. President, come this way."

The young cowboy opened the back door, and from Wild Man's intel, they knew the homestead was empty, and there was no one else on the ranch.

They entered the dark-stained barn, and Johnny took them directly to the tack room. Two Eastern saddles were selected because they allowed maximum contact.

Declan noticed right away that the mountain horses sported strong chests and well-muscled hind- quarters. The paddock was full of beautiful Quarter Horses and most of them were bay colored.

Johnny saddled up two hill climbers and attached the main cinch. The young cowboy tugged on the flexible collar.

"If you're looking to ride straight up the mountain, this breast collar comes in handy. There's a slight movement to the saddle, but it conforms better to the horse's back."

Desi took the voice modulator, "Is there only one path to the top?"

The kid laughed nervously, "Sorry, Mrs. Reagan, I forgot to fill in the details."

He distributed two contour maps. "There are three trails leading to the summit, and the same number descending the other side."

"Blue is for beginners, and it snakes up the mountain slowly, and there are a shitload of switchbacks. Green is for mid-level riders, and it takes you straight up, but the trail has some rocky places."

The red trail is for advanced mountaineers, and there are lots of rocky outcroppings."

Declan spoke in Reagan's voice, "Two questions: Which trail is the fastest? And which trail has the most tree cover?"

Johnny exclaimed, "This is cooler than shit. I can't wait to tell my friends that I met the Reagans."

Desiree touched her 9 mm, "Sorry cowboy, you have no friends, and this encounter must never be discussed. Savvy?"

"Oh, of course. What was I thinking?"

"Back to Ron's question. Even though the red markers are more challenging, they aren't the fastest. With dry weather, the mid-level trail is best, and there's far more tree coverage. So, if you're worried about being seen, I'd take the green."

Declan tossed Johnny the keys and the empty credit card. "Son, there's a big bonus waiting in Salt Lake at the Humvee dealership."

"When you arrive, Robin Hood will contact you and load the card. Your brand-new Hummer will remain in Salt Lake for three months, and then it's all yours."

"No way! This is amazing. I'll make up some stuff and head that way later."

Declan patted his sniper rifle, "Son, there's no time like the present. I want to see your taillights disappear in the distance, and we're out of here."

"And remember, this meeting never took place."

"Mr. President, I totally understand. On the contour the yellow markers indicate several drop off points. You can leave the mountain horses on the other side. Or if you take the scenic trail, you can cross the next summit, and leave them at a wooden lean too."

Declan tipped his Reagan mask, "Better get a move on it, Johnny. I can hit a mark twenty-four football fields away."

"Holy Shit, Mr. President, I'm outta here. And Nancy it was nice meeting you."

The kid scattered the horse remuda and leaped into the Hummer. Within seconds, his taillights were outside the property, and he was headed south. It was the opposite way they were headed, and their plans were unfolding nicely.

Desiree slipped her riding boot into the stirrup and whirled into the saddle. It was a streamlined Eastern saddle, and the knee pads were extremely comfortable.

Her sorrel's name was Comanche, and his reddish-brown coat caught the sun, and it highlighted his muscular physique. Comie was a gorgeous stud, and she was eager to see how he performed.

It shouldn't have surprised her that Comanche was a stallion. Mountain climbing required exceptional strength, and the testosterone of an ungelded male was absolutely essential.

Furthermore, the ranch could breed their best males and create the bloodlines, which enabled their horses to climb to the top.

Declan wheeled into the saddle, checked his riflery, and performed a smooth rollout. Hidalgo was a magnificent bay stud, with a physique capable of carrying a strong warrior.

They left the lush valley and followed the horse path to the trailhead. Desi hadn't been horseback for the past seven years. But it came back to her in a rush.

She loved horses, and the rolling hills were a perfect place to practice her body posture and work her core. The bronze beauty adopted a half-saddle gait and bounced her rear ever so slightly.

From behind, Dayo groaned, "But damn, girl! You have an

incredible ass. And your derrière is so freakin' shapely, even those night camos can't hide your comely beauty."

"Kay Bear thinks you're awfully direct, and he thinks you have a raging libido."

"Tell K-Man, he's right. But as a commander, there's a time and place for everything. So, sweetheart, let's not dally, it's time to hit the high country."

The moment they entered the forest, their horses disappeared from view. Desi entered a world of dappled light and shadow. Ferns and spritzers covered the forest floor, and the hillside was lined with conifers.

She paused to assess the markers. Leaving the trailhead, the mid-level markers trailed straight up. The path was covered in dry dirt, head-sized stones, and an occasional cluster of tree roots.

From her past, she knew that Comanche would need to pick his footing, pull with his shoulders, and push with his hindquarters. Her job was to use her core, lean slightly forward, and seize his mane.

Declan studied the map briefly, "Let's take the green trail to the first lookout, and let our horses acclimate."

She leaned forward with the reins, and swiftly, Comanche started up hill. She used her bodyweight to assist his footing, and to her amazement, the mountain climber went straight up.

Comie came to a root lattice, and he tilted his head downward, and eyed his footwork. She didn't rush him, this was a delicate maneuver, and the sorrel stud was her only means of transportation.

Over the span of an hour, Comanche and Hidalgo worked their way over root lattices, small outcroppings, and narrow rock ways. But their mountaineers kept ascending, and it was a thrilling ride. Directly ahead, there was an opening in the trees, and a granite overlook appeared.

They rode their horses to an intermediate resting point. Declan discovered a spring as water trickled into a rocky pool.

He led Hidalgo forward, and the bay stud quenched his thirst. Apparently, the mountain climber knew how much to drink and when to stop.

Within less than a minute, Hidalgo lifted his head.

Declan patted his sweaty neck, "That a boy, you handled the trail like a pro. And I appreciate all your hard work."

She gazed across the high Sierras. They weren't at the summit, but through a gap, she saw snow-covered mountain peaks and alpine green meadows.

The sunshine cast a gorgeous glow over the land, and the clear blue skies were riveting. Standing on the promontory, they had an eagle's view of the landscape.

Over on an adjacent hillside, there were elk wandering through a high meadow. It was spectacular.

And even though she was on the run, Desi felt like she was becoming more like herself. There was a time when nature rides filled her afternoons, and she forgot how much she enjoyed them.

Desiree let Comanche drink from the pool. And suddenly, she felt a wave of suspicion hit her with a gut punch.

Wild Man and Declan coordinated way too smoothly. From all appearances, they were a well-oiled machine, and this op had a very tangible goal.

She was referred to as the package, but the one blurry point was the destination. *What if Dayo planned to take the reward money?*

Desiree was worth a half billion dead, and it would take a lot to walk away from that kind of money.

She rode up beside him, "Commander, what's your stake in all of this?"

He furrowed his handsome brows and cocked his head curiously. "What do you mean?"

"I mean, you're a SWAT team expert, and the Witness Program was only a sideline. It seems pretty suspicious that your safe house was so close to mine."

"And the way you and Eugene communicate, you had this thing planned to a tee."

"And to make sure, you get the bounty money, Wild Man is calling in the military unit."

She shrugged beneath her night camos, "I mean a half billion goes a long way. And I'm sure the guys need the funds."

His dark brown eyes bored into hers, and his handsome lower lip dropped. He wasn't shocked, but she could see the disappointment. "Is that what you think?"

Was she making a huge mistake? The rescue mission went off without a hitch, or did it? With a fearless Marine and a legendary headhunter, it was hard to say.

She folded her arms in defiance, "I refuse to go one step further, unless you tell me what's going on!"

He eyed her carefully, "What do you want to know?"

"You're a military strategist, give me the brief."

Declan stroked his handsome stubble. "In a thumbnail sketch, there's a huge bounty on your head, and every minute, you stay alive, the figure keeps going up."

"The Witness Program has been compromised, and Pietro Sanchez may be a bought bitch. And of course, the safe house was a set-up."

"Since we demolished the safe house, we've got hostiles and cops coming after us. We left a sketchy trail, cleaned our tracks, but the further we get from L.A. the better."

"Wild Man is our lookout man. And our goal is to lose the hostile trackers, board a train, and get several states away."

Dez pointed an elegant finger at her bosom, "Am I nothing more than a package? A stacked, brick house chick who is worth millions?"

When she uttered those words, her lower lip quivered, and she was scared to death. Dayo was her only hope, and if he went south, she was screwed. She might as well give up.

"Package is code speak for key witness. And please forgive Wild Man's chauvinistic comments. He saw your Rodeo Queen photos, and he still can't get over how amazing you look."

"All right, that sounds plausible, so where's the delivery point?"

"I don't really know, but the destination sure as hell isn't a scheduled meeting with Antonio."

"I'd drill five bullets into his worthless skull before I ever handed you over. He's a cartel piece of crap, and you're a valiant woman."

"And to put it plainly, the rendezvous point isn't an assigned handoff. It's a place to hole up, lay low, and cattle ranch until we know our next move."

"That's all I know, and all I can accurately tell you."

Desi held her koala toy, "Kay Bear, do you think Dayo is telling the truth?"

His little button eyes were vibrant with faith, and his pink lips reassured her with a happy smile. "You're in luck, Captain. Kay Bear thinks you can be trusted."

She was about to rein her horse, but then she stopped. "One more question, Commander."

Dayo led Hidalgo beneath the outstretched branches of a ponderosa. The long needles grazed his military helmet, and he said, "Shoot!"

"Am I more to you than a generous rack, and a well-rounded ass?"

She was feeling very unsure of herself, and words like package and brick house made her feel undervalued.

He curled his lips with male appreciation, and she wanted to slap him hard.

Declan palmed her bronze cheek, "You're an amazing woman, and a courageous combat pilot. And now, you're one of us."

"You're an honorary headhunter, and there's no going back. And from a personal standpoint, your feelings run deep, you love teddy bears, and you're dedicated to saving lives."

"You struggle with post-traumatic episodes, and you're trying to fit in. And most of all, I happen to like you...."

For the first time, she realized Dayo had a heart. Beneath the Marine intensity, there was a man who cared. He wouldn't sell her out, and he would go to any lengths to protect her.

He blew up a Spanish custom home, and he said that he really liked her. She felt warm and fuzzy all over.

As Hidalgo came to the next trail marker, Declan halted.

"Babe, you've got to put all your warm fuzzies aside, put on your game face and focus on the rocky ascent."

"Concentrate on the perfect hill climbing posture, clench your tummy muscles, and lean slightly into Comanche's mane. The trail looks rockier, but we're making good time, and shortly we'll be at the summit."

Desi rode up to him, "Just when I started to like you, you go back to being a callous butthead."

"Kay Bear thinks you have major control issues."

"Tell K-Man, I'm in charge, and I'm responsible for both of you."

It was childish, but Desiree raised her middle finger in a rebellious salute. "Captain, can you read my body language?"

"I've seen worse and flippin' me the bird isn't gonna help. Lieutenant, just focus on what's before you, and let's get after it. Daylight is burnin', and the enemy is hot on our tail."

The commander was right and flipping him off was childish. She used her adductors to grip Comanche's shoulders, and she distributed her weight, so the sorrel could pick his footing.

Desi ascended straight up the mountain as she clenched her abs, gripped his mane and leaned into the mountain. Her Quarter Horse threaded one rock outcropping after another, and the astute animal found good traction and pushed with his powerful hind legs.

In a short hill climb, they attained the summit and a mountaintop view exploded before them. With the last incline, she hugged Comanche, and pressed herself to his withers, and made herself one with his exertions. They finally made it.

Just then, she heard a plane engine. It was a Hercules C-130, and the transport plane hovered at a slow jet speed, less than a thousand feet above the ridge. From its trajectory, she figured it was a sky diving plane, and the pilot was preparing for a jump.

Mysteriously, two sky divers leaped from the aft ramp, and the trip line released their chutes. Looking into the sky, the silhouette of two paratroopers was unmistakable. Her heart raced, but she glanced at Declan, and he used his M16 to track them.

He called out, "Lieutenant, they're headed for the shoulder. We've got to descend to that precipice, set up a sniper nest, and take 'em down."

"Now don't panic, we've got time, and I don't believe they saw us."

"We've stayed in the forest during the entire ascent. I think Antonio's bounty hunters have taken a wild guess, and they think we might have survived."

His dead calm assuaged her. They returned to the green markers and started the descent. This time Dayo took the lead.

Hidalgo took a diagonal path, and her Marine kept a relaxed posture, allowing his bay stud to pick his downward footing.

The Quarter Horse arched his neck, stared at the rocky path, and his forelegs purchased a sound grip. They took the fast track downward as the parachutists worked their guidelines.

She didn't dare take her eyes off the trail, but only glanced occasionally. Finally, they hit a ridge, and Declan followed the arête until he reached a precipice.

It was a scary granite outcropping, cantilevered like a diving board. But the aerial view and the high ground were perfect.

Desi tied Comanche to a pine tree and grabbed her scope. Within seconds, they created a sniper nest, and she became the spotter, and Declan was the sniper.

The precipice offered a rock cleft on the back side, and they were hidden from view. If they were wearing granite camos, it would have been perfect.

Desiree peered through the scope and called out the calibrations. It was a lot like avionics, and she liked the physics behind the earth's curvature, the temperature, and the wind speed.

Declan set up the tripod and held the enhanced sniper rifle with precision. He eyed the hostile target. Dayo made the adjustments and waited for them to fold their chutes.

A stationary target would be easier to hit. Just as the first sky diver landed, the guy hit and rolled. The hostile looked around and kept a low stance.

Declan held his eye six inches from the scope and had him dead to rights. The shot was a mere fifteen football fields away.

The Marine used the single bolt action and exhaled slowly. He pulled the trigger and cleaned the hostile off his feet.

Desiree held one hand over her eye. "Captain, it's a confirmed kill. He's dead and not moving. One down, and one to go."

They scanned the high meadow, and the second sky diver had just landed. He used the bolt action, re-calibrated per Desi's announcements, and aimed at the insurgent.

When he took out the first bounty hunter, the second guy raised his head, scanning for his buddy. It was a dumb move, but Declan took advantage of the opportunity. The sniper exhaled slowly, and a second hit knocked the enemy to the ground.

"Desi keep your rifle in hand, and we'll ride horizontally across the mountain. I nailed them both, but we've got to make sure."

Hidalgo and Comanche left the green markers, found an elk trail and cut across the mountain face. Thankfully, the trail was fairly well worn, and the horses adjusted to the terrain.

When they were fifty yards from the fallen, they tied off. It was an easy shot, but the commander had to make sure.

He unslung the M 2010, scoped the fallen, and fired another projectile into each body. Now, it was a confirmed kill.

She used her scope and watched his methodical execution. He was a professional marksman, and a loyal warrior. And she was damn proud to be on his team.

Declan slung the rifle over his hunting pack and decided to use the M16. "Lieutenant, I'm headed downhill. I'll search the hostiles for clues. Then, we'll hit the trail, and call Wild Man."

"I'm going with you."

He signaled with a finger point, and she trailed behind him, working from boulder to boulder and from tree to tree. Declan motioned for her to halt, and she drew her assault rifle into position.

Dayo scanned the skies, waiting to see if the Herc 130 circled back. But there was nothing but blue sky. Quickly, he scrambled across the meadow, seized the fallen hostile, and dragged him into the shadows.

He worked through his vestments and discovered a set of coordinates. It had to be a wild guess, there was nothing out here.

But one thing was certain, the hostile was a bounty hunter, and Antonio's number was in his breast pocket. Declan grabbed the info for safekeeping.

He made it to the second sky diver and performed the same inspection. Other than discovering the same thing, there was nothing to gleam. Both men were South American and may have affiliations with the syndicate.

Declan met Desi back at the horse site. In silence, the pair hugged the tree line and descended into the valley. Their mountain climbers descended at a steady pace, and there was even a dirt bluff at the very end.

Hidalgo picked his footing carefully, but the stud took sliding strides downward, and he skidded with each step. Tiny pebbles rolled down the dirt bluffs, and finally they bottomed out.

They rode through the lush valley hardly saying a word. Over his shoulder, he could hear Desi talking to Kay Bear, and she was definitely upset. He had to keep his team together and get as far from the Southern Sierras as he could.

Desiree enjoyed the valley trail, the babbling brook, and the mountain meadows. But dammit all, Antonio's bounty hunters were still on their tail, and she wondered if this would ever end.

Directly ahead, she spotted a wooden lean too. They dismounted, grained, and watered the mountain climbers. She wasn't sure if they were headed for the second scenic trail or not.

Desi finally broke silence, "Commander, what comes next?"

"That's what I need to find out."

He touched his communicator. "Wild Man come in. I've got a report on a Hercules C-130, and two hostile bounty hunters. How close is that train connection?"

She examined the contour map, and it wasn't far away. Desi peered through the evergreens and spotted two parallel tracks.

Wild Man came over their communicators. "The police station is in total confusion, and fire fighters spent all night putting out the fire."

"Half the syndicate headed after the Uber, and they figured you went to the airport. Cops are combing commercial stops and looking for signs of getaway vehicles."

"Of course, they don't know what they're looking for, and I've scrambled their dispatch reports, and cops are running everywhere."

"Hostiles haven't discovered the salvage yard, and your Hummer is halfway to Salt Lake. Even though I loaded Johnny's credit card, I expunged all record of the transaction."

"Good going, Eugene."

Desi chimed in, "What's our next move? I want to get the hell outta here. We just took out two bounty hunters, and I'm getting sick of this."

Eugene yelled, "Hang on to your hat, girl. There's a northbound train coming your way. Drop off the horses, and head over to the train tracks."

"I'll hack the computer and slow the locomotive down. Make sure you position yourself around a bend when you leap aboard."

Declan heard a train whistle echo off the canyons.

"Hey, Eugene, we're out of position, and we've got to hustle. We'll talk when Desi is safely aboard."

"Roger that!"

They scurried down a small hillside and came to a blind curve. A triple locomotive thundered their way. The two warriors waited in the shadows as the engine sailed past.

When Declan spotted a cattle car, he yelled, "Start running!"

He veered toward the box car, seized the metal flatbed, and leaped onto the floor. Dayo bellied up and rolled his legs aboard.

Desi pumped her fists furiously, and he caught her hand, and lifted her up. Thank goodness, Dayo was a strong guy. The combat pilot chose to drown her sorrows in buckets of ice cream, and stateside, she'd added a few pounds.

Declan surveyed their surroundings, and the car was stacked with hay bales. One side was nearly full to the ceiling. There was a strong, dusty smell, and the slide panels were slotted to allow airflow.

To her surprise, Dayo arranged alfalfa bales into a two-person sofa and threw a tarp on top.

The fearless Marine pointed to her new sofa set, "It took longer than I thought, but I promised you rest, and here it is."

Desiree set her rifle to the side and climbed onto the sofa. Fatigue hit her like a ton of bricks. She had been awake all night, fought off insurgents, and rode mountain climbers to the summit.

Declan called in, "Wild Man, we're safely aboard a cattle car and headed north. What's our estimated time of arrival?"

"Boss, I've selected a cattle ranch. It's our primary target. The owner is half blind, and his driver's license was suspended. He has a beautiful spread, and cows are scattered everywhere."

"But his homestead has seen better days, and it's a real fixer upper. There's one aging cowboy on the property, and the outbuildings look like hell."

"The odd thing is there's a huge headcount for mares and colts."

"Eugene, it sounds like the rancher has a diverse revenue stream. He raises cattle and does horse ranching as well."

"Oh, that probably explains it. Because one covered arena is in fantastic shape."

Declan whispered into his communicator, "Make sure it's remote and far from any major cities."

"Boss, the entrance consists of two dirt lanes, and I don't think the man gets many visitors."

Suddenly, a new voice piped into the conversation. It was Lt. Tanya Williams.

"Hi y'all, it's Tanya. When I heard about the safe house, Eugene put out the word, and I just had to join the action."

"You two are on the run, and we've got one helluva ranch prepared. By the way, how are your cowboy skills?"

"You guys know how to drive cattle, brand calves, and do open-range roping, don't you?"

Wild Man chimed in, "Or was all that cattle driving talk just a load of bull?"

Eugene continued, "Old Man Cobb Pettigrew won't take kindly if a pair of greenhorns hit his property."

Desiree bolted upright. She was in no mood for taunting. "Kay Bear says you better watch your mouth. He knows what I can do. And I'm no newcomer to cattle drives, branding, or roping steers."

Tanya replied, "Sorry about that Desi, I didn't realize you were a black cowgirl!"

Declan watched her eyes widen, and the bronze beauty was about to explode.

"Hey, Tanya, it just so happens that twenty-five percent of the ranches are owned by black cowboys. But we prefer to think of ourselves as cattlemen and veteran warriors. We tend to leave out any references to our suntan."

Desi sent a verbal volley, "And girl, if memory serves, you've got a wild fluff of auburn ringlets, and a dark cocoa complexion. So, let's drop the racial references, and just accept that people are people."

Dayo could tell Desiree was suffering from sleep deprivation. "Hey guys, we're about to hit the hay for a few hours, is there anything else we should know?"

Eugene popped another question. "It looks like our horse rancher once specialized in reined cow horse competitions. Can you do that?"

Declan answered, "Western horsemanship requires finesse, subtle rein work, and highly responsive Quarter Horses. We never had such refined animals at our ranch, but if it's needed, I will definitely up my game!"

Desi was still upset from the racial reference.

She elevated her voice, "The Captain can do freakin' anything. He's an insane Marine, and he'll master any damn thing you throw at him."

Tanya eased up, "All right, girl, I hear you loud and clear. You're a mean-lean fighting machine, and you stand by your man."

Williams added, "Just so you know, we're air dropping two crates about seven hundred miles north. Desiree will have cowgirl clothes, ultimate sports bras, new wranglers, and cool tall boots."

Declan watched her yawn, "Hey guys, my bronze beauty is all worn out. So, we're going to sign off. I'll check back in, in a few hours."

The transmission ended, and Desiree processed her future. After a violent safe house demolition, a car chase, and the elimination of bounty hunters, her nerves were frayed.

She was emotionally exhausted, and her next challenge was becoming a real live cowgirl. *Good lord, this was crazy!*

Declan climbed onto the hay bale sofa and pulled her close. She cuddled into his chest and nuzzled into his arms.

"Dayo, I want to be held, can you wrap your arms around me? Kay Bear and I have been through hell. And I deserve a fully loaded Longbow with coordinates set for Antonio's mansion."

"I want to punish the bastard, blow the hell outta his home, and drill him with an M 230 chain gun."

He kissed her forehead, "Hey Babe, I like the retaliatory idea. I don't like fighting a defensive battle. And strike force attacks are the way to go."

"But your plan will take pinpoint accuracy and careful planning. When the time comes, I'm behind you all the way."

Desi smacked her lips and yawned, "Thanks, Dayo, you're the best. Kay Bear thinks you have a great ass." She tickled him and giggled while she assaulted his funny bone.

She peered through her lashes to watch his response. Desi was so tired; she was becoming delirious.

Declan dug her back with a low tummy tickle. His nimble fingers ducked beneath her body armor, and he assaulted her treasure trail with a flurry of tickles.

"Babe, you've got a ranch vacation coming up, and an opportunity to live like an American cowgirl. What do you say to that?"

Weakly, she smiled and whispered, "Yippee Ki-Yay! Here I come!"

She trailed off dreaming of Longbow helo missions and launching a Hellfire missile right into Antonio's bedroom. What a happy thought!

Chapter Five

Seven Hundred Miles Away, Deep in the Cascade Mountains.

The Pettigrew Horse Ranch

Cobb Pettigrew wore an Irish-weave sweater and a leather barn coat. He tugged on his black felt Stetson and exhaled in a long sigh. It was early in the morning, and the sunrise was breaking over the mountain ridge. There was so many things to do, and not enough daylight to get them all done.

Not to mention the fact Pettigrew entered his seventh decade, and he had barely enough manpower to run the property.

After his heart attack, the downtime forced his wranglers to seek out other work. His faithful wife, Hallie May, tried to keep things going, but the cattle work and the horse training were just too much.

He removed his felt Stetson and hand-combed his wiry grey hair. Cobb set his cane against the horizontal rails and flicked on the arena lights.

This was his sanctuary and the place where he trained his Western riding horses. Overhead, there was a steel trussed canopy with corrugated metal. Bright globe lights illuminated a rectangular horse arena, and the dirt had been harrowed to loamy perfection.

His last cowhand, David T. entered the arena, riding Shepherd Cat.

The Quarter Horse was the finest animal he owned. And Cobb didn't want Sheppie to get rusty, so the least he could do was put the eighteen-year-old through the paces.

Pettigrew cocked his jaw philosophically. He stroked his peppered circle beard and considered his present situation. He had to let go of his bucket dreams and face the facts.

The master horseman was too old to win another riding contest. It was time to dip into his savings, hire a good performance rider, and win some prize money.

With his winnings, he'd paint the barn, the stables, and his homestead. Sadly, it was time to say farewell to his life's work and accept the inevitable.

While he reflected, his lovely wife of six decades called out. "Cobb, you ol' cowboy, here's a piping cup of coffee. Don't go throwing in the towel until you hear the latest."

God bless the woman, every morning, she met the Almighty. And the Good Lord directed her to a passage. Hallie May would read the scripture several times and hold the Bible to her bosom.

When she memorized the daily word, she'd leave the dining room, and wander through her vegetable garden. While plucking carrots, beets, and Russet potatoes, the prayer warrior would listen to the Holy Spirit.

He wasn't a religious man, but he couldn't fault Hallie one bit. On more than one occasion, she received divine guidance, and her wisdom was absolutely crucial.

Cobb took the piping hot mug and gazed into her radiant dark eyes. Age had been kind to her, Hallie still projected the same radiance as when he first met her. Her generous lips formed a birdwing Cupid's bow, and her large smile never failed to brighten his day.

His wife wore a purple country dress and a floppy gardener's hat. *Good lord, she was beautiful woman!*

Cobb's greatest regret was never having children. Hallie deserved a great big family, and his wife had so much love to give.

Hallie placed an aging hand to his Irish sweater, "Hang onto your hat, Cobb. I know you're plumb worn out, but help is on the way. Your sorrow will turn to joy, the dawn will awaken, and you'll bring in the sheaves. And best of all, your heart will be filled with gladness."

Cobb grinned and spoke in a thoughtful drawl. "If I was a farmer that would be good news, but as you can see, we're ranchers." He pointed through the open aired arena at the distant pastures. "We have fields of sires, broodmares, and frisky little colts."

Hallie clasped her hands, "Aren't they beautiful?"

"In place of a family, the Almighty has given us a gorgeous herd of mares and colts. See how the little ones kick up their heels and run beside their mommas?"

Each time a new colt stands on his wobbly legs, I rejoice in the gift of life. Our Quarter Horses are like one great big family, and I love them all."

Cobb watched a tiny foal lean his little head against his momma's large nose. A delirious look of maternal love crossed the chestnut's features.

She licked the little fellow, and she relished the gift of life. Bright-eyed colts and fillies danced around the flowery pastures. Every grasshopper and butterfly offered amazement. *Oh, to be young and innocent, and thrill to every blessing!*

Pettigrew chuckled, "We do have a big horse family, but if we don't do something quick, we won't have enough feed to get through the winter."

Hallie pointed to the arid foothills. There were brown Herefords grazing among pinyon and juniper. As though they knew Mrs. Pettigrew was talking about them, they lifted their white faces and eyed the distant homestead.

She beamed a great big smile. "Aw, Cobb, admit it. We have a great big herd of yearlings, and in the fall, we'll harvest the steers, and our finances will be fine. There's nothing to worry about."

His pretty wife jumped up in the air and spilled her coffee. "Just wait to you hear what I received in prayer."

Cobb pretended not to be interested, but in all his years, Hallie came through with many a divine insight. He was all ears, but as a doubting Thomas, he had to play it cool and detached.

His full lips parted, "Ohhh! So, what did the Almighty tell you this time?"

She raised an elegant finger, "Now, don't be disrespectful."

"Oh, believe me, I respect the Holy One, but I wish we could see eye to eye. If I had infinite power, I would have done a few things differently."

Hallie's optimism remained undaunted. "I know you're thinking about selling the horse ranch, but the dawn is about to break, and help is on the way."

He groused, "From your lips to God's ears. But as a backup plan I'll put a few ads in the Amarillo Quarterly. We can hire a Western rider and a website designer."

Hallie beamed, "Let's hold up on the Amarillo stuff, and let's give the Almighty a chance."

"If you could take a therapy bath and loosen your hip, maybe you could compete one more time. We don't have to win first place in the Reined Cow Horse (RCH) event, but surely, we could place. You're a master horseman and Shepherd Cat is an amazing cutting horse."

Cobb felt as though her suggestion cut him to the quick. "Oh, honey, we've been over this. The last time I competed, it was before my heart attack, and that was five years ago."

"The basic problem is that I'm like Satchel Paige, taking the mound in Cleveland. I've already had my prime in the Negro Baseball League, and now it's the big time. I'm a leathery-faced old buzzard, and the judges want to see a bright, young face."

Hallie leaned forward and kissed him full on the lips. "Cobb Pettigrew, you're my knight in shining armor. So, don't you go runnin' yourself down."

"I married you after Nam, and we toured the rodeo circuits, and we've had an incredible life. And I don't regret a single moment. And for better or worse, you'll always be my champion!"

Cobb was deeply touched. Why in God's name did he get such a faithful and beautiful bride? If he hadn't chased bronc riding, and steer roping for so many years, Hallie would have been younger, and they could have had children. A woman gets up in years, and it gets harder. He still hadn't forgiven himself for that huge mistake.

Pettigrew held her hands with gratitude. "Hallie, ol' girl, we need a Jackie Robinson. We need a bright-eyed, young man, so full of goodness, the judges won't be deterred by his suntan. They'll see his horsemanship and talent, and we'll take the trophy."

Hallie chortled, "I was getting to that part. I had a vision of a young couple who are headed this way. You'll meet a handsome young cowboy, and you're not going to like him. He's more of a high-action rodeo type."

"Oh, good lord, here we go again. I left the rodeo twenty years ago, and I'm not in the mood to coach a young stud in team roping."

"Oh hush and let me tell you about my vision. He's a mysterious fellow with a military background, but with the proper guidance, he has the making of a great horseman."

"And for some strange reason, I received a mental image of Harry Belafonte's Calypso album. It made me wonder if our new horseman will have a certain Caribbean charm?"

Cobb pursed his full lips, "It's too much to hope for, but I'd take Belafonte any day. If he can sing the 'Banana Boat Song,' and ride like the wind, he is my man."

"Remember, sweetheart, you were once a bull in a China shop, but you became a superlative horseman. You can coach this man to bring out his poise, his finesse, and his horsemanship."

By this time, Pettigrew was deeply interested. He had to meet the lad, but with a military can-do attitude, and rough ranching skills, there was a chance he could undo the high action tendencies. *Good lord, this was going to be a lot of work!*

"All right, my luv. Let's just say I'm willing, and that I'll open my heart to the possibility. But one great looking horseman is hardly enough to turn around this whole ranch."

"Oh, I forgot the best part. The great looking cattleman has a wife. At least, I think they're a couple. There are some problems, and she has a few issues, but she's going to come around. They can stay at the foreman's custom lodge, and I know for a fact, they'll be hard working."

Cobb tilted his head, "Not to rain on your parade, but that makes two cowhands with a remote shot at Western riding events."

She slapped his barn coat. "You know how the Holy One is. He works in mysterious ways, and his will unfolds slowly, but surely. He will accomplish what he sets out to do, so don't get in his way."

Pettigrew held up his hands, "Far be it from me to hinder the Almighty. Whatever he's gonna do, I hope he does it fast. And put in a good word, we need an army of cowpunchers to turn the place around."

In her unsinkable fashion, Hallie clapped her hands. "That reminds me, there was a second part to my vision."

"It was hard to understand. But it appears that an army will arrive, and a military helicopter will land, and a unit of highly trained warriors will visit our property."

"Isn't that wonderful? We'll need to fix up the bunkhouse, remove all the sheets, and retrieve all the jar vegetables. I'll have tons of men to feed, and it will be like old times."

Cobb curled his lips, and the thought consoled him. He wasn't one to count his chicks, but if even half of what she said was true, maybe they had a chance. It wasn't the fulfillment of his bucket dreams, but it was something.

Pettigrew stroked his circle beard, "Any chance, one of them knows something about computers? How about building a website, is there a designer among them? We've got futurity colts to auction off, and the old-fashioned way isn't working."

"Now, you're going to laugh, but I did have a vision of this wild and crazy hacker. He's a genius with silvery blue eyes and a big white smile."

"He's crazy as a loon, but the men trust him. And I think he can build us a great website. Before you know it, we'll have folks milling about our stables, and buying up three-year olds."

Of all the unbelievable things, his dearly beloved wife reported, the crazy guy seemed like a strong possibility. If he could get one crazy hacker to promote the Pettigrew Ranch, they could create two revenue streams: cattle and horse sales.

Cobb sipped his coffee, "Hallie, ol' girl, did I tell you recently, how incredible you are?"

"Only last night, but a woman never tires of hearing it."

"Well then, my sweet, you're an amazing woman, and I thank my lucky stars I married you."

"Right back at ya, Jackie Robinson. You're gonna see some amazing things, so hang on to your hat."

Pettigrew turned his attention to David T. and his Quarter Horse champion. Things were looking up. If nothing else, all of Hallie's prayers served to lift his spirits.

Declan napped through the long train ride. In an alpha sleep, he listened to the clacking of steel wheels, and he felt the rocking of cattle cars. At road crossings, he heard the low wail of the locomotive, but for the most part, it was a quiet ride.

He felt the temperature become brisk, and a gentle breeze whipped hay dust into his face. He rose from his slumber and checked his surroundings.

Instead of the lower Sierras, their locomotive cruised through deep rocky gorges and steep mountainsides. Below the tracks, there was a frothy white-water stream, and the skies were bluer than ever.

The commander loosened up with a round of calisthenics. He performed jumping jacks, a hundred push-ups, two-hundred sit ups, and a fifty squat thrusts. The blood was pumping, and it was time to check in with Eugene.

Declan let Desiree catch some shut eye. The bronze beauty had been through hell, and just looking at her, she slept like an angel.

Her faithful friend, Kay Bear, had his little black nose nestled against her cheek, and his button brown eyes beamed with joy. If he was a koala toy, there was no where he'd rather be than cuddled up to this curvy beauty.

He snapped his mind back to the present, "Wild Man, This is Cazador. The air has changed, and we're about four thousand feet higher."

"The air is brisk, and I'm wondering if we're still in the Sierras?"

"No, boss, you're in the Cascades, and your transport left California, and you're headed for Oregon. Between the Siskiyous and the Cascades, you're surrounded by mountains. And it just so happens, the Pettigrew Ranch is around the next bend."

"There's an airdrop scheduled for a flowery meadow. So, I suggest you leap off the train, and track down the crates, and get washed up."

Dayo turned to Desi, "Babe, our stop is just ahead. It's time to grab Kay Bear and prepare to jump."

Desiree felt a man rock her shoulder. Instinctively, she reached for her 9 mm and rolled to a seated position. She had the offender in her sights and held her Beretta with a double-handed death grip.

She fought for recognition, but the oddity of whirling hay dust and a smiling warrior confused the hell outta her. She blinked several times, and nothing made sense.

Dayo curled his lips in a charming, half-smile, "Babe, it's me, Declan Cazador. You're in a cattle car loaded with hay bales, and you've just entered Oregon."

"We've been sleeping for half a day, and the rendezvous point is right around the bend."

Desiree holstered her 9 mm and slung her hunting pack over her shoulder. While the fog lifted, it felt good, knowing that an assault rifle was nearby.

Declan led her to the sliding door. She watched the ground whiz by, and below the evergreen timbers, there was a lush field of long-stemmed grass.

The commander turned to her, "Desi, when the train slows down, we're going to jump. Hit the ground in a crouch and roll into the thick grass."

Finally, her sluggish brain registered. She was traveling with the famous headhunter, Declan Cazador. The fearless Marine was totally insane, and the lackwit kept asking her to do impossible things. *What she needed was the first trip outta here!*

Before she could check with Kay Bear, he gave the count, "One-Two-Three, Jump!"

Desiree watched the commander leap beyond the tapered gravel berm, land in a half crouch, and he rolled once, and popped up. He made it look simple.

Desi turned to Kay Bear, "Hang on, little buddy. Psycho dude wants us to jump out of a moving train."

She counted again, and on three, the lady warrior leaped beyond the gravel berm, and rolled three times and popped to her feet.

Unlike Dayo, her field helmet was covered in weeds, and she had a mud streak down one shoulder. She dusted herself off, "Kay Bear, I think we made it."

Just then, she looked into the sky, and watched a Black Hawk sweep low. Two soldiers pushed a pair of crates out the bay and a military chutes opened.

She watched a wooden crate sail pleasantly to the ground. It flew gently into a flowering meadow, surrounded by aspen trees, and conifers. It was a gorgeous setting, but what she really wanted was that damn helicopter.

Desiree took off at a sprint. "Hey, bring back that helo! I don't want a wooden crate; I want to fly that Sikorsky to the nearest army base."

"What the hell was Wild Man thinking? That could be our ticket outta here."

Declan caught up with her and led her into a maple grove. "Desi, get a hold of yourself, girl."

"We may be hundreds of miles from L.A., but we're still in enemy territory. There's no telling how many bounty hunters Antonio deployed. So, keep your head low, and let's make this thing work."

Desi caught her breath, "Why didn't that hawk land? We could have boarded it and flown to the Lewis-McChord AFB."

"I'd trade out a utility helo for an Apache Longbow." She spread her arms, "I could blow the shite out of Antonio's estate, and this would be all over."

Dayo curled his handsome lips, and she wanted to smack him. *Here it comes, the voice of reason!*

The great Commander had other ideas.

He chucked her chin softly, "Let's stick to the plan. I love the retaliatory idea, but we've got to let the dust settle. The Pettigrew

Ranch is around the bend, and we're going undercover as cattle ranchers."

Her arms went slack, "Ohhh, phooey on that. I want to blow something up. I'm a good combat pilot, and it's been seven years since I've been on a horse."

"No problems, sweetie. We'll pry open the crate and take this one step at a time."

Desiree watched Declan trot through a field of flowering pink lupine. He seized the wooden crate and hauled it into the forest. Reluctantly, she followed him.

She hauled her cache into a beautiful deciduous forest. Light shafted through leafy trees, and there was a pretty stream bouncing between mossy rocks. She rolled up the parachute and stuffed it into a tree hollow.

Declan pried open his treasure and riffled through the contents. He noticed she wasn't moving, so he trotted over to her, and gave her a side hug.

"Hey, babe, I wonder what's inside that wooden box? Maybe, there's a cute cowgirl outfit, boots, and a cattleman's hat."

"I've never seen you in Western attire, I'll bet you look fantastic!"

She dropped her hands to her hips and stuck out her tongue. For full effect, she elongated her glottis, and her tantalizing member dipped well below her chin.

Dayo stopped in his tracks, "Good lord, girl, French kissing you would be an erotic adventure." Desiree stepped back, and she was deeply offended. It wasn't the reaction she was shooting for.

The Commander pried open her box and laid the contents on a grassy embankment. If they were camping, this would be fun. But she was returning to cattle ranching, and she wanted her old life back.

Declan chirped, "Let's see what Eugene and Tanya packed for you? Oh, here's a few pairs of cowgirl clothes, three ultimate sports bras, and an interesting set of ginger ringlets."

He set the hair piece down carefully and laid a large cosmetic case next to it. "Well, I'll be! Tanya wants you to go undercover, and this is a fantastic disguise."

Declan added, "I should have made the request, but a total makeover will make you totally unrecognizable."

He arranged her ultimate sports bras with complementary outfits.

He held up a full-breasted white athletic brassiere, "Honey, with your endowments, this baby will catch the girls perfectly. You can trot, canter, and ride full tilt. And your jugs will be safe and sound!"

Her eyes enlarged. She snatched the athletic bra. "Stop handling my lingerie, you animal!"

She fetched a stance, "And I don't have jugs, I have well-shaped, lovely breasts!"

Desiree shooed him away, "Why don't you go back to your crate and leave me alone."

She unpacked the cosmetic case and opened the lid. Tanya neatly packed a photo of a ginger red model with a peach bronze complexion.

The girl looked peachy and delicious, and Desi felt like her IQ dropped a hundred points. The bronze beauty didn't want to be someone else; she had enough trouble being herself.

Desiree wasn't normally given to a public meltdown, but it was time to go ballistic. She stomped over to the little creek and seized a mossy rock.

She held the slimy stone way above her head and heaved it into a dark plunge pool. To her satisfaction, the stone made a huge indentation, but the backsplash hurled mud all over her chest.

Desi was so furious; she couldn't even throw a tantrum and have it work out.

She wiped the slime from her cheek and glanced over at Declan. The fearless Marine stripped out of his night camos and wore ass-hugging Wranglers, a blue muscle tee, and cool shades.

He placed a backward cap in place and held out his arms, "What do you think?"

For the first time, she was back on the mission. "Dayo, you look good. The two-day stubble, the shades, and the baseball cap are good for lounging around, but it fails to capture the cattlemen's look."

She went through his belongings and seized a lavender button down and a black Stetson. "Try these on, stud. You'll look like a famous steer roper, and maybe Pettigrew will think you're an actual wrangler."

Declan modeled his Western look, and she gave him a thumbs up. At least, someone was getting into this charade. The Commander hauled the wooden crate to a thicket, broke down the elements, and hid the contents.

He dusted his hands. "There's a steep hillside, and I'm going to hike up the incline, and do some recon. Eugene's description may be off, and I want to prepare for our debut."

Desi allowed him to trek up the hillside. She hauled her cache to another thicket, and she was about to break it to bits, but noticed a velvet box.

She extracted the jewelry items and discovered an heirloom wedding ring with ornate platinum work. The style was from another century, but the high-mounted cradle held a dazzling three karat diamond.

The facets caught the forest light, and the prismatic effect caused a brilliant display. It was an old-fashioned ring, and it spoke volumes about traditional values.

It symbolized the marriage she always dreamed of having, and the revelation stopped her cold. For the first time, she started to wonder if something spiritual was happening.

Maybe, the whole Witness Program was a means to a different end. There was a man stomping up the hillside who she very much admired, and in fact, she once had a crush on him.

Desiree reached for a second jewelry box and discovered a man's wedding band. The ring had leafy gold darts and a handsome diamond. The edgework formed a masculine double rim, and it would frame beautifully against Declan's hand. It was perfect for her stud Marine.

To the Pettigrews, the ring would look like it had always been there. Something was happening, and she couldn't put her finger on it.

But she sensed that someone was praying for her. She turned to Kay Bear, "Do you think we're supposed to be here?"

Kay Bear projected an air of perpetual happiness. His button brown eyes radiated a sense of joy, and his pink lips smiled with reassurance.

A higher power guided them here, and everything was just as it should be. For the first time in a long while, Desiree felt she was on the right track.

She hustled into the shadows and donned her cowgirl outfit. Desi skipped the flaming red ringlets and wore a chocolate Stetson instead.

She looked incredible. With a white ultimate, and an open lapel blouse, she was the very image of a Western cowgirl. She stuffed her clothing into her backpack, seized her weaponry, and headed up the hillside.

Desiree spotted Declan surveying the surrounding mountains. He held his scope and traced the bowl-shaped ridge. It was a sensible precaution. Seven hundred miles ago, bounty hunters parachuted into the hills and tried to ambush them.

He stood behind a cluster of branches and made sure to obscure the glare of the lens.

"Well, Commander, do we have the all clear?"

Dayo lowered his scope. "It's an interesting geographical phenomena. Way off in the distance is the little town of Pine Whisper."

"It's situated inside a large basin surrounded by evergreen-studded hills. Hostiles would have to come through the pass before they could drop into the valley. We have a strategical advantage, and we'll have advance notice if they show up."

Desi pointed downhill, "Is that the Pettigrew Ranch? It looks like a fairy tale horse ranch."

She asked for his scope, "Wait a minute, are those white-faced Herefords scattered among the pinyon junipers?"

He handed her the lens, and she scanned the arid foothills. "Why are the white faces grazing the dry hillsides? The grass has turned gold, and it can't be more than sustenance forage."

"Well, it's obvious that Pettigrew owns a lot of acreage. Starting with the homestead, his custom home is situated at the end of the double-tired dirt road."

"His pride and joy is an open-air arena, decked out with night lights, and the dirt is harrowed to perfection. But over to the right, the rodeo arena is full of weeds, and it's been a while since there's been any team roping."

"And directly beside the open-air arena, there's a wooden round pen with moderate usage. I'd say he trains three-year-olds and gets tired, and goes back inside."

"Ohhh, that's terrible! He has all those beautiful horses. I can see a pasture full of studs, and a large herd of broodmares. This was once a fine breeding ranch."

"And look at all those frisky little colts. Awww, they're so cute. I bet Kay Bear would love to meet them. Furry creatures tend to bond with one another."

Dayo continued, "In addition to the open-air arena, Pettigrew has a craftsman horse barn. It's in fairly good shape, and I bet he has rodeo horses inside. His champion sires receive first class treatment, and the Herefords have become an afterthought."

"Ah yes! He gave the lush lower pastures to his best breeders, and the arid foothills to the white face cattle."

Desiree pointed way off in the distance. "Beyond that stream, I wonder if he owns the high pasture. If he expects us to herd cattle through the river, we'll be freshwater cowboys."

She giggled, "I can wear my bikini and my cowgirl hat, and I'll be one sexy cowgirl."

The fearless Marine curled his lips and grinned. If she planted an alluring image in his mind, perhaps, he would treat her differently.

So far, he treated her as a lady warrior, and not a real woman. If they were going to continue this charade, his callous disregard had to come to an end.

Dayo replaced the rifle scope. "Based on the lay of the land, we'll take the dirt entrance and introduce ourselves. We'll pose as an engaged couple, and hopefully, the Pettigrews will allow us to live at the foreman's lodge."

"What did you say?" She took the scope and panned next to the homestead. Hiding amongst the overhanging trees was an adorable steep roofed log home.

The honey-stained siding needed another coat of sealant, but the place looked like a dream. Her heart fluttered, and she could really see herself living there.

There was a front porch with pine log rails, a romantic A-framed great room, and an upstairs filled with dormer windows. That's where she'd put the kids. *Oh, my god, where in the blazes did that thought come from?*

Her dream home was nestled inside a beautiful forest, and dappled light gave it a dreamy appearance. They could ranch all day and swing on the love chair by night.

She finally caught herself and wondered what was happening?

Desiree touched her shiny black ringlets and handed back the scope.

"Commander, your plan sounds good, but there's one teensy-weensy flaw." He stared at her as though she had defied his genius.

"Well, I confess there are a lot of unknown variables. And I was getting to the second phase of my strategy."

"Cobb Pettigrew may be down on his luck, but judging by his exceptional bloodlines, I'd say he's a bit of a perfectionist. If I were a cattle rancher, and two wranglers suddenly appeared, I'd test them out."

"So, we've got to prepare for a team roping test. We'll let him know we have a military background, and it's been a few years since we've herded cattle. But we were both raised on cattle ranches, and we'd like to freshen up our roping skills."

Desi touched his arm, "Dayo, I know the drill, and I agree. We've got to practice heeling and heading and roping live cattle. But that wasn't what I was hinting at."

She opened a velvet case. Desi curled her lips, and her eyes twinkled. "I'm not sure an engagement is strong enough. Older folks may want to split us up until the wedding."

Dayo stroked his shadow beard. "I think you're right. We've got to hang together at all times, and marriage offers the most protection."

Desiree broke into a radiant smile. She was excited about their undercover story.

"Okay, I've got it. We're already married, we've encountered a few setbacks, and we're looking for a new start."

The shapely beauty placed the gold wedding band on his ring finger. She peered through her long slashes, "With this ring, I thee wed."

Declan gazed at the ring, and she could tell he was in shock. He probably figured marriage was a long way off, and suddenly, he was wearing an heirloom wedding band.

She pointed to the double-banded filigree and the tiny diamond. "This ring looks like it's been on your finger for a long time."

Desiree produced her three-karat wedding ring and handed it to him. Declan slid the vintage ring on her pretty bronze finger and paused to admire it.

The man was immersed in deep thought.

Dayo's voice dropped to a hoarse whisper, "With this ring, I thee wed." It was evident, the Commander took marriage vows seriously, and the rounder had been caught totally off guard.

Declan held her hands and gazed into her deep brown pools. "To be convincing, we can't pretend to be married, we have to become the real deal."

"And our physical touch must convey the fact we're very familiar with one another. Desiree could see where this conversation was headed.

She arched a S-shaped brow, "What do you have in mind?"

Dayo dropped his voice, "This is how I'll touch you, so don't be surprised."

He palmed her face, slid his hand behind her, and hauled her close. She felt the distance disappear, and they were very intimate.

His strength, power, and commanding appearance mesmerized her. He was a gorgeous, Caribbean god, and she could feel his heartbeat, and inhale his masculine scent.

Dayo angled above her apricot pink lips, and descended into a robust, mouthwatering kiss. He massaged her Cupid's bow in a vigorous rhythm, and then her lips parted. His tongue plunged into a deep, tongue-tangling French kiss.

The commander skillfully undid her sports bra, and her generous globes spilled into his hands. The seductive hunk teased her peaks, and she felt heat shoot to her core.

Within seconds, her panties were soaked with lady dew, and a world of sensuality exploded. For years, she had been shut down, but Dayo awakened her passions like a raging forest fire.

The commander took charge and eased her derrière against a velvet covered boulder. Pinned against a mossy wall, she had to submit to his desires. There was no place to run.

He kissed the holy hell out of her and caressed her breasts with a finesse rarely displayed. Her swells enlarged, and he teased her areolas until her peaks pebbled into hard tips.

His manhood lifted, and she seized his delicious ass, and hauled him closer. She may have been out of practice, but her hips undulated in a sweet rhythm. And she couldn't stop fantasizing about how good they would be.

When she came up for air, Dayo held her aroused breasts and whispered, "These are all mine!"

She should have taken exception to his possessive demeanor, but then again, Declan was her undercover husband.

He cupped her damp mons, "Your lady flower is definitely mine, and I've laid you a thousand times, and every love session leaves you sated and delirious and deeply in love."

Dayo was a scoundrel and a barbarian, but his words thrilled her to pieces. The cad was clearly enjoying his new role, and as long as he was sincere, she could enjoy it too.

To her surprise, Declan stood back, and curled his fingers in a taunting gesture.

"Darlin', it's time to bring it! I'm your lovin' man, and you can't get enough of me. So, it's your turn to take the initiative."

She placed her hands to her shapely hips, "You don't think I'll come after you, do you?"

He curled his handsome lips, "You can't be built like a brick house; you've got to have game. So, let's see what you've got!"

Desiree was incensed. She rocked her hips in a seductive sway and placed a delicate hand to his chest. She ripped open his shirt and lavished his chest with dripping, love bites.

The naughty combat pilot kissed her way to his flat nipples and took a whole mouthful of man meat. She slowly released her hold with playful pluck.

"You stud Marine, you've got a nice chest, but let's see if you really know how to kiss."

Desi peered wickedly through her Arabian eyeliner, and swept a hand around his nape, and hauled him into a hungry, ravenous kiss.

Her pent-up desires exploded, and the moment his lips parted, she plunged her long tongue down his throat. They tangled in an aggressive French assault, and she could feel Dayo's arousal enlarge.

She pinned him to the mossy boulder, tiptoed for more contact, and rubbed her damp mons against his ridge.

The little vixen didn't stop. Her French kissing continued, while her fingers unzipped his pants, and she cleverly seized his enthusiasm.

It took two hands and then some, but she stroked his expanding arousal. Desi slammed her tongue deeper into an exhilarating marathon, and she couldn't get enough of this guy. He felt so good, and his endowments filled her hands, and it had been way too long.

Just then, there was a shotgun blast. They both dove for cover. She came up with her 9 mm, and Declan had his M 16 at the ready.

Way off in the distance, she watched Mrs. Pettigrew blast a twelve-gauge into the air. A flock of crows scattered, and she yelled at them. It was too far to hear her words, but the point was clear. No one messes with the woman's vegetable garden.

Declan broke into a laugh, "Nothing like a shotgun blast to dampen the mood." He tucked his man parts back in place, and she quickly reassembled herself.

She rose to her cowgirl boots and cast a wicked little smile. "Since I've ridden you a thousand times, tonight will make it a thousand and one."

Desi palmed Dayo's package and broke into a seductive smile. "Don't forget to bring your A game, stud. You'll need every ounce of energy you can muster."

And with her flirtatious comment, she sashayed into the forest, and peered over her shoulder.

She was playing with fire, but it sure felt good. Desiree dated the Commander once, and she always wanted to see how good he was. And now, she was about to find out.

Chapter Six

They emerged from the deciduous forest, leaped over a barbed wire fence, and landed on a remote country road. The lush valley was gorgeous as the sun illuminated the fairy tale setting.

Declan and Desi ducked beneath a tilted iron sign, which advertised the Pettigrew Ranch. Two steel columns supported sagging ironwork, and the archway was in dire need of a welder.

The Captain hooked a finger, "In addition to cattle work, I can weld that sign, and make this place look respectable." He patted the split rail fence as they walked the length of a dirt entrance.

Desiree admired the rustic setting, the distant cattle pastures, and the high Cascades.

"Ya know, Dayo, this ranch looks even more like paradise, when you get close. Kay Bear loves the pretty horses, and he could see himself settling down here."

She wanted to control her bear speaking tendencies, but when she was nervous, the words simply spilled out. The combat pilot was in a whirlwind of emotions.

Her daily routines were blown to hell, and she spent the morning riding mountain horses. The Sierras were beautiful beyond belief, but concentrating on treacherous terrain, and picking the right footing was demanding.

Even though she caught a few hours of sleep, she could use a full night of rest. And using those binocs, she remembered how charming the log home was.

If they could convince the Pettigrews, they were suitable cattle drivers, then she and Kay Bear would have a new home.

Desi carried an assault rifle in her bedroll. Instead of one bedroll, Dayo carried two. One was for his sniper rifle, and the other was for his M16. After the parachuting bounty hunters, neither of them were taking any chances.

It was better to be cautious than to get caught with their pants down. And from all appearances, they'd look like a lovely couple hiking the backcountry. No one would suspect their sleeping bags were filled with artillery.

Desiree turned to him, "Dayo, I need a word with Kay Bear. I said some things up on that mountain, and I'm pretty sure I gave you the wrong impression."

She giggled nervously, "Kay Bear watched us kiss, and he says you're a great kisser. And any man who loves my deepthroat kissing has gotta be a good guy."

Declan fell into an easy smile. "My lips are still tingling, and I'll remember that tongue tangling for a long time."

Desi felt expectations were building, but she was actually two different people. One moment, she could be a brazen vixen, and the next minute, she was a shy beauty. And if Dayo thought her kissing technique was a proposition, she better downgrade his expectations.

She flipped a delicate hand, "I may have a great figure, but I'm a really a nice person. And Kay Bear recognizes the real me. So, I've got to get current with my little buddy."

"Go for it, honey, we've got a half mile, and the Pettigrews are nothing more than dots on the front porch. They're rocking in their chairs and enjoying their golden years."

"But one thing is clear: they're fully aware that we're on the way. So, you best have a word with Kay Bear, and share your innermost thoughts. He loves you, and the both of you have been through the mill."

Desi couldn't believe what he said. The man had compassion for her problems, and he didn't pass judgement, and he accepted her just the way she was.

It took a load off her shoulders, knowing the Commander had her back. And the fearless Marine was there for her.

"Hey little buddy, I can see that you're enthusiastic about your new surroundings. There's a pretty farmhouse at the end of the road, and two very nice people are waiting to meet you. There's even a friendly gold retriever, wagging his tail."

She whispered into Kay Bear's ear, "Back up on the mountain, I came on pretty strong. I was a flirtatious vixen, and I fired up Dayo's passions."

"I may have made a big mistake. With so many things changing, I'm really not sure I'm ready to make love."

She tickled his koala tummy, "What do you think?"

Desi pressed her ear to his adorable face. Desiree felt a sense of balance return. There was no pressure. She repeated her koala's feelings.

"Kay Bear doesn't think a thunder tupping should happen tonight. He thinks we should act like a loving couple, share our feelings, and really get to know each other."

Declan listened carefully. It was obvious, the man anticipated a searing hot, frontal assault. But he was a smart leader, and if he pushed too hard, she might snap.

Dayo lowered his cool guy shades, "I must admit, I'm a little disappointed. How about a hot shower and a bone-melting massage? And later, we can snuggle and share our feelings."

She held up her round-eared friend, "Kay Bear thinks that's a great idea, and he's very impressed with your sensitivity."

Dayo curled his lips, "I'm glad K-Man approves. So, what do you think of the Pettigrew homestead?"

Desiree kept a steady pace. She studied the two-story farmhouse with yellow siding. There were white shutters beside the windows, and a delightful front porch.

"It sure is a cute farmhouse. I love the front lawn, the flower beds, and the country setting. It's quite lovely, and seeing an old couple, full of years, makes me want to help them."

Declan eyed the older couple, a squint-eyed wrangler, and a friendly retriever.

"From Wild Man's report, the older gentleman is Cobb Pettigrew. His dusty cattleman's hat, grey circle beard, and Irish sweater tell me Cobb is up in years and gets cold easily."

Desi chimed in, "According to Eugene, his wife's name is Hallie May, and she's wearing a cute country dress. And her smile is so big, I can see it from here."

A few steps later, Declan hailed the owners with a friendly wave. He opened an outer white gate, and there were mere moments before they arrived.

He leaned over to Desi, "Honey, we're gonna meet the Pettigrews, and here's the plan. We'll offer our services for cattle herding, team roping, and branding."

"We'll offer to move the cattle from low pasture to high ground. And we'll use our ranch skills to mend fences and do all the remodeling."

"If I were in his shoes, I'd test out the new wranglers to see what they've got. So, be prepared for a team roping test."

"You got it, stud. I'll take the header and you can heel the little rascal." They exchanged fist bumps and hand explosions.

They were undercover, and the mission was underway. They had three months before the trial, and they had to make this thing work.

Desi understood the logistics, and hoped she could hold it together. It was mid-afternoon, and she'd ridden mountain horses, and slept on a freakin' hay bale sofa.

Later, they jumped from a train and chased down an air drop. It had been an unbelievable day, and now, she had to switch gears, and become a roping sensation.

"Kay Bear, we've got our work cut out. Now, you're a smart little guy, so keep your eyes peeled, and make friends with that big ol' header."

"Dayo thinks he may be a high-dollar rodeo horse. So, hang on tight, little buddy, we're going to ride like the wind."

Declan palmed her back, "Before we meet the Pettigrews, I should talk about our undercover appearance. You don't have time to change, so you'll have to go with what you've got."

"I'm going to play it cool, wear these rainbow shades, and keep my Stetson pulled down low."

Dayo continued, "The Witness Director may have posted an all-points bulletin. If your LifeNet helo or California ID are out there, you may be easy to identify."

Desi produced the ginger red photo from her blouse. "This is my new disguise."

"But damn! Can you really look like that? It'll throw 'em off the trail, and you'll look amazing."

"With ginger ringlets, and the peach glow complexion you'll look so darn delicious. I could eat you up and taste your forbidden fruit and make love all day long."

She belted his arm, "Put your tongue back in your mouth. I'm not ready for a new look, but I'm working on it."

Declan narrowed his eyes. "Your call. As soon as you're ready, it would strengthen our mission."

Desiree was about to scream, "I've had this mission up to my eyeballs. It's been six years since I've ridden a horse, and now some old codger wants me to catch horns, dally up, and turn a six-hundred-pound steer."

She heaved her bosom, and her eyes went wild. Dayo quickly took charge and hauled her into a side hug.

"Honey, it's going to be all right! Everything will work out. And try not to look like your California ID."

"That's easy, all my helo photos look like mug shots. I'll just flash a radiant smilc, and the Pettigrews won't know the difference."

They opened an inner gate, and an old retriever trotted down the steps. He wagged his tail so hard; he beat the zinnias to pieces.

Desiree took an immediate liking to him. She tousled his furry ears, "You're such a nice dog, you love everyone, and you're welcoming us to your new home."

She peered up at the old man wearing an Irish sweater and a dusty Stetson. "What's the retriever's name?"

Cobb Pettigrew rose from his rocking chair and grabbed a white column. "His formal name is Jefferson, but around these parts, everyone calls him Jeffrey."

Desiree gave the dog a good pet down, and she held up her koala toy.

"This is Kay Bear, he's my best friend, and he loves golden retrievers. K-Man thinks you're a very loyal dog, and a wonderful companion."

"He looks forward to going on long walks with you and Jeffers. And Kay buddy will become your best friend."

The Pettigrews stood side by side, leaning against the white rails. If she was supposed to contain her little idiosyncrasies, the cat was out of the bag.

She had an imaginary friend, and a good luck charm that got her through thick and thin. She hoped they would understand.

Cobb spoke in a heavy cadence, "This is my wife, Hallie May, and this is our lifelong friend, David T."

Hallie exclaimed, "It's so nice to meet both of you. Welcome to our horse ranch. The property has seen better days, but I have a thriving garden."

"And after you folks get settled in, we can harvest some veggies, and put out a spread."

Cobb curled his full lips, "Please forgive my wife's enthusiasm, but we don't get many visitors. She's been prayin' up a storm and thinks you might be help from above."

Desiree rushed up the steps and gave Hallie a great big hug. "You remind me of my Aunt Clara, she was a prayin' woman. And just the other day, I felt your prayers."

"And looking down on your ranch, it was like the heavens opened, and I knew this would be a wonderful place to stay."

Hallie replied softly, "And what we're you doing when you felt the heavens open?"

Desi blushed, "I can't say that the heavens truly opened, but I felt a gentle nudge, especially when we spotted your foreman's home."

Hallie eyed her husband, "The hand of the Almighty has set things in motion, and we best keep an attentive ear."

Pettigrew cocked his head thoughtfully, "I won't deny the power of the Big Guy, but I'm a practical man, and a few matters must be addressed."

Hallie interrupted her husband. "I notice you're wearing a koala wrist cuff. Is that a fashionable thing these days?"

Desiree lifted her wrist toy excitedly. "This is Kay Bear, he's my best friend. We met one another during the war. And he's very intelligent and has great insights."

"And even though, K-Man has seen it all, he remains happy and cheerful."

Desi pointed to his brown button eyes, "Isn't he cute? He has an excellent attitude, and if I get down, he beams his adorable smile, and keeps me on track."

Hallie May tickled Kay Bear's white tummy.

"He's a cute one, that's for sure. And it just so happens, I have a teddy bear collection too."

"K-Man can meet all my friends. We even have a little dining table, and the bears sit around, drinking tea, and they talk about their adventures."

Desiree turned to her protector, "See! I told you they'd like Kay Bear."

Declan nimbly leaped up the steps and took his place alongside his woman.

"Hallie, I really appreciate the hospitality, and your willingness to share your collection. It means a lot to Desi, and she's been through a lot. Every little kindness helps."

Hallie May patted his hands, "Young man, that's no problem. I believe you were sent from above, and you're perfectly welcome here."

Mrs. Pettigrew could barely contain her enthusiasm, but she eyed her husband. "Now, I know we'll get along famously, but my beloved would like to discuss a few practical matters."

"Sir, before we go any further, I'd like to say a few things about my wife. Desiree served her country, and she's a heavily decorated pilot."

"The Lieutenant flew Apache Longbow missions against Russian Scorpions, and she won every battle. She also flew Sikorsky Black Hawks, and transported men in and out of battle."

Declan smiled at her affectionately, "This little lady has seen a lot of combat and witnessed more things than anyone should ever see."

"She may have a unique view of the world, but I assure you, she's one hundred percent functional. When all hell breaks loose, she comes out fighting, and she won't give up. I'm damn proud of her, and she and Kay Bear can do almost anything."

Desiree relaxed into the shoulder massage, which addressed her deep muscle aches. When Dayo was finished, she felt fully validated.

Desi flipped her black ringlets, "Declan is no slouch either. He's a Marine special ops leader, and commander of a famous headhunter unit."

"He's taken out more Islamic hostiles than you can shake a stick at. So, when it comes to roping steer, and branding little butts, you couldn't find a better man."

Desiree realized their undercover story had taken a dramatic turn. But honesty was the best policy, and it was easier to remember.

She just hoped the Pettigrews wouldn't share their profiles. If Antonio learned of their hidey-hole, they'd have to make a run for it.

Cobb listened to the young couple. He spoke in a ponderous manner, "I served in Vietnam, and I'm well aware of the horrors."

"Listening to your wife, I fully understand her perspective. And if your military expertise translates into ranching skills, we'll get along pretty well."

Mr. Pettigrew eyed their backpacks, "You've got camping gear, and this isn't exactly a national forest. You're miles from nowhere. So, what brings you folks to this particular property?"

Desiree watched her man formulate an answer. "We're enjoying

America's back country, and we're taking a break from our ordinary lives."

Dayo nodded toward the distant Herefords. "I see you have a full pasture of older cattle. The forage is starting to turn brown. And you may need a few hands to drive 'em into the high country."

"Sir, my name is Declan Corazon, and this is my beautiful wife, Desiree."

Her warrior changed his last name, but Corazon would be easier to remember. If anything, he was all heart, and she was equally passionate. Desi didn't do anything halfway, it was full steam, and she didn't let anything get in her way.

Pettigrew listened carefully, and he must have realized Declan's explanation was pretty vague. Cobb removed his beat-up Stetson and hand-combed his receding hairline.

"Lord knows there's a ton of work that needs to be done. I can't pay you much, but my wife Hallie is a phenomenal cook."

The veteran cowboy gestured to the honey-stained log cottage. "Since our cattle boss left the premises, you can stay at his lodge. At least, it will be a roof over your head."

David T. squinted against the afternoon sun. A dusty haze settled over the mountain range, and it created shattering rays of sunshine.

If Desi didn't know differently, she'd say the Almighty was smiling down at them, and blessing this meeting.

She glanced at Hallie May for confirmation, and the vivacious old beauty exploded in a knowing smile. Whatever the men folk had planned, she was sure glad that this lady had a strong voice.

David T. wore a buckskin barn coat and when he smiled, his face appeared weather-beaten from years of sunshine.

David held out a calloused hand, "I'm pleased to meet both of you."

He pushed up on his black Resistol, "Naturally, I'm angling for more help, but I was wondering. Do you have any rodeo experience?"

Desi realized they had to weave the truth with a few lies. They didn't want to alert anyone to the fact they were fugitives.

Declan removed his shades and flashed his Caribbean charm. "Before the war, I competed in team roping and tie down. Desiree was a Rodeo Queen, but she's also competent in barrel racing and breakaway." *Good lord, Dayo was throwing it out there.*

Cobb looked pleased, "In that case, let's fire up the All-Terrain Vehicle, and brush up on your roping skills."

"David T. will drive the Polaris and pull the dummy steer. And when you're warmed up, we'll rope a Charolais. How does that sound?"

Desiree squeezed Kay Bear. Her tough talk started to waver. Now, it was time to put up or shut up, and she started to panic.

It had been six whole years, and steer roping wasn't the same as flying a Flight for Life chopper.

Hallie came to the rescue. She patted her husband's forearm. "Please pardon my husband's abrupt manner. But we've suffered a series of bad years, and we're down on funding."

"But my husband wants to see if you have a talent for rodeo. We know a number of folks in the business, and if you can master team roping, and put in a favorable time, then we have a way to raise funds."

Declan squared his shoulders, "Sounds good to me."

He turned to Desiree and patted her world-class behind, "Babe, we got this. Don't hold anything back. You can do anything, you set your mind to."

Before her man donned his cool guy shades, Hallie commented.

"Declan, has anyone ever said you look like Harry Belafonte? I admit you're more muscular and rougher cut, but you do resemble the Calypso singer."

Desi bounced in her cowgirl boots, "It's funny you should say that. Back when we were in high school, the kids called him Dayo."

"His nickname was from the 'Banana Boat Song.'" She rocked her hips and did a jazz number with her hands.

Hallie turned to Cobb, "The Lord works in mysterious ways, and he informed me that our guest might resemble the Caribbean singer."

Pettigrew wagged his head, "My dear, I will be the first to admit the resemblance, but the question remains, can the man rope a steer?"

Mrs. Pettigrew winked at Declan, "Of course he can. And as for the young lady, I want you to go easy on Desiree. She's a tender soul. So, you better be nice!"

Desi lit up like a candle. She thrived with encouragement, and with Hallie's support, this might be easier than she thought.

The entourage didn't bother entering the house, and there was a bit of tension between Cobb and Hallie May.

The matriarch announced, "I'll meet you folks around back. I'll bring the lemonade and a plate of finger foods. I know you folks must be really hungry."

Cobb turned to David T., "Can you fire up the ATV and hook up the dummy steer? And while you're at, can you set up the roping target?"

"You got it, boss." The squinty-eyed wrangler trotted down the steps and headed for the machine room.

Declan took his cue, "If you're planning to use the rodeo arena, I noticed the dirt could use a good harrowing. The arena is full of weeds, and the ground is dry packed. It would be inadvisable to put your horses through a high-performance drill with bad ground."

Cobb eyed him with agreement. "That's why I'm taking you to my open-air arena. The soil is loamy, and neither Shepherd nor Hunter will suffer injury."

They rounded the clapboard, soft yellow home, and came to the hallowed arena. Due to the afternoon clouds, the lighting was on a sensor system, and the bright lights came on. The place was a sanctuary.

Declan assessed the arena from close range. His earlier assessment that the covered arena was a special place had been confirmed.

There was two horse boxes and a cattle chute. It was a good-sized arena, but definitely smaller than a competitive stadium.

"By the way, what do you use this facility for?"

Cobb rocked his head back, and a proud smile crossed his lips. "This is actually a Western riding arena. Sheppie and Hunter are reined cow horse (RCH) champions. Have you ever heard of that event?"

Declan had to keep Desiree going. He knew her well enough, and any minute, she'd want to talk to Kay Bear.

Thankfully, Cobb and Hallie accepted her nuanced behavior, but he didn't want to push the envelope.

"Babe, this man is a master horseman, and he competes in reined cow horse events. The contest calls for poise and superlative horsemanship. In fact, it all boils down to showmanship. And if Cobb has an arena like this, it means he's won a trophy or two."

Desi responded, "I'm familiar with Western riding events, but it's a step up from my ranching experience."

Cobb said, "It's like your husband said. Western riding breaks down to rein work, cattle work, and cutting. Are you good at any of those?"

Desi felt put on the spot, and she refused to be singled out.

"Sir, if you put me on a decent cattle horse, and he's got cow sense, then I'll cut so well, it'll make your beard turn black and curly."

Declan burst out laughing, "I'm sorry Cobb, but my woman is a feisty cowgirl, and when she's under the gun, she comes out fighting."

"Oh, I don't mind a bit. And to answer your question, Hunter Cat has great cow sense, and he's an instinctive cutting horse."

"Yes, siree. I'll put you on a high-dollar horse and see what you're made of."

Just then, Hallie May rushed over with a tray of finger foods. "Is my husband giving you a hard time?"

Desiree responded, "No, ma'am. But after all the hype, I'm dying to meet Hunter. He must be one amazing Quarter Horse."

Hallie gestured to the plate, "Oh, he is. And he's been with us so long, he's become like family. So, go ahead and dig in."

Mrs. Pettigrew squeezed her hands, "I imagine camping rations get old after a while, and club sandwiches are a perfect refresher."

Dayo and Desi dug into the pile, and they didn't realize how famished they were. Moments later, the tray was empty.

Cobb finished a glass of lemonade. "Let's meet my pride and joy and see if we can rope a few Corriente before the sun sets."

They left the harrowed arena and crossed the commons. Directly before them was a roofed horse barn. The two-story structure sported a grey metal roof, dormer windows, and a tiny cupolas.

Declan had to admire the facility, and he realized that the Pettigrews had poured substantial investments into their breeding program.

David T. brought two Quarter Horses from their stalls.

"Declan, Desi, here are your horses." Dayo sized up the bay stud and the sorrel.

"Desiree will do the heading, so she needs a muscular horse that can fade hard to the left, and really turn a steer's arse."

Cobb chuckled, "Hunter Cat is the one for heading, and Shepherd loves to heel. They're both exceptional animals, dead-broke fantastic, and riding them is like a dream."

Declan checked the main cinch and the breast collar. They were going to burst out of the boxes like two bats out of hell. And his Western saddle better stay firmly attached.

"Looks good. And if you don't mind, I'll mount up and ride a few figure eights. When Sheppie is warmed up, I'll practice scooping the heels."

He turned to David T., "Can you fire up the dummy steer? I'll practice roping, then the missus and I will be ready for the real thing."

He hauled Desiree into a sideways embrace. He squeezed her lovely derrière, "Darlin, you got this. I believe in you, and Hunter Cat will be amazing."

"You're going to catch those horns in nothing flat, and fade to the left, and whip that steer's heinie around like a top. I'll sweep in, find the sweet spot, and scoop the heels."

The commander lifted her chin, "Kay Bear tells me you'll be fantastic. Just relax and have some fun." He descended into a reassuring kiss, and he willed her to succeed.

When their lips parted, Desi trotted away, full of optimism. The bronze beauty was fueled by encouragement, and his support meant the world to her.

He'd have to remember that. From now on, Dayo would have her back, and be ten steps in front of her.

They both entered the open-air sanctuary and rode figure eights. Desiree was amazed at Hunter's push-button responses. She used a light signal, and the horse cut on a dime.

"My lord, this animal's incredible!" She had never ridden such a lightning-fast Quarter Horse. They cut circles, changed direction, and she tested his top speed.

Desiree centered Hunter down the middle, and by barely lifting the reins, the cutting horse took off like a shot. There were two ground-eating strides, and Hunter cruised through the gaits, and rapidly hit a full-out run.

With head extended and tailfeathers flying, she covered the length of the arena. When she slid her stirrups forward and reined backward, Hunter performed a phenomenal skid stop.

His flanks slung into a low posture, and dirt splashed in a huge wave.

"Wow! What an incredible horse! I've seen this done on the Cowboy Channel, but I've never ridden a horse like this."

Desiree performed a roll out with a minor signal. Hunter rolled back and burst into another high acceleration run. He shifted through the gaits and came to another splash stop.

Cobb was as pleased as can be. "Hey Desi, lean back and give Hunter the command to walk backward."

Hunter showed off his stuff. The bay stud curled his neck, exhibited excellent form, and walked backward ten steps.

"Holy shite! This horse is amazing!"

She caught sight of Declan, and the commander worked a half circle. He remained mounted on Shepherd Cat, while David T. pulled the dummy steer. With each ass-bobbing motion, Declan timed the hips.

When the steer raised his hips, he knew the hooves were soon to fall. There was a small window, and he rifled one throw after another. In between each throw, he rubbed his shoulder to keep his muscles hot.

Hallie ran over, "I imagine you folks have been camping a lot, and your muscles are a bit tight. Why don't you rub this ointment in, and you'll stay good and limber."

"Why thank ya, ma'am." Declan remained mounted and worked the ointment into his shoulders. At the same time, he rolled his rotator cuff, and worked his shoulder blades.

The man rode over to Desiree and removed her open-cleavage blouse.

He kissed her shoulders affectionately, and the horny cowboy admired her ultimate push-up. The girls were lifted high, and her breasts formed a delicious valley.

He whispered, "Girl, you're so stacked and sexy, I could place a glass on your breasts, and they'd make a perfect shelf."

"Good lord, Dayo. Keep it in your pants, man."

She turned a bright shade of rosy bronze, and the girls swelled, and heat shot to her core. This guy did things to her, and his velvet voice, and cocksure Caribbean ways made butterflies take flight.

Desiree enjoyed the shoulder rub, and Dayo's muscular hands did a number on her aching muscles.

"Okay, babe, I'm warmed up. Why don't you catch the dummy horns a few times, then we'll do a live drill."

She felt radiant and cared for. Why didn't men realize that they get more mileage out of sweet gestures than rugged commands?

She was wired that way, and no one except Kay Bear knew her secret. Desi realized that it was high time to tell him what she wanted.

Desiree worked a one-eighty and caught the plastic horns from every angle. She called out, "Let's fire up the ATV, and rope that butt-bobbin' steer."

They worked the dummy steer four times, and Desi missed the head once, but on every other run she caught the horns.

Dayo was magnificent, and he used the drill to practice his timing. He knew this wasn't the real deal, so he saved his best throws for later.

By the fourth run, Cobb was duly impressed. His new arrivals mastered dummy roping in a heartbeat. "All right, David, let's disconnect the dummy, and load up the Corriente. We're going live."

Declan talked it up. "Desi, you're doing great. It's the same as before, but when Hunter sees a real Corriente, he's going to take off like a bat outta tell. He'll hit a gear you haven't seen."

He patted her fine ass, "You got this, girl!"

She flipped her ringlets, "Damn, right, you big stud. I've got this, and Hunter Cat will be freakin' awesome."

Dayo liked her moxie. "As soon as David loads up that bad boy, you start your air cuts. This is a short flippin' arena, and as soon as the barrier drops, Hunter will cover ground."

"Do the same thing you've been doing, keep your back straight, and when you feel the sweet spot, rifle a flat-handed throw."

She eyed him with concern, but the smart Marine added, "Honey, I'm proud of you, and you got this!"

That's all she needed to hear. She didn't appreciate his little pep talks, but the sweet nothings fueled her resolve.

From the sidelines, she overheard Hallie May.

Hallie turned to Cobb, "See how Dayo pumps her up. He loves her so much; he wants her to succeed. The man is highly protective. And that's not a bad thing!"

Cobb responded, "There's something going on between those two. I don't know what it is, but they're not cattleman. They're more like cattle warriors going in for the kill."

Hallie chuckled, "As long as the Corriente doesn't die, and his ears stay glued to his head, we're okay."

Desi had a few more seconds, "Kay Bear, there's a lot riding on this contest. So, hang onto your fur coat. Hunter and I are going to whip that steer's little butt, and you're going to experience a G-force whiplash. We'll come out of this box like thunder. So, you stay glued to my wrist, while I do the rope work."

David T. loaded the black Corriente into the chute. Hunter Cat trotted in place while Desiree performed two air cuts.

Suddenly, David dropped the blue handle, and the little rogue blasted across the arena. The Spanish steer shot ten feet beyond the barrier, and Hunter accelerated with two explosive strides.

The adrenaline surge coursed through her veins, and Desi performed a series of air cuts. Her lariat whipped overhead as she swung into the sweet spot.

Hunter rated with the steer, and then she let loose with a flat-handed lightning bolt. She caught the horns, dallied up, and hauled hard to the left.

The big healer jerked the steer's ass around so fast, Dayo shot in like a bird of prey. No sooner did the Corriente's heels fly wide, Declan timed the hips, and rifled his noose.

He scooped two and Sheppie reared back. They pulled the ropes taut and signaled for time.

It all happened so fast; Cobb was astonished. His cattle warriors punished the clock and there were no apologies.

He yelled out, "That was fantastic. It was a great first run."

The old horseman turned to Hallie May, "I hope that wasn't beginner's luck."

Hallie beamed her birdwing smile, "I don't think so, they look like a couple of pros. They roped a live steer four times in a row, and each time, they became more proficient."

He trotted over to Cobb. "Well, how are we doing?"

"I can't believe it. You two rope like rodeo veterans, and you're faster than hell. And with these times, you could win prize money anywhere."

Dayo fist bumped Desi, "Way to go, girl. You're one awesome header."

Desiree danced in her saddle and broke into a radiant smile. "When we herd the cattle in open range, the rundown will be longer. But with Hunter's acceleration, and Sheppie's speed, I really don't see a problem."

Hallie jumped in, "Hunter Cat loves open range. And that cutting horse has great cow sense, I guarantee it!"

Cobb was pleased, "I wonder if you were to use leg commands, if we could shave a few tenths off the time?"

Hallie May objected, "Sweetheart, we mustn't push the young folks. They've done a great job today, and they've proved their mettle."

"Open range will be a piece of cake and twice as fun. They can herd the cattle from low pasture to high. And there won't be a problem."

Pettigrew drawled, "I know that dear, but to win a PRCA rodeo event, shaving a few tenths assures top dollar."

"We can compete, earn the winnings, and fix this place up. Desi and Dayo will take seventy-five, and we'll take twenty-five. Afterall, they're borrowing our horses."

Declan trotted next to Desiree. "Sir, I understand shaving a few tenths off the clock, but what will leg commands prove?"

"Son, you're a high-action cattle warrior. Your movements are exacting, firm, and precise. But what you don't realize is that your hand work is wasting a few milliseconds."

"Shepherd is a smart horse, and heeling is second nature. He's been doing it for fifteen years. But he's also a Western riding horse, and you can show him off, and you'll be amazed at what he can do."

Hallie May countered, "Aren't we mixing disciplines? Team roping is one thing and rein work is another."

Declan lowered his heavy brows, "I see what he's getting at. Since I've never ridden a high-dollar horse, I've never tried it."

He turned to Desiree, and she was clutching Kay Bear.

"Honey, if we both use verbal commands, you don't have to push your hand to Hunter's mane. Simply lean forward, give the verbal commands, and the Big Cat will take you into the sweet spot."

Desiree became defensive, "I didn't do anything wrong. We rode the pattern perfectly, and I've been making incredible throws."

He palmed her bosom and gazed into her eyes. Her heart hammered a mile a minute, but with his touch, she felt cared for and reassured.

Even though his hand palmed her cleavage, the warmth was comforting. Her breathing slowed down, and a post-traumatic episode had been averted. His eyes were locked into hers, and there was nothing but adoration and encouragement.

Finally, she found a safe place. It was the same space that Kay Bear led her to.

In a soft voice, Desiree volunteered, "Maybe, I don't understand what Cobb is asking?"

Hallie May cautioned her husband, "Sweetheart, let Declan explain it. Desi prefers to hear things from her husband."

Dayo started in, "First off, our times are incredible. And I don't think there's any point in more roping. But on another occasion, we could employ Cobb's ideas."

"I could shave a few tenths, and if you did the same, we'd be untouchable. First place would be in the bag."

Desiree fingered a ringlet strand, "Explain it to me one more time."

"In a nutshell, I'm wasting time, using a hard rein. Tenths of second are being lost, and Shepherd is highly instinctive."

"I can focus on my air cuts, reduce my hand movements, and with nothing more than a left knee command, Sheppie will hit the sweet spot. And I can concentrate all my efforts on a cleaner, faster throw."

Desiree laughed, "You've got to be kidding! You're practically riding no handed, and all you're doing is feeding the rope and making the throw."

"That's right, and it's because Shepherd is a champion warhorse, it will work."

"Oh, I get it. I can do the same thing with Hunter. It'll save time and minimize hand movements. And after I dally up, and fade hard to the left, you'll sweep in and scoop two so fast, it'll make the little guy's head spin."

"That's exactly what I'm talking about."

She turned to Cobb, "I'm sorry, sir. I thought you were jerking my chain and trying to piss me off."

Hallie leaped in. "No, honey he wasn't trying to get your goat. He's just an old Western competitor, and sometimes his perfectionism is a little overbearing."

Cobb folded his arms, "I don't know about that."

Desi giggled, and she felt free as a bird. "Okay, let's do it one more time. Bring out a really fast Corriente, and Hunter Boy will kick his butt."

Their last run went like clockwork. The two cattle warriors used leg commands and eliminated all wasted effort.

Desiree caught the horns faster, and Hunter's hard left was powerful as all hell. Dayo scooped two so fast, the steer was barely beyond the barrier.

Cobb clocked his stopwatch, "You guys did it! You shaved off eight tenths, and that puts you in the winner's circle."

"You're both hired. And what's more, I'll schedule a rodeo, and we can make some money." The old man grinned from ear to ear and hobbled away.

Cobb was arm in arm with Hallie May, and she could feel the love. When she grew old, she wanted to be just like them.

She lifted her wrist, "Kay Bear, we did it!"

"You're looking at the new cattle drivers. And what's more, we may even compete in a rodeo, and you can meet lots of nice people."

Kay Man beamed with perpetual happiness, and Desi reached the end of a really long day. She was beat. After she groomed Hunter, she was going to face plant for two days.

The only problem was her recurring nightmare. If she awakened, screaming into the night, what would the Pettigrews think?

Chapter Seven

Cobb stood next to the enchanting log home. He used his cane for balance and clapped a hand over the pine log handrail.

"This cottage belonged to Beau and Katie Jackson. He was my ranch foreman, and the man in charge of my breeding program."

"After my heart attack, and diminished capacity, there simply wasn't enough work. Unfortunately, Beau couldn't hold out any longer, and he took a position in Montana."

Hallie chimed in, "They were wonderful people, and their children became like family. I was always hoping that another young couple would move in."

"Little ones bring so much joy. I really missed the kids, and all the great picnics we had."

Pettigrew cocked his head thoughtfully, "For the time being, you can stay here. And if you take to ranch life, then you can carve out a place for yourselves."

"There ya go, always thinking about Reined Cow Horse competitions. Desiree and Dayo are high action rodeo types, I'm not sure horsemanship is really their calling."

"I hear ya, Hallie, but I have a few ideas. If Declan is a special ops man, he's probably a fair marksman."

"And I have a little exercise that will teach composure, centering, and using a light rein. I bet our Marine would enjoy that exercise, and it carries over directly to Western showmanship."

Declan lowered his brows, "Sir, we plan to be here for three months. But over the course of the summer, I'm willing to learn anything you want."

"And I've seen RCH events before, and I've always wanted to try it. So, let's just say, I'm interested."

Desiree removed Kay Bear from her wrist, so he could listen to the conversation. She loved this old couple, and the thought of leaving seemed horrible.

Her life was in a turmoil. And she had no idea where she stood on the testimony issue.

Desi held her koala, "Kay Bear isn't sure about the three-month period. He's been looking around, and he loves the way the maples shade the property. He thinks this would be a lovely place to live, and to build wonderful memories."

Dayo slid his hand behind her back, "It's been a long day, and I promised Desi a hot shower and a massage. Does anyone want to give us a tour?"

Cobb pointed with his cane, "It's more like a custom lodge. At one time, we considered leaving our country home and moving over here."

Hallie said, "But we have so many memories over there, I couldn't bear to move."

She turned to her husband, "Would you care to join us?"

"I thank you for the invite, but I'm going over to the trophy room and do some thinking. I'll look through my directory, locate a few friends, and make those rodeo calls."

He nodded curtly, "Dayo, Desi, I'll see you folks tomorrow."

Hallie lifted the hem to her country dress and trotted up the timber steps. They crossed a spacious, elevated front porch, and peered at a post-and-beam great room. Huge picture windows caught the last rays of sunshine.

Desiree was overwhelmed by the lovely cottage, and she imagined the sunsets were spectacular.

"Kay Bear, I think you're going to love it here. It's not a eucalyptus forest, but you're nestled beneath hearty maple trees, and the shade is delightful."

Hallie May opened the craft door, and they entered directly into the great room.

Desiree entered a two-story vaulted living area. She couldn't believe the grandeur, and the ambiance of the post-and-beam construction.

The hardwood floors were covered with rawhide rugs, crackled leather sofas, and an aspen log coffee table. Beyond the luxurious furnishings, a cobble stoned fireplace reached toward the ceiling.

Vaulted trusses and ceiling planks cast a honey-stained glow that made the room so comfy and inviting. "Oh, Hallie, I love what you've done with this place."

"Back in the day, Beau and Katie invited their friends, and over the holidays, a huge Christmas tree stood in that corner."

Desi clasped her hands to her face, "Oh my goodness, I can practically see it."

Declan took a few long strides. "Sweetheart, if you think the post-and-beam construction is amazing, you've got to see this teddy bear collection."

Desiree carried Kay Bear over to the display. "Little Buddy, I don't want you to be jealous. You're my favorite koala, but I simply have to look at these teddies."

She couldn't believe the assortment. There were toy grizzlies, black bears, carpenter bears, and picnicking teddies.

And to her amazement, Hallie May even had an assortment of koala bears. "Oh, Hallie, this is fantastic. It must have taken you years to collect them all."

Hallie radiated pure joy, and her birdwing smile lit up the room. "Oh, honey, it's been a hobby of mine for quite some time. You can move the teddy bears anywhere you want, and even take some into the master bedroom."

Desi spotted another display with French teddy bears, drinking from little teacups and wearing striped outfits and red berets. "Oh, my goodness, I think I'm going to die of a cutie attack."

Declan carried a lifelike koala bear and presented it to her. "What do you think of this little guy?"

"He's patterned after the marsupials, and if I didn't know better, I'd say he was alive."

"Ohhh, he's so adorable. Look at his big button eyes, and his pink chin, and the way his claws cling to your hand."

Desi realized she was making too big a fuss. "Kay Bear, I want you to know that you're the cutest, the bravest, and the most loyal friend a girl could ever ask for. And none of them can hold a candle to your loyalty and your friendship."

Dayo clapped his hands, "Honey, why don't you scoop up a few teddies, and we'll visit the master suite. It's getting late, and I still owe you a piping hot shower and a back rub."

He didn't have to ask twice. Desiree scooped up an armful of teddy bears and carried them into the next room. She spotted a wonderful four poster, a roaring fire, and a honey-stained ceiling.

The suite was cozy, and there were Navaho recliners stationed near the bed. Desiree carried her treasures to a recliner and piled her friends into an easy chair. She wasted no time, arranging them in tiers, so everyone had a view.

Hallie May took stock of the room. "I've placed a new set of towels in the spa, and breakfast provisions are in the fridge."

"So, treat yourself to an egg breakfast with pancakes. And once I've had a chance to harvest vegetables, and collect steaks from the locker, we'll have a grand celebration."

Desiree rushed over to her and gave her a great big hug. "Thank you, so much, Hallie."

"Staying here is like living at a mountain resort."

"Oh, I don't know if I'd go that far, but make yourself at home, and enjoy yourselves. I believe your man is anxious to give you a massage."

Mrs. Pettigrew turned to Declan. "Young man, could you walk me to the door?"

Desiree set her pack in a Native recliner. She unzipped it and removed a teddy. It was a silky, lingerie wraparound, and perfect for wearing to bed.

She held up the transparent negligee, "What do you think, Dayo? Isn't this cute?"

He lowered his voice an octave, "I'll be right back!"

Desi giggled and rushed into the loo.

Declan arrived at the foyer and held open the door.

Hallie turned to him with a look of concern. "Your wife is a lovely person, and I realize she's gone through a lot."

"I want my prayers to be effective, so I was wondering if she suffers from shell shock?"

Dayo stopped cold and processed the question. "Oh yeah, that's the old-fashioned term for her condition. Nowadays, they call it post-traumatic syndrome."

"And yes, I'd appreciate prayers. Occasionally, Desi lapses into an episode, and I haven't found a remedy."

"That's what I was thinking. I'll scan the internet and see if there are any treatments or medications."

"I appreciate that, she's currently taking meds, but I'm not sure they're working. I'm just learning about her condition, and I'd appreciate the help."

Hallie patted his chest. "Young man, I'll find a solution. I'm good at this sort of thing."

Mrs. Pettigrew continued, "I looked into her eyes, and at one point, I thought she was on the verge of a meltdown."

Dayo still had to maintain privacy. "Hallie, we revealed some things about our military past, and I'd like you to keep those things confidential."

"We're in transition, and I'd rather that the locals know us only as hired hands."

"All right, I'll tell Cobb, and we'll leave out your military background. But he's really pumped about the rodeo contests."

"It's all right to talk about team roping, and barrel racing, isn't it?"

"Oh, yeah, I don't see any problem there. Country folks love to talk about rodeos. And in nothing flat, we won't be the subject of conversation, the residents will be spinning tall tales, and trying to outdo one another."

Hallie paused, "Desiree is fully functional, isn't she?"

"Since we've been married, her episodes only occur at night. During the day, she can fly Flight for Life helos, ride mountain horses, and do just about anything. She has a level head, and she's a pleasure to be around."

"I can see you're very protective and deeply in love. I'll tell Cobb that there's no problem with her condition. A horse ranch presents a lot of challenges, and we don't want to see the girl get hurt."

"I believe in teamwork, and the buddy-buddy system. So, if she were to get injured, I'd be right there." Declan lifted his communicator, "What's more, we're always in contact with one another."

Hallie laughed, "If I had one of those, I'd drive my husband crazy."

"Good night, Declan, and be nice to your lovely bride."

Declan closed the door, and he had mixed emotions. He wanted their act to be convincing, but his interaction with Desi exceeded all expectations.

His protective actions were spilling into adoration. He couldn't fight it. Dayo adored his little bronze beauty. And right now, he had a lovely bombshell in a steamy shower, and he couldn't wait to rub her down.

Dayo entered the boudoir, and to his surprise, Desiree was buried beneath a sensuous gold comforter and a mound of teddy bears. She turned the lights down low, and there were bowl-shaped candles burning on both nightstands. Even the fireplace cast a romantic glow.

The determined Marine promised her a delicious back massage, and he felt compelled to follow through. Declan pulled back the saffron comforter and laid it to one side.

"Sweetheart, I promised you a back massage, and I think it would help you sleep better."

Desi licked her lips, "Kay Bear thinks I'm in for a rough night. I'm out of post-traumatic meds, and I'm really frightened. Everything went so well today; I'd hate to cap it off with a horrible episode."

"I hear ya, babe. After few hours of shut eye, I'll get on the horn with Eugene, and order your meds."

"Ohhh, thank you so much!"

"Dayo, you're so kind, I really appreciate all your support. If it weren't for you, I would be dead."

"It's the least I could do. Afterall, you're my lovin' woman, and my lovely bride."

She turned her head sideways and pushed the pillows aside. Since my backside is fully exposed, am I going to get that massage?"

"Absolutely, darlin'."

Dayo disrobed down to his briefs and knelt above her shapely hourglass. Gazing down at her, Desi's generous breasts spilled beyond her ribs, and her bronze shoulders tapered down to a scandalously small waist. Her hips flared outward, displaying an incredibly voluptuous derrière.

Declan paused for a moment to admire this alluring beauty.

"Are you going to stare at me all night, or give me that massage?"

"If I hadn't told you before, your shapely hourglass is such a work of art, it belongs in the Louvre."

"Oh, that's so nice. It sure beats your brick house compliments."

"Hey, I'm working on it. So don't give me such a hard time."

Declan scooped up a mane of shiny ringlets and created a messy bun. Now that her shiny ringlets were arrayed in a glistening topknot, the massage oils wouldn't mess up her hair.

The Caribbean warrior reached for the oil rack, and a golden candle heated the massage oils. He used a tiny pitcher and poured a drizzle of heated oil down her spine.

With his large hands, he seized her neck tenderly, and worked her cervical muscles until she was moaning in sweet surrender. He gently worked out the knots, and the poor girl was tighter than a drum.

As soon as her cervical muscles relaxed, Declan palmed her

shoulder blades, gripped her hot oiled flesh, and massaged her entire back. With his big hands, he rocked her shapely frame and delivered a bone-melting massage.

Desi moaned, "Ohhh, that feels so good! Dayo, I forgive you for all the horrible things you've put me through."

He wagged his head. "That's one way to look at it. But you're alive, and lying in a romantic four poster, and you've got a fire burning. Things don't look half bad."

Declan seized the tiny pitcher, and drizzled hot oils over her voluptuous, well-round cheeks. He noticed that there were love toys nearby, and he seized a vibrating pad.

Gently, he lifted her luscious hips, and placed the vibrator against Chloe.

She whispered to Kay Bear, "What is he up to?"

He adjusted the dial to a medium setting and watcher her lips curl into a delicious smile.

"Honey, I'm going to give you a mind-blowing glute massage."

"Oh, that explains it."

It was evident, Desiree was enjoying the back massage, and she smacked her lips like a little kid. Clearly, the bronze beauty was about to fall asleep.

He realized sexual intimacy was out of the question, but gazing at her gorgeous body, he had a lot to look forward to.

His big hands gripped her cheeks, and he worked the upper glute layers, and descended deeper. And all of sudden, he had a powerful grip on her whole bottom, and he was massaging her to sweet perfection.

Unconsciously, Desiree dropped a hand to her Chloe and gave herself a whirlwind massage. It was self-serving, but she bit down on the comforter, and rocked her hips furiously.

She couldn't help herself. The pressure started to build, and she was past the point of no return. Her whole frame shattered into a delicious orgasm.

Desiree moaned into the saffron sheets, and suddenly, she was out like a light. The poor thing was so exhausted, she was snoring like a log.

It wasn't ladylike, but then again, his courageous girl had been through hell and back.

Desiree felt her man spoon against her. He cradled her breasts and snuggled against her backside. His sideways embrace felt so good, and she felt so safe and warm. She could get used to this sort of thing.

Moments later, she drifted into a deep sleep. Her cozy dreams were interrupted by a recurring nightmare.

She was back in Afghanistan, and Desiree landed her fully armed hawk. The flagman gave her the all clear, and the Army Rangers hit the ground, ducked, and ran for the debriefing tent.

The sleeping beauty tried to alter the dream. She yelled to her men, "Get back aboard, it's unsafe. We've got to touch down somewhere else."

But the Rangers raced toward the debriefing tent, and there was nothing she could do. It was excruciating to watch the same scene unfold.

It happened in slow motion, and there was nothing she could do to stop it. There were feelings of prolonged horror as her hawk exploded into a million pieces.

Desiree broke form Dayo's grasp, bolted upright, and screamed into the darkness.

She slammed her palms to her temples and sobbed, "Why won't these nightmares stop? I hate it. I'm soaked, and I'm terrified."

Instantly, she felt two massive arms engulf her, and he crushed her into a bear hug. Desi squeezed his midsection and cried against his chest. She nuzzled deeper into his embrace and wished the world would go away.

Her trembling finally subsided, and she peered up at Dayo. "I'm all right, but I sure wish these nightmares would stop."

"It can't be healthy. I relive the same day repeatedly. Each time, I'm powerless. And I start the day feeling like I'm inadequate."

"I understand, babe. It must be a horrifying experience to relive that day. Let me, fire up the coffee pot, then I'll call in the reinforcements."

Desiree slid out of bed and padded into the bathroom.

She called out, "By reinforcements, do you mean Eugene Merriweather? Maybe, the super-hacker can get my meds? And we can get this trauma problem under control."

"You got it, honey. I'm headed for the kitchen, and I'll get things going."

Declan pulled on his Wranglers, grabbed an Aztec button-down, and shot into the kitchen.

In a flash, he called out, "Wild Man, come in. We have a major emergency, and we need your help."

The fearless Marine padded across the hardwood floors and prepared a pot of searing hot coffee. He set two cups on a black galaxy countertop and padded past the cherry shaker cabinets.

Dayo seated himself in a cozy kitchen nook and gazed out the window. The Eastern sunrise came over the high Cascades, and another gorgeous day was about to begin.

If his lady love wasn't going through hell, his mind would be at ease. *Did he just call Desiree his lady love?*

Wild Man grumbled, "You cattlemen sure get up early. I worked late, covering your tracks, and deploying the old unit."

"They're working the lower Sierras and the coastline. And you won't believe the number of bounty hunters they've dispatched."

"Thanks for your dedication, and I really want to hear how the old unit is doing."

"But Eugene, we have a serious emergency. Desi isn't doing very well, and last night, she had a horrible traumatic episode."

"She woke up, screaming like a banshee, and she wailed and sobbed for half an hour. Finally, I calmed her down, and she told Kay Bear all her problems."

"Man, that's the second time I've heard about Kay Bear. Who the hell is Kay Bear?"

"It's her koala wrist cuff. He's a cute little guy from the Middle East. And he has button brown eyes and a perpetual smile of happiness. She uses the toy as a good luck charm and channels all her emotions through it."

"Wow! She's worse off than I thought."

Declan felt defensive. "She's highly functional, but with a few little quirks."

"Back to the post-traumatic stuff, can you place an order to the Pine Whisper pharmacy?"

"Under the name of Dez Corazon, can you order a new supply of meds?"

"You got it, boss! Anything else?"

"I'm combing my mind for solutions, and the only thing I can think of is a therapy dog. I read there are hyper-sensitive dogs that can detect a change in human chemistry."

Declan heard the wheels squeak as Eugene flew across his command center. He heard the tapping of keys.

Wild man came over the communicator, "More precisely, a seizure alert dog would be even better."

"By the way, I've assembled a local search engine, and I'm combing through therapy dogs."

"Bingo! You're not going to believe this, but Bailey Compton wants to pass her seizure alert dog to a deserving individual."

Here's a photo of a fawn colored, Belgian Malinois. The pupper has alert brown eyes, a lolling tongue, and jet-black muzzle. It's a great looking animal."

"Why is Bailey Compton giving up such a fine therapy dog?"

"It says here, the owner has discovered a new set of epilepsy meds, and no longer needs her faithful friend, Molly."

"Wild Man, you're the best. Fake a few phone calls and send Molly over here, pronto."

"You got it, Chief. One seizure alert doggo is headed your way."

Desiree emerged from the barnwood shower enclosure. She stepped over the slate tiled curb into a honey-stained bathroom. She strolled over to the amber slabbed countertop and spotted a cup of piping hot coffee.

Desi turned to Kay Bear, "Dayo is one thoughtful Marine. I'm getting used to the guy, and he's trying to butter me up."

"Do you think I should give into his romantic wiles?"

K-Man beamed his bright brown eyes and smiled from his tiny pink lips. "I take that as a yes. The question is, how should we choreograph our first romantic interlude?"

The bronze beauty sashayed into the honey-stained master suite. By morning light, sunshine shattered through a transom window, and her boudoir was bathed in golden rays. Despite a niggling anxiety, the world seemed like a friendly place.

She used a hair dryer to blow Kay Bear's furry scalp. "Do you like that, buddy?" His look of perpetual happiness beamed forth, and she knew how much he enjoyed their morning rituals.

Desiree carried her coffee cup, strolled through the great room, and entered the front porch. Dappled light threw playful shadows across the floorboards. Declan finished his push-ups and leaped to his feet.

Swiftly, he lowered his cool guy shades, and pulled a black Stetson into place. She couldn't believe the rapid transformation; the Marine was ready for action.

"Hey, babe, I just heard the squeal of truck tires. I'm going to investigate, care to join me?"

Desi trotted down the pine log treads and landed on a giant flagstone. She glanced through the dappled light of early morning and scanned the Pettigrew homestead.

There was a delivery man, wearing a short-brimmed cowboy hat and striped button-down. He opened the door, and a gorgeous Belgian Malinois leaped to the ground.

Desi wanted to introduce Kay Bear to the new doggo, but realized she wasn't wearing her disguise. It was one thing for Cobb and Hallie to see her au natural, but as for Pine Whisper locals, it was best to keep a low profile.

She pulled her chocolate Stetson down low and summoned a generous smile. Her radiant beauty and adorable dimples were sure to throw him off.

But when she started to cross the lawn, she had second thoughts. Even though she didn't look like any of her IDs, it was better to stay in the shadows.

She tugged on Declan's sleeve, "Hey stud, why don't you see what's going on?"

He leaned over and kissed her sweetly, "For you babe, I'd do anything."

She didn't know what to say. They weren't a real married couple, but Declan sure acted like it. Maybe their affair might actually work.

Declan walked over to Cobb and Hallie. They stood on the porch while leaning on the white handrail. Cobb wore a green Irish Sweater, and Hallie wore a brown pioneer dress.

The woman's aging-figure filled out the décolletage, and her large hips filled out the skirt. At the base of the wooden steps, there was a local cowboy holding a leash.

Dayo couldn't believe it. Less than two hours ago, he requested a Belgian Malinois. *Could this be Desi's seizure alert dog?* He had to hand it to Eugene, the man worked wonders.

The blue-shirted cowboy issued a command, "Vorwarts"" and waved his hand forward. It was a Schutzhund command for military dogs. *Man alive, Desiree was going to love this dog. It was freakin' perfect.*

In English, the cowboy said, "Go ahead, Molly, you can play with Jeffrey."

The Belgian Malinois performed an agile leap and ran over to the golden retriever. They raced around the green lawn, bounding, barking, and playing.

Hallie caught sight of Declan, "Morgan, I'd like you to meet our new cattle driver, Declan Corazon. He can heel a Corriente something fierce, and Cobb has big plans for him."

Morgan wore a small-brimmed hat, a comical grin, and a peppered brown beard. The medium-built man extended a hearty handshake, "I'm pleased to meet, ya, Declan."

The cowboy nodded toward the two dogs and cleared his throat. "Early this morning, the assisted care facility got wind of Molly's availability."

"My sister, Bailey, suffers from epileptic seizures, but she no longer needs the service dog. Assisted care suggested that Molly would do well at the Pettigrew Ranch."

"And I knew right away, it was a perfect match. The horse ranch has wide open spaces, green pastures, and her best friend, Jeffrey."

Morgan chuckled, "I almost forgot." He handed a pharmacy package to Hallie. "I picked up this script, and if you would be so kind, can you pass it on to Dez Corazon?"

He smiled, "I bet she's your wife." Declan felt more and more like it was the truth.

The bronze warrior lowered his gaze, "Yes sir, she is my lovin' woman, and I'll make sure she gets these."

Morgan patted Dayo on the shoulder, "My sister and I run an art gallery, Whispering Watercolors. If you're ever in town, be sure to stop by."

The cowboy issued a command, "Hier." The alert Malinois perked her ears, and in a blinding bolt of coffee-colored fur, Molly arrived at the man's side.

"That a girl. You're going to love your new home, so I'm giving the Pettigrews a list of Schutzhund commands."

"Now you be a good girl and cut them some slack. Not everyone speaks German, so the commands may sound different."

Molly cocked her ears as though she understood. Morgan disappeared into his delivery truck, and Declan couldn't wait to introduce Desi's new pupper.

This could be the solution they were looking for. The fearless Marine knew better than to get his hopes up, but it sure as hell seemed like a good fit.

Desiree clutched Kay Bear. Back at her Spanish Med home, there was an article lying on the table. It was about therapy dogs, and standing over by the Pettigrew homestead, there was a beautiful Malinois wearing a red vest.

She emerged from the shadows and skipped quickly across the front lawn. The second the Belgian Malinois spotted her, the therapy dog shot right for her.

The Malinois stepped to Desi's thigh and stared her in the face. The pupper's nostrils flared and the Belgian took in a hundred body scents and memorized them.

Desi ruffled the dog's fawn colored neck, "You're such a friendly dog, What's your name?"

Hallie lifted the hem to her pioneer dress and trotted gingerly down the steps. "Her name is Molly."

Declan whispered, "The Belgian knows Schutzhund commands, and here's the list."

Desiree reviewed the list swiftly, and she already knew every command by heart. This was too good to be true.

Desi initiated the training session, "Achtung! Sitz!" It was evident that the therapy dog was on duty, and she was alert for the next command.

Not only did the Malinois start her day shift, then she was ordered to sit. Molly dropped into an alert position with black ears pointed and tongue lolling.

The therapy dog waited for the next command. Hallie burst into a radiant birdwing smile. "My lord, this is a sign. Molly has taken to you like you're a lifelong friend. You two were meant for each other."

Cobb leaned on his cane and tilted his head thoughtfully. "Does Molly take commands from anyone?"

Declan answered, "Preferably, the Schutzhund commands should come from one person, and that would be her owner."

Pettigrew followed up with another question, "But what confused me was the way she stared into Desiree's face so long. It's rather unusual."

Desi explained, "The human face and décolletage emit hormones, enzymes, and a host of chemical fragrances. I think Molly knows I had a nightmare last night."

Hallie touched her cross-shaped brooch, "Her previous owner, Bailey Compton, had epileptic seizures, but she claimed that Molly could halt every episode."

"With a good face lick, Bailey was back at her easel painting."

Hallie eyed her with motherly concern, "Are your nightmares chronic?"

Desiree experienced not only terrifying nightmares, but tingling anxiety, and her mind wasn't fully focused. Earlier, she talked her way down from the ledge.

Kay Bear heard it all before, and her little buddy let her vent, and get it all out.

Desi glanced at Dayo, and she knew it was all right to share. "I suffer from post-traumatic syndrome and memories besiege me."

Hallie clapped her hands, "Then, Molly is your answer. She's a miracle dog sent straight from heaven."

Mrs. Pettigrew motioned to the front lawn, "Why don't you two get acquainted. Give Molls some more commands. In the Middle East, she was a military dog, and she loves to work."

"In the meantime, I'll be indoors, preparing breakfast." The old timers disappeared into the yellow homestead, and she had Miss Molly all to herself.

Desiree knew that Molly was an obedient therapy dog. Her pupper didn't need a leash, so she unlatched the nylon tether. Before she made a new friend, she had to reassure Kay Bear.

No one could replace him. But maybe, he was willing to accept Molly, and they could be one big happy family.

She lifted her wrist, "Kay Bear, I want you to know how much I love you. You saw me through two tours of duty, and you never wavered."

"Your enthusiasm and perpetual optimism has been a guiding light.

And today, I want to make a new friend. Do you mind if Molly joins the team?"

K-Man beamed his adorable smile, and his button brown eyes were full of encouragement. She kissed his cute face, "Thank you, so much for understanding."

Desiree issued the command, "Fuss," which means to heel. Without a leash, the pair marched across the lawn toward the round pen.

Molly fell into line and heeled right at her side.

Dayo watched in amazement. "Over in Afghanistan, I watched dog handlers, and girl, you seem to know what you're doing."

"I should think so. When I wasn't flying combat helos, my bunkmate, Amy, taught me the German commands."

"Her Malinois never took a shine to me, but he did allow me to work with him. And now, I have a Belgian pupper of my very own. And Kay Bear thinks we'll make a great team: me, K-Man, and Molly."

Dayo laughed, "I guess my services are no longer needed. I'll just take the next flight outta here and fly back to my Spanish home."

She was horrified by his comment, didn't Declan know he was the glue that held her life together. Maybe, the tough guy needed reassurance.

She halted Molly's advance, "Bleibsitzen," and the Malinois came to a sudden halt. She pointed at Declan, "Gradaus," which means to run forward.

They both shot across the lawn toward the Marine. And when Molly arrived first, Desi shouted, "Hopp," which means to jump up.

The Malinois leaped through the air and landed in Declan's arms. The big man fell to the ground, and Desi issued a make-believe command, "Licken ze face!"

Molls sat on his chest and stared at her mistress. Her doggo comprehended and deluged Dayo with a sloppy face licking.

He pursed his lips as doggie kisses covered his chin and spattered his cheeks.

Finally, Declan yelled out, "Enough already. For Pete's sake, 'Sitz.'"

Molls sat down on her haunches, but she was really pleased with herself.

"There ya go, Dayo. My pupper loves you, and I...like you a whole lot." She broke into a radiant smile, "See what a mighty weapon I wield?"

"Oh yeah, I'm pretty impressed. If the attack command doesn't work, Molly can lick them to death."

Desiree could feel the love pouring from this wonderful, fawn colored cannonball. Molly was dying to lave kisses all over her face.

And after that, they'd be well met. And Molls could discern if any of her chemistry was amiss. The combat pilot curled her fingers, "Hopp."

Molly covered the distance like a furry lightning bolt and leaped to her thighs. Her doggo climbed up her legs and kissed her face to pieces.

It was a slurry of face licks, and Molls loved every moment. Not only did the Belgian dial in her olfactory scents, but she also tasted her facial chemistry. And from now on, Molly would know if a post-traumatic episode was on the way.

Anything out of the ordinary, and any anxiety-filled smell meant trouble was on the way.

Finally, Desi issued the command, "Daun," which meant down. Molly sat on her haunches as pleased as could be.

She patted the Malinois' head, "Good girl! Now, you know my happy scent, so get used to it."

Declan appreciated the bonding moment, but he shifted the conversation to more practical matters.

"From now on, I want you to surround yourself with your support group: Kay Bear, your teddy collection, and your new seizure alert dog. Whenever you rest or sleep, I want that pupper at your side. Got it!"

Goodness, the man loved giving orders. "Aye, Aye, Captain." She giggled with her new friends, Kay Bear and Molly.

She whispered under her breath, "He's such a control freak, but the commander means well, and I adore him, and I forgive him."

Declan and Desiree finished the training session and trotted up the white staircase. The six paneled blue door was left ajar, and Dayo called out.

"Hallie, Cobb, do you mind if we come in?"

Hallie came trotting down a ceramic tiled hallway, "I've almost got breakfast ready. How did the Schutzhund commands go? Does Molly know her stuff?"

Desiree gave the aging beauty a big hug. "I'm so glad you're letting Molls stay with us. She's a great dog, and she's already memorized my scent. And after a horrible night, I'm looking forward to her intervention."

Hallie gestured to the family room, "Cobb is watching the news, and I'll have breakfast served in a jiffy. Just bring Molly in and make yourself at home."

They entered a cozy great room with a roaring fireplace, a faded oriental rug, and textured sofas. It was an airy room with vista windows, an incredible view, and a tapered plank ceiling. Beside the wood mantle, there was a flat screen spouting the local news.

Cobb stroked his peppered beard, "Not much happening in Pine Whisper. Why don't you folks take a seat, and we'll see what's happening in L.A."

Desiree sunk into an armed sofa chair, and the commander was right at her side. Molly instinctively laid down and rested her chin on the floor.

In a bold blue banner, the words "News Alert" flashed across the screen. The announcer adjusted his striped tie and looked into the camera.

"Earlier this week, a key witness to the Gonzalez trial was murdered. Desiree DeNiro perished in a safe house fire."

"Lieutenant DeNiro was a Flight for Life pilot, and she lost her life in a neighborhood explosion." There was a photo of Desi, wearing her flight uniform, and holding an aviation helmet.

Her image stood expressionless, and her full-lipped gaze appeared defiant. It was a horrible LifeNet pose, and as suddenly as it appeared, the transmission faded.

A blast of static filled the screen. The commentator came back on, "Apparently, we lost our signal, so let's go to Sam Wainwright. He has the weather, and Kansas tornadoes are ripping across the countryside."

Hallie ducked into the great room, "Everyone, breakfast is ready. So, wash up, and join me in the breakfast nook." Cobb clicked off the screen and processed what he had seen.

Declan went on full alert, and the Malinois could feel the tension. The "Achtung" command wasn't issued, but his team was ready for action. He already made the decision, they were leaving.

When he entered the kitchen nook, he took in the charming, country décor. There was a weathered sign mounted to the wall, and a paint-chipped long table dominated the dining area. Two long benches were stationed at each side, and an alphabet rug covered the floor.

He glanced through the arched portal into an ivory kitchen. There was a tiny flatscreen, mounted above the butcher block countertops.

The tornado story filled the screen, and judging by Hallie's quiet manner, Mrs. Pettigrew had seen the news bulletin.

They needed the protein. And after they ate their fill, he'd call Eugene, and plot their next move.

He planned to take the Malinois and ensure Desiree's condition. It was a brief stay, but he enjoyed working with high-end horses, and sleeping in a king-sized bed. His 9 mm was at his hip, and within fifteen minutes, they'd have their military packs in place.

Desiree sat at the long bench like she'd been struck by lightning. Molly recognized the overload, and the Malinois was in her face, delivering doggie kisses.

She wiped her lips, "Thank you, Molls, I'm fully grounded." She glanced at Declan, and he mouthed the words, "We're out of here." She fully agreed.

Hallie said grace, "Lord, Please bless this meal. I wish to thank you for our visitors and realize that nothing has changed. Your good, pleasing, and perfect will, will unfold according to your desires. Amen."

Dayo considered the prayer and realized where Mrs. Pettigrew was coming from. The old prayer warrior didn't give a rip about news alerts, she'd follow the Almighty wherever he led. As for Cobb, he may not feel the same way.

Hallie forced herself to be cheerful, and she curled her lips into a great big smile. "There's plenty to go around. Bowls of scrambled eggs, applewood bacon, and heavenly biscuits."

Cobb glanced philosophically at his two guests.

Declan addressed the old horseman respectfully, "I appreciate the hospitality, but you saw the news alert. We've got unfinished business, and after breakfast, we'll be leaving."

"I hate to be impolite, but I've got to make an emergency phone call."

"By the way, where is David T?"

Cobb touched his lips, "David is cleaning out the stables. He'll be in shortly, Why do you ask?"

"Is there a flatscreen in the horse barn?"

"Inside my trophy room, there is one. But the old wrangler is partial to country music, so he's mucking out stalls, and listening to George Straight and Charlie Pride."

"After my phone call, I'll have a word with David T. I've got to contain this situation, and then we'll depart peaceably. And rest assured, I won't put your lives in jeopardy."

Before Cobb could object, Dayo pushed open the French doors, and strolled into the flower garden. He surveyed the perimeter, and kept an eye on Desi. Inside the kitchen nook, no one touched a phone.

Hallie's garden was bursting with colors, and the natural beauty belied the fact that all hell was breaking loose. His sniper rifle was fifty meters away, and he wouldn't hesitate to take down the local police force.

He clicked his communicator, "Wild Man, cut all phone lines to the Pettigrews. I need radio silence until we clear outta here."

"And if you can find a black hawk, I want to get as far from here as possible. As soon as the unit is assembled, let me know. I've had enough of this shite!"

Declan continued, "David T. may have seen the news bulletin, and I don't need an old wrangler making a report and looking for a reward."

Wild Man came across his communicator. "Just so you know, the L.A. news just aired a brief news flash. I caught it in time and killed the story."

"And per your request, I've closed down the entire Pine Whisper phone system. The relay tower suffered high wind damage, and a backhoe cut the phone lines."

"Perfect! We're in the middle of breakfast, and as soon as we're finished, we're leaving. Call back when you know our next destination, and whether a hawk is available."

Declan opened up the doors, and Desiree must have heard his parting words. He glanced in her eyes, and he could see the walls close in. Instantly, Molly was in her face, bathing her with doggie kisses.

The distressed pilot absorbed the sloppy face-licking and managed to stay centered. Declan dropped next to her and squeezed her hand.

"Stay with me, girl. The episode will pass, and we'll be on our way." Tears streaked across her peach bronze complexion, and her lips were thick with saliva.

Desiree moaned, "I don't want to go. This is a nice place, and I'm tired of running."

Hallie looked from Declan to her husband and back at Desiree. "You folks just got here, you can't just up and leave. You were sent by the Almighty and there's so much around here that needs to be done."

Cobb said, "I agree with the missus, and I think I understand what happened. You're not fugitives, but survivors of a crime lord's murder attempt."

"And you've got to realize that no one has seen either of you, except Morgan Compton. And since you arrived, your beard has grown thick. You were wearing sunglasses, and your Stetson was pulled low."

Hallie chimed in, "Besides, Declan's face wasn't aired on television."

The old prayer warrior wrapped her arms around Desi, "This is like Harriet Tubman's underground railroad. She was a godly woman who ushered slaves to their freedom."

"The way I see it, you need a disguise."

Desi wiped her nose, and Molly delivered a few more face licks, just for good measure.

Desiree drank a glass of orange juice and cleared her mind. "I've got ginger ringlets and a cosmetic case."

"That's the spirit. I'll give you a complete makeover, and no one will know the difference."

Mrs. Pettigrew set up a round top stool, and the matriarch flipped the switch to three hanging lights. The country kitchen lit up like a vanity, and the matriarch prepared to transform the shapely beauty into a ginger red model.

"Desi, why don't you sit right here." Molly took her station at Desiree's feet. Her pupper was poised and ready.

If she suffered another panic attack, Molls would rush to the rescue. Her Malinois pawed her leg and whimpered. "I'm all right, girl."

Desi realized her disguise was back in her log cabin. She rushed back to her bedroom and retrieved her backpack. The combat pilot laid the ginger ringlets and the cosmetic palette on the table.

Quickly, Desiree flipped open the lid and stationed the model's photo. In addition to a mane of gorgeous amber ringlets, the make-up model had a glowing peach complexion.

Hallie was so excited, she rushed into the kitchen, carrying a skull cap, pins, and stick 'em glue.

"Oh, boy, this is just like putting on stage makeup. Back in the day, I worked for an acting company, and it was so fun to put on theatrical make-up."

The prayer warrior tucked Desi's black ringlets into a tidy shell and pulled the cap over the top. With agile hands, Hallie drew forth the sexy ginger ringlets.

She wrapped the amber hairpiece over Desi's scalp and allowed a large bang of over swept ringlets to fall to one side. Hallie plucked the ringlets until they fell way past Desi's shoulders and dropped to the middle of her back.

"Goodness, you look sensational! When Declan sees how beautiful you are, he's going to lay into you something fierce."

Desiree giggled, "I'm not into heavy make-up, but this time I don't have a choice."

Hallie seized a fluffy brush and dusted an application of luminous, peach glow foundation. The transformation was immediate, "You don't look like Desiree what's her name, at all."

"And I think Dayo will love the new you." Mrs. Pettigrew applied honey glow blush, pearl pink lipstick, and feline flared lashes.

Hallie stood back, "There is a feminine grace to your appearance, and if I don't say so myself, you look positively scrumptious."

Desiree held up the hand mirror, "Good lord, I look like a ginger red model ready for a camera shoot."

"I couldn't agree more. Now, let's complete the look with peach-colored fingernails." Hallie took out her nail kit and went to work.

"Oh, Hallie, I feel like I'm being pampered. As a combat pilot, I never make it to the beauty salon." Molly sensed a sense of sadness and leaped to her thigh.

Her doggo stared into her eyes and sniffed the new cosmetics. Molls turned away and sneezed.

Desi laughed, "I don't blame you. That's exactly how I feel."

Hallie pressed on the nails. In nothing flat, there was an assortment of peach solids, peach snowflakes, and bejeweled fingernails.

The matriarch chuckled, "Would you consider singing in our church choir? You look magnificent."

Desi giggled, "If you want me to drive people away, I'll take the microphone, and blister their ears."

"A joyful noise is all that's required. Any hymn sung out of love finds its way to the hearer."

Desiree took one more look in the mirror. "I wonder if I can get the ginger ringlets under my flight helmet?"

"Don't worry about a flight helmet, Cobb wants you to wear your amber ringlets beneath a rodeo hat. How about that?"

Desi finally burst out laughing. "This is crazier than shite, but I love it."

"Ohhh, I'm sorry Hallie, I didn't mean to offend you."

"What's wrong? I recognize an emergency when I see one. And there's no problem with enthusiastic speech."

"Just ask for the Lord's forgiveness before you retire, and all is right with the world. Now, let's go show the men the new you!"

Cobb and Declan remained in the kitchen nook. Pettigrew chewed on a toothpick and gazed at the garden.

"Son, I could take an educated guess as to what happened. I don't need too many details, just the important parts. Just so we're clear."

Dayo wrapped his knuckles on the chipped table. "Despite your wife's good intentions, there's a lot at stake. Desiree witnessed the murder of an innocent man. She watched Antonio Gonzalez gun him down in broad daylight."

"Innocently, she volunteered as an eyewitness to take down the kingpin. But Gonzalez infiltrated the safe house, and I had to go into action."

"Desi is an Apache Longbow pilot, and the girl served her country, and she didn't deserve to be executed. I ran a special op, destroyed the hostiles, and fled to a safe location."

"No one but you, Hallie, and David T. know we're alive. So, it is in everyone's best interest if we pack up and seek out a new destination."

Cobb stroked his circle beard and spoke in a drawl.

"Son, I think you're prepared to move on, and take it to the enemy. But from what I see, Desiree's nerves are shot, and she needs to pull herself together. And what's more, this old ranch is just the place to do it."

Declan eyed him from beneath his shades. The master horseman was shooting straight, and he wasn't about to turn them in.

"I'll consider the offer and figure out the logistics."

"While you're figuring out the logistics, the newscaster said Desiree DeNiro was dead. So, any viewers who saw the news bulletin will simply accept it."

"No one is looking for a girl who perished in a fire."

Dayo countered, "I'm still suspicious of the announcement, and whether the police department, or Gonzalez is trying to flush us out."

"In my opinion, her death makes it all the easier. No one is looking for you, are they?"

"I'll have to get back with my people. There's something fishy going on, and I've got to figure out what the police, and the bounty hunters are up to."

Cobb grumbled, "There's not much of a reward for a dead woman."

Dayo rose to his feet and paced the alphabet flooring, "I hope you're right!"

Hallie, Desi, and Molly entered the nook. Desi fingered her lush, ginger ringlets and struck a stylish pose. Her luminous peachy foundation, pearl pink lipstick, and spiky flared lashes belonged to a fashion model.

The transformation was incredible. Declan was up on his feet, and he palmed her honey glow cheek.

"You don't look a bit like Desiree Corazon. Who are you, and what have you done with my woman?"

Desie flashed a radiant smile, "I think this disguise will work. But it calls for a whole new set of mannerisms. What do you think?"

The Marine had his doubts, but he rolled with the suggestion. "Yeah, I agree. Why don't you lick your lips and make dramatic hand gestures. The outlandish display will mesmerize your audience, and no one will suspect a thing."

Dayo paused, "You're like a walking-talking diversion. And I happen to feel you're very sexy and extremely beautiful. And best of all, no one will know your real identity."

The fearless warrior continued, "All I know is how badly I want to taste those pearly pink lips."

Declan threw one arm behind her waist and dipped her into a dramatic swoon. Desi's eyes went wide as he descended into a dramatic, ravishing kiss.

She pounded his chest in resistance, and then melted into his devouring kiss. She enjoyed the drama so much, Desiree countered with a tongue plunging French assault.

If they didn't bring their tempestuous display to a halt, they'd need a pleasure palace to work out his libidinous desires.

When Declan finished, their lips parted, and she stared into his eyes. The fearless cowboy reeled her to her feet and smacked her delicious bottom.

"Darlin', I can't say that the peachy goddess is my favorite, but you sure are a treat."

Desiree regained her composure and flipped her wrist, "Just so you remember. The real me prefers to wear shiny black ringlets, apricot lipstick, and a bronze foundation. And I don't put on flamboyant displays, and I do everything from the heart."

He smacked her well-rounded derrière, "And that's what I love about you."

Hallie said, "Since you look so beautiful, let's go to town, and test out your disguise."

Desiree glanced into Declan's eyes, "I know you want to leave, but I can't take another step. Molly, Kay Bear, and I are bonding, and the country life is exactly what I need."

Cobb interjected, "Besides that, you two promised to drive cattle to high pasture, and win a few rodeos. So, until you fulfill your obligations, you're staying right here."

Hallie clapped her hands, "After you win a team roping contest, Cobb wants to mold you into a real horseman. You don't want to spoil an old man's lifelong dream, do you?"

Declan knew he was outnumbered and as long as Desiree was safe, he'd take it one day at a time.

Dayo broke into a huge grin, "You guys are pouring it on thick. And for what it's worth, I'd love to see Cobb's dreams come true."

Pettigrew slapped his knee, "I knew I liked you from the get-go."

"Son, you and I are going places. So, tomorrow, I'm going to put you through the paces."

"Uh-oh, what does that mean?"

Cobb leaned back in the captain's chair, "You'll find out!"

Chapter Eight

Declan drove the twin cab down the dirt road. As they passed a large herd of beautiful grazing horses, Desiree called out, "The Pettigrews ranch is so lush, and the Quarter Horses are so gorgeous, this feels like we're coming home."

Dayo hauled the twin cab into a parking lot next to the bunkhouse. The only cowboy to grace the flagstone front porch and use the rustic bedrooms was David T.

Just then the old wrangler tipped his hat and curled his lips into a face-stretching smile. He called out, "How was your town visit?"

Hallie May slipped out the back door, "David, meeting the townies was a huge success. Everyone loved Desiree."

David T. scratched his stubbled chin and contemplated Desiree. "Miss, did you do something to your hair?"

Desiree flipped her ginger ringlets, "Yes, I did. For a visit to Pine Whisper, I wanted to go all out, so I wore my flaming red ringlets and a peachy complexion."

"Women are like that. Always changin' things."

"By the way, I was muckin' out stalls this morning, and listening to Charlie Pride. Man alive, can that man sing. By the came I came into the house, you folks were gone. Did I miss anything important?"

Cobb shut the truck door, "I believe there are tornadoes in Kansas." The master horseman left out the biggest news of all.

"Well, hells bells, that ain't news. Kansas is always getting hit by tornadoes."

Hallie chuckled, "You are right as rain. I'll run inside and get the sun-brewed tea ready. Care to join us on the front porch?"

Pettigrew settled into a large, comfy rocker, while Declan brought two chairs. Desiree set out a stainless-steel dog bowl and poured in the dog chow.

In nothing flat, the sleek Malinois devoured her diet food. Molly licked her chops and sat at attention. Desi reached into a bag and held up a chew toy.

"What do you think, Molls? Do want to play with your new toy?"

Desiree took two leaps and hurled the chew toy across the lawn. Desi pointed, "Voraus", which means go. The Belgian Malinois took off like a shot, seized the chew toy, and shook the stuffing out of it.

Her faithful canine carried her toy with pride and took her post. Even though her mistress seemed happy, her pupper knew better. A post-traumatic episode could come out of nowhere. And if it wasn't a flashback, it could be a burst of uncontrollable fear.

Desiree sat down in a rocker and kissed Kay Bear. "We did it, little buddy. We convinced everyone that my natural hair color is ginger red. And I inherited my beautiful ringlets from my Aunt Clara."

Hallie set her iced tea on a scissor-legged table. She and Cobb moved to a love chair and enjoyed a slow swinging moment.

Mrs. Pettigrew laughed, "Maddie Trudeau knew better, but she was impressed by your gorgeous ringlets, which were cultivated from real hair."

Desi said, "And your make-up artistry left her speechless. But what puzzles me was her bungalow hair salon."

"On the outskirts of a little town, she bought a white Spanish Colonial with large European tiles and iron windows. And if the outside wasn't lavish enough, the inside décor was over the top."

Hallie laughed, "You should have seen your eyes when Maddie entered the hair salon. She's quite a character."

"Maddie loves her blonde braids, low slung Stetson, and her badass gunslinger outfit. Ya, know, her pearl handled revolver is real, but she doesn't carry ammo."

Desi said, "When she circled me and touched my ringlets and admired my cosmetic beauty, I didn't know what to think."

"That's because she was thinking about how to get more bronze cowgirls into her shop and give 'em the peach glow treatment."

Cobb pushed off the wooden floorboards and sipped his tea. "I'm glad to see how well Pine Whisper took to you. Of course, our charming Caribbean cowboy hovered so close, no one dared to pry."

Dayo chuckled, but he wasn't making any apologies.

Hallie curled her generous lips and smiled with heavenly gratitude. "What really impressed me was Captain Deveaux and the Flight for Life helo."

"The Captain really wants your services, and your willingness to be on standby."

Desiree said, "Most fire departments field emergencies. But rarely do they have such a beautiful LifeNet helo parked behind the station."

In her mind, she could still visualize the three-tanker garage and the red brick station. And directly around the back, there was a red cross helipad, and a fully equipped chopper. An S-76 Sikorsky helo sported a torpedo nose, an aerodynamic cockpit, and a complete ambulance bay.

When she visited the station, Deveau popped open the clamshell, and showed off the stretcher, the oxygen, and the vital monitoring screens.

It brought back wonderful memories while flying her Flight for Life missions, and for a moment, it seemed like her life might turn around. There was a slim possibility Desi might find a new normal.

Declan squeezed her hand as though he could read her thoughts. "You want to get back in the air, don't you?"

"You bet I do. But this time, I'll have a pupper at my side. And I'll modify the seat belts so Molly can sit beside me and watch for signs."

He caressed her face, "And if those nasty flashbacks rear their ugly heads, then Molls will lick your face off."

Desiree rubbed Molly's neck, "You're a good girl. Nothing is happening, so you can take five." Molly retrieved her chew toy and carried it out into the yard. Jeffrey joined her, and the two of them engaged in a tug of war contest.

Cobb answered her unasked question. "You're probably wondering how this one-horse town can afford a medevac helo, aren't you?"

Desiree raised an S-shaped brow, "Yes, I am."

"Well, it was donated by a wealthy townsman, and he insisted that injured people deserved to make it to Sacramento as quick as possible."

Desi twirled her long-spiraled ringlets, "At one-hundred-sixty-seven mph, flying at top speed, I could make it in less than an hour. And time is crucial when it comes to saving lives."

Hallie chimed in, "When you spouted all those aviation facts, you floored Deveau. He thought to himself, 'My god, the ginger red beauty has a brain.'" Everyone laughed at the comment, and Molly woofed in agreement.

Declan realized he made a tactical error. "It's good to see you so relaxed and having fun. Traveling into town was a good idea. And more than testing your disguise, it was a way to meet people and fit in."

Desiree said, "Even though I'm not fond of this fashion disguise, I finally got into it. The more that people accepted me, the easier it was."

"I licked my pink pearl lips, and gestured with my peach-colored nails, and folks were mesmerized by my flamboyant behavior."

Declan reminded her, "Remember how the forest fighters quizzed you about the Bambi Bucket?"

"I couldn't believe that guy. I've flown fire retardant drops from a Chinook CH-47."

"And a Chinook can extend a waterspout and flood a burning ridge. How much harder could it be to fly a Firehawk with a Bambi Bucket?"

Declan calmed her down, "Darlin', the forest fighter just wants to be sure you can handle a water sling. Believe me, if there's a forest fire near town, he'll give you a call."

Declan hauled her into his lap and gave her an affectionate tummy tickle.

"Babe, it's time for this ginger-red goddess to prepare for bed. Clean your pretty face and take a good long bath."

"I'll come in later to set up Molly's doggie bed. She'll sleep right next to you, and your pupper will be at eye level."

Desiree peered beneath her flared lashes, "Along with Kay Bear and my new teddy friends."

"You're limited to one Malinois and three stuffed bears."

Desi stuck out her tongue. "Aww, you're such a meanie! I want all my teddies with me."

Declan chucked her chin tenderly, "I'm thinking about what's best, and rest is key to a sound mind and good cattle work."

She had become so accustomed to Dayo's companionship; she didn't like the idea of him leaving. "Where are you going?"

He lifted his chest communicator, "I'll be in contact if you need me. But I'm going to perform a little recon and catch up on the latest intel."

Desiree lifted her communicator, "Declan, we're a team. And as soon as Wild Man fills you in, I want to know what's happening."

He nipped her delicious lower lip, "There's nothing to worry about, you take that cute fanny and treat yourself to some girl time." Desi kissed him sweetly and cherished his controlling ways.

The combat pilot called Molly, and her pupper raced to her side.

"Molls let's go look at your new doggie bed. We're going to be sleeping pals, and I want to make sure you're happy."

She turned to her koala friend, "Kay Bear, isn't this wonderful?"

"I'm going to have a night free from horrifying nightmares. But thanks to our new friend, I'm due for a restful sleep."

Declan retrieved his backpack and carried his sniper scope. He rounded the clapboard farmhouse, crossed the commons, and headed into the shadows. Dayo ducked into the metal-roofed horse stables.

He trotted down an immaculate aisle as his cowboy boots slapped against the brickwork. When he made it to the end, he vaulted to a wooden ladder, and raced hand over hand into the world of glistening hay bales.

From the uppermost stack, he peered from the shadows, making sure his lens didn't refract light. He scanned the rugged mountain peaks, looking for any signs of hostiles.

If he spotted a refractive lens, or airborne drones, then he would know they had company. Dayo surveyed the pink lupine and purple larkspur, and there was nothing out of the ordinary.

He used the scope to extend his range, and he scanned the laid-back streets of downtown. In particular, he looked for covert movement, but came up with nothing.

Declan clicked his communicator, "Hey Wild Man, I'm sorry I had to cut you off earlier. The emergency has been handled. Because of the news alert, Desiree has assumed her ginger red disguise."

"We tested it out on the townies, and they accepted our cattle detail. To Pine Whisper, we're nothing more than a wranglers, staying for the summer."

There was no visual webcam, but Declan could see Eugene in his mind. The hacker was probably wearing a pair of wild shades and an outlandish outfit.

His intel man said, "I'm glad to hear it. To locate a better cattle ranch would have taken a lot of work. And the best ranches are several states away. If you can't make this Oregon thing work, you're next destination is Montana."

Eugene switched gears, "Getting back to the current situation, here's the brief. Our Marine unit covered your tracks from L.A. all the way to Reno. The high Sierras have been swept clean, and there's not a living bounty hunter in the high country."

Declan mused about the body count, but at this moment, he really didn't care. His old unit was doing what they loved, and his woman was safe.

Eugene continued, "Now, they're leap-frogging up the California coast. A number of hostiles have been eliminated, and not a single message has been relayed."

"From Antonio's viewpoint, he's living in radio silence, and he doesn't know a damn thing."

Dayo preferred to keep the enemy in the dark. They had a decided advantage, and he wanted it to stay that way.

"Now, here's a curious discovery. Antonio doesn't know anything about the safe house fire, except what Chief Dwight and Director Pietro have told him."

"Wild Man, slow up for a second. Back to Dwight, what is the police chief telling

Gonzalez?"

"It appears that two bodies were taken from a morgue, both of them African American, and they were planted in the bombed-out safe house."

"The bodies were beyond recognition, and even the dentals were fragmented. It appears our bad boy has accepted the death of the key witness. So, the party line is that both Declan Cazador and Desiree DeNiro died in the fire."

Declan broke-down his rifle and reassembled it. The field maneuver gave him time to listen and helped him process the details.

He snapped the automatic together, "Do we know who precisely planted the bodies? Is it a collaborative effort between Dwight, Pietro, and the coroner?"

Wild Man wheeled over to a screen and studied an intercepted message. "It sounds like the Chief didn't leak the safe house location."

"He just wants to bury it all and cover up the situation. As for the Director, I intercepted Pietro's correspondence, and there was no intentional leak."

"Therefore, the crime boss hacked into the program, and replaced his people with the night shift. And his syndicate gangsters tried to kill our lovely key witness."

Dayo contemplated the safe house, and what a freakin' mess it was. The program had been compromised so easily and swiftly; it was a wonder that Desi was alive.

Eugene made a weird Bruce Lee sound, "Eeeooow!" The commander could tell how much Wild Man got into his job. His superheroes were short guys like the famed martial artist.

Wild Man continued, "And get this, the funeral for both parties is scheduled for tomorrow. Talk about moving fast."

Declan assembled his assault rifle, jammed the magazine in place, and peered through the scope. "It sounds like Dwight wants to bury this thing and get Gonzalez off his back."

Dayo considered the twin funeral events, and the fact the DeNiros would mourn her death. If Desi heard about this, the girl would try to make contact.

And that was precisely what Antonio was hoping for. If the key witness were alive, then she'd make herself known.

"Hey, Wild Man, don't mention this to Desi. She's very fragile right now. Months from now, we'll straighten things out."

Just referring to her fragile emotional state, put things in perspective. If he was to be an effective leader, working with her would require kid gloves.

Eugene continued, "By the way, the unit will arrive in a day or two. They've established drone surveillance at the DeNiro Ranch, so we've got Desi's family covered."

"That's great news. How about my folks?"

Wild Man laughed, "For some reason, your family is of no interest. It appears that not a single hostile has visited your homestead."

Declan figured it was a mixed report, and Antonio was still unconvinced. He agreed to a quick funeral to flush the girl out. And Dwight and Pietro covered up their deaths.

In some ways, Desi was free to start a new life, but they had to keep a low profile. Even though Declan wanted to review the trial, it was more intel than he wanted to gather.

Antonio was on the lookout and undercover disguises were absolutely necessary."

"Thanks, Wild Man, gotta go and tuck Desi in."

"Whooeee! Go for it, man!"

Declan slung his backpack over his shoulder and descended the ladder. Leaving the world of golden hay particles, he dropped to the cobble-bricked corridor.

Horses stirred in their stalls, and when he walked past Shepherd Cat, the champion wanted to say hello.

Dayo pet the sorrel's white nose, "I hear ya, big guy. All this military planning doesn't interest you a bit."

"But bring out a rogue steer, and you're all over it."

Sheppie's big brown eyes looked into his soul as though to say, "I'm gonna hold you to it. Tomorrow, I want to flush cattle, and show you my amazing footwork."

Declan patted his reddish-brown neck, "We'll go after it, I promise."

The Commander reflected on his beloved cowgirl. Desi needed to be loved, but with her precarious condition, the question was how to go about it? And right now, he didn't have a clue.

But getting physical too quick could frighten the poor thing. Wisdom dictated a longer period to settle in. Desi found a new normal, and he wanted her life to become routine.

The following day, Desiree slipped from Dayo's embrace. Her feet hit the floor, and the sleepy bombshell padded into the barnwood loo.

She missed his body heat. Her beloved commander spooned all night, and she loved the way he cradled her breasts and pressed his manhood against her.

She wasn't counting, but her horny Marine had five erections. His enthusiasm graced her round cheeks, and even slipped across her damp petals. It wasn't just men who have aroused cycles, her Chloe was rarin' to go, but she still felt way too shy.

Desiree considered how well the night went. She brushed her teeth and stretched her arms. The light bronze beauty felt incredible. What was so different?

It hit her like a lightning bolt. There were no nightmares, and she made it through the whole night. On one occasion, she was back in the Middle East, but the moment a wave of anxiety hit her, Molly must have caught the scent.

Her Malinois delivered a fierce face-licking deluge and sat on her chest until she awakened. There's nothing like a sixty-pound dog licking your lips and staring into your face. But it worked, and she got up in the middle of the night and went back to sleep.

Desi opened the studio door and pointed, "Voraus", which means

Go! She called out, "Molls, you be a good girl, and poo in the designated area."

"Later, today, we'll scoop it up." Her pupper relieved herself like a lady and kicked grass blades over her mess. "That a girl, you relax for a while, and then we'll get breakfast ready."

Desi and Dayo met in the tack room and saddled up the horses.

Cobb ambled down the corridor, "The first order of business is to flush out the cattle. The Herefords are scattered among the pinyon-juniper, and we've got to assemble them in the valley."

Declan stepped in the stirrup and wheeled himself into the saddle. "That sounds easy enough."

Pettigrew handed each of them a bull whip. "Do you know how to use this thing?"

"Sure do, I was raised on a small cattle ranch, and we moved cattle the same way."

Desiree held the braided handle, "Dayo, I know dogies are dumber than dirt, but I don't want you to flay their little heinies."

"Darlin', I would never damage the product." He raised the whip, "There will be nothing but supersonic air whips, and all those brown heinies will be spared."

He continued, "But I'll tell ya one thing, I never met a Hereford that liked the sound of an ear-piercing crack."

Cobb watched them trot out of the horse barn. He and David T. mounted a Polaris all-terrain vehicle. The old cattleman stacked a block of hay bales in the little flatbed.

Pettigrew whistled, "To me."

Molly looked from Cobb to Desiree. The bronze beauty walked Hunter to the Polaris, and issued the command, "Hopp." Molly understood the command, and leaped into the front seat, and climbed to the top.

Her Malinois pupper was at eye level, and if an ugly episode occurred, Molls would bathe her with doggie kisses.

Declan clarified the situation. "We'll be in the brush country, but if for any reason Desi starts to have a meltdown, I want Molly to be close by."

David T. fired up the all-terrain vehicle. "You got it boss!"

Cobb took the passenger seat, "We can flush the herd today, but it wouldn't hurt if we had more manpower."

"My unit should be here any day now. You'll have two Oklahoma cowboys, a Kansas steer wrestler, and one dude rancher."

She didn't like the sound of this. Desiree enjoyed having Declan to herself, and she was just getting settled in. For the first time, she had a seizure alert dog, and things were going well.

Dayo saw her purse her lips, "Babe, even though I plan to meet the guys, you're still number one. So, don't think for one minute that I'll abandon you."

"You better not! We've been through hell and back, and I've been right by your side. I've earned my stripes. So, we're an unbeatable team, and I don't want you to forget that."

"Yes, ma'am, I agree with you one hundred percent."

Declan and Desi trotted past the grazing horses and deep into the back forty. The lush valley gave way to a sandy alluvial arroyo, flanked by desert hillsides.

Cobb gave his horses the best grazing areas, but he pastured his cattle among pinyon-juniper hillsides. The Cascades featured southern exposures, and instead of leafy trees and flowering meadows, there were arid landscapes.

David T. stopped at the base of a dry southern slope. There were rolling fields with sagebrush, yucca blooms, and juniper trees.

The moment Declan and Desiree headed into the hills, about fifty Herefords lifted their heads. It was a mix of yearlings and old cattle.

Dayo realized the process of flushing cattle was about to begin. And even though they agreed to working the ranch, his real mission was his bronze beauty.

He rapidly assessed everything. They lived in a fairy tale cottage, and an affectionate therapy dog slept near their bed. They spooned every night, and not a moment passed that he wasn't with her. He was far more than her protector, the fearless warrior was falling hard and falling fast.

Desiree was a combat girl, who was motivated by kindness, encouragement, and love. He had to get it through his thick skull, issuing commands wasn't working.

And in a way, this was so much harder than commanding a unit. It required him to reach deep into his soul, and summon compassion, and touch areas that had never been awakened.

He wasn't going to change the bronze beauty. It was he, who had to do the changing. It hit him like a ton of bricks, but there it was.

The truth stared him in the face. Was he willing to open his heart and seize the moment? It was a clarion call to action, and before they hit the PJ scrub, he better make his feelings known.

More than anything, Desi had become his everything. She was his top priority, his combat partner, and the love of his life. As for the cattle drive and Cobb's exercises, those things didn't qualify for a close second.

Good lord, this mission had become so exceedingly personal. Any attempt to distance himself had failed.

And the truth was he didn't want to remain detached. Declan wanted to fall in love, and enjoy the intimacy of closeness, and share his heart.

It was a huge change, but their arrival at the Pettigrews brought out feelings which had been long buried.

Dayo lifted the reins and rode Sheppie over to Desiree's horse. She sipped from her camel pack and wondered what was going on.

Declan leaned over and palmed her cheek. "Sweetheart, I want you to know that you're more important than any cattle drive."

"We're in this together, and you've become the most important thing in my life."

"And I'm making a few adjustments, so I ask you to be understanding. I'm accustomed to giving orders, and having my men carry them out."

"But you aren't like them. You are motivated by encouraging words, bottom pats, and tender kisses."

Desiree lit up like a thousand candles. She beamed a radiant smile and leaned into his palm.

"Dayo, I really appreciate the way you're handling this. This can't be easy for you, but having an overly sensitive cowgirl must be a huge challenge."

"I'll admit, I've had to switch gears. But from now on, you're my top priority."

The commander lowered his brows, "Babe, don't ever allow me to forget how important you are. You got that, sweetcheeks?"

The bronze bombshell glowed from within. She threw her arms around him, and dove into a horseback kiss. They kissed like two lovers who had reached a profound understanding.

He descended over her generous lips and kissed the holy hell outta her. Desiree responded in kind and plunged her tongue into a deep French kiss.

God love this woman! She was built like a brick house, and she kissed like a dream.

After an eternity had passed, they separated. Desiree lifted her koala cuff, "Kay Bear wondered when you were going to figure it out. And he's overjoyed. K-Man thinks you're a keeper."

Just them, Hallie May bounded over the terrain in a four-wheel drive pick-up.

The matriarch exclaimed, "I'm glad to see you two figured it out. But my husband was wondering if you're ever going to flush cattle?"

Cobb stood in the ATV, "Not to foreshorten your romance, but the hills are calling, and my cattle are scattered everywhere."

Desi giggled, "I think we better get to work."

"With you at my side, it will be a day of pleasure." He patted her well rounded ass, and it was going to be an unforgettable day.

Chapter Nine

Desiree felt a few reservations about flushing cattle, but her fears had been allayed. With the fearless commander at her side, she could do freakin' anything. And the thick-headed Marine finally got his priorities straight. She was happier than a loon.

The bronze beauty rode Hunter into the brush and ascended high the hillside. When she had the high ground, she drew forth her bull whip, and let it fly. The tip snapped faster than the speed of sound, and it cracked the sound barrier.

It let out a fierce snap, and the Herefords lifted their heads immediately. They let out a bawling cry, and a mass of brown bodies ran down the golden hillside. A few mommas ushered their calves to safety. But it was amazing how many steers were hidden.

Directly to the right, Dayo performed the same air splitting ritual. They were a team, and they were in this together. It was a gorgeous day to flush cattle and experience the Great American West.

The Hereford mass flowed downhill and gathered in the valley. She eyed a distant branding pen, and figured they were headed that direction.

Cobb stood up in the Polaris. "You guys made that look simple, so I've got a surprise for you."

Desi didn't like surprises, and after Cobb's roping session, she wasn't sure if she'd like his newest game.

Dayo threaded the rabbitbrush and rode to her side, "Babe, we got this. I don't want you to worry and no matter what he throws at us, we can handle it."

Instantly, her worries subsided, and there was no reason to call Molly.

The Old Man explained what he wanted. "Declan, you've seen reined cow horse events on TV. What I want you to do is to cut out a fast steer, box him in, and work the fence."

Desiree thought it was the height of stupidity. They weren't in a horse arena, it was an open range, and for some ridiculous reason, there was an L-shaped horizontal fence. There was no reason for its existence.

Now, that she heard Pettigrew's request, she was glad Hunter Cat wasn't the target. She'd pull Cobb's Stetson down over his ears and tell him off. She was in no mood for bullshit. After Dayo opened his heart, she was riding on cloud nine, and she wasn't about to leave.

Declan sized up the situation. The white fence ran through a sandy, dry riverbed, which provided the perfect footing for fast cuts and quick changes.

Shepherd Cat wouldn't get hurt. But she noticed the sorrel stud wore shin splints and bell boots, and the threat of a hoof injury was non-existent. Naturally, a stallion was better suited to a high-octane cattle maneuver, and Sheppie's endurance was about to be tested.

Her commander eyed the challenge. "Cobb, you're crazy as hell, but I'll take the challenge, and I'll show you what I've got."

Dayo cut a speedster out of the herd and moved the steer along the bottom fence. Shepherd Cat worked the cow one way, and then cut him off.

The Hereford shot the opposite direction, trying to evade the cutting horse. To no avail, Sheppie took control. The champion didn't get too close; the big cat stayed off the fence by ten yards. And gave the steer ample room to run.

The purpose of boxing the steer was to feel out the opponent.

Both her commander and Sheppie sized up the enemy, and knew how fast the steer could run, and how smart it was.

Desiree watched Shepherd transform. The cow horse came to life and loved working a stray. Declan came behind the steer from the left and allowed an avenue of escape.

The white face spotted an exit and blasted along the white fence. Dayo kicked his heels and held the reins forward.

It didn't take much lead, and Shepherd lunged forward with two ground eating strides, and accelerated like the little rogue was standing still.

The Big Cat shot past his prey, went shoulder-to-shoulder and forced a sudden stop. The poor little steer was outmanned and outmaneuvered.

The dogie had a clear exit, and the Hereford shot the other way. Dayo worked the fence, performed a quick rollout, and the game was on.

Desiree chewed her lip, and wondered how long this idiotic game would go? But Declan amazed her, he pulled from behind, exploded two strides, and Sheppie blew past the steer for a second time.

Then, the cattle horse cut him off. The steer was bewildered and looking for a way out. Adrenaline seized his little bovine butt, and he didn't know which way to go.

Cobb called out, "Dayo, you're doing great. Now take the steer into a full circle and exert full control." Despite the compliments, Desi still didn't like this little game.

She yelled out, "Of course, Declan is the man. The insane Marine can do anything."

Cobb turned to her, and he gave a leather-handed salute. "Thanks Desiree, your man is doing great, but I'd like to see one more maneuver. Is that all right with you?"

"No, it's not. Just make it quick, and we can herd the cattle." The old buzzard curled his full lips, and she failed to see the humor.

Declan flew to the steer's right flank and forced the Hereford into the loamy basin. Shepherd Cat went shoulder-to-shoulder and performed a big circle.

The steer started to tucker out, so Dayo cut behind its flanks, and turned the Hereford the other direction. Now, Shepherd took full control and guided the cow in a second circle.

The Big Cat was in complete control, and finally, the Hereford simply ran out of gas. Declan guided the steer back to the herd, and the little runaway couldn't have been happier.

She overheard Cobb speaking to David T. "Dayo shows promise, it's rodeo style, but he's assertive, and our cattleman takes control."

David stroked his weather-beaten jaw, "Not much for finesse, if that's what you're looking for?"

Cobb answered, "Declan is a high-powered cattleman, and I wanted to see if he could maintain control. And there wasn't a second that steer could have gotten away. I'm pleased with his horsemanship, and the finesse will come later."

Desiree eavesdropped, and realized what this was all about. That crafty old fart was grooming her man to become an RCH competitor.

First, the Old Man tested out his boxing abilities, and his fence work, and lastly his cow control. In her humble opinion, her fearless stud passed with flying colors.

Cobb stepped out of the Polaris and addressed Desi. She sat transfixed to the saddle and awaited his over-the-top request. She squeezed the leather reins and waited.

David T. knew the girl by now and backed up the vehicle. Molly was at eye level, staring into her face. The bronze beauty extended a hand and pet her sweet Malinois.

"Molls, the old buzzard is trying to get my goat, but we won't let him, will we?"

Pettigrew watched the interaction, but he was dead set on pressing forward.

"If you hadn't guessed by now, Declan's RCH drill followed the exact pattern for Western riding events. But it just so happens, you're riding Hunter Cat, and he's a champion cutting horse."

Desi opened her eyes wide and assumed a look of pure defiance. "Mr. Pettigrew, I can cut a steer outta that herd. That's no problem."

Dayo trotted to her side and fist bumped her, "Damn right, girl. You're a force of nature, and you can do damn near anything."

She appreciated the moral support. With Kay Bear, Molls, and her stud Marine, she had her full unit in gear.

Cobb pointed to a cluster of Herefords, "What I'd like you to do is to cull out a rebellious steer, and herd him about thirty yards from the gathering."

"The thirty-yard position will simulate the far zone of a cutting contest. Since Hunter has a lot of working room, his goal is to keep the steer from joining his buddies. And the more times, you cut him off, the more anxious he'll be."

"Old Man, tell me something I don't know."

Pettigrew curled his thick lips and smiled. She wanted to knock him for a loop.

Declan stood beside her, and lifted Molly to his saddle. Her pupper placed her paws on the saddle horn and licked her face. The combat girl tried to stay in the moment.

"Why don't we just herd all of these dang beasties over to the branding paddock? That's where they want to go."

Pettigrew removed his black Stetson, "Honey, something tells me you're a natural cutter. And teamed up with Hunter Cat, you guys will be sensational."

Desiree eyed him like he'd eaten a bushel of locoweed. She was about to object, and then the whole world started to close in.

Her periphery was clouded by darkness, and she could feel her hands shaking. Her support team leaped into action.

Declan placed a palm to her heart and infused her with peace. Molly recognized the escalating tension, the dilated pupils, and the fearful scent.

The Malinois tiptoed into her saddle, plowed into her face, and laved her with doggie kisses. Finally, Desi relented.

"All right, you guys, I'll do the damn cutting drill. But so help me, if I hear any criticism, I won't speak to any of you again." The sassy, bronze beauty snapped her head like it was final.

She stared right into Cobb's aging eyes, "Old Man, don't be surprised if I give you a flying salute, when this is all over. And what's more, there's a barrel cactus on that sunny hill, and I suggest you sit on it and rotate."

David T. clapped his thigh. "Man alive, she's a feisty one. Boss, I think she just told you off."

Pettigrew smoothed his peppered beard. "Yes, she did, and I heard every word."

Desiree led Hunter Cat, her dangerous bay stud, into a cluster of Herefords. The brown sea parted, and she culled out an agile, nimble-footed speedster.

Since competition Charolais ran around six-hundred-pounds, they wanted a fast animal, not one who was too mature and heavy-bodied.

Hunter Cat skirted behind the steer and directed the dogie thirty yards away. Her Fast Cat stopped, and the duel was on.

It was the O.K. Corral, high noon, and Desi lowered her center of gravity. It was moments like this, that having a big round ass came in handy.

The steer trotted to the right like Hunter wouldn't notice. The cow horse floated smoothly, shoulder lowered, and weight distributed.

Her Big Boy could change direction on a dime, and he waited for the next move. The steer changed direction and skipped toward the left.

Hunter intercepted the bad boy in a large leftward sweep. The bay stud wouldn't let it happen. And the cow sprinted toward an end around, but Hunter wasn't having any of it.

In a lightning move, the Cat cut him off. Her cow horse juked to the left, and his legs sailed into a diagonal cut. If she wasn't seated upright, and watching it happen, she wouldn't have believed his athleticism.

Thanks to the alluvial sand, dirt sprayed to the left. The little dogie's eyes went wide, and he blasted to the right. Hunter dodged from right to left, and his eyes were fixed on his prey.

Their duel went on for five minutes, and Hunter went into high gear. It was an amazing feat, and Desiree loved the back-and-forth movement.

Her soul was joined with the champion, and the cutting action was a thing of beauty. Finally, the steer gave up, and simply stood there.

Snot drizzled from his little nose, and the fella was done. Desi felt compassion for him, and she wheeled Hunter to the side, so the little speedster could join the herd.

Cobb clapped his hands, "That was magnificent."

"Desiree, you're a natural cutting girl. You passed my test with flying colors. Now, you two can herd the gathering into the branding paddock."

They drove the cattle through the sandy wash into a golden grassy paddock. Declan rode ahead, opened the pipe rail gate, and Desiree took the back flank.

Hunter Cat worked the sides in a back-and-forth weave, and the Herefords didn't want any part of him. They bunched together, slamming heads into rear ends, and pushed their way into the corral.

The grazing was better, and quickly the white face found tall tufts and ate to their hearts contentment. The All-terrain vehicle came to a stop.

Next to the holding paddock was the branding pen.

Cobb turned to David T. "As soon as the unit arrives, you'll fire up the branding irons, and we'll bring the 'calvies' into the pen."

"I know the drill, boss. There'll be a branding party, and Dayo and Desi will rope steer, isolate their hooves, and I'll brand their little butts."

"That's right, and for old times' sake, Hallie May will bring the chuckwagon, and we will have a big ol' barbecue."

Just then, Hallie stepped out of her pick-up and dusted her hands. "That's right, David T. I've got a feast planned. I've selected the best cuts, and I'm soaking the beans, and getting the cornmeal ready. You're going to enjoy ribs, brisket, and burnt ends like you've never imagined."

David T. heard his stomach growl, "Just hearing you talk about a chuckwagon dinner has my belly riled up. So, when are the military cowboys going to arrive?"

Dayo stood next to Desiree, "Any day now, my old unit will arrive.

And David, their presence should make your chores easier, and the major projects will be a breeze."

Cobb clapped his leathery hands. "You've done remarkably well. But I've got one more drill. The purpose is to find the sweet spot."

"Like expert marksmanship, you can feel the right moment. And using a light rein and showing off your Big Cat is the same thing. You're fully in control, and your hands barely move. It's sort of like pulling a trigger."

Desiree giggled, "Old Man, you don't want to see what I can do with a rifle."

"Actually, I do want to see what you can do."

He waved his hands toward the shaley bluffs, and she saw David T., setting up three archery targets. They were spaced thirty feet apart.

"Oh boy, we've played cowboy long enough, and now I get to be a Native brave with a long bow."

Cobb handed her a Henry repeater. It was a Civil War carbine, which enabled firing bullets in rapid succession. Up to that time, it was shell ejection, and slow-paced action.

She handled the firearm and peered down the iron sights. It was antiquated, but the woodwork was impressive. "So, tell me, what museum did you steal this from?"

Cobb cocked his head philosophically. He had seen it all, and he found her sassy patter rather amusing.

"I didn't confiscate this historical piece, it's a replica. And for our purposes, it will take more concentration than a modern rifle."

Desi giggled, "And if we don't hit the freakin' target, we can always throw the dang thing."

Cobb chuckled, "Dayo, is she always like this?"

"Ever since I've known her, she's been a firebrand."

She touched her open cleavage, "Who me?"

Dayo grinned like the devil, "Yes, darlin', you."

Declan continued, "I think I see what he wants. Cobb wants us to nail a perfect bullseye in the center of that yellow circle. And using the repeater, he wants us to form a cluster."

Cobb jumped in, "That's part of the goal. But I want you to ride full speed, running parallel to the targets, and hit a bullseye three times in a row."

Declan used the iron ladder sights, and he had his doubts. "This Henry repeater isn't calibrated that well, and from an all-out run, hitting the center will take focus, excellent marksmanship, and a ton of luck."

Cobb added, "If you've never tried this before, I suggest you start way back there. Give Shepherd enough time to hit an all-out run, and when he flattens out. It will be a smooth ride, and you can aim better."

Desiree was glad that Dayo went first. He was an expert marksman, but that was with modern artillery. And he was highly proficient with a Trijicon scope, not a ladder sight.

But he trotted to the starting line, and performed a smooth rollout, and Shepherd accelerated. Sheppie's head extended, and his tail feathers flattened, and Declan was flying over the open terrain.

In an all-out running position, it was smooth sailing. The commander sighted, and he hit the first target. He used one hand to hold the grip, and he clenched his thighs.

He waited until there was the divine moment of reckoning. He exhaled, and in rapid succession, he fired one bullseye after another. It was so beautiful and effortless; it was Zen marksmanship at its finest.

Desiree lifted her hands and yelled, "Way to go, Dayo! You're one badass cowboy. Good shooting, you stud Marine. Now, it's my turn!"

Desi felt determined, but she wanted Kay Bear to know how silly this was. She lifted her wrist cuff, and her koala greeted her with his button brown eyes.

She kissed his pink lips, "The Old Coot is out of his ever-lovin' mind, but I'll humor him, and do this dumb-ass drill."

Desiree trotted Hunter to the starting line and took off like a bat outta hell. The Big Cat accelerated through the gaits and hit a flat out run. Cruising at fifty-five miles an hour, she leveled the Henry Repeater, took aim, and sighted at the first target.

She waited for the divine moment, and then it happened. She felt at one with Hunter and one with the bullseye, and she exhaled softly, and pulled the trigger.

It felt so good, and so right, it was amazing. Desi raced toward two more targets and nailed them all. They were barely off center.

It wasn't nearly as precise as Dayo, but she was a damn good shot. And any Civil War soldier would have met his end.

Cobb was delighted, "See, that wasn't so bad, was it?"

"All right, Old Timer, I'll admit it was a good exercise. I see your point, and in the future, I'll try to feel Hunter's soul. I'll sense the divine moment and use the reins like a sensitive trigger."

"Bravo, you understand what I'm trying to do, don't you?"

Desi curled her lips into a wicked smile. "Oh, yeah, I know what you want, but there's still the question. Do I want to cooperate?"

Cobb furrowed his brows and grinned. "Maybe, you don't want to, but at least, you have options."

He leaped into the Polaris, "Why don't we head back to the horse barn and cool down the horses?"

When they returned, she spotted a fully armed hawk land beside the homestead. The Sikorsky UH-60 sported a dark grey hull, Hellfire missiles, and a cargo bay filled with fierce Marines.

In addition to the combat helo, there was a tricked-out Airstream. The sparkling aluminum RV was festooned with satellites, generators, and white box units. Instantly, she knew that Wild Man had arrived. And he brought his whole command center.

Declan turned to Pettigrew, "Cobb, my old unit has arrived. They're looking forward to the branding party, but I better get acquainted before they meet you and Hallie."

Cobb led his champions to the grooming area. The master horseman turned the faucet and selected the temperature.

Cobb called out, "David T. and I will dress down the horses. You just make sure the little lady is ready to meet your men. She looks a might skittish."

Dayo glanced at Desiree, and she looked as though her world had fallen. She appeared crestfallen, and he realized something else.

She wasn't good at sharing. And once, she found her support group,

Desi didn't want any newcomers. His combat girl had Molly and Kay Bear, and at the center of everything, he was the glue that held things together.

Declan was suddenly stuck between a rock and a hard place. And he wasn't sure how to pull this thing off! But he had to make a command decision, but he wasn't sure which way to go.

Chapter Ten

Desiree wheeled from the saddle and dropped to the ground. She wasn't interested in meeting the famed headhunters. They would never understand Kay Bear.

Nor would they comprehend what an amazing therapy dog Molly was. Despite her sassy banter with Old Man Cobb, she was starting to love this place.

She knew the lay of the land, the horse pastures, and the cattle country. And now a new dynamic threatened to take Dayo away. Until that very moment, she didn't realize how much he meant to her.

Since they were fugitives, the fearless warrior was always at her side. Desiree feared that was all about to change.

She loosened the breast collar and the cinch attachments and carried the saddle into the tack room. The bronze beauty did her best to avoid Declan.

She settled the saddle on a tree and turned to Kay Bear. "Why did those stupid Marines have to arrive? They don't know anything about driving cattle and practicing for rodeo events."

"Don't you think Dayo, and I have a good thing going?"

Kay Bear eyed her with a bright-eyed smile, and his pink lips smiled reassuringly. She kissed his furry little cheek, "You think I should fight for my man, and lay down some rules, don't you?"

Desiree felt winded and all out of ideas. How was she going to fight for him? It sounded so co-dependent and needy, she wanted to hurl.

But there it was, it was the truth. Desi marched back to Hunter and snagged a yellow hose. She turned the faucets to cold, and drenched his hooves, fetlocks, and cannon bones.

She patted Hunter, "Those shin splints were mighty hot. I bet the cold water feels good, and what's more, it prevents injury."

"But now for the good part, I'll turn the water to a tepid temp, and I'll hose you down."

Desi made kissing sounds and amused the Big Cat while she doused his withers and flanks with lukewarm water. Her bay stud loved a good water bath, and he peered into her eyes, and gave her the reassurance she needed.

Why couldn't Dayo see how important their relationship was? She was his woman, and moments ago, she put in an amazing performance.

Earlier, he professed his adoration and loyalty. *So, what the hell was he doing?*

Not to mention the fact, she fired an antiquated firearm while riding full tilt. And Desi nailed the yellow bullseye three times.

Admittedly, the combat pilot wasn't a dead shot, but she found her groove, and her spiritual poise. Next time, she could make three dead ringers.

The fearless Marine came to her side. "For the unit to land the helo next to Cobb's homestead was a bold move. But then again, the cat is out of the bag, and Cobb knows we're a special ops team."

"What do you think? For a civilian to witness a fully armed black hawk, it must be pretty intimidating."

Desi turned the water hose and sprayed him up and down. Within seconds, Declan's shades were drenched, and his lavender shirt was soaked. And she even doused his package.

She curled her lips with satisfaction. "I don't see what the big deal is. I see black hawks all the time."

It was obvious, Desiree was pissed. His heart leaped at the opportunity of seeing his men, but he had to reassess his priorities. He reached for a towel and dried off his face.

While polishing his sunglasses, he glanced at the bronze beauty. He saw her disposition change, and it wasn't playful.

Declan removed his Stetson and hand-combed his dense black hair. He realized he was at a very important crossroad, and it was imperative that he did the right thing. While his clothes dried off, he had a few moments to think.

Looking back at their whirlwind affair, he saved her life because she was one of them. And since he started with noble intentions, it was best to finish that way.

The Commander removed her water hose and pressed her against a cedar plank wall. He pinned her with two arms held in a spread position.

Desiree couldn't get away, and the bronze bombshell had to look him in the eye. He lowered his head and curled his lips into a charming half-smile.

"Desi, you're one of us. You're a Marine warrior chick, and our newest celebrity. The men want to meet the badass queen who took down a den of hostiles."

"And darlin', you were awesome back there, when you gunned down the insurgents."

He trapped her with his arms and peered into her enormous brown eyes. "You, Kay Bear, and Molly are officially headhunters."

"And what's more, you're my lovin' woman, and the men are dying to meet you."

Desiree curled her lips into a shy smile. "You say, I'm your lovin' woman, but we only did it one time, and we were both half asleep."

He was shocked, "I thought that was a wet dream?"

"Oh, no, it was real. We spooned so closely, the Big Guy slid into my flower, and I started doing the doggie backstroke."

"Oh, man, why didn't you wake me up?"

"Is that so important, Dayo? I just wanted you to know, so that when you introduce me, you can say that we have a thing going." She peered through her starburst eyelashes and smiled at him.

This little tidbit changed everything. He glanced through the stable doors and eyed his old unit. As much as he wanted to see them, Desiree came first.

He cupped her face, "Babe, you're the most important thing in my life. And if we're having wet dreams together, then I say, it's time to do it right."

"Why don't you run inside, and I'll pick some flowers, and we can create a love nest."

She stared at him in disbelief. "Are you sure?"

"Oh, hell yes. I don't have to be a genius to read the signs. We're way overdue, and somewhere along the line, I started to fall for this amazing woman."

Desiree giggled, "You're talking about me, aren't you?"

"Yes, I am. So, I'll pick the flowers, and you can find a vase, and we'll spend a romantic evening all alone."

She leaped into his arms and peppered him with sloppy kisses. "Declan, sometimes you're as dense as a brick, but right now, you're singing my favorite song."

He whirled her in a circle. "Desi-girl, why don't you skip the horse grooming, and I'll meet you back at our romantic log home."

"You, got it, stud. Bring you're A-game, and I'll be rarin' to go."

Declan made arrangements with Cobb and Hallie. He hated to dodge his unit, but they fought together for six years, and surely, they would understand.

Cobb volunteered to take them to the bunkhouse and get them settled in. The Old Man knew how to run a ranch, so he wasn't at a loss for giving orders.

As for Hallie May, she was overjoyed. There were so many mouths to feed, she could pull out her old cookbook and go to town.

Dayo trotted over to Hallie's vegetable garden and spotted a flower knoll. He picked an armful of gorgeous flowers and headed back to the lodge.

Somewhere along the way, the honey-stained cottage had become a home. He trotted up the log treads, padded across the porch, and threw open the front door.

"Honey, I'm home. And you're not going to believe how beautiful these flowers are."

"But sweetheart, there's not a single blossom that compares to you."

Desiree rushed out of the master suite, "Dayo, I'm so nervous. I've been walking in circles, talking to Kay Bear, and I really don't know what to do."

Declan set the flowers into a vase and held her hands. He gazed deeply into her enormous brown pools, "Honey, I know this is our first time, but believe me, you'll be sensational."

She pointed a delicate finger toward her V. "There's something you don't know about me."

He lowered his brows and tried to be understanding. "I was hoping for two X chromosomes. You are all woman aren't you?"

"Oh, definitely. But I have a whole lotta stuff in my panties."

He was unsure of what her fear was. He wasn't a cavalier Don Juan, but he knew a few things about women, and Desiree couldn't be that far out of the ordinary.

Declan searched her eyes, "Honey, whatever, you've got in your panties, we can make it work. Let's prepare our love nest, and a little activity will set your mind at ease."

He led her by the hand as they entered the master suite. He pointed the control and ignited the fireplace. Flames lapped around the ceramic logs and bathed the room in an amber glow.

"How about that? The room is getting more romantic by the minute."

She removed her cowgirl boots, and in her bare feet, she padded over to the nightstands. She set the lampshades to a low dim.

"You're right, our boudoir is getting more romantic. But there are a few things missing."

The bronze beauty drew a deep breath, and she pillowed beautifully. He paused to admire her voluptuous hourglass, and now, he wanted her more than ever.

Declan opened a vanity and drew forth an armload of candles. He arranged them around the yoga chaise lounge. After he dimmed the lights and lit the bowl candles, the room took on an enchanted glow.

He glanced at his unsure beauty, "And now, for the moment you've been waiting for. We can be a couple of exhibitionists. We'll make love in front of a teddy bear audience."

She giggled, "I don't know if this is going to work, but at least, all my friends will be here."

Desiree moved an armload of teddies into a recliner, and they had a front row seat. Naturally, Kay Bear would be attached to her wrist, and if anything became awkward, he could talk her down.

She paused, "Kay Bear thinks we should make a beautiful love nest. But he thinks you should take a good look at my squiggly flower before we get jiggy."

"I'm quite fond of squiggly flowers, and however the good lord made you, that's fine with me."

"Dayo, you're a good man, and that was a very nice thing to say."

Desiree placed Molly's doggie bed next to the chaise lounge. The chair was shaped in an S-curve with a high backrest, a low saddle, and a curved footstool.

The love chair offered a thousand Kama Sutra positions. And the beauty of the design was that it relieved back pressure and body weight. So, Declan wouldn't crush her with his muscular mass. And if she rode cowgirl, her weight would be evenly distributed.

But there was still one problem, her petals dropped well below her majora, and some guys hated the way she looked. And there was also the problem of a flower petal getting in the way.

She squeezed her delicate hands, "The room looks perfect."

"It sure does, and it's even color coordinated. We can start in the king bed with its saffron comforter, and then move to the love chair."

"The love chair is upholstered in buttery soft leather, and I can't wait to feel your sweet ass nestled in the saddle."

"Oh, is that your favorite position?"

"Actually, I'm quite versatile. I ran the one-hundred-meter in nine flat, so I'm built of rock-hard muscle, and I have tons of endurance."

He reassured her, "But we can take turns, switching between cowboy and cowgirl. It will be a lot of fun, and the main thing is for you to be comfortable and to enjoy yourself."

If nothing else, Dayo was understanding.

They were headed for the shower, and she braced herself for the worst. Her body wasn't the least bit relaxed. In fact, her squiggly flower was bunched in a big clump, and her heart was beating a mile a minute.

Declan stepped through the saloon doors and turned on the spray heads. Within seconds, the shower enclosure was filled with steam. The wall jets were going, and even the rain head created a glorious waterfall.

She removed her socks and her Wranglers and came to a dead stop. Declan slid behind her. He kissed her bronze shoulders and unlatched her bustier. Her generous breasts spilled into his hands, and the girls were free.

"Darlin', I've waited for this moment, and I must tell you, you are one beautiful woman. Your breasts are a work of art, so perfect, so full and round. I could spend hours devouring your delicious fruit."

Desiree blushed, "My boobs are covered in sweat, and there's even a sand particles. I think you should hold off until I enter the shower."

Dayo watched her hesitate, so he removed his button-down, toed off his cowboy boots, and dropped his drawers. She beheld a bronze Adonis.

He looked like a Greek god, and his endowments were huge. She tried not to stare, but his length and girth were enormous, and he was only partly aroused.

He was built, and the Marine knew it. But she didn't detect an air of conceit. His concern was fully on her. Declan could tell she was reluctant to remove her thong. So, he led her into the shower stall.

"Honey, it's time to shed your panties, and I promise you, I'll love the way you look."

She removed Kay Bear from her wrist and said a quick prayer. Desire removed her thong slowly and watched his eyes carefully. Molly stood on the terry cloth rug and watched their interplay.

Declan saw her convoluted petals, which were bunched together like a Celosia flower. Her squiggly petals were folded together and formed a fleshy cluster.

And no doubt, he saw her Chloe perched on top. Her lady jewel was top and dead center, and impossible to miss.

She was a whole lotta woman, but Declan didn't blink an eye.

He curled his lips into a rakish smile, "Your fig leaf is a work of art. I look forward to unraveling your petals and treating you to a flower devouring special."

Good lord, this guy was persistent! Nothing stood in the way of a determined Marine. Where there was a will, there was a way. And by god, Captain Cazador was going to find a way.

Declan placed her in front of the wall jets and rinsed her off. He lathered her from behind, and kissed her shoulders and massaged her lovely pillows. He washed her navel and used his talented fingers to part her copious folds.

Her bronze lover unhooked a telescopic showerhead and sprayed her flower with one hand and massaged her with the other. Her copious folds relaxed, and her petals fell way past her majora.

To her amazement, he feathered her plump folds until they expanded into pretty wings, and he spread her wings, and glued each flying petal to her thigh.

Could this really be happening? She refused to watch, but when her fuchsia flower was fully open, and her petals remained glued, Desi had a ray of hope. Her petals wouldn't interfere with penetration, and she could really do this.

She opened her eyes and watched Dayo place a roller bottle in the caddy.

He laughed, "Hallie thinks of everything!"

"Sweetheart, if that was what you were worried about, we've found a solution. The body stick 'em is working in the shower, so I don't see any reason it won't work in the boudoir."

"I'll carry the roller bottle, and if we need to reapply, it's slick and easy." *The man was an absolute genius.*

He lathered a dollop over Chloe, and her lady jewel went crazy. Declan delivered a circular massage to her tiny bud, and her jewel was bursting with happiness.

Dayo held her from behind and massaged her into a mind-numbing circular assault. Her whole body rocked with pleasure, and the pressure started to build higher and higher.

She gasped for air and seized the grab bar. She was beyond the point of no return, and she pointed her toes, and clenched her sheath, and exploded into a long, fulfilling O face.

Her orgasm came in waves, and the aftershocks rolled all the way to her toes. To her horror, one of her wing petals lost its grip and fell downward.

Desiree moaned, "Oh no, it's not working. I don't look pretty anymore."

Declan seized the roller ball and applied more stick 'em. He glued her wing petal to her thigh, and she was as beautiful as ever.

"Honey, it's as good as new. There's nothing to worry about. And for safe measure, we'll take the roller bottle into our love nest."

Desiree watched her aroused warrior step out of the shower. His enthusiasm was engorged, and his proportions were massive. His length and girth were sizeable, and she wondered if this was really going to work.

They entered their love chamber. The fire was burning, and Declan led her to the chaise lounge. He angled above her delicious pout and descended into a ravenous kiss.

Good lord, the man wanted her like a house of fire. But he slowed down and savored the moment and made her feel loved.

Gradually, she parted her lips, and his tongue tangled with hers, and it was a delightful ballet. His arousal bobbed with enthusiasm, and she could tell, her French kissing was inspiring.

As the flames bathed the room in an amber glow, Declan looked into her deep brown eyes, "Babe, You've got me revved up like a raging storm."

Without preamble, Dayo swept her off her feet and whipped her around his waist.

Desiree squealed, "Whooeee! The way you sling me around, I forget how strong you are."

"Darlin', I want you to experience the freight train of love."

"Oh goodness, that sounds exciting."

While holding her in the air, Dayo angled his manhood against her open flower, and thrust from the balls of his feet and buried himself halfway. Her folds parted, and she squeezed him with a tight grip.

"Good lord, Desi, you're so tight, and athletic, and willing. You're one in a million."

Declan lifted her sweet derrière and pressed her against a padded column. With a second thrust, he buried himself to the hilt. His power and athleticism were overwhelming.

And when he said he was a powerful sprinter, she believed him. The problem was: where did that leave her? The bronze Adonis would tup her into blissful oblivion, but what was her contribution?

It was now or never. "Dayo, I know you'll be fantastic, but what will I do?"

"Babe, all you need to do is hang on, and enjoy the ride. I can feel Chloe against my shaft, and I'll tup you until you blow apart. Just clench your sheath, grip me hard, and the sex will be amazing!"

Desi panted and her breasts heaved against his chest. "Dayo, I hate to be party-pooper, but I'm more of a giver than a receiver."

"Is there anyway, I can be on top? It will give me confidence, and you can coach me. And I'll do it exactly the way you want."

He cupped her face and nipped her lip tenderly, "Honey, can we just try it my way, first?"

"I'll work off some energy, and you may find, a good air-tupping is a thing of beauty."

He rocked from the balls of his feet and ground her flower in a pleasurable circle. The bronze warrior burst into a high-speed sprint, and she could feel the column shake with his power.

Declan squeezed her shapely ass and found another gear. Desi wrapped her legs and clenched her sheath. And sure enough, Chloe was taking a pounding. Her lady jewel loved the action, and it wouldn't be long.

Declan found a sweet rhythm, and she experienced his all-out sprint. They hit the back curve, and Dayo accelerated, and he was like a piston-pounding, sensual lover.

His bronze physique was streaked with sweat, and he looked absolutely gorgeous. As she admired his Adonis build, the pleasure took a quantum leap.

The passion overwhelmed her, and her pleasure circuits were on overload, and then she passed the point of no return.

She wrapped her legs tight, squeezed her sheath hard, and threw back her head. Desiree wailed in a sweet release, and she felt pleasure rock her very core.

Waves of pleasure rolled through her extremities, and she blew apart into a million pieces. The aftershocks rocked her frame, and it felt so good, and so satisfying. *Man alive, the guy had power and endurance like a freight train!*

Desi peered up at him. "Dayo, I love you."

He gazed into her dark brown pools, and suddenly, her stud slowed down. He buried himself deep and came to a complete stop.

He wiped the sweat from his brow, "Girl, you just don't play fair."

"I'm hammering like a warhorse, and you blew apart, but now I feel like I've let you down."

Dayo stammered, "I long to say, I love you, but I'm not there yet. I do love you more than the stars and the heavens above. But I'm not sure if that's love."

She giggled and her sheath vibrated with joy. "I'd say that's love. I think you secretly love me, and since you said it that way, I feel very fulfilled."

Dayo ground his arousal deep inside her love canal.

He searched her eyes, "Woman, you drive me crazy! You can't pull out the love card when I'm being self-centered and tupping the holy hell outta you."

Declan growled, "Dammit all! Now, I've got to do the right thing."

She wasn't sure what he was doing, or even what he was feeling. But the fierce stud cradled her and carried her over to the love chair.

He held her bottom and lowered himself into the saddle. Desiree felt her breasts settle against his chest, and she was riding on top.

And not only was she riding cowgirl, but her legs splayed around his waist, and she could purchase traction with her feet. She could sling her flower so fast and hard; it would make his head spin.

And not only was she on top, but the love chair compensated for their height difference. She was face to face with her beloved. Now, she could kiss him and love him on every level. This was cooler than all get out.

Just then, her flower petals came loose. Her lips fell against his shaft and encapsulated his bangers. They were already buried to the hilt, but she worried that this was way too much labial contact.

Desi whimpered, "I think the stick 'em wore out. My petals came unglued and I'm not very pretty."

Declan gazed into her brown eyes, "Babe, it's no problem." He gazed into the Cheval mirror, "Sweetheart, you're as gorgeous as ever."

Moments later, Dayo rocked from the balls of his feet and pounded upward. She rode his upward thrusts and nearly popped into the air.

The guy was truly an athlete. He ceased his metronome pounding and curled his lips into a wonderful smile.

"Actually, this feels incredible. I'm buried deep inside, and your lady petals engulfed my man parts, and I can feel your love. Your pretty petals take lovemaking to a new level."

She stared at him in disbelief. "Really?"

"Oh, absolutely! This is sensual and romantic. But if you want to apply the stick 'em, we can do it that way. Or we can go au natural, and it will be thrilling."

She gained confidence. Dayo liked her just the way she was. And there was no need for further adjustments.

Desi lowered her mouth and descended into a delicious ballet of love. She kissed his handsome mouth, and when his lips parted, she slid her tongue way down his throat.

Desi wanted to love him with everything she had. She probed deeper and entered a tongue- tangling, deepthroat kiss.

She felt Dayo's arousal leap inside. The guy was getting harder than a steel cylinder, and it thrilled her to pieces. She had complete control, and she could use the love arts to bring him to a searing climax.

She slung her flower up and down his steely shaft. And as she became more confident, she accelerated her speed. They were joined so intimately, and this was so beautiful. Their lips were joined, their tongues tangled, and her lady flower was wrapped deeply around him.

Declan wrapped his arms around her and hauled her closer. Her generous breasts crushed against his chest, and then he smacked her well-rounded ass.

She knew what he wanted; slow-motion flower slinging wasn't doing the trick. He wanted it fast and furious, and that was exactly what he was going to get.

Desiree leaned forward and slung her flower into a piston-pounding sprint. Her nectar dripping sheath slammed up and down, and then she found another gear.

If Dayo could sprint like a track star than so, could she. Desi cut loose, and she slung her vagina faster and faster. She slammed her mons against his base, gripped his length, and tupped him at a furious pace.

The bronze beauty gasped for air, released her tongue, and stared into his gorgeous eyes.

Desiree wanted to watch it happen. She wanted to bring her man to a tumultuous orgasm, and she wanted to watch him blow apart.

When their lips separated, Declan rocked his head backward. She knew he was almost there. Desi launched into one more flower slinging sprint.

She blasted around the curve and headed down the straightaway. Suddenly, his bangers lifted, and she knew he was beyond the point of no return.

The agile beauty clenched down, and hurled her flower so fast and hard, Declan reached the edge. She watched him sail over the precipice as he roared out his climax.

She felt a jet stream splash into her sheath, and then Dayo made the most delicious O Face. He growled, and he yelled, and finally his mouth opened with nothing but pure ecstasy.

Her Adonis warrior was a thing of beauty, and she would cherish this moment for as long as she lived.

Desiree panted for air, and now, it was her turn. She held off just so she could watch him, but now she gave herself permission.

She slammed her Chloe into his shaft and ground out a pleasure-filled massage. Her sheath went into a full spasm, and her lady jewel blew apart into the most delicious, body racking orgasm.

She kept slinging her flower as waves of ecstasy consumed her. It was so beautiful, tears trickled down her cheeks.

Desiree slung her flower slower and slower and savored the aftershocks. She felt his manhood go to half mast, and yet, she wanted this to last forever.

Dayo's manhood fell from her lady sheath, but Desi wanted another round. She peered from beneath her long lashes, "Is there any chance the Big Guy will get excited again?"

Declan stroked her arms, "Babe, I love the enthusiasm, but I'm not as young as I used to be." He glanced over at a rack of love oils.

"But I'll tell ya what, why don't you pick out an edible oil. And I can drizzle your sweet vulva and do some flower tasting."

She tingled at the possibilities, but once again, Dayo would be the giver, and she would be the recipient.

The bronze beauty surveyed the rack of love oils and noticed an assortment of tiny pitchers. She read the labels and discovered an amber candle with fiery hot oils.

There were flames dancing on the white bottle, and she knew this was the one. She could feel the anticipation grow.

Desiree lit the tiny candle and inhaled the delicious scent. A spicy fragrance touched her nose, and she knew Dayo was going to love it.

She walked over to the love chair where Declan reclined like a Greek god. She seized Mr. Big and held him upright.

Declan yelled, "Hey, wait a minute, what are you doing?"

"It's my treat, you just sit there and relax."

She poured heated oils over his flared head and down his shaft. Declan arched his back and his whole body tensed, waiting for the warmth to sear his family jewels.

"Ohhh, that feels pretty good!"

Desi set down the candle aside and launched into a double-fisted pounding action. Her tight-fisted hands gripped him hard, and she slammed her hands up and down, pounding until Mr. Big got even larger.

A blue veiner appeared, and she took that as a good sign. He looked so sex-dripping and sensual, she couldn't take it. Desiree stroked him into a hand sprint, lowered her mouth, and then engulfed his length.

Her lips opened, and she swallowed, and she plunged downward. The oily flavor seared her tongue with hot spices, and it burned her lips and tingled her tongue.

She could only imagine what Dayo was feeling. She loved this spicy foray and launched into a head-bobbing, throat-thrusting marathon.

He was so delicious, and hard, and large, she had to take in all of him. She took a deep breath, and swallowed, and plunged her open throat all the way to the hilt.

Declan grabbed her ringlets, "Whoa, girl! That feels awesome!"

Desi slammed his length up and down her throat. Several times she wolfed him down and plunged to the hilt. With her nose touching his mons, and her throat filled with his arousal, Dayo was all man.

Finally, she came up for air and stroked him in another flurry.

"Wow! I had no idea that would be so spicy. My hardon is at a full salute. And now, we can go for seconds."

Desiree eyed the love chair and spotted a Cheval mirror. She could ride reverse cowgirl, but they'd have the benefit of facial contact. And what's more, Declan could watch her breasts bounce, and she planned to give him one helluva show.

After she moved the Cheval into place, she grabbed the roller stick 'em. In all the excitement, her lady petals came unglued. She applied the stick 'em and glued her flower into position.

Desiree curled her lips into a seductive little smile. She stepped over the love chaise, seized his engorged manhood, and lowered herself.

She felt his flared head enter, and she gripped him hard, and plunged downward. Once she seated herself, and wriggled for comfort, Desiree arched he back, and kicked out her amazing ass.

He had a tantalizing view of her derrière, and she planned to give him a thrill he would never forget.

His enthusiasm filled her in a different way, and she arched her back, leaned forward, and started slinging. She glanced at the Cheval, and her breasts bounced beautifully.

Her swollen globes heaved upward, and her nipples pebbled with increasing desire.

Now that the stage was set, she launched into a butt-slamming, flower-slinging marathon. Like a racehorse, she blasted down the straightaway, took the curve at full throttle, and then burst around the last bend.

She found another gear and pounded like a thoroughbred. She was getting close to a climax. *But dang it all, they weren't intimate enough!*

"Dayo, I want to be close, how do we pull this off?"

Leave it to her Marine, the guy was a wealth of creative ideas. "Babe, I want you to stay mounted, but lift your feet to the footstool, and lean backward."

"This is like reclining doggie style, and we'll be really intimate."

Desiree lifted her feet into position and braced her toes. She arched backward and reclined against his chest.

She laid her head against his shoulder, and he turned her face, and they engaged in an intimate, fully joined kiss.

Dayo started the sprint by pounding from the balls of his feet. His enthusiasm pounded upward, and he hit her erogenous zone in a mind-blowing assault.

Geezus! The guy was powerful. He wrapped his arms around her breasts, held on tight, and hammered like a warhorse.

Desiree felt the pressure build, and it wouldn't be long. She broke from his heated kiss, and threw her head back, and felt the pleasure build.

She was so aroused by the G-spot slamming, she leaned against his chest, and slung her flower in a backward pounding marathon.

Desi led him into sexual nirvana, and she wouldn't stop until he blew apart. She clenched her sheath, and she burst into a mind-blowing sprint.

She slung her flower backward, harder and harder, and then she felt his bangers lift, and her man sailed past the point of no return.

He approached the precipice, and he flew over the edge. Dayo roared out a loud orgasm, and she felt his seed fill her womb. It was so wonderful, and they were so close, she couldn't last any longer.

Desi felt her sheath go into a horrendous spasm, and then she blew apart into a million pieces. The aftershocks reeled through her members, and the spasms came in waves. It felt so good, and so fulfilling. She would cherish this forever.

Good lord, she felt like a real woman! Finally, she was able to please her man, and sate their pent-up desires. Until this very moment, the bronze beauty didn't realize how badly she needed this.

Dayo rose from the love chair and seized a towel. He tossed her a washcloth, "Come on, babe. Clean up can be fun."

He wiped down the silhouette S-curve like it was his pride and joy.

Dayo pointed to a love puddle, "Honey, you missed a spot."

She giggled, "Where on earth did all these juices come from?"

Declan laughed heartily, "It wasn't all me, it was both of us." Desi remembered gushing during one of her orgasms, but she had no idea her lady fluids would be so extensive.

She peered through her lashes, "Dayo, do you think I'm a messy lover?"

He burst into a glorious smile, and she loved the way he laughed. "Honey, you've got nothing to worry about. Love juices are natural, and between the two of us, we sure gush a lot."

Dayo tossed his towel in the hamper and scooped her up. He carried her to the four poster and pulled back the sheets. Gently, he lowered her to the comforter.

Molly jumped into her doggie bed, and Declan set Kay Bear next to her cheek. He walked over to the teddy bear audience.

"Now, let me see, who wants to sleep with the shapely warrior chick?"

"No volunteers, I'll grab you guys and tuck you in."

Desi cuddled against her support group, and Dayo snuggled behind her. He cradled the girls and pushed his member against her backside.

She felt so safe, and so satisfied, things couldn't be better. It was the end to a perfect day, and she was surrounded by everyone she loved.

"Dayo, I want to thank you for a lovely day. You're the stick 'em that holds my life together."

He kissed her crown of ringlets. "Sweetheart, right back at ya. And ya know what?"

"I love you."

Oh my god, he said it! Declan uttered those three incredible words. She savored the moment, and this truly was the end to a very beautiful day.

Chapter Eleven

Declan arose the next morning and padded into the kitchen. He glanced out the kitchen window and watched the first rays shatter through the forest.

His dream cottage was nestled in the woods, and he'd just made love to the most incredible woman. And not only did she ride cowgirl, but she woke him up in the middle of the night. He was harder than hell, and her willingness made him feel like a king.

Since his bronze beauty was a giver, he had to find a clever position. Dayo led her to a low elevated bench, and he lifted her on top.

He slid into her flower, and his woman surprised the hell outta him. Desiree seized his rock-hard butt, opened her legs, and went full Amazon.

From a standing position, she tupped him in a furious, flower slinging sprint. *The chick was amazing!*

Dayo poured a cup of coffee. He was deliciously sated and dumber than a fence post.

Good lord, he needed that release. But that wasn't a fair assessment. They were really good together. And most of all, he loved her, and couldn't imagine life without her.

The fearless Marine carried his coffee into the great room. The sunshine lit up the vaulted ceiling, and there was more than a sense of architectural beauty. There was pervasive peace. He hadn't felt like this in ages.

Declan opened the French doors and strolled onto the porch. Dappled light played over the floorboards, and the maple trees swayed in a gentle breeze.

Good lord, he could get used to this. And with a woman like Desiree, there was a chance he could become a cattleman, and maybe a prize-winning horseman.

Over in the yellow-sided homestead was a master equestrian. If he could learn the secret to Western riding, then he had a shot at the big money.

More than that, he might be able to partner with Cobb, and really make a go of this place. It was a longshot, but what else did he have?

His headhunter career was over, and he was too decisive for the SWAT team, and the witness program sucked. So, it was back to his first love: cattle ranching, roping steer, and riding Quarter Horses.

Desiree wore one of his button-downs and slid beneath his arms. She exploded into a delirious smile, "I feel so good, why don't we just lay around, and make love all day?"

Desi squeezed his rock-hard butt, "Goodness, you're an incredible lover. And also, one helluva man. I won't trade you in, you're a keeper."

She tiptoed to his mouth, slung a hand around his nape, and kissed her man with deep gratitude. Desi held up her koala toy. "Kay Bear thinks we're headed for the danger zone."

"Huh?"

"K-Man says we're running low on stick 'em, and we have to make a run for the sex shop."

He curled his lips in amusement, "Do you think Pine Whisper, actually has a sex shop?"

She giggled, "When I went to Maddie's hair salon, and the back room was full of sex toys, lotions, and crazy gadgets. There's got to be a bottle of stick 'em, and I think I'll buy a whole case."

Declan kissed her, "Darlin', you've gone from a shy beauty to a passion puppy."

"I don't know about that, but I can't get enough of you. And I want this party to last!"

Just then, Trick threaded the maple trees and arrived at the bottom step. His second-in-command wore an open-chested button-down, a black Stetson, and a pair of Wranglers.

His keen eyes flashed with brilliance, and the Lieutenant wasn't on holiday, he had a mission to accomplish.

He trotted up the steps, and Dayo engaged in a heartfelt back pounding. "Good to see ya, Trick. This is my woman, Desiree Corazon."

"She's an Apache combat pilot, and a former key witness. But she blasted her way out of the safe house. And now, she's looking for a new life."

Trick tipped his cattleman's hat, "Ma'am, I'm pleased to meet ya."

The Lieutenant turned, "We have a lot of intel to catch up on. But you're deliriously in love, so I'll let you enjoy the afterglow."

Declan thumped his chest, "Hey, man, I'm ready for action. Just hit me with the facts, and I'll take the lead."

Whip came through the woods and his gunnery man flashed a party-going smile. From a summer Stetson, and a stubble face, the Oklahoma cowboy laughed.

"Cap'n, while you're boneless, we'll have a team meeting and walk Cobb's property."

Dayo was slow to put together the pieces. He left his unit in the care of Cobb and Hallie, and they must have discussed a few logistics. On the one hand, he wished he was there, but on the other, he discovered what his heart was longing for.

He wrapped his arm around Desiree, "Whip, I'd like you to meet Desiree. She's a combat pilot and an amazing woman."

Desi tickled him, "Last night, you said I was an amazing lover. Are you downgrading me?"

Declan curled his lips, "No, darlin', I'm not. But I don't want to share our intimate details with others."

Whip shook her hand. "I remember you from Afghanistan, it appears you're integrating pretty well."

"Up to last night, I've been going through the motions. But with my therapy pupper, Kay Bear, and a stud Marine, I've got an incredible team. And I'm ready to face the world."

Trick leveled his eyes, "Cobb wants you to do some RCH work. There's a Western riding event coming up, and he says you have a heavy rein, and you're not worth a shit. But while you're punch drunk in love, you'll be more fluid and graceful."

Dayo listened in disbelief. "Are you talking about the me or Shepherd Cat?"

Whip flashed a party-going smile, "Cap'n, we're talkin' about you. And for what it's worth, I think Cobb's right."

Desiree kissed him in a deepthroat French assault. Declan hauled her tight, sucked on her tantalizing tongue, and enjoyed her passion. *The girl was incredible.*

Desi giggled, "I'll round up some more body stick 'em. And I'll let you initiate the love play, but I get to finish with a cowgirl thumping."

She squeezed his ass and cooed, "You're incredible, you big stud. Now, go over to the open-air arena and kick some ass!"

He raised his hands in self-defense. "All right, I get the message, everyone wants me to practice Western riding, and get my act together. So, I'm outta here."

Declan walked to the tack room and saddled Shepherd Cat. The eighteen-year-old sorrel was a champion through and through. It was an honor to ride such an expensive sire.

The fearless Marine wheeled into the saddle, trotted down the cobbled corridor, and entered the morning light. He glanced at the metal roofed horse barn and considered the remodeling costs.

A few metal panels were loose, and the furred walls needed a new coat. But other than that, David T. had done a great job.

Dayo trotted down a dirt path and entered the hallowed sanctuary. The open-air arena was groomed to perfection, and the night lights glowed with a surreal intensity.

This was where it happened. And this covered arena represented Cobb's bucket dreams. He didn't know if he was the man to fulfill those dreams or not. But he sure didn't want to disappoint the Old Man.

Cobb stood at the center paddock and leaned against the pipe rails.

He called out, "Why don't you ride a few figure eights and loosen up. Shepherd Cat could use the work. And in the meantime, David T. will run a Charolais into the chute."

Calmly, Declan saluted. He knew the Old Man had an agenda, but he felt relaxed, and at one with the world.

Dayo went right into the rein work, and Sheppie shot straight down the middle. Declan's splash stops, spins, and backward trot were all done with an easy rein and fluid mastery.

It was so easy, and he was so centered, it was unbelievable. The bronze warrior entered the arena with low expectations. There were no cattle to herd, and there was no reason to get excited.

Declan didn't force the issue, nor did he use a high-action signal. Shepherd seemed to appreciate the fact his hands were held low. And with barely a signal, the veteran cow horse performed fluidly and showed off his prowess.

Dayo was stunned, but he learned one major lesson. It didn't take much for Sheppie to perform the maneuvers. There was no need to exert excessive control.

He and this sorrel stud were bonded on a deep spiritual level. Declan simply let it happen, and they performed the rein work like it was no big deal.

Dayo swore he knew what Shepherd was thinking. The veteran Quarter Horse felt relieved. The animal knew there was a bond of trust, and he showed off his abilities.

Cobb tipped a finger to his beat-up Stetson. "Way to go, son. You're doing well."

"David T. will release a Charolais, and even though it's one-on-one, you don't have to bring your open range game."

"Just relax in the saddle, lift your hands slightly, and deliver a tiny signal."

There it was the key to reined cow horse events. He could deliver a tiny signal, and the old pro would exhibit his cow-horse savvy.

Dayo's role was to deliver a slight cue and help the Big Cat whenever he needed it. They were a team, and each one had to know their roles.

David T. loaded a beige colored Charolais into the chute. Except for a single steer, the arena was empty. Shepherd Cat spotted the little hombre, and his nostrils flared.

The veteran sire lived for this kind of thing. He was a bloodline cutting horse all the way back to his great granddaddy.

The weather-beaten cowboy released a frisky, athletic steer. Shepherd Cat glided fluidly down the length of the arena. The hesitant steer stood at the far end.

Declan remained relaxed and his mind intuitively evaluated the frisky bovine. The steer's eyes and shoulders provided a tell, and Declan knew exactly where the rogue was headed.

In the duel of wits, Sheppie didn't overplay his cut-offs. Dayo reined him lightly, hands held low, and barely gave a signal. To his amazement, that was all the Big Cat needed. It was a thrilling discovery, and the Marine showed off his sorrel to maximum advantage.

Compared to open range, he didn't need to work as hard. Shepherd showed off his skills, and his cow sense, and that's what the judges wanted to see.

After the box work, the steer ran the long wall, and the Big Cat came from behind, accelerated smoothly through the gaits, and overtook the runaway.

In a deft graceful move, Sheppie cut off the steer and turned him the other direction. It was a thing of beauty, riding such a magnificent Quarter, and taking control so easily.

To complete Cobb's cow work, Declan led the steer into center, and performed a half arena circle. Sheppie showed off his cow sense, and ran shoulder-to-shoulder, exhibiting full command.

They were done, and in his mind, the cow work was perfect. In fact, he was so relaxed, he really didn't care what Cobb had to say.

Cobb hailed him over to the grandstands. "Dayo, your run was perfect. There's always some little damn thing the judges ding you for, but if you ride like that, you'll take first place every time."

The Old Man cocked his head thoughtfully, "Do you know what's different?"

"Yeah, I had amazing sex all night long. I'm relaxed and I don't give a rip about anything."

Pettigrew inquired, "Is there anything else?"

"Since I had zero expectations, I decided to have fun, and see how sensitive Shepherd's response really is. And to my amazement, he can heed a barely-there signal."

"And if I could think like a horse, I'd say it made him happy. He felt I trusted him, and he reciprocated."

Cobb stroked his circle beard. "Let's review what you've learned so far. Yesterday, you rode Shepherd at full tilt."

"When the stud flattened out, you rode no handed, and reached for the divine moment. That's what you did while target shooting, and you did it again, inside the arena. There is a special moment to give a signal, and you found it."

The leathery old horseman became excited, "What's more, you're enjoying yourself. You're allowing your love for riding to come through."

"And as a consequence, you showed off Shepherd's cow sense to perfection. That's how you'll impress the judges."

Declan didn't know what to make of Cobb's comments. He worked a steer in open range and performed a full cow horse run. And now, the old man was talking about a judged event.

Dayo made light of the idea. "If we hit the big time, I'll have wild mountain sex and knock the judges for a loop."

Cobb chuffed, "That's not exactly the formula I had in mind. But an interlude with your lovin' woman wouldn't hurt."

Cazador felt removed, but the Old Man's resolve began to affect him. It was worth pursuing, and seeing how far he could take RCH competitions.

"Suppose I competed in an RCH event, how much of a prize are we talking about?"

Cobb stroked his jaw, first place brings a hundred thousand dollars, or more. Naturally, our business arrangement means that I'll take twenty-five percent."

"But son, a seventy-five percent winning gives a man a lot to build on."

The commander had no idea the stakes were so high. He came off his love bubble, and momentarily considered the possibilities.

He was a fearless Marine, and he laid plans, analyzed logistics, and charted a course. It was a no-nonsense approach.

"All jesting aside, you're saying that if I won ten RCH events, I could earn over a million a year?"

"I don't see why not. But the goal should never be the money, but rather making the perfect run."

"And as your coach, I'm interested in the perfect performance."

The old horseman scratched his head. "But from my side, it goes a lot deeper than that. I've been flush with money before, but the one thing that eluded me was a first-place trophy."

The Old Man reflected. "Shepherd and Hunter Cat deserve that honor, and in a way, I feel as though I failed them."

The commander walked Shepherd over to a food bag, and they resumed the conversation.

"All right, you've got my attention, but I feel as though the trophy isn't everything. You're holding back, and if we're having an honest conversation, we both have to put our cards on the table."

It felt good to be forthright, and his sated afterglow gave him a measure of detachment.

Cobb tilted his head. "Fair enough." The Old Man pointed to the distant horse pastures, and the far-flung paddocks.

"This ranch is my life's work, but I never realized its full potential.

My first goal is to honor Sheppie and Hunter. And my second goal is to honor them with colt sales."

"And lastly, I'd like to find a ranch foreman, who can drive cattle, compete in Western riding, and conduct horse auctions."

The Old Man waved his hand, "It's all right here. A young man could make a living, sink deep roots, and forge a future."

"Hell, if he was good at it, that same ranch foreman could raise a family, and one day, he could buy me out."

Declan surveyed Cobb's property. He could see it. The building blocks to forge an incredible future lay right before him.

He laid aside the dream of cattle ranching years ago, but then again, he didn't have a life coach, and he didn't have a track to run on.

The Old Man and he got along. They were both straight shooters, and he was willing to learn.

However, there was one fly in the ointment, and that was the three-month mark. Desiree hadn't given up the idea of testifying.

And if his woman planned to fly back to L.A., and testify against Antonio, there was gonna be one helluva fight. His unit would have to plow the fields, prepare for a helo drop, and guide the key witness into a courtroom.

He didn't care for that plan; it would make his unit into marked men. But then again, it was three months away, and Desiree was just getting settled.

But he was denying a great opportunity. Cobb's objectives and veiled offer would take longer than a full summer.

For the first time, he saw a way to do something he loved. He loved Quarter Horses, roping, and driving cattle. Back in High School, he and his brother Jovanni competed in circuit rodeos.

He was a good roper, and he could hurl a laser beam. Dayo could catch horns or scoop hooves. Back then, he didn't have high-dollar horses, but all that was about to change.

Declan was in search of his life's calling. His first calling was to command a Marine Raider unit. But the war ended, and he bounced from one unworkable solution to the next.

Clearly, SWAT missions and Witness Programs were a no-go, but he could really get into this.

What's more, the woman he loved, Desiree DeNiro, would become more than a summer affair, she might be the One.

He wanted to avoid blue-sky thinking, but Cobb's veiled offer opened up a slew of opportunities. It was a lot to take in. In fact, it was an opportunity to forge a whole new life.

He'd be blind to say the tools weren't right in front of him. *Why the hell hadn't he seen it before?*

The commander ended his reflections and turned to Cobb. The Old Horseman was wise beyond his years. He knew when to talk, and when to let it settle in.

"All right, you've laid it on the table, and now it's my turn. I can safely guarantee you three months. And anything you want to teach me, I'll put my whole heart into it."

"Your methods are crazier than hell, but then again, my drill sergeant was the same way. I can man-up, and I'm willing to compete."

Cobbed eyed him curiously and waited.

Declan squeezed the saddle horn, "At three months, we may have a special appointment. We already talked about the fact Desiree is a key witness."

"She saw Antonio gun down an innocent man. One way or the other, the kingpin has to answer for that. But when Gonzalez is out of the picture, I can give you one hundred percent."

Declan broke into a half-smile. The commander extended his hand, "Do we have a deal?"

Cobb shook his hand, "Son, I accept your three month offer, but I want you to know, a lot can happen in the span of one summer."

Dayo curled his lips, "Are you referring to more insane horse lessons?"

The Old Man chuckled, "No, I was referring to fate."

"My faithful wife keeps praying and things keep happening, and you never know what the Big Man's gonna do. The Almighty has his divine will, and in the end, we're just part of a greater plan."

Before the commander could contemplate a higher power, a two-ton dually rolled up. The women piled out of the white twin cab, and Hallie headed for the homestead. And his lady love was headed right his way.

Chapter Twelve

Desiree entered the open-air arena. Molly ran alongside her, and Kay Bear looked extremely happy. She held up her hair salon package. "I see you guys are hard at work."

"Just so you know, I went to Maddie's, and purchased love oils, body stick 'em, and a booklet about sixteen cowgirl positions."

She giggled, "Stud, when I'm through with you, you won't' be able to walk a straight line."

"Whooeee! I can barely wait."

Molly woofed her agreement. And Desi patted her doggo, "You tell him, girl."

Cobb paused, "Are you up to riding Hunter Cat? It won't take long for David T. to load thirty-cattle into the far end."

"All you have to do is put in five minutes, and then you're done for the day."

Desi eyed him with suspicion, but she really didn't give a rip.

"Ya know, Old Man, I had such a fulfilling love session last night, I'm riding on cloud nine. And nothing you can say will dampen my mood or kill my joy."

Pettigrew whistled and Hunter trotted into the arena.

Declan wagged his head, "You Old Fox, you had this planned from the get-go."

Desiree pointed to a stack of hay bales. She issued the command, "Hopp," and her Malinois leaped up the staircase.

Her pupper was seated above the pipe rails, and if there was the slightest problem, her safety net was in place. She wasn't about to have a post-traumatic flashback or give Cobb the satisfaction.

Desiree ducked through the rails, placed her foot in the stirrup, and wheeled into the saddle.

"Is Hunter warmed up?"

Cobb nodded, "David T. warmed him up earlier. Are you ready to have a go?"

"You bet your sweet ass. Bring out those dogies, and I'll show 'em who's boss."

Declan trotted over. "Before I give you the full arena, I should share a profound discovery. These expensive horses are extremely sensitive."

"And to show them how much we trust 'em, all you have to do is give a barely-there signal."

Desi felt light as a feather, and stupid male bravado seemed so silly. She applied an imperceptible rein command.

Her fingers were light, and the reins barely moved, and it was no more than a tingle to his bit. But sure enough, Hunter performed an easy roll out, and he was anxious for the next command.

"Good lord, that was amazing! Do you mean I can keep my hands low, and just use teensy-weensy signals, and the Big Cat will understand?"

"More than that, the Big Cat will feel you trust him. And he'll show you how amazing his cow sense is. I made the same mistake, but with these horses, trust goes a long way."

The commander chucked her chin softly, "Darlin', I know you don't like someone tellin' you what to do. But as a suggestion, you should try to bond with Hunter, feel his predatory savvy, and you'll know exactly where he's going."

"And the bonus is, he won't throw you out of the saddle."

Desiree giggled, "I like that bonus. And going after a frisky steer is like taking on a basketball opponent. I can box him off, force him to retreat, and I can take full control."

She hooked a thumb, "I feel pretty loose today, and you may be surprised at what I can do."

Dayo kissed her reassuringly, "Babe, you never stop surprising me."

He swatted her lovely round ass, and Desi burst into a smile. "You want me, don't you?"

"I sure do. Now, get into that arena and show me your stuff."

Hunter walked forward like an equine predator. His brownish-black coat shimmered beneath the lights, and the bay stud was all business.

She saw an opening form, and Desiree parted the bovine sea. A mass of blonde Charolais parted, and she singled out a crew of three. As she evaluated their speeds, one dogie broke into a run, and he was the one.

Hunter Cat went shoulder-to-shoulder with the steer, and took him all the way to the outer zone.

She patted his neck, "Way to go, Big Cat. That was a badass move, and it presents a high degree of difficulty, and we're gonna kick his little butt."

The steer didn't like the trip one bit. Way off in the other side, there were twenty-nine of his buddies, and his herd instincts went into high gear.

The blonde bullet was terrified, and he had to get back. There was safety in numbers, and he was all alone.

Hunter lowered his shoulders and floated to the left. The steer hoped for a quick end around, but this was going to be a lot harder.

The Charolais feinted and made beeline for the left wall. She laid her hand to his withers and gave a barely perceptible lead.

The Big Cat appreciated the respect, and now it was his time to show off. The bay stud intercepted the steer and turned him around. The Charolais bawled and sprinted to the right side.

Quickly, the arcs became larger and larger, and the cow's desperation increased. Hunter juked back and forth, and using his superlative cow sense, the eighteen-year-old drove the bad boy deeper.

It was an awesome duel at the O.K. Corral. And Desiree found herself bonding with her awesome mount. It was an experiment in imperceptible signals, and she was lovin' it.

Hunter must have felt the same thing because he emerged with a new personality. The Big Cat worked that little dogie for five full minutes, and finally, the Charolais gave up.

"Good lord, that was a lot of fun!" And if she hadn't been so deeply in Hunter's head, he would have thrown her for a loop.

The bronze cowgirl felt good about herself. And she'd just experienced a huge breakthrough, and a life changing revelation.

She patted Hunter's withers, "Sorry boy. Yesterday, I didn't accord you the respect you deserve. But I see where you're coming from, and from now on, things are going to be different."

Just for safety, Desiree trotted over to the hay bales and offered her cheek. Her Malinois stood at full attention, and her tongue lolled in anticipation.

"Hey girl, I was having fun out there, but I could never forget you."

She tapped her copper glow cheek, "Care to give me a little sugar." Her doggo kissed her cheek with a flurry of doggie kisses, but Molls wasn't one to stop at a cheek licking.

Her pupper slayed her with mouth kisses, and even though dog breath isn't the greatest thing, Desi felt safer than a bug in a rug.

Dayo rode his red sorrel and stopped before the grandstands. Cobb was grinning from ear to ear, but the Old Man didn't say a word.

Finally, the Old Man clapped his hands, "That was a magnificent run, but I said you were here for five minutes, and I aim to keep my promise."

"Why thank you, Cobb. I appreciate the candor, and after I cool down Hunter, I'll go about my day."

Declan nodded his cowboy hat. "Before you arrived, Cobb and I put things on the table. It was a solid conversation filled with honesty."

Desi arched her S-curved brow, "Oh, and what did you guys talk about?"

"He extended a solid offer to teach me Western riding. For the next three months, I'll be the ranch foreman, the cattle driver, and an RCH competitor."

"We'll hit as many horse shows as we can, and we'll win as much prize money as possible. And it is interesting to note, first place winnings are nothing to sneeze at."

"The RCH Association has come a long way, and there's big money, sometimes as much as professional rodeo. Maybe a hundred thou a piece."

Desiree took a keen interest. She could complain that she hadn't been included, but that's the way men were. They made plans, and then expected lady folk to go along.

But it just so happened, she was in complete agreement. But she made a side note, when she had Dayo alone, she'd have to set down a few rules.

They were husband and wife, and married couples did things in complete agreement. She dismissed the notion they had a fake marriage. Everything was real.

Her stud warrior curled his lips, "There's also an interesting offer on the table."

She couldn't believe her guy. He was making plans without her.

Dayo reached over and massaged her neck. "Babe, nothing is set in stone, but with your agreement, we could build a future here."

Her eyes widened, "What does that future look like?"

"Well, there's more to this ranch than it appears. There are three main revenue streams: cattle raising, equine contests, and colt sales. These two champions have sired a large number of bloodline cutters.

She glanced through the open-air arena at a vast playground, filled with frisky youngsters. It hadn't dawned on her, this was a breeding ranch, and one with serious possibilities.

"Do you plan to train them and finish them?"

"That's the third revenue stream. And if we stayed on, we could be ranching managers, cattle drivers, and performance riders."

"And once the funding is established, Cobb is willing to teach us his breeding program, and how to sell futurity colts."

"At every turn, we could earn an income. Naturally, it's his ranch and these are his horses, but our take is substantial. On a good year, we could hit a million."

Declan drawled, "We could forge a new life, and I could find something I love doing. And a calling that I can sink my teeth into."

She listened to her Marine pour out his heart. His stateside return didn't go well, and he hadn't integrated. But horse ranching was in his blood, and she could see that.

Finally, Desiree asked timidly, "What do you want me to say?"

"Well, darlin' it's your turn to trip the light fantastic. Just talk from the heart and lay out your dreams."

He gestured to the wide-open valley. "If you could paint the sky blue, just tell us what you want."

She felt honored, and free as a bird. "For starters, if we became the ranch managers, I'd like to decorate the log manor a little differently."

Cobb leaned on the top rail. "I don't see a problem."

"I'd add more feminine touches, pretty accents, and I'd paint the children's rooms." She glanced at her fearless warrior, and she wasn't sure what he was thinking.

"A new coat of paint would spruce the place up, and I'm sure Hallie will assist in any way she can."

Desi continued, "If it were a perfect world, I could fly the Flight for Life helos twice a week and Molly would be my co-pilot. Between my therapy dog and Kay Bear, we'd make a fantastic team."

Cobb mused, "You've already impressed Captain Deveau. Of course, no one wants to see injuries, but for crucial runs, they should be able to keep you busy."

For the first time, Desiree looked past Cobb's gruff manner and realized he was a very caring man. Of course, she didn't want to take instructions, he drove her crazy.

The bronze beauty placed a finger to her lips and thought about her dreams. "I do enjoy horseback riding, and I could throw myself into cutting horse competitions."

"Naturally, I prefer to hear instructions from Dayo, and it's easier for me to process. So, you two can work out a system, and I only want to hear nice things."

Pettigrew replied, "The translator system seems to be working; we'll do it that way. And you won't have to hear from my melodious voice." The old man chuckled.

"Most of all, I want to be surrounded by people I love, and by people who love me. A support group is absolutely essential."

"I've spoken about Molly and Kay Bear and Declan, but I'd like the military unit to accept me, and encourage me."

Declan answered, "I'll have a talk with them, and we'll focus on the positive. You're my badass warrior girl, and they'll come to admire you."

"I sure hope so. Trick and Whip seemed nice enough. But I have yet to meet the others."

Dayo interjected, "The cattle drive is about to take place, and there's no better way to meet the unit than working a project. And when they see what a topnotch cowgirl you are, they'll think you're over the moon."

She gazed at her idyllic log manor, "I want to have a period of honeymoon sex, and after a while, I'd like to start a family."

"With all these wide-open spaces, horse trails, and things to do, raising a family would be perfect. I love children, and Dayo's a bit childish, so we'd make great parents."

She giggled and tickled Declan's stomach.

He folded his arms and listened carefully. Desiree read his nonchalant, laid-back reaction. It was more than a poker face; he was sorting things out.

And she was pretty sure, she caught him off guard. The commander was a rational guy, and he didn't like surprises any better than she did.

Desiree resumed her discourse and suddenly stopped cold.

"Geezus! I hate Antonio Gonzalez. That son of a bitch is a dark cloud, hanging over everything."

"We have to keep a low profile, and both of us are undercover. I want to testify in court, but that doesn't happen for three months."

"We're putting our lives on hold and living life the wrong way. We spend too much time looking over our shoulders."

She wrung her hands, and Molly jumped into action. Her pupper delivered a flurry of doggie kisses, and she was drenched.

She squeezed her dog's fur coat. "Thanks girl. I was just having a down moment."

Dayo glanced at Cobb, "I should point out the obvious. There's a full Marine unit over at the bunkhouse. The headhunters specialize in taking out hostile leaders."

"Planning an op against Antonio would be no different. And it would be a lot cleaner than a court case."

"While I listened to your dreams, I shared every one of them. Of course, I thought children would be ways off. But I'm reconsidering a new timetable."

"We can discuss how long the honeymoon lasts and take it from there."

Desiree touched his hands. "Oh, Dayo, you're so understanding. And I know we shouldn't rush into it."

"First, we have to run the ranch, win a few contests, and move onto the granddaddy, the RCH events."

She thought about her favorite dreams, and Gonzalez was like a huge burden, hanging over her head. "Just out of curiosity, how easy would it be to terminate Antonio?"

Dayo cast an alpha-warrior grin. "It would be a piece of case. Our headhunter unit has done it hundreds of times, and Antonio's demise would be no different."

Declan turned to Cobb, "I hope the severity of our conversation didn't cause you alarm."

Pettigrew waved his hand, "Naw, I fought in Viet Nam, and I know all about those helos. I'm not a judgmental individual, and the call is entirely yours."

The Old Man added, "But the sooner Desiree starts having babies, we'll be one happy family." Dayo had a stunned expression on his face. Cobb pointed, "Gotcha!"

Chapter Thirteen

Desiree and Declan cooled down the champions and headed for their home. The bronze beauty returned to the log manor overwhelmed with teeming emotions.

She couldn't wait to talk to Cazador, but subtlety and timing were of the utmost importance. Not only did she want to disclose her dream of raising a family, but she had to apologize.

With the exception of her combat role, Desi had fallen into the trap of being overly passive. Her post-traumatic episodes threw her for a loop, and she became a victim, instead of an active pursuer.

But her therapy pupper changed everything. The bronze beauty went for weeks without a flashback or a devastating episode. And now, life had become so exciting, she was about to burst.

Desi wasn't cured, but she had a workable program. Ever since her trip into town, Hallie inspired her to become more assertive. And she wanted Declan Cazador, and she wanted a real marriage, and she wanted to have children.

While she brewed the coffee, Desi bubbled with excitement. It was all coming into focus. Ever since the cutting horse practice, her brain kicked into high gear. She had clarity, and it was best to strike while the iron was hot.

And when Mrs. Pettigrew mentioned the fact she delayed having children, her words struck a profound chord. But bringing her fondest dreams into the light was frightening.

She had to cowgirl up, and make her feelings known. Otherwise, they didn't have a fighting chance.

Dayo entered the post-and-beam kitchen. He hung his black Stetson on a pinewood wall hanger. As Desiree fired up a pot of coffee, she made the suggestion.

"It's such a glorious morning, why don't we talk outdoors?"

The rustic kitchen opened to a romantic view of a mountain stream. Dayo donned his cool guy shades, and the man was as stunning as ever. But what bothered her was that he was hiding. Her man was as overwhelmed by the offer as she was.

Desiree crossed the hardwood planks and settled onto a sofa. She sipped her coffee, while her stud cowboy perched his fine ass on a bench rail.

Beyond Declan, a lovely stream flowed between the rocks, and tall grass overhung an enchanting riverbank. There were so many possibilities staring them in the face, she didn't know where to begin.

Fate gave them the building blocks to forge a wonderful life. And as Hallie would say, the Almighty has given you everything you need, now it's up to you to do the rest.

Desi strolled over to her fearless Marine. "Honey, could you remove your shades? I know Cobb through you for a loop, but I want to gaze into your eyes, and know what you're feeling."

Declan removed his glasses, "Darlin', you have my full attention. But before you start in, I'll let you know, I'm good with about ninety-eight percent of Cobb's ideas."

That was reassuring. Now, it was up to her to do the rest.

She sat down with her coffee cup and nuzzled close. She could hear the flow of water, and the chirping of birds, and more than anything she wanted to make this her home. And to accomplish her greatest dreams, this incredible warrior had to be on board.

Molly knew something was up, so she sat obediently, and placed her chin on Desi's knee. Kay Bear peered at her, and he was as encouraging as ever. His button-brown eyes beamed with optimism, and K-Man told her to go for it.

The bronze beauty curled her alluring lips, "Something happened when we said our vows. I felt a spiritual anointing when I said, 'I thee wed.'"

"And it wasn't a rehearsal. Suddenly, it became the real thing. In my heart, I wanted to be married, and the moment I put on that ring, it became real."

She gestured through the French doors. "We're not pretending to be undercover partners. Somewhere along the line, you became my husband, and that means, I'm your loving wife."

She finally stated the truth, and it was out in the open. It felt liberating to admit that she never felt like his girlfriend. She was actually his wife.

Before her fearless warrior could bolt upright and start pacing, Desi threw a leg into his lap. "Just search your heart, and review what we've been through."

"Together, we demolished a safe house, we rode mountain climbers, and fled north in a cattle car. Circumstances drove us together, and we launched into our next op."

"We engaged in team roping, flushed cattle, and I had a traumatic relapse. You went into high gear, not as my protector, nor as a fellow warrior, but as my loving husband."

"You found a seizure alert dog and brought my PTSD under control."

She raised a delicate bronze finger, "Something spiritual has taken place. We have become a married couple."

Desiree could see he wanted to get up. So, she slipped into his lap and peered into his dark brown eyes. She wrapped her legs around his waist, and they were as intimate as two people could get.

Declan swept a hand behind her shiny ringlets, "Woman, I can see you won't be dissuaded. You've got something on your mind, so I'm willing to hear it."

She parted her generous lips and kissed him sweetly. This wasn't easy for either of them, but they had to be gut-level honest. And transparency isn't easy, but it lays a sound foundation.

Desiree didn't know what drove her, but she had to get these things out.

She peered beneath her lashes. "Something spiritual has taken place. We have become a married couple. I don't know how it happened, but it did."

"You started out as my commander, my rescuer, and my bodyguard, but somewhere along the way, you became my husband. And what's more, you became my lover... and my future."

Desiree made sure to speak slowly, so that each word could sink in. Declan was her husband, her lover, and her future. There was no going back, and what lay before them required courage.

And together, she believed they could build a remarkable life. But to do so, it required the willingness to share one another's dreams.

She ate, drank, and slept just like a married woman. And her thoughts were always about him, how to please him, and to help him.

The bronze beauty cuddled closer and rested her endowments against his chest. Desiree was afraid to ask him how he felt.

She just finished laying it on the line. And her only hope was that she had a real partner, and she wasn't going through this alone.

Desi whispered against his lips, "What do you feel?"

He wrapped his arms around her. And Dayo curled his charming mouth into a Belafonte smile. "I feel you're right!"

"We're spiritually joined, and it's way more than bodyguard protection. And I must confess, I've been kidding myself. I just haven't wanted to admit what's in front of me."

He drew a deep breath, and she hung on his every word. "I'm in love with you. And like you said, I don't know how it happened, but that's exactly where I'm at."

"I love you, and I can't imagine a life without you. And since we already exchanged our vows, that makes you my wife, and ...I'm your husband."

There was a brief hesitation, but her valiant Marine said it. And he didn't say things lightly. When Cazador said something, he spoke with sincerity and conviction.

Declan lowered his thick brows, "Let's think about where this is going. It doesn't seem fair that we're married, and there was no wedding."

"Every little girl dreams about her wedding day. And we skipped the rehearsal, the wedding gown, and the honeymoon."

He gazed at her with deep concern. "Somehow, I feel as though we should have a public ceremony. How do you feel about that?"

"I realize that we skipped the ceremony, but I have what I really want, and that's you." Not only did she say those words, but she really meant them.

"If we announced our wedding, we'd no longer be undercover. Gonzalez has hackers trolling the internet. And if he realized I was still alive, he'd make me his number one target."

Desi broke into a radiant smile, "We'll renew our vows someday, and I'm good with that."

She wiggled her breasts against his chest and teased him with her pert nipples. "Does it frighten you that we're husband and wife?"

He broke into a cavalier grin. "Yes and no. Loving you is easy, and that part isn't scary. But marriage comes with a lot of responsibility."

"And as your husband, we need to find a way to build a life together."

She nipped his attractive lower lip. "Before we go on, I'd like to say. How much I love you, and how much I appreciate your honesty."

"This can't be easy for a tough-ass Marine. But Dayo, what you said means the world to me."

Right then, Molly pushed into their laps and delivered a doggie kiss to Declan's mouth. If she didn't know better, she'd say her pupper understood their conversation. Furthermore, her doggo was pleased that the right things were being said.

Desi reflected on her next words. When she visited Maddie's salon, Hallie May discussed the virtues of womanhood.

Hallie spoke heavily about a woman's duties, and what a pleasure it was. And lastly, the old woman acknowledged the guiding hand of God.

There were no accidents, and surely a higher power had brought them together. Hallie stated the obvious as thought it was plain as day.

And when Mrs. Pettigrew spoke, it was without drama, but simply the truth.

Desiree wanted the full blessings of her higher power. And if she failed to acknowledge his guiding hand, it would be wrong.

Her enormous eyes were bursting. "Hallie said there are no accidents, and that we were brought together as part of his divine plan. Do you feel that way?"

Dayo gazed off in the distance to collect his thoughts, then he lowered his masculine brows.

"I'm fully aware there is a divine presence. And never have I felt it more profoundly than when I'm with you."

"Oh, that was a nice thing to say. I had no idea you were open to God."

He curled his lips, "Let's not get carried away. I simply acknowledged there was a higher power at work. And I'm convinced the Almighty will have his way, whether I like it or not."

This conversation was full of surprises. And at every turn, her Marine surprised her. She didn't want a holy roller, but it was good to have a touch of the spiritual.

Desiree switched directions, "I have issues too." She was a passive victim of traumatic episodes, but it was time to take the bull by the horns.

"I want to be completely honest. As your wife, and your best friend, I have responsibilities too."

It was time to make amends and turn a new leaf. "I'm sorry, I didn't fulfill my wedding vows right away, but that has all changed."

She lit up, "We can get intimate anytime you want, and I want to love you as deep and hard as I can. I want to tup you so hard; you'll blow apart. But more than that, I want to love you with everything I've got."

Desiree arched her S-shaped brows. "I want cowgirl time, but we can switch to cowboy dominant in a couple of weeks. As your loving wife, it's something I need to do."

"And by slinging my flower hard, that's how I say, 'I love you.'" Desiree laid it on the line.

She continued, "Loving you isn't a chore. I love tupping the hell outta you. And I want to thank you for your patience."

"I realize you're a love machine, and with your track star physique, you could tup me to hell and gone. But I'm still finding my game, and I need a little more time."

Desi searched his eyes and was amazed at Dayo's listening skills.

He bounced her in his lap. "All right, the cowgirl mania can last a little longer, but then this locomotive powerhouse will get his turn. Do you agree?"

She patted his chest fondly. "Yes, you big stud. You'll get your chance to slay me. But in all our thunder tupping, I hope we can take turns."

The sex talk loosened Dayo up. He remarked, "I agree to the terms, but just don't take too long. When you're slinging your flower, there are moments, when I want to thunder tup you to pieces."

"I'd like to bring Chloe to such a harrowing climax, your eyes will roll back in your head, and you'll scream like a wild banshee."

Desiree giggled, "You have a lot of kinky ideas, don't you?"

"You bet I do."

She loved being close and getting on the same page.

Desiree took a deep breath and heaved her pillows. "Now, for a difficult topic. While I'm lovin' you like a wild woman, there is a chance that I might conceive. Under the right circumstances, when I'm at peak fertility, it could happen."

"Now, I want you to know, I'm not trying to have a wee bairn. But it could happen, and I don't want there to be any pressure."

She paused, "Regarding children, we can cross that bridge later. But after we build this ranch, and I arrive at a safe place, you can be the stud cowboy and get me pregnant."

"You can thump me hard, and love me good, and make a wee babe." She giggled, "I know how much you love my ass, and I hear doggie style is one of the best ways."

Declan burst into a glorious laugh. "I like the sounds of that. We can bring in rodeo funds and build a future."

"And when the time is right, we can do the doggie two-step, and make a wee bairn."

Desiree blushed, but she was really pleased with the way things were going. She had a keeper, and she knew it. And the most important thing was to point her Marine in the right direction.

Dayo arched his thick brows, "Are you on the pill?" He must have seen the contraceptives in the wooden crate.

Desi wiggled in his lap, knowing her answer would pose problems.

"When I went into town, Hallie told me how difficult it was to bear children. She and Cobb worked the rodeo, and when they finally had the money, she couldn't get pregnant. When she told me not to wait, I felt it was a word from on high."

She pursed her lips, "I know it sounds irresponsible, but I'm not on the pill. I'm leaving this up to fate, and if the Almighty wants to bless us with a wee babe, then I'm all for it."

She peered through her lashes. "Please, Dayo, tell me this is all right. I don't want to miss the chance of having a baby."

Her fearless Marine was taken aback. He chewed his lip and considered the situation.

"If you conceive and we have a wee bairn, we've only got nine months. And from what I hear, children change everything."

"Yes, they do. But sweetheart, I don't want to wait, and miss a wonderful blessing. I've always wanted a family, and having a family with you, would be a dream come true."

"That reassures me, sweetie. There's no one else I'd like to have a baby with."

He looked at her suspiciously, "You're focusing on this family start-up a lot. Are you already pregnant?"

The bronze beauty giggled. "It is way too early, but I don't think so! However, the thought of having a family has kicked my brain into high gear."

"And bucko, I have faith in you. Just like a military op, this ranch is a special mission." She pounded his chest affectionately, "You can do this, buddy! This is exactly what you do."

"Look at what's been given to us. Fate has dropped a once-in-a-lifetime opportunity into our laps. We have a ranch to run, and an older couple to guide us, and a log manor all of our own. It staggers the imagination, but it's really happening."

She could see it in his eyes. Dayo was so overcome; he didn't want to jinx the outcome. But if they didn't acknowledge such an amazing blessing, it would be wrong. Desi was on a rampage.

"Cobb hired you as the ranch manager, and when it comes to horse competitions, he agreed to give us seventy-five percent."

Desi raised a pretty finger, "And after we win a few events, it will boost the colt sales. Not only do we make money from the prize winnings, but we get a sales commission."

"We can sell our homes, make a living, and build a new life. Antonio destroyed my California job, but don't you see, this could be even better."

The commander loved her enthusiasm. He cupped her cheek, "Babe, you're on fire, and I'd like to know what changed?"

She peered at him, "Maybe a night of relentless tupping blew out the circuits. But most of all, I chose to be in love."

"This may be a glowing moment of clarity, but buddy, we got this!"

Dayo felt confident and the intimidating future no longer seemed so daunting. He had a beautiful woman, and she believed in him.

Desiree continued, "The men count on you. They're here to take out Antonio. And I have no illusions about that, but they're also searching for their own calling."

"And we can help them make a living and find a career that works. You're their commander, and they look up to you."

He smacked her sweet ass, "Babe, when did you get so smart?"

"Oh, the incredible sex, the fulfilling vows, and Hallie's motherly ways are part of it. Finally, something broke free."

"This damn PTSD thing made me feel like a victim and a neurotic casualty. But no more!" Desi chopped the air with her hand, and it was final.

"I owe you a huge apology. Molly is my therapy dog and my nightmares have ceased. And, I can't tell you how freeing that is."

"Now, I'm able to live life on my own terms." She lifted her koala cuff, "Kay Bear loves the new me."

Dayo booped her nose, "K-Man isn't the only one. I've found an amazing woman, and I'm glad to have you by my side. Listening to your plans makes me feel as though we can do anything."

"Hey look, I'm not giving the orders, you're the mighty commander and you're in charge. I've got it easy, but you have a lot on your plate."

"You have the hard part, and all I want to do, is cover your fine ass, and support you in every way I can."

He looked at her curiously, "Really? Don't you secretly want to be in charge?"

"Good lord, no! My role is to point you in the right direction and support you. I'm your Girl Friday, and I'm your right-hand combat girl."

"I'm your warrior chick. So, tell me what to do, and I'll do it."

She grinned mischievously, "But you have the important part. You'll coordinate the op; you'll get with Pettigrew and make it happen."

"I have the easy part. I just follow your lead, fill in the gaps, and make your dreams come true."

Desiree seemed to be enjoying herself. She raised a delicate finger,

"While you're overseeing the horse ranch, I'll get the log cottage ready and make this into a real home."

Since they were being gut-level honest, he had to bring the inside out. "I've been a fearless Marine, but I'm wondering if I'm up to this?"

Desiree surprised him once again. She seized his shoulders, "Oh, you are so freakin' ready, I don't know where to begin."

"You're a born leader, a decision maker, and a strategical planner. Captain Cazador, there's nothing you can't do."

During the entire Middle East campaign, he had the support of his unit. But no one had ever believed in him the way Desi did.

It gave him a new sense of pride, and even greater resolve. This was the second phase of his life, and he may have found his calling.

It was a package deal, but they were in full agreement. All he had to do was treat this as a military op, study the obstacles, lay a plan, and freakin' execute.

After he broke it down, the prospect of marriage, raising a family, and jumpstarting a ranching career didn't seem so overwhelming.

He always planned to get married, and one day, he planned to have children. But with Desiree's brick house figure, and fertile ways, it could happen faster than he imagined.

But now that their fears had been brought to light, it seemed workable. And to make it easier, he had a good woman at his side. The combat pilot was one gutsy cowgirl, and she was all in.

All he had to do was choose this life, embrace it, and own it.

Ever since he returned from the war, he'd been searching for something to fight for and something to believe in. And Desiree was the answer. He would fight for her, and forge a future, and win her heart.

He kissed his woman full on the mouth, "Babe, we have a phenomenal opportunity. And I choose to go after it, and to fully embrace it, and make it into a reality."

Desiree wiggled closer and crushed her globes into his chest, "Dayo, I know it sounds dreamy and school-girlish, but you've always been my hero. And now, more than ever, I feel honored to be your wifey bear."

Declan cocked a cavalier smile, "If you're my wifey bear, I guess that makes me you're hubby bear."

"You bet it does, bucko."

She plowed into his mouth and delivered a tongue-tangling, deepthroat kiss. His woman lived to show him love. And good lord, he had hit the jackpot. Their journey wasn't over by a long shot, but it sure was one helluva beginning.

Desiree curled her lips, "Just because we're married, it's not a done deal. We've got to go after it and make it happen."

"You better believe it, and you're the fire in my heart, and the wind in my sails. Darlin', we're going to make this happen, and you can bet your bottom dollar."

Chapter Fourteen

Trick Johnson rounded the corner. He gazed at the timber porch with a piercing stare.

"I thought you guys needed some time. Cobb said he made you one helluva an offer, and you guys needed to sort out the details."

They finished kissing, and Desiree slid from his lap. The commander left the world of future dreams and settled back into the unforgiving moment.

Trick wore an open-chested shirt and three-days of stubble. Unlike the Middle East, Trick grew a neck-trailing mullet, and it looked good. Not many men could pull it off.

His second-in-command pushed up on his cowboy hat. "The unit is staged around front. We're ready to brand calves."

Declan asked, "Before the team landed the hawk, did you guys perform a surveillance check?"

Desiree touched Dayo's muscular biceps, "Babe, I'm going to change, and don't expect anything sexy. We'll be branding dogies, and kickin' up dust, and gettin' dirty."

He kissed her tenderly, "Doesn't bother me one bit, I can spot that amazing ass five miles away. And I never get tired of your hourglass. It always brightens my day."

Declan swatted her sweet derrière as Desiree trotted to the door jamb.

Trick eyed the two of them, and he seemed unclear about something. "Cobb tells me that he saw a news flash, and he knows that Desiree was reported dead."

"He knows you leveled the safe house and made a run for it. He also knows that we're a Marine unit. But what confuses me is that he thinks you two are really married."

Simultaneously, Desi and Dayo held up their ring fingers.

The commander stated in no uncertain terms, "When we exchanged our vows, it became real. And you can tell the team, we're not playing house, we're a real couple. And this sweet thing is my wifey bear."

Desiree paused long enough to hear his confession. She was as pleased as punch.

She pointed a cute finger, "And that stud over there is my hubby bear. And when he growls, I tup him good. And he loves the way I ride cowgirl. He thinks I'm sensational."

Dayo curled his lips into a Caribbean grin. "Tis true, tis true."

Trick wagged his head, "Up to this moment, I had my doubts. But you two are definitely married. You finish each other's sentences, and leer at each other with puppy dog happiness."

"On the one hand, I'm glad for you, but on the other hand, I'm envious, and it makes me sick."

Desi called from the kitchen, "Trick, we'll try to keep our puppy love to a minimum."

"Thanks, lieutenant. The unit wants more combat girl, and less wifey bear."

She giggled and ran into the bedroom.

Declan grabbed his things and leaped over the bench rail. He landed on the ground. "So, back to the recon subject, where do things stand?"

"Our pilot, Vance Killian, flew the hawk around the ridge. We deployed trigger sensors and motion-activated drones."

"If any hostile steps foot in the valley, we'll have live camera, and the sucker may get nailed with poison darts."

Trick continued, "We went to the airdrop coordinates. The team discovered your night camos, and the broken crates. We destroyed the evidence and hid the cache deep in the forest."

"I appreciate that. Let's go meet the team." He said it with enthusiasm, but a lot had changed. He still wanted to assist them, and get them integrated, but with Desiree at his side, things were going to be a whole lot different.

When Declan reached the front deck, dappled light played over the porch. The foreman's house had been transformed, and now it was home sweet home.

Desiree skipped out the front door wearing a pink riding bra, a tummy tie blouse, and an ass-hugging pair of Wranglers.

She parked a chocolate Stetson over her ringlets and stopped at the pine railing.

"Declan, are you going to introduce me to everyone? I know Trick and Whip; we met them the other day. But who are those two?"

He nodded toward the Big Man. "The powerlifter wearing a white tee and flaunting his muscular physique is Heavy Duty. His real name is Lawrence Reynolds, but no one calls him that."

"He's from Kansas, and he specializes in artillery and steer wrestling. And the sassy girl next to him is Lieutenant Tanya Williams."

"You may remember her from the requisition department. She used her street smarts to make deals and get whatever the unit needed."

Tanya allowed her auburn ringlets to fall. She was a light bronze beauty who didn't allow anyone to give her crap.

Desiree said, "I didn't recognize you with the leather vest and the cowgirl chic."

"That's me, and I'm all attitude. Like Heavy Duty, I'm from Kansas City, and I'm familiar with cattle driving and working a ranch."

"Never thought I'd be back in the saddle, but the Big Man and I make quite a team." They fist bumped with flickering fingers and an explosion.

Desi giggled, "So, are you two a couple?"

Lawrence rolled his steely blue eyes and adjusted his sailing Stetson.

"Back in Afghanistan, we were friends with benefits. But this new op has put a kibosh on our affair. It just so happens that Wild Man has a crush on Tanya, and to make this Gonzalez hit work, we've got to play it cool."

Tanya leered beneath her auburn curls. "That's right. You can look, but you can't touch." She laughed softly. "Sorry, HD, I'd love to roll in the hay, but it's just not in the cards."

Heavy Duty did a rollout and turned toward the bunkhouse. "Are we gonna brand cattle or not?"

Desi whispered into Dayo's ear, "We gotta fix those two."

"The real fix is to reduce Eugene's geek behavior and normalize the guy, so Tanya can fall in love."

"Oooh, boy, that sounds like a huge order."

"Tell me about it."

"But HD is right. I want Wild Man to stay on point, and as long as Gonzalez is out there, Eugene needs to be hitting on all cylinders."

The commander turned to Desiree and spoke under his breath. "I just realized we have to help them find their callings, and find their sweethearts."

He laughed, "This ranching op has become a lot more complicated."

Desi reined Hunter, and she was lovin' it. She batted her long lashes, "Just leave it to me and Hallie. We'll find cowgirls for these guys, and they'll be so happy, they'll be walking on air."

He fist bumped his lady, and they did a finger explosion and they both grinned like teenagers. "Darlin', matchmaking isn't my forte, so I'm willing to accept all the help I can get."

Declan and Desiree rode beside his team. He lined out the men and gave orders for various revenue streams. The Marines were excited, and the opportunity to ride expensive horses was exhilarating.

The entourage rode through the horse pastures, and finally they arrived at the branding pen.

Cobb, David T., and Eugene fired up the electric irons. There were lead wires running from a generator to the center of the pen. The usage of burning coal and red-hot irons had given way to the future.

Hallie May pulled up in a horse drawn chuckwagon. The prayer warrior must have gotten up around three o'clock in the morning. She wore a purple pioneer dress and tall cowgirl boots.

Mrs. Pettigrew set up a fire pit with triangular holders, S hooks, and black Dutch ovens. Even from a distance, Desi could smell the Texas chili, the cornbread, and the cowboy baked beans.

Desi rode over to Hallie's chuckwagon. The lady chef opened the cupboard doors and lowered a drop-table. There were long stirring spoons and tongs for moving kettles.

Hallie turned around, "Lands alive, girl. I've been praying for you all morning."

Desiree blushed, "It must have worked. Cobb offered Dayo a foreman job. And later, Declan and I had a heart to heart."

"Ohhh, what did you young folks talk about?"

Desi flipped her glistening ringlets. It was like meeting her mother, except a hundred times better. So, the bronze beauty gathered her thoughts and tried to condense it all.

"Well, it all boils down to two things. Number one, I had to get behind Dayo and motivate him. He's a freakin' Marine, and the guy can do anything."

"But when it comes to marriage and raising a family, those are entirely new areas. But ever since I started lovin' him hard, and riding him with fury, something has changed."

Hallie's birdwing lips took flight, and she grinned with motherly anticipation. Of course, the pioneer chef never stopped moving, and whatever Hallie did, Desiree grabbed a spoon, and jumped right in.

The two women worked seamlessly, and Mrs. Pettigrew was truly her long lost mother. Desi stirred the beans and added a few jalapenos. Folks out West love spicy, hot chili.

Desiree replaced the black iron lid, "So much has been happening, we haven't had time to catch our breath. I told him we had to be honest."

"And it was time to stop playing house and become a real husband and wife. From now on, I'm his wifey bear, and he's my hubby."

Hallie carried a Dutch oven and attached it to an S hook.

She chuckled, "Cobb and I were wondering if you two were really married. From the moment, I saw you, I knew you were meant for one another."

"But you folks had to realize it yourself. And it appears, the good lord pushed you two together."

Dayo rode over to the chuckwagon and tipped his hat. "Hallie, I want to thank you for taking my girl under your wing. She amazed me with her clear-headed thinking, and a vision of what this ranch could be."

"It's about time you two pulled together. I suppose you want to take my assistant, and do some cattle branding?"

"Yes, ma'am, I do. We're a pair of team ropers, and inside the pen, Desi has the right stuff."

He turned to his lovely cowgirl, "Desiree, my luv, could you mount Hunter and meet me in the paddock?"

It didn't take much to convince her. She loved working with Dayo, and together, they were pretty amazing.

Cobb opened the gate, and his men culled out the calves. The older steers already had brands, but the "calvies" were unmarked. And no matter how well you mended the fence, there was always a runaway.

The Old Man stretched out the lead wires. He turned to Wild Man, "Son, I'm glad you decided to dress like a normal cowboy."

"That Roy Rogers outfit was colorful, but it made you look like a greenhorn."

Eugene flashed a bright white smile, "Mr. Pettigrew, I'm vertically challenged. A short guy has to do something to get noticed."

Cobb stroked his peppered beard, "Son, that's a lot of horseshit. You're wearing work clothes, a cattleman's hat, and boots. You look like a regular cowboy, and girls respect that."

Just then Tanya rode over to the branding area. She touched her fluffy auburn curls, "Eugene, you're looking mighty good. If you dressed normal all the time, I'd be interested in dating."

"Awww, come on, you're just pullin' my chain."

"No, I'm not. When you carry that mega-geek thing too far, it's embarrassing. But when you act casual and you're yourself, this is the man I'd like to go out with."

Cobb reassured him, "Son, I think she's shooting straight. And if you have all those investments, then I suggest you just act naturally, and the girl will come a-runnin.'"

"All right, but if she ignores me, it's all your fault."

Wild Man stroked his circle beard. The guy was damn good looking with his blue eyes. If he'd only relax, maybe he could hit it off with Tanya. And it would be better for the whole unit.

The Commander made the announcement, "All right, we're ready to go into action. There will be three teams of ropers: Heavy Duty and Tanya, Trip and Whip, and Desiree and me."

"When you mobilize your steer in one spot. The tie down man will follow the rope, heft the little calvie to the ground, and wrap the hooves."

"Signal for Eugene to brand the calves' flanks. Afterward, make sure you lead the calf into the holding pen. We've got about twenty-one calves to brand, and that makes seven a piece."

Dayo clapped his hands, "Let's get after it!" Desiree enjoyed watching him shout orders.

She teased, "Can we catch the horns using underhand, sidearm, and loop tosses?"

He wagged his head, "Sweetcheeks, there's always one comedian in every group. I just didn't think it would be you. But you can catch the horns any way you want."

Dayo and Desiree trotted to the far side of the branding pen and culled out seven calves. The Hereford youngsters were feeling stressed out, and they didn't like being separated.

Desi practiced her light rein, and Hunter shot into action. The bay stud brought a white face youngster into the open, and his girl rifled a headshot, right around the horns.

The Big Cat faded left, but it didn't take much to whip the little guy's hindquarters. Shepherd was there in a flash, and Dayo timed the little hips, and rifled a laser throw beneath the hooves.

He dallied up, and they isolated the youngster. With loving care, the Commander dismounted and followed the lead line. He seized the little guy, hefted him into the air, and gently laid the calf to the ground.

He whirled his glove, "Cobb, we've got one ready."

Desiree patted Hunter, "I hope you don't mind, but I'm going to dismount. I want to make sure the calvie doesn't freak out."

Declan straddled the little Hereford and pinned him to the ground. His eyes went wild, but Desi cradled his face.

"Don't worry, little buddy. You'll get your butt branded, and it will be back to momma."

The creature seemed to understand, but things weren't happening fast enough. Suddenly, Wild Man stood over the calf.

His hands were trembling. Dayo pointed to the flanks and guided Eugene's hands. "Wild Man, you got this!"

Eugene applied the Pettigrew brand, and David T. timed it. "That's it, you're done!"

The cowboy hacker called out, "That was easy. Let's go brand another one."

Trick and Whip were in another corner. "Hey, Wild Man, get your cowboy butt over here. We've got an ornery little guy, and he's anxious to get away."

Dayo raised the calf to his feet, and he undid the heeler rope. Desi kept the noose in place and trotted him into the holding pen.

The moment he was back with the cow calf units, the calf bawled. His momma came a runnin' and their little family was restored.

The commander mounted Shepherd, and they rounded up six more calves. He and Desi made an awesome team.

When he surveyed the branding pen, his unit behaved like a well-oiled machine. There was constant movement, and if you didn't know better, you'd swear they were cattlemen, and not headhunters.

Two hours later, every calf was branded, and Eugene and David T. got a workout. But the cowboy hacker loved every minute.

For the first time, he got to do real men's work. Not that running a command center was easy, but it wasn't physically demanding, that's for damn sure.

Dayo and Desiree rode over to the grandstand. Cobb stood against the pipe rails and watched the branding with a keen interest.

He called out, "Dayo, you guys are amazing. I've seen seasoned cattlemen, who weren't half as efficient. Your cowboys know how to work together, how to coordinate, and anticipate a calf's every movement."

"There was nothing but non-stop movement and not a drop of confusion. Hell, your unit puts most branding parties to shame."

Dayo flashed his Caribbean smile. "Pettigrew, we may be new at ranchin' together, but we've been taking down hostile leaders for six years. We know how to read one another, and there's almost a telepathic way of communicating."

Pettigrew stroked his circle beard, "Ya know, I'm not much for rodeo, but we've got to raise money somehow."

And when we hit Pendleton, there are some Western riding events nearby. I want to hold off on the RCH stuff, but your men could enter ranch sorting and team penning.

One event requires two men, and I think Trick and Whip make a fluid team. And for team penning, Heavy Duty could join them. And I know you guys would win. It's all a matter of scheduling, and getting our entries in.

Desiree felt like she was part of the unit. These men were Dayo's comrades, and he'd do anything for them.

She flashed a radiant smile, "I bet Eugene can figure it out. Between your personal contacts, and his hacking skills, we can enter any event you want."

Cobb eyed them with gratitude. "I'm full of years, and I haven't had this much manpower in a long time. Just watching your men in action, sort of chokes me up."

Dayo clapped him on the shoulder, "You've got the unit for the whole summer. And there's a good chance, these men could find their calling, and make your ranch their home."

Trick and Whip can win rodeo contests, auction colts, and conduct a roping clinic. As for Tanya and HD, they can wrestle steers, manage obstacle courses, and teach antiquated riflery. Folks will come from all around."

Pettigrew choked up, and Cobb patted Declan's arm. "Can't say I'm interested in all those things. But I've got the acreage, and you're free to do anything you want."

He drawled, "Of course, the horse pastures and the alfalfa fields have to stay as they are."

Desiree clapped her hands, "This is fantastic. It's all coming together. And Mr. Pettigrew, you won't be sorry."

"Oh, I trust you. But seeing visitors climb walls, and swing over water features, isn't a common sight. Not to mention the fact, that no one in their right mind uses Civil War rifles."

By that time, his unit settled the horses around a feed trough.

Desi giggled, "While we've been laying plans, it looks like everyone is getting ready for a chuckwagon dinner."

Heavy Duty strolled by with a loaded plate. "Yee haw! Ya better get over to the barbecue pit, before I eat it all up."

She looked around, "Where's Tanya?"

"She did the team ropin' with me, but the girl has gone AWOL. She has this thing for short guys with blue eyes, and she's over there, flirtin' with Eugene."

"Oh, aren't they sweet?"

"It's nauseating if you ask me."

"Do you have a crush on Tanya?"

"Like I said before, we're friends with benefits. But if you line up a fitness girl with a chocolate complexion, then I'm all in."

Desiree had to admire them. They served their country and went after cattle branding with a rare talent. But underneath it all, the headhunters were good men who wanted to settle down.

Desi realized this was her new home. And she was willing to fight for it and do everything she could. And at the center of it all was an amazing Commander: Declan Cazador.

Good lord, she loved that man.

Chapter Fifteen

Hallie ladled the Texas chili into bowls and filled their plates. She broke into a birdwing smile, "I'm so glad you folks are here. We haven't had a branding party in a long while."

"And it feels like old times, to have so many strapping young men working the ranch."

Desiree used her spoon to make an air jab, "And don't forget the pretty cowgirls. Tanya and I are holding are own, and we're gonna show these military studs how to drive cattle."

Tanya perked up, "You tell him, girl. We'll organize this drive and take 'em to high pasture."

Mrs. Pettigrew held her husband's arm, "Isn't this wonderful? We have the manpower to fix up the ranch, and I don't want to hear anything about selling."

Cobb patted her arm, "My dear, this military unit changes everything. And believe me, I want one more shot at glory."

"You just keep prayin', my dear, and I can check off my bucket list."

"Oh, there ya go, Cobb. You're not going up yonder, and we have a lot of work to do. And besides, Desiree hasn't had a child yet."

Everyone's ears perked up. Trick's ears didn't miss a thing. He leveled his piercing eyes, "Is Desiree on the nest? Does your combat girl have a muffin in the oven?"

Desi blushed at the attention, and she turned a rosy shade of bronze.

She stood up, "Everyone, I want you to know I'm not pregnant. At least, I don't think so. But Dayo and I are taking our time, enjoying our honeymoon. But pretty soon, we're gonna get serious."

Her Belgian Malinois chewed a cattle bone, but suddenly perked up. Molly trotted next to her and placed a paw to her leg.

"What's up, girl? I'm doing fine. You just enjoy your doggie bone, and we'll start the cattle drive in a little while."

The unit burst into applause. Wild Man yelled out, "With a brick house figure like yours, it's gotta happen." Eugene turned to Declan, "Make us proud, Cap'n, and give this woman a wee babe."

Dayo glowed with male pride, and the idea of a newborn didn't seem half bad.

Declan walked over to Hallie May and kissed her cheek. "Mrs. Pettigrew, I want to thank you for the fine meal."

She said, "Don't think anything of it, Dayo. Your men are like family. They're respectful and so darn polite, it's been a pleasure cooking for them."

"And if y'all would like to give me a hug, and say thank you, Cobb and I will head over to the grandstands."

The men rose from the fire ring, and one after another, they gave Hallie a kiss. Declan was proud of his men, and the way they conducted themselves.

And Mrs. Pettigrew was right, they were like one great big family. This wasn't his doing, there was a higher power at work, and he felt so darn thankful.

Hallie May, Cobb, and David T. carried their plates over to the bleachers. The headhunters and the girls were gathered around a fire ring.

It was just like a cowboy round-up. Suddenly, a silence fell over the team. They enjoyed the cattle driving, but there was an elephant in the room. They had to talk about Antonio Gonzalez, and there was no getting around it.

Declan surveyed the grandstands to make sure the Pettigrews were out of range. His men carried their chairs closer to the fire and prepared for the report.

Dayo kicked it off, "As you know, we're all here because Desiree witnessed the murder of an innocent man." He squeezed her hand, "My sweetheart wanted to do the right thing, and testify against Antonio Gonzalez."

"Director Sanchez set her up in an East L.A. safe house. The night before she was relocated, there were bets as to whether she would make it through the night."

"When the betting line went nuclear, I knew Antonio hired hitmen to murder her. Wild Man and I planned a special op, and I brought enough firepower to detonate a city block."

Heavy Duty stroked his auburn beard, "Yeah, I saw the photos. You leveled that Spanish Med, blew up five cars, and took down more than twenty hostiles. Shit damn, I wish I had been there!"

Trick raised a hand, "Let's take this step by step. Wild Man, what does your current intel reveal?"

Desiree squeezed his hand so tight, her nails dug in. Molly rose from her dog bone and placed her muzzle in Desi's lap.

"Thanks girl, I'm all right. But I need to hear this, and if it gets too intense, I may have to take a break."

Tanya wrapped an arm around Eugene, "I came on board right after the safe house incident. I've worked hand in hand with Wild Man. So, I know most of the facts. And we'll try to phrase things in the least alarming way."

Desiree was a fighter, but she preferred to fly a combat helo. And hearing life threatening news while she had nothing more than an assault rifle was deeply disturbing.

She lifted her wrist cuff. "What do you say Kay Bear? Are you ready to hear the nitty gritty?"

K-Man beamed his button brown eyes, and she loved the little guy. She announced to everyone, "Kay Bear says we've been through Middle Eastern hell, and nothing can be worse than that."

Whip broke from his party-going smile, "Here, here. I'm in complete agreement, but we gotta hear the facts and take the necessary action."

Around the flaming fire pit, men and women huddled together and sipped their coffee.

Dayo nodded to Wild Man, "Eugene, you've got the floor." Wild Man adjusted his turquoise bolo, which complemented his eye color perfectly.

The bronze hacker began, "So far, I can't tell if the safe house was a set-up, or if Director Sanchez had anything to do with the leak."

"More than likely, the Witness program was filled with informants and the local police had a number of dirty cops."

"After Declan went commando and destroyed the safe house, he eliminated the Gonzalez hit men. But one thing is clear, Sanchez called off his night shift, and Antonio's hostiles stepped in."

Desiree clenched her fists and listened carefully. She felt like such an idiot. The bronze beauty tried to do the honorable thing, and the results were disastrous.

Eugene glanced into Desi's eyes. "There's no evidence that Oberon and Sanchez jointly compromised the safe house, but I intercepted text messages, and they definitely staged the dead bodies."

This was all new. "What do you mean, the dead bodies? Declan and I survived, and unless there was a misidentification, all the bodies were hostile hitmen."

"Actually, Oberon coordinated with the local coroner, and the remains of two unidentified African Americans were placed in the ruins."

"The dentals were fractured, and no ID could be performed. Hence, the Police Chief shared his findings and announced that the key witness was dead."

It was unnerving to say the least. Listening to someone discuss your fictitious death was very disturbing. She had to assert herself, "That's not true. We're both alive, and we're sitting right here."

Declan hauled her into a sideways hug. "You got that right. We're alive and well, and we made it outta there."

Eugene resumed his discourse, "But we do know that Sanchez and

Oberon collaborated in the cover up. And it appears the Chief wanted Gonzalez off his back."

Dayo knew some of the details already.

Trick narrowed his penetrating eyes, "So, where is Gonzalez right now?"

"He's out on bail and moving freely. He has resumed his criminal activities. But he isn't one hundred percent convinced of DeNiro's death. Bounty hunters were hired, and there was a sizeable reward posted."

Heavy Duty flexed his arms. "We eliminated hostiles up and down the Sierras and tracked them along the coastline. By my count, no word got back to Antonio. Does the kingpin know who terminated his bounty hunters?"

Eugene adjusted his bolo, "I've hacked his command center, and there's no evidence that anyone sent back a positive ID. From Antonio's perspective, he's living in radio silence with zero intel."

"I deduced from a Mexican phone call that competing bounty hunters eliminated one another. Our Marine unit remains in the clear."

Desiree breathed a sigh of relief. "What about Vance Killian and the armed black hawk? Where did you get that helo?"

Tanya coiffed her fluffy auburn curls. "Sweetheart, you don't really want to know. Let's just say deals were made, gifts were exchanged, and all fingerprints were scrubbed from the hawk."

Out of sheer nervousness, she giggled. "So, a black hawk disappears, and someone rolls back the odometer, wipes the prints, and re-arms the weaponry. And presto, the Sikorsky UH-60 is back on the tarmac."

Eugene cracked a smile, "That's it in a nutshell. Vance Killian is back at the Lewis-McChord AFB, conducting business as usual."

Declan sensed the worst part was about to be revealed. He pulled Desiree into his lap.

She eyed him curiously, "What are you doing? You're not normally this affectionate unless you want it."

He chucked her chin softly, "You're not going to like this next part, babe. But I'm here for you."

Eugene took his cue, "Chief Oberon acted quickly, and the

Cazadors and DeNiros were contacted, and quick funerals were conducted last Friday."

Desire leaped out of his lap, "What the eff? My parents think I'm dead, and they wept at my funeral, and they're probably heart broken."

Molly was right at her side. Her pupper stepped to her thigh and stared directly into her face. The canine gesture caused her to evaluate herself.

She wasn't having a post-traumatic episode, she wanted to take action. "I've got to get a chopper and fly to my parent's ranch."

"We can speak with the Pine Whisper LifeNet people, and we can borrow their helo. We'll tell mom and dad, I'm okay, and then we'll go back into hiding."

Molly sensed a flurry of emotions, but the Malinois' only focus was Desi. Molls barked two times and gave her a thorough face licking.

The bronze beauty rubbed Molly's fawn-colored shoulders, "Thanks girl, but I'm still here."

Heavy Duty chimed in, "That's exactly what Gonzalez wants you to do. He's not sure if you're dead, but he agreed to a quick funeral to flush you out."

Trick flipped his mullet, "We searched the cemetery for Antonio, and he was a no show. But we spotted three of his men. The DeNiros and the Cazadors grieved, and their mourning was heartfelt and convincing."

Tanya confirmed the findings, "Desi, honey, Gonzalez is watching your parent's ranch. He's keeping at a distance and waiting for you to make contact. It's a trap, sure as hell."

Desiree paced back and forth. "Where does that leave the trial date?"

Eugene lowered his voice, "Antonio's attorneys have moved to dismiss the case. A hearing is scheduled in a few weeks. Since the key witness has been reported as dead, there's no case against Gonzalez."

"What do you mean no case? I've got to keep that court date. Gonzalez murdered an innocent man, and justice must prevail."

"He must go to jail and pay for his wrongdoing. This is a free country, and you can't go around killing good people."

Declan hauled her into a big hug. It felt good to get crushed beneath all that muscle. But she was getting madder than hell.

She searched his eyes, but it was unclear what course of action he believed in.

He released her, "Sweetheart, maybe you should hear what the unit has to say. You can hear several options, and we'll select the best path."

"What did you say? There's only one appropriate legal remedy."

Heavy Duty stretched his muscular arms. "I sympathize with your feelings, but the cover up may be a blessing. Let's think this thing through."

"If we fly a chopper to the courthouse, suddenly, you'll rise from the dead. Your testimony will convict Gonzalez, and he'll go to jail. But do you think that's the end of it?"

She pleaded with them, "Tinder Williams' family would see justice. His lost life would be vindicated."

Trick played out the scene, "If you testify, and Antonio goes to jail. He'll call the shots from prison. You'll be a marked woman, and since we flew to the courthouse, our cover will be blown. Your good intentions will jeopardize all of our lives."

Desiree felt like she was trapped. She circled around the campfire looking for a viable solution. Molly was at her side, and the Malinois heeled in perfect step.

Whip felt bad for her. He knew exactly what had to be done, and she was slowly coming to the same conclusion.

Trick just came out and said it, "It's easier to take Gonzalez down, and Wild Man can liquidate his assets."

"The loss of Tinder's life will be compensated, and funds will be sent to the Williams' family."

"Sadly, nothing can be done to redeem the man's life, but frontier justice can be served."

Tanya jumped in, "Honey, don't you see?"

"In the end, it's the same result. And these Marines are trained headhunters, and this is what they do. You can take down Antonio, avenge Tinder's death, and set yourself free."

Desiree lowered her pretty brows, "Will that really work?"

Trick continued the logistics. "If we take down the kingpin in a swift military op, and clean our tracks, there will be a void in the cartel."

"There's a chance for retaliation. But if we execute the op perfectly, the new kingpin won't even know who we are. And after Gonzalez is eliminated, your life can go back to normal."

Those were the words she wanted to hear. After debating the logistics, there seemed to be one course of action. During the entire discussion, her man didn't say a thing.

But obviously, Dayo wanted her to hear it from his men.

She turned to Declan, "Commander, what do you think we should do?"

"Babe, I'm the leader of a professional strike force and surgical ops are what we do. Gonzalez is no different than any other hostile leader."

"I agree with Trick's plan. If there's the slightest sign of an armed assault against you or your family, we'll eliminate Antonio. It's that simple."

Declan held her shoulders, "Sweetheart, you mean more to me than a flawed legal system. Gonzalez is going down."

She winced at his conclusion, and Dayo said, "There's a good side to all of this."

"Huh? What are you talking about."

"When we plan the mission, you get to fly an Apache Longbow and blow his Malibu mansion to kingdom come."

Her vicious idea came full circle, but this time, it was the right thing to do. "Ya know, I like the sound of that. So, what are we waiting for?"

Eugene jumped in, "Antonio's movements are under constant surveillance. However, he moves fluidly between L.A., Mexico, and New York."

"To execute the perfect op, we have to pinpoint his location, and know he'll definitely be there. And my plan is to hit him at his Malibu home, just as you said."

"We've got the blueprints, and it's a classic in-and-out mission. But we can't pull the trigger until we're dead certain."

"All right. Get me a combat helo, and I'm all in."

Molly jumped to her leg and woofed.

"That's right, girl. That bad man is going to experience a horrible death."

She giggled, "With cluster bombs and Hellfire missiles, I'll vaporize him, and he won't feel a freakin' thing."

David T. trotted over to the campfire meeting. He turned to Desiree, "Mrs. Corazon, Cobb just got a call from the Flight for Life team."

"There is an elderly heart attack victim at the hospital. And the operation calls for a special procedure, but the nearest surgeons are in Sacramento. Can you fly the helo?"

Finally, there was a tangible problem, and she could take action. She turned to the men, "Do you guys mind if I take this helo mission? I'll miss the cattle drive, but you can tell me all about it."

Trick assumed his command, "Get outta here, girl! You're already stressed out, but from what Dayo tells me, flying medevacs calms your nerves."

Desiree turned to the Marines, "I'm sorry, but I'll catch the next cattle drive. In the fall, we can bring 'em all back."

Heavy Duty pointed a trigger finger, "You got it, girl. Go save some lives, and we'll herd the cattle to high ground. We've got this."

Declan stood up, "I'll fly shotgun and assist the medic. I've got first response training, and it may come in handy. Let's take Cobb's twin cab and get the hell outta here."

En route to the twin cab, Hallie met her at the door. "Honey, I knew something like this was bound to happen. I was down on my knees, and I saw you flying a helo."

"But you didn't have your undercover disguise, so I brought your ginger red ringlets, and your peach glow makeup kit."

Desi squished her eyes, "Ohhh, Hallie, you're the best. While Dayo drives into town, I'll get myself together. And I can't tell you how much your prayers mean. You're like my long-lost mother, and my best friend."

Hallie broke into a generous birdwing smile, "I feel the same way, and if you were my daughter, I'd tell you to do the things you love, and magnify the Lord with your talents."

"And flying helos is one of your callings. So, girl, you best get at it."

"Yes, ma'am." Desiree opened the twin cab, and patted the seat, "Hopp!"

Her faithful Malinois leaped into the seat and sat down. Desi locked her belt and lifted her wrist cuff.

"Kay Bear, they need us. It's just like old times, we'll fly a cardiac patient to Sacramento, and we'll be like a bird in flight."

K-Man beamed his brown eyes, and Desi knew what he was thinking. Her koala felt that flying Flight for Life was far more important than a cattle drive. And she couldn't agree more.

Fifteen minutes later, Desiree fired up the Flight for Life helo and airlifted. The chopper hovered above the helipad, tilted slightly, and then she ascended in altitude.

In nothing flat, Pine Whisper appeared like a toy town, and the mountains were reduced to evergreen studded hills.

She already went through the triple checks, and Molly was strapped in, and Declan rode shotgun. Old habits die hard, and she consulted with her good luck charm.

"Kay Bear, do you think this will be a safe mission?"

Her brown button-eyed bear peered at her, and she could have sworn he gave a thumbs up and a pink grin. "That's right, K-Man, we're going to kick butt."

The LifeNet helo sailed over the Cascades as they left the town's airspace. She decided to fly over the Pettigrew Ranch to see the cattle drive.

There they were. Several hundred Herefords cruised down a green embankment and trotted through a mountain stream.

She could see Whip and Trick herding the adults through the knee-deep water. Just as she was about to accelerate to a higher altitude, she spotted Heavy Duty and Tanya herding the cow calf units.

Desiree cooed, "Ohhh, look how cute they are! All those little calves are sticking to their mommas. And the little guys are chest deep, but the stream looks calm, and they're gonna make it."

Declan squeezed her knee, "Honey, you're a softie when it comes to little creatures."

Dayo peered from beneath his visor. "I'm glad we swung by the ranch to watch the cattle drive. From the rearview, I can see the yearlings have reached high pasture. We weren't there, but in a way we were."

Desi whimpered, "It's hard to do everything. I wanted to see the white face hit the high pasture. But like you said, we were able to see them in the mirror."

"The uplands are so lush and green; they can graze to their heart's content. And it won't be long until the little ones have a new home."

The LifeNet pilot turned her attention back to her mission. She accelerated to maximum speed, and the Sikorsky helo hit one-hundred-sixty miles an hour.

She spoke into the communicator, "Damian, I've cleared the flight pattern with the tower, and we'll arrive in fifty-five minutes." Desiree wanted to make sure their blond-haired medic knew the ETA.

Damian responded, "Good going, Desiree. It's a smooth ride back here, and Gladys is taking a nap."

"Roger that. I'll let you know when we see the Sacramento hospital."

Declan flipped his visor and pointed. "You can see Mt. Shasta on the horizon. The twin peaked volcano never fails to amaze me. Even in summer, it's capped with snow."

Desiree felt their mission was well under way, and they could afford to talk. Her stud Marine allowed her to settle in, and there had been little dialogue.

She felt alert and relaxed. "The Pacific Northwest has a fair amount of volcanic activity. Most of them aren't active, but Shasta, Helens, and especially Yellowstone are rife with geothermal activity."

It felt good to talk about something other than rodeos and military strategies.

The moment her helo airlifted; they broke away from the earth's gravitational pull. She was a bird in flight, and the worries of earthborn reality fell away.

Her problems became small and insignificant, and that was a huge reason she loved flying. As she gazed out the slanted window, she remembered Crater Lake.

She spoke into her communicator. "Dayo, have you ever been to Wizard Island?"

"No, I haven't, but that's a good example of an ancient volcano that blew its cone to bits. There's nothing left but a scenic caldera and a giant crater. It's filled with the bluest water you've ever seen."

She agreed, "The photos are incredible, and when things settle down, I'd like to go there again."

Her family went there for vacation once, and she rode a tiny speedboat across the bluest lake in the world. They arrived at Wizard Island, and it was like they were pioneers making landfall. It was a good memory, and one she should treasure.

Too bad her parents thought she died in a gunbattle. But Desi had to remain positive; Dayo promised to make contact when things were settled.

An hour flew by in nothing flat. She spotted the Sacramento skyline and punched in the coordinates for her destination.

They skirted downtown, and finally, she spotted the hospital. A three-story brick building came into view, and there was a white porte cochère attached.

She wasn't the only one making an emergency run. She saw yellow ambulances shoot beneath the carport. Desiree made radio contact and whirled around the backside. The aqua colored helipad was within sight.

There was a strong breeze, and she pointed into the wind, and made a smooth landing. The runners alighted softly upon the ground, and she was happy that Gladys experienced a gentle flight.

Desiree cut the engine and allowed the rotators to slow down. When Dayo threw open the bulkhead door, she watched medic Damian make his preparations.

Damian called through the portal, "The ER medics are here, so we need to open the clamshell."

She released the doors, and the bifold opened with ease. Gladys was lowered to the ground, and fortunately, the Stryker gurney was highly versatile. It could be ushered directly into the operating room.

The Lieutenant walked to the side of the stretcher. "Mrs. Alderfer, we'll be praying for you. And I know you're going to pull through. You'll get your heart fixed, and you'll be stronger than ever."

The old woman smiled beneath her mask and gave a weak thumb's up. Desi loved this line of work; she was part of something big. And saving lives gave her purpose, and a strong sense of definition.

Back in L.A., she clung to her job, and it was the only thing that made sense. But up in the Cascades, her life had become multi-dimensional.

There was ranching, rodeo, and making love. She was one lucky girl, and Southern California didn't hold a candle to her new life.

The Commander returned to the helo and closed the clamshell. Declan eyed his lady and slipped a hand to her back.

"Luv, you've been eyeing that mechanic's hangar, and I believe it's a good idea to duck inside."

Desi placed a hand to his chest, "I agree. It's time to face bad memories and realize I'm safe and sound."

He handed her the hunting pack. "The last time you went into a helo hangar, you were under armed and outmanned. But this time, we won't make the same mistake."

Desiree gushed, "Declan, you are one badass Marine, and if you had been there that day, there would have been seven dead hostiles. And Tinder would still be alive."

"Perhaps, but I'm not one to relive history."

"Darlin', you've got a 9 mm on your hip, and an assault rifle over your shoulder, and if any bad shit goes down, were trained headhunters, and we'll go into action."

She sighed, "Flying with you is a quite an experience."

"In fact, we're rewriting history, and I've learned from my mistakes."

Declan hauled her into a sideways hug. "Atta, girl, let's do this."

They crossed the tarmac and entered a two-story hangar with a bay full of helos. Molly walked beside her, and Declan watched her every move.

He couldn't rewrite history, but he could build her esteem. And in a small way, erase what happened that day.

Dayo fell into formation, and even though his weapons weren't drawn, he surveyed the hangar. There were four LifeNet helos parked beneath a white metal ceiling.

He surveyed the state of repair and spotted helicopters with their nose cones popped open. Beside every helo, there were wheeled toolboxes, and portable diagnostic equipment.

"Does this look like the hangar where Antonio Gonzalez gunned down Tinder Williams?"

Desiree surveyed the brightly lit hangar. "The layout is similar, and it does trigger memories."

He eyed the facility, and it was dead quiet. "It's lunchtime, and the mechanics are on break."

"What I want you to do is to unholster your 9 mm and get your M4 into position. As I remember, you hunkered behind a portable toolbox, and listened to the execution."

This time, you won't feel helpless. You'll draw a bead, and take down the guards and that son of a bitch, Gonzalez."

Desiree curled her lips, and she loved this little exercise. "Are you a psych major?"

"No, but this is the perfect opportunity to assert yourself and take control."

His woman confirmed the hangar was empty. Desiree unslung her assault rifle, and crept behind a wheeled toolbox.

She peered behind the red piece of equipment, and waited as though she was having a flashback. Finally, she sprang into action.

The safety was on, but she visualized Gonzalez, and dropped him cold. In a swift move, she gunned down the hostile guards. It was over, and there wasn't a man standing.

Dayo was in her head; she could almost feel it. "Lieutenant, how does Tinder Williams look?"

She turned toward the empty hangar, "My god, I can almost see him. He's happy and full of life, and I saved him. I know it didn't happen that way, but somehow, I've found some closure."

She slipped into the shadows and stored her weapons.

When Desiree emerged, she admitted. "It's funny that I did that little exercise. And coupled with Tinder's death was the same helplessness I felt in Afghanistan."

The Commander dropped to his haunches and stroked Molly's fur. The Malinois wasn't his, but together they were a team. "That's an interesting observation."

She curled her lips, "I feel like punching you. You're a smartass Marine, and you think this is amusing."

"Not in the least, but please explain the comparison."

"Well, it's rather obvious. My recurring nightmare involves the return of an Army Ranger unit. When they disembarked, they were instantly hit by a Stinger missile."

"I watched in absolute horror, and there was nothing I could do. Both situations involved death of innocent men, and my powerlessness to stop it."

Declan raised a bronze finger, "But that's not the case anymore. Today, you're the Captain of your own destiny, and you call the shots, and go after what you want."

"And thank god, you came to your senses, and you came after me."

"You're a smug superhero, Declan. You think the world revolves around your fine ass. And you think flirting will result in a thunder tupping, don't you?"

"Won't it?"

"Oh, absolutely. I may even wear peach glow makeup, but I refuse to wear the ginger ringlets."

"Awww, I thought it was an ensemble."

Desiree slung her pack over her shoulder, "Is there anything else we need to see?"

The Commander used two hands to frame a picture. "If that helo wasn't a Flight for Life chopper, but an Apache Longbow, what is your reaction."

"Is this a game in visual associations?"

"Yeah, sort of. But play along. You're standing in front of a fully armed, combat helo, so what's your first thought?"

"My first thought is how easy it would be come off the California coast and blow the living shit outta Antonio's mansion."

"And not only that, but a Longbow can also fly low, remain undetected, and detonate the target with relative ease. It's not like he has a squadron of Scorpions guarding his fortress."

"That's what I wanted to hear. I don't believe in underestimating a hostile leader, but then again, I don't want to make him into a mega threat either."

"Gonzalez puts his legs in his pants, one leg at a time like the rest of us. He's a man of flesh and blood, and he will go down just as easily."

She trotted over and punched him in the arm. "Captain, you've made your point. So, let's go home." Molly leaped in the air and woofed her agreement.

An hour later, their LifeNet helo flew over Pine Whisper. From the air, the small mountain town appeared tranquil and even picturesque.

Nestled in a lush valley surrounded by mountains, there was a fairytale quality. The return flight was filled with a pleasant euphoria. Desiree put her past to rest, and in a small way, she felt more prepared for life's next big crisis.

"Captain, before we land, do you have any earth-shattering insights?"

He lifted his cool guy shades and flashed his Caribbean smile. "Actually, I've been thinking about the Pettigrew Ranch."

"A penny for your thoughts, you big stud."

"I think I have one thought that's worth a whole dollar."

She arched her S-curved brows, "Pray tell, what is this momentous thought."

"The position of a ranch foreman is a good start. But if we win a few contests, I'd like to consider buying Cobb's ranch."

"As an owner, we could keep Pettigrew on as a consultant, and you and I would provide the energy to really run this place."

"Wow! That is an ambitious goal. Do you think Cobb and Hallie would go for it?"

"I don't know, we haven't discussed it, yet."

"But I'm putting the cart before the horse, and I'm painting the sky a vibrant shade of blue. However, it could work."

"And if his bloodlines are as strong as I think, his breeding program is incredible. We stand to inherit a lifetime of possibilities."

Desiree removed her helmet and shook her ginger ringlets. Her ginger red mane fell to her shoulders, and she threw out her arms.

"You sly Marine, come over here, and give me a kiss. I thought you were a dumbass soldier, but apparently, you're a pretty smart guy."

"Do ya think?"

Declan descended over her mouth, and they kissed for what seemed like an eternity. In one month, her whole life had changed.

She owed it all to an unseen power and one wicked-ass Marine. The man had ideas, and she had to take him home, and reward him properly.

Chapter Sixteen

Two Weeks later.

Declan poured himself a cup of coffee and stood on his pine log porch. A gentle breeze swayed the red maples, and there was a romantic play of light and shadow.

He loved waking up every morning and enjoyed watching the Eastern sunrise. Light shattered above the high mountain ridge and bathed the Pettigrew Ranch in a golden glow.

He surveyed the horse pastures, and there were fewer colts than before. The last two weeks were filled with a victorious Pendleton rodeo, a swift fixer upper, and a successful horse auction.

In addition to the horse sales, they threw a barn dance, and every red-blooded Marine was out to woo a sexy cowgirl.

Dayo was thankful for Hallie's matchmaking skills. During the award ceremony and the post-rodeo round-up, his men were assailed by buckle bunnies, decent ranch girls, and fitness chicks.

Mrs. Pettigrew directed their pent-up hormones and chided his unit against sowing oats. In her delicate words, they were too old to be indulging in wild rodeo sex. It was time to find a good woman.

Naturally, Heavy Duty, Trick, and Whip were disappointed. But when Hallie introduced them to the good girls, they were thoroughly surprised.

A good ranching woman could have brains and a great figure. So, they decided to give Hallie's girls a shot.

Just then, a sixteen-wheeler hauled into the parking lot. *What the eff?*

Lawrence, Whip, and Trick came flying out of the timber-chink bunkhouse. The men rushed to the tractor trailer's backdoors and released the lock handles.

Two delivery men rushed to meet them. A tall guy dressed in a green uniform presented a signature sheet. "Which one of you is Lawrence Reynolds?"

"That's me."

"Your sofa set, new four poster, and love chair go first."

Trick narrowed his eyes, "HD, tell me, you didn't buy a love chair!"

"Hell yes. I want to engage in the Kama Sutra, and what could be better?" Lawrence tugged on his sailing Stetson, "I intend to test out my courtin' cuties and see how well they perform."

Dayo listened to their banter. It was early morning, dew glistened, and the sound carried well. It was like a morning entertainment show.

And the best part was the Commander didn't need to meddle or do a freakin' thing. His men had this. And his role was simply to step back, and let nature take its course.

Personally, a huge burden fell from his shoulders. His Marine unit had finally integrated back into society. They capitalized on their ranching skills and rode the finest Quarter Horses in the Northwest.

They took home rodeo victories in team roping, steer wrestling, and tie down. And they used their winnings wisely.

Trick lined up next, and he received his allotment of new furniture, bedspreads, and dishes. *What the eff?*

His men decided to purchase new kitchenware, plastic containers, and china.

Whip pushed back his Summer Resistol, "Hey, man, I can see new furniture and cowhide rugs. But I don't understand why we're buying new china, cutlery, and kitchen goods."

Trick tucked his mullet into a loose fall, "We aren't animals. These cowgirl hotties won't think much of us if we can't barbecue, and take care of ourselves."

"And nothing says, I know what I'm doing like a new china set and cutting knives."

Whip flashed his party-going smile, "I purchased a new bedroom set, but I went over to Maddie's salon, and outfitted my love parlor with a full set of sex toys."

Heavy Duty carried out a pile of boxes, "Whip, I heard that. And if Hallie catches you, there'll be hell to pay."

"Hey, man, I'm way ahead of you. I bought an armoire to house my stuff. If a sexy cowgirl passes Hallie's qualifications, then I'll take her to my parlor, open the doors, and let the good times roll."

Lawrence scratched his close-cut beard. "Doesn't sound like a half bad idea. Let me know how it works."

Dayo sipped his coffee and watched the movers. His unit carried out the old furniture and loaded up the flatbed.

By the looks of it, there was empty space in the horse barn, and Hallie's old-fashioned furniture was headed for storage.

Just then, a second box truck hauled into the drive.

Desiree skipped over the front porch and called out. "Hey, moving guys. The order for Rae Corazon is over here."

"You can pull into our driveway and start unloading."

Dayo set his coffee cup down, "Honey, what's going on?"

Desi disappeared and carried a breakfast charger to the porch table. "Dayo, here's your breakfast, the newspaper, and a footstool."

"Just eat your breakfast and let me take over."

"About that, darlin'. How come we didn't talk about this delivery?"

She flipped her glistening ringlets, "What's there to talk about? We won four rodeo events, and there was a seventy-five percent take."

"I put most of it into savings, but with the leftovers, I decided to decorate our new home."

Before he could object, she pulled out a chair, and set his boots on the stool. "Honey, you're the Commander-in-Chief, and you don't want to be bothered by such trivial, feminine matters."

Desiree flashed a radiant smile, "So, I took over."

There were so many things wrong with that statement, he didn't know where to begin.

"Desiree, I thought we agreed to discuss any purchase for more than two hundred."

"We did, but don't you remember allocating several thousand to home repairs?"

"Yes, I do remember that part."

She waved her delicate hands, "The guys already applied new sealant to the exterior. And they fastened down the standing seam, so there was no point in dipping into those funds."

She placed a finger to her scrumptious lips, "So, I decided to use the multi-thousand dollar allocation for interior decorating."

Dayo tried to object, but she stuffed a marmalade muffin in his mouth. And just then, a team of movers carried one piece of furniture after another through the double-wide craft door.

Judging by the sofa set, a turquoise coffee table, and cowhide recliners, they were getting a new great room. *What was wrong with the old one?*

Two guys carried ruby satin comforters, oriental rugs, and upholstery covers through the door. *Good lord, she was going crazy.*

Desiree planned to replace their saffron bedspread, and his favorite sex chair with ruby pink. Was nothing sacred?

And if that wasn't bad enough, Molly pranced next to Desi while a mover carried two boxes of teddy bears.

The guy stopped and modeled a koala bear. "Of all the koalas, this is the most realistic marsupial I've ever seen."

The mover congratulated him, "Way to go, dude. You won the Pendleton, and now your woman is starting to nest."

Declan didn't want to hear his psychological assessment, but maybe the guy was right. And if Desiree was nesting, was she pregnant or preparing to conceive?"

The commander finished his breakfast and prepared for a course of action. But for the life of him, he wasn't sure what to do.

Desiree rushed out to the pine log table and poured him a glass of orange juice. "Isn't this wonderful? I can finally add the feminine touches I've wanted."

Dayo cocked his head, "I thought Hallie's décor was rather pleasant."

Desi spread her hands, "Don't you know anything about women? Mrs. Pettigrew created a charming log home, but it wasn't me."

"Every woman wants her home to reflect her tastes, her personality, and her loved ones. Don't you see?"

He volunteered, "Maybe I should come inside and help you make a few decisions."

Desiree carried his hunting pack to the porch. Her faithful Malinois trotted alongside, and the girls were in complete agreement.

They were on a mission, and it didn't require feedback. Desi tossed the hunting pack into his lap.

"Your weaponry is inside, and I think you should visit the firing range, and relieve some stress. It always makes you calmer after you've shot something."

Before he could stop her, Desi, Molly, and the mover rushed through the door. This time, the man carried a box of photo frames.

Right then, Wild Man trotted up the pine treads. "Hey, boss, your woman ordered these prints, and I've got them developed."

Eugene paused, "Which way is the great room?"

"Here, I'll take you in the general direction." He tried to squeeze through, but Desiree stopped him cold.

"Dayo, you can't come in. I'm decorating the house, and Eugene is going to help with the photo wall. Now, I want it to be a big surprise, so I'd like you to go away."

"If that's the way you feel, I'm outta here. And don't think I'll be coming back. The firing range sounds great to me."

"It's a place where a man can group a tight cluster and gather his thoughts."

Declan slung the pack over his shoulder and trotted down the pine treads. As he cruised past the Pettigrew wraparound, he spotted Hallie May.

The Commander addressed her. "Hallie, I'm holding you partly responsible. Desiree is remodeling, and she won't let me inside."

The prayer warrior broke into a birdwing smile, "May I pour you a cup of coffee, Dayo?"

"As an older woman, I can put your heart at ease, and explain what's happening."

Declan paused to consider the offer. Drilling a rifle target was mighty tempting, but it wouldn't answer any questions. His marksmanship was already up to speed.

Only a few days ago, the whole unit visited the range, and tested out their automatics. Heavy Duty even broke out the vintage riflery, and they all had a blast.

"I'm too full of coffee, but if you have a buttery croissant and berry jam, you got yourself a deal."

Hallie beamed from ear to ear, "Dayo, when you enter your newly decorated home, I want you to cherish what the Almighty has given you."

"And I want you to appreciate what Desiree has done. Your house has become a celebration of love. And as a housewarming present, I donated a collection of blue glassware."

"You'll have a decorative shelf of blue dishes, little flower vases, and tulip-shaped glasses."

Dayo owed the world to the Pettigrews, and he wanted to be completely transparent. "There's something you don't know about our marriage, and I'd like to set the record straight."

"I know you two never walked down the aisle. But, son, that's not important."

Declan underestimated Hallie's powers of perception, but he was listening.

Hallie continued, "What I see is two people who have fallen deeply in love. You can have a wedding anytime. But what you have inside is a woman who loves you with all her heart."

"You are the center of her life. And what's more, Desi loves it here. And best of all, she's like the daughter I always wanted."

He couldn't believe her words. You could have knocked him over with a feather.

Dayo stammered, "It's all happened so fast. Our undercover marriage became real, and you're absolutely right, I have fallen for Desiree."

"The other day, we dissolved our temp marriage, and agreed to be husband and wife. And ever since, I've thought of my bronze beauty as my better half."

Declan took this opportunity to say what was needed. He continued, "In a half a summer, Desi has become like the air I breathe."

"And being her hubby, has forged an unbelievable relationship. I just wish I could slow things down."

Hallie nibbled on a jam-covered croissant. "From where I stand, I suggest you speed things up. There's this military business, and we all know what needs to happen."

"I saw the safe house news, and you have one last mission. Maybe, it's the most important mission of your entire life."

"This time it's personal, and you're fighting for your woman and battling for your future."

Dayo realized that Hallie May was far more aware than he had guessed. And Mrs. Pettigrew put things in crystal clear perspective.

The prayer warrior rose from her chair, "Don't make the mistake that Cobb and I did. We pursued rodeo for twenty years and put off having children."

"If I started a family at sixteen, I would have had a passel of children."

Hallie pointed across the commons at his master bedroom. "Your woman is ripe and fertile, and ready to bear children. I suggest you get at it, while you're both young and Desiree is supple."

Declan knew a few things about older women, but rarely had anyone spoken so candidly. And there was a special anointing to her words.

Furthermore, Hallie wanted to pass on her wisdom, and make sure they didn't fall into the same trap. His head reeled from her insights, and his emotions slammed into a wall.

Mrs. Pettigrew retrieved the tray. "Dayo, one other thing, the ranch is all yours. Of course, Cobb and I will stay on for a spell, and help you with the transition."

Dayo's brows arched in surprise.

"Hallie, I don't know if you and Cobb are in complete agreement. But last night, after the barn dance was over. We had a heart to heart."

"Cobb appreciated his moment in the sun, but he'd been there before. Years ago, he won prize money, and sold his futurity colts."

"So, nothing about the Pendleton celebration really surprised him."

"Yes, I'm aware of that. And you're right, Cobb and I have been at this juncture several times. But if he failed to say it, I want to thank you for getting this place fixed up."

"You and your men remodeled the horse barn, the stables, and even the log manor. This place hasn't looked this good in ages."

"And when Cobb and I came together, we said a prayer of thanks, and we were pleased as punch."

She set the tray inside the door. "Dayo, we experienced a great deal of closure since the unit arrived. It was like an overdue reunion with long lost relatives. I felt as though my family had returned."

Hallie touched the corner of her eye. And immediately, Declan stood up and gave her a big hug.

The Caribbean warrior held her hands and cleared his throat. "Cobb went on to say, that he's had a number of offers. And some of them were pretty generous, and more than likely, a lot more than I could offer."

Mrs. Pettigrew flipped a dismissive hand. "Oh, phooey on that. There hasn't been a single offer from a respectable horseman yet."

"They're not interested in his breeding ledger, or the fine stallions he's studded out. They're only interested in Hunter and Shepherd and getting their greedy hands on the land."

Dayo heard the same thing from her husband. "Well, ma'am, it sounds like you're in agreement about most things. But when it came to the buyout, he wasn't sure if I was ready to inherit his legacy."

"This property represents a lifetime of horse breeding, rodeo contests, and reined cow horse events. And to put it bluntly, he wasn't sure I deserved it."

"He challenged me to examine my life. He asked when the killing would end. And when I would start doing things for myself? And lastly, he told me to do whatever it takes to set myself free."

"I made the decision to terminate Gonzalez. But last night, it became crystal clear that Desiree won't be free until he's dead."

Hallie held his hands and listened carefully. "My husband wanted to reinforce your decision. And even though Cobb hesitated, I can see it in his eyes."

"In our minds, the ranch is yours. You and Desiree are good people, and that's what really counts."

"We're old, and money doesn't matter much. It's all about family and receiving closure. And naturally, I'd like to see little ones running about the place."

Hallie squeezed his hands, "We believe you will love the land, and will do what's right."

The old prayer warrior eyed him lovingly, "Dayo, the ranch is yours, and you can make payments whenever possible."

Declan was left speechless. It was a huge blessing, and he didn't know what to say.

Finally, the Commander stammered, "Hallie, I won't let you down. And before we eliminate the hostile, I'll make sure Cobb receives his bucket request."

"I'll do my darndest to win an RCH competition. Shepherd Cat deserves a first-place trophy, and so does Hunter."

Mrs. Pettigrew hugged him, "It's up to the lord, but if you could become Jackie Robinson, just one time, and charm those judges, then he'd have the trophy he always wanted."

Geezus! He loved these people.

Hallie wiped her eyes, "Dayo, I think your lady love is about ready. Go see what your new home looks like."

Declan was all choked up, and he couldn't wait to tell Desiree the good news. He trotted over the commons and took the pine treads two at a time.

He rushed through the craft door and entered his home. He stopped cold.

Desiree skipped over to him and kissed him sweetly, "Dayo, as king of your new castle, I want to welcome you to our new home."

He walked through the house, and he was totally blown away. "Wow! This place looks amazing!"

"You've added feminine touches everywhere. And you've transformed a foreman's house into a loving home."

Desiree burst into a radiant smile. "I'm glad you like it but let me take you on a personal tour."

They entered the vaulted great room, and above the fireplace mantle, there were huge picture frames.

Desi made a grand gesture, "These are my favorite people."

He gazed above the rough-hewn mantle, and there was his picture. Eugene must have dug up an old photo. Declan radiated pure Caribbean charm, and the Belafonte resemblance was incredible.

And his portrait was flanked by their Malinois pupper, Molly, and Kay Bear. It seemed surprising to see a K-Man enlargement, but he was key to her recovery, and deserved a place of honor.

Declan couldn't believe how honored he felt. "Where's your photo?"

"I should have placed my studio portrait above the mantle, but it was a memorial to the ones I love. But if you'll follow me, you'll see our favorite peeps."

"I'm standing in the middle, and that was a studio pic when I was prettier."

"What are you talkin' about, woman? You just get better and better. Besides your studio pic isn't nearly as brick house beautiful as you are today."

Desiree blushed, "To keep our tour going, you can see Cobb, Hallie, and the Marine unit."

Dayo checked the photos and sure enough, they were all there. He felt a huge sense of closure and commemoration.

He touched the pics fondly as he gazed at Heavy Duty, Whip, and Trick. And using Photoshop alterations, there was a pic of Eugene and Tanya holding hands.

Dayo remarked, "This is phenomenal!"

Desiree gestured toward the boudoir, "Shall we see our new love nest?"

He responded with enthusiasm, "Most definitely!"

She led him into their master suite. There was a warm fire going and bowl candles glowed from the end tables.

The honey-stained vault cast an amber glow, but something was different. There was a sensual ruby comforter on the four poster and a matching pullover on their love seat.

Dayo ran his hand over the satin material, "This comforter is so silky and sensual, I'm getting aroused just looking at it."

"I never thought French sensuality would become my new favorite. But girl, you've outdone yourself."

Desi bounced on her heels, and her scrumptious cleavage shimmied with delight. She skipped over to the love chair.

"I hope you don't mind, but there's a ruby pullover, and it matches the overall theme. I don't think it will impair your abilities, and we can still have loads of fun."

She curled her lips in a mischievous grin.

Desiree gestured to the curtains, "I removed the stark cranberry and softened the colors. My goal was to capture elements of Yin and Yang. Do you think it all works?"

"Oh, absolutely! Darlin', you nailed it."

She trotted over to an amphitheater of teddy bears.

Dayo burst out laughing. "I've never seen so many teddies in my entire life."

Desiree seized a few, "We've got happy grizzlies, cute koalas, and even smiling pandas. Every night, we can choose a different pair to sleep with us."

Declan raised a finger, "I still adhere to the rule of three teddies. Molly sleeps on her doggie bed, and you get three bears, and Kay Man. That's it!"

"You're such a meanie, but I don't mind. Over a month's time, every bear will get his turn. And our family will be complete."

Desiree peered beneath her lashes, "Before I show you my latest lingerie, I'd like to hear your thoughts about our new décor."

He exhaled, "Well, here it goes. I love what you've done to this place, and I feel like it's the most beautiful home I've ever lived in."

"And as a wandering warrior, I feel as though I've finally come home. And most of all, I'll cherish you for as long as I live."

Dayo toed off his cowboy boots and tossed his shirt over a chair. He flaunted his muscular physique and came to a halt at his belt buckle.

The fearless Marine walked over to a calendar with a big circle. What does this red highlighter mean?"

Desiree tiptoed to the calendar wall. "Dayo, I'm off the pill, and this big circle means I'm at peak fertility." She curled her lips into a seductive smile, "Do you want to make a baby with me?"

He tried to mask his surprise. No woman had ever asked him that question. But then again, he should have known. Hallie May was pulling for little ones, and the moment had arrived.

He curled his lips like a hungry panther. "Darlin', I want to say yes in the worst way. But before I annihilate your beautiful ass, perhaps, you should tell me the rules."

Desiree popped her flared hip, "Big boy, the rules are as follows. We'll have privacy, and you can make love to me as many times as you want."

"In fact, I'll even let you be on top. But the goal is deep penetration, and we want to make sure your swimmers have the shortest distance to the baby chamber."

"Wow! You're going for the brass ring, aren't you?"

"Yes, I am. And the best fertility positions is doggie style." Desiree smacked her voluptuous ass, "Woof! Woof! You big stud, let's go for it!"

Molly danced around the floor barking, and the baby making marathon was on.

Chapter Seventeen

Desi held up a delicate finger, "Dayo, I've got a big surprise for you. Just give me a minute, and I'll change into something more comfortable."

The bronze bombshell trotted into the amber glow, barnwood bathroom and stood before the mirror.

She giggled to Kay Bear. "Since we're going for multiple eruptions, it's time to bring out the big guns."

Desi dropped her brassiere and her panties and slipped on her newest lingerie. She wiggled her peach under bustier into place, and the girls billowed with seductive beauty.

Her generous fruit bowls heaved upward, and her dark chocolate nipples peaked with arousal.

Desiree whispered to Kay Bear, "The big stud thinks I need foreplay, but the girls are excited, and Chloe is perky with anticipation."

The bronze beauty wiggled her crotchless panties around her hips and plucked the waistband.

"Kay Bear, Dayo is gonna love this number." She stood before the mirror, "And now for the showstopper."

Desiree pulled her ginger ringlets into position and teased her luxuriant bangs. The hair display cascaded over her right shoulder in a massive freefall.

She exclaimed, "What man wouldn't want to run his fingers through all that ginger red glory?"

Quickly, Desiree applied the peach glow foundation, pearl pink lipstick, and enormous flared lashes.

To draw greater attention to her mysterious dark eyes, she applied Arabian eyeliner at the outside crease.

She turned to Kay Bear, "Girl, you look sensational. All we have to do is remind Dayo that he's making love to me, and not a runway model."

Kay Bear beamed his button brown eyes. "I can see you approve. And with a heavenly blessing, there may be a little one, pretty soon."

"He'll pull on your round ears, and tickle your white tummy, and we'll be a happy little family."

Molly stood at attention, but seemed to know exactly where this love tryst was headed. Her pupper knew the drill.

Once they entered their boudoir, her doggo would settle in, and watch their escapades.

Desiree patted Molly's coffee colored head. "This time, we're going for the gold. And even though I said he could be a locomotive powerhouse; I think I've changed my mind."

"We should take turns, and I'll get him revved up. And for the grand finale, he'll go cowboy crazy and blast his swimmers into my baby chamber."

"What do you think about that?" Molly cocked her head and delivered three encouraging barks.

"I'll take that as a yes!"

Desiree entered their love parlor, and Dayo had the candles lit, the fireplace going, and the ruby satin sheets were turned back.

Her stud Marine cranked out a few push-ups and leaped to his feet.

The bronze Adonis had beads of sweat trickling across his muscular chest. And his abs looked like a delicious washboard. *Goodness, she could eat him up.*

Desi laid a hand to the four-poster and popped a delicious hip. "Hey, big boy, what do you think of my lingerie?"

Her bad boy stood at rapt attention, and Mr. Big bobbed in admiration. His enthusiasm was engorged with male desire, and his head was flared and swollen.

It didn't take much to get Dayo going. She giggled, "I take it, you're glad to see me?"

"Oh, hell yeah. And even though my nether regions have paid you a compliment, I want to say your peach glow complexion and ginger ringlets look scrumptious."

Desi lifted her wrist cuff, "Kay Bear thought we should bring out the big guns. And I want to remind you that beneath this peachy get-up, it's really me. And I'm your adorable wife."

Declan's voice dropped an octave as palmed her cheek. "Honey, you have nothing to worry about. When I look into your deep brown pools, all is see is the woman I love."

He lowered his mouth and descended into a ravenous mouthwatering kiss. The pearl pink lipstick tasted like cherries, and he was devouring her with pure male adoration.

His lips parted with a sweet invitation, and he combed a callused finger beneath her chin. It was their secret signal for romantic kissing. Desiree had to hand it to him, he was a charmer through and through.

She delivered a kissing flourish, and then she plunged her tongue deep into his throat. Their tongues tangled and Dayo performed a sensuous sucking action that drove her crazy.

Her hands dropped to his arousal, and with a double-fisted grip, she pumped him to full length. She knew how much he loved French kissing, and it turned him on like a wild stallion.

When they broke from their tantalizing kiss, her lips lingered.

In a hoarse voice, she whispered, "There's been a little change of plans. I know you're a locomotive powerhouse, but I would like to take turns. It gives me a bit of control, and we can share the grand finale."

He smacked her shapely derrière, "I was wondering if you'd pull that card. But it just so happens, I'm wise to you, and your seductive ways."

Desiree curled her lips into an alluring smile. Her dimples formed a wicked touch to what she had planned. The brick house beauty sashayed over to the silhouette love chair.

She dragged a toe for sensual drama and mounted the high crested curve. She seized a tiny pitcher of glowing love oils and drizzled an oily trail across her generous pillows.

She layered it thick, and Desi trailed a finger through the amber oils, "Adonis, would you like to taste my fruit bowls?"

"Darlin', you don't have to ask twice."

He straddled the love chair and slid between her legs, and when she tossed back her head and offered herself, Dayo descended.

His big hands cupped her breasts, and he lifted her peaks to his awaiting mouth. Declan devoured her breasts in huge mouthfuls and teased her nipples until they pebbled with arousal.

Her legs bounced against his thighs, and her labial petals began to fall. Lady nectar pooled low and mean, and she wanted him bad.

Dayo finished with a nipple-twisting flourish and plucked her chocolate peaks.

She gazed into his eyes, "Sir, if you would be kind enough, could you trickle love oils from my breasts all the way to my glistening flower?"

Desi giggled, "And don't forget the stick 'em. A girl likes to be pretty and make a good impression."

Declan slipped his fingers through her frilled, crotchless panties and caressed her labial petals. He lifted his dripping fingers to his mouth and tasted her juices.

"Darlin', you are spicy and delicious, and I can't wait to taste your delights."

Desiree balanced on the chaise lounge and opened her legs wide. He lifted her behind and removed her frilly thong in one graceful motion.

Her man held her thighs open as Desiree layered dripping love oils over her squiggly flower. Dayo parted her long petals and applied stick 'em to each wing.

He glued her wings, and she felt beautiful and fully accepted. Long gone were the days of self-conscious fears.

Her stud Marine lifted her to his mouth and paused. "Honey, it amazes me every time I go down on you, just how beautiful you are."

"You've got a bright pink vulva with lovely lips and a pretty bronze trim. Your treasures are so inviting, a man can hardly resist."

"Then stop talking and do the down and dirty."

"Your wish is my command."

Declan lifted her derrière high and plunged his tongue into her opening. Her lady sheath clenched around his glottis as the guy pounded into a medley of passion.

Desi's thighs banged around his face, and she felt pressure start to build. In a deft move, his tongue trailed across her flower basin and landed on her lady jewel.

Chloe was so excited; she was practically out of her mind. Declan pulled back her lady folds and engulfed her entire love bud.

He teased Chloe in a tongue-batting marathon, and when Chloe became turgid, he sucked her deep between his lips.

In a grand finale, he performed a tongue-twirling tornado, and her jewel went crazy. Millions of tingling nerves sent pleasure rifling to her core.

Desi slammed her legs around his face and formed a silent scream. It was a delicious O face that lasted forever.

Time stood still and her body erupted into wave after wave of pleasure-filled orgasms. She gasped for air, balanced herself on the chaise, and slammed Dayo's face deeper.

She blew apart into a zillion pieces, and shock waves caused her to spasm repeatedly. It was so delicious and life affirming. Her most self-conscious part had become a treasure of sharing.

The Commander opened her fuchsia flower, angled his flared head, and slid his engorged length into her love canal. She was slick and damp, and as Dayo's hardon gained momentum, he seized the back of the couch, and performed a swooshing thrust.

His enthusiasm powered into her tight sheath, and the Greek god buried himself to the hilt.

Declan lifted her bottom and lowered himself into the saddle. Desi's generous breasts crushed against his chest, and her flower splayed around his manhood.

It was her favorite position, and the goal of their love tryst was to make babies. He'd save the male thunder sex for another time. In fact, he had grown accustomed to cowgirl super-sex, and his woman knew how to put out.

Desiree buried her aroused peaks against his chest and gazed into his charming brown eyes.

"Dayo, I hope this doesn't affect your male pride. Because you're the most virile stud in the whole world."

"And you're so freakin' confident, you let your little filly do all the slinging because she has a teensy-weensy little problem.

He smacked her voluptuous ass, "No problem, sweetheart. You can thunder tup me to the brink, and when I'm on the edge, we'll switch places."

"Oh, Dayo, you're the best."

Desi had to show him how much she loved this guy. She descended into a ravenous kiss, and plunged her tongue deep, and started to gyrate her hips.

When she had him buried deep, and they were joined on every level, she leaned forward, and started slinging her flower.

She accelerated and slung her sheath in an amazing piston-pounding marathon. As she went faster, she willed herself to pour all her love into their affair.

The bronze bombshell hammered faster and faster, and her sweet derrière pounded into a mesmerizing sprint.

The pleasure increased and love filled her heart. She tangled so deep that Dayo went into a steely hardon. They rounded the last turn, and she was about to hit the straightaway.

Suddenly, she felt his bangers lift. She yelled out, "Declan, it's your turn."

Declan separated, "Oh, my god, I'm teetering on the edge, and we gotta do this fast."

Desiree yelled, "Man the torpedoes, buddy."

He lifted her into the air, whirled in a fluid spin, and settled her against the backrest. Her stud Marine threw her ankles over his shoulders, and she was splayed into ripe fullness.

His enthusiasm hammered harder and harder, and they were past the point of no return. He thundered down the straightaway, and her man blew apart into a thunderous climax.

She watched his O face. Dayo roared with power, and his seed blasted into her womb. Desiree milked him for all she was worth, and she had to get every last swimmer.

His eyes were dilated, and his handsome face turned to a rosy shade of bronze.

She blew apart, and the aftershocks slammed her a thousand ways. She flailed beneath his embrace, and her core went into a hundred little spasms.

It was glorious beyond belief, and to think that the seeds of life were inside her baby place.

Dayo's voice was hoarse with arousal. "Babe, you're not going to believe this, but I think round two is already here."

She arched a tempting S-brow, "Do you want to try doggie style?"

He carried her to the ruby comforter and stepped on top of the bed. Like an acrobat, he wheeled her around his hardon, making an aerial cartwheel, and instantly, she was on all fours.

Desiree found her bearings and gazed into the Cheval mirror. Her breasts swung forward, and Dayo was mounted behind.

She whimpered, "I know the view must be frightening, but this will only take a few minutes."

"On the contrary, the view is incredible! I'm looking at a tiny little waist that flares outward, and your world-class ass is off the freakin' charts."

"Your pretty cheeks are full and round and so darn sexy. I want to thunder fook you into tomorrow."

She loved the compliments, but she had to find a way to be in control. "Let me go first, and I'll back sling, and bounce into your steely hardon."

"The logistics are flattering, but you'll need some help."

She whimpered, "Please let me do the doggie backstroke. It will make me feel better."

Desiree rocked forward and started banging her sweet arse into his manhood. She watched her breasts bounce, and she started to slam faster and faster.

She hit maximum speed, and she was starting to wear down.

"Dayo, help me! I'm open to suggestions."

Her stud Marine seized her arms, arched her back, and launched into a bottom pounding, flower slinging sprint. She matched him thrust for thrust, and since he was doing most of the work, all she had to do was time their union.

Glancing in the mirror, her Greek god relished the thunder fooking sprint, and then suddenly, he released her arms, and pressed her ginger ringlets into the comforter.

With her face planted in the sheets, and her round ass tilted high in the air, it was male dominance at its finest. Her hand shot to her lady jewel and her stud hit another gear.

She whimpered, "Not to be a spoil sport, but you're pressing my face into the mattress."

"Babe, this is the best angle for maximum depth, and the highest percentage position."

She listened to his explanation, and she gave him the thumbs up. "Way to go stud, just dominate me, and make those swimmers fly."

Declan pushed down with one hand, and with his hands locked around one hip, he rose into a half crouch and pounded like a marathon sprinter.

It was a powerful demonstration of manhood, and it inspired her to give Chloe a tornado twirling massage. As she teetered on the edge of an orgasm, Desi heard him yell.

"We're past the point of no return, here it comes!"

The man released her ginger mane, and he seized her elevated butt with both hands. The stud Marine hammered deep, and thundered hard, and then he bellowed.

It was a long warrior's yell, and she felt his swimmers splash into her womb. He kept thrusting until every drop left his handsome body.

Desiree let go, and she flew into a body racking series of orgasms. One after another, waves of torrential pleasure rocked her frame.

And while the aftershocks caused her to shake like a leaf, it suddenly happened.

She felt the spirt of life enter her womb. There was a spark of life, and one special swimmer entered her ovum, and a brand-new life was formed.

It was glorious and overwhelming, and she dissolved into a pool of tears.

Dayo remained in his doggie dominant position, but he tilted her face to the side. "Babe, are you all right? Was I too rough?"

Desiree wiped her nose, "These are tears of joy. I felt the gift of life enter my womb, and we've been blessed with a tiny muffin."

"Our little person is nestled deep within my baby chamber."

"Babe, do you want me to withdraw? I'm at half mast, and I'm going to spill pretty soon."

Desiree wiggled backward and squeezed his flagging manhood. "Just hold on a sec, I want to savor this moment."

"Ya know, having a baby is a blessing from the Big Guy. It's not simply a matter of the right fertility peak, or a high sperm count, it requires the smiling face of God."

"So, you think Hallie has been prayin' her ass off."

Desi giggled and his words sounded so inappropriate, but somehow, they were so comical. When she laughed, his half-mast hardon bounced inside. And it felt so good, and so right, she didn't want to separate.

They had just finished making love, and on the second round it happened. Certain women are spiritually sensitive, and they experience the exact moment of conception. She felt honored that she had been blessed in such a way.

Declan removed his manhood. And immediately, she clutched her petals and folded them into place. For safe keeping, her squiggly flower was reassembled, and she tucked herself into a neat little coil.

Dayo handed her a pair of cotton panties, and they rolled into bed. The stud Marine propped her bottom with a tilted pillow, so all the swimmers slid downward.

He rose to his full height. "Babe let's take a moment to appreciate this. To fully imbed inside your womb, you may want to rest for a while. I'll make lunch and serve you."

"Oh, my god, I've died and gone to heaven. My husband is actually serving me dinner!"

He shot a look from his handsome face, "Don't overdo it, darlin'. This is a special occasion, and not one to be abused."

Desiree felt as free as a bird. "While you're at it, can you pile a bunch of teddies around me?"

Dayo crossed the floor and grabbed an armload.

"For this special occasion, we'll exceed the teddy bear limit." He raised her on a backrest and arranged her stuffed friends. Desiree was buried in a mound of teddy bears, and life couldn't have been better.

She raised her wrist cuff, "Kay Bear, we're going to have a baby. What do you think of that?"

Moments later, Declan arrived with a lunch tray. "How is our little momma doing?"

She held up her koala bear, "K-Man says, you're the best, and you're gonna make one helluva father."

"He said that did he? Well, I think my wifey bear will make a fantastic momma."

He poured her a milkshake. "Even though you may have received the gift of life, I'd like to keep this on the down low. Let's not jinx our blessing."

"What about Hallie May? She prayed her ass off, and I think she should know."

Desiree started laughing hysterically when she realized what she had said. But she arched her S-curved brow, "Well?"

"My suggestion is to keep it speculative. Until we know for sure, and it's confirmed by the OB/GYN, let's just say, things look promising."

"You just want to look at my big ass, and mash my face into the mattress, and thunder tup like a Greek god."

"You better believe it. And we're going to keep practicing until we get it right!"

Chapter Eighteen
Las Vegas Reined Cow Horse Competition

Three Weeks later

Declan hauled his fifth-wheel RV into a rest area. The Pettigrew entourage consisted of Cobb's Airstream, Eugene's tricked out RV, and the unit's mobile bunkhouse.

The Commander pulled into the diagonal lot and opened Desiree's door. Molly jumped to the ground and surveyed her surroundings.

The Nevada desert was far more arid than Pine Whisper. Desi's dog knew right away they were in an alien environment, and things were completely different.

Desi lifted her wrist cuff, "Kay Bear, will you look at that glorious sunrise?"

"The first light hits the red sandstone, and lights it up with so much beauty, I just know it's going to be a great day."

She tickled his little white tummy and glanced into his button brown eyes. The bronze beauty curled her lips and exhibited her adorable dimples.

"K-Man thinks we've come to the right place. And he says you're gonna win the RCII, and all you have to do is be your charming self."

Dayo stroked his heavy stubble, "As soon as we arrive at the South

Point Equine facility, I'll shave, apply facial moisturizer, and practice my Caribbean charm."

Desiree tiptoed to his chest and kissed her beloved. "Dayo, you and Shepherd Cat are gonna knock 'em dead."

"And when the judges see how all-American you are, they'll leap passed your bronze complexion and focus on your horsemanship."

The Captain broke into a warm laugh, "It's been ages since I've practiced my Caribbean charm, but it's all for a good cause. Cobb deserves a first-place trophy, and becoming the RCH poster boy is how we're going to do it."

The bronze beauty considered their geographical location. They were north of Vegas and the sunrise caught the glowing sandstone.

Red Rock Canyon displayed flaming red and orange hues, and it came alive with a burst of natural colors.

Dayo walked around to the back of the luxury trailer and dropped the tailgate. "Honey, I'm going to exercise the horses before we drive through Vegas."

"Why don't you put on your ginger ringlets and get ready. Even though I plan to break cover, it's imperative that you remain incognito."

She was about to thank him, but suddenly her stomach went into revolt. Desiree ducked into the travel stall and hurled into a stainless-steel head.

The ginger-haired cowgirl heaved two more times and wiped her mouth. From her purse, she retrieved her morning mouthwash and cleansed her breath.

When she rejoined him, the horses were back in the trailer. "Ya know, morning sickness isn't that bad. After I purge, then I feel great."

"My OB/GYN says our little tyke is firmly attached. I can compete in the cutting event, but she absolutely forbids bronc busting."

Dayo chuckled, "Fortunately for you, the Vegas competitions are all about horsemanship, and not rodeo insanity. Besides, I wouldn't let you ride saddle bronc even if you begged me."

She rubbed her baby bump and felt protective and maternal. Even though she wasn't showing, she couldn't wait to pack on the pounds, and show off her tummy.

She patted her Malinois, "Both Molly and Kay Bear think I'm going to have a boy. He'll be adventurous and carefree just like his poppa."

"Or you could have an adorable girl who looks just like her pretty momma."

Desi enjoyed their paternal patter; it took her mind off other things. For the past week, she and Hallie painted the kid's rooms, applied teddy bear borders, and hung children's mobiles.

Simply preparing the children's wing put her in another state of mind. But now, she had to snap back to more pressing matters.

Desiree patted the front seat, "Hopp!"

Molly jumped inside, "Molls, we're going to have a baby. I don't want you to worry about the morning sickness, it's all part of the journey."

"My body has been flooded with hormones, and my metabolism has changed. But pretty soon, it will stabilize, and things will return to normal."

Declan pointed through the windshield at the Vegas skyline. "For the record, there's nothing normal about this trip."

"We're going to an adult playground, and we're competing against the best professionals in North America. And if that isn't daunting enough, the Equine Center features a casino hotel and a huge swimming pool."

Desi finished her peach-glow makeup, "After we compete all day, a cool dip in a luxury pool will be refreshing."

Dayo patted her leg, "Just don't get your hair wet, and everything will work out. You have to keep your ginger ringlets dry. So, don't blow your cover."

She wanted to win it for the Pettigrews. But going undercover so close to L.A. was nerve-wracking. The Vegas outskirts were only a four-hour drive from Sage. And that's where it all started.

She thought about her Spanish Med home and her former life. But rapidly, the reality of Tinder's death, and the fact she was on Antonio's hit list came roaring back.

Geezus! She wanted to win this thing, and help Cobb realize his bucket dream. But they were risking it all.

When Dayo broke his cover, there was a remote chance, Gonzalez might be watching. And it didn't take a genius to recognize Dayo as detective Declan Cazador.

And if he was alive, the kingpin would know that she was alive. In short order, things could get dicey.

Declan drove the Vegas strip and admired the revelry. He cruised the two-ton down a tree studded boulevard, and right then, the tranquil pools erupted into a carnival of white fountains.

The jets streamed skyward, forming a water arc, and three circular fountains burst into watery glory. It was Vegas at its best.

He cruised down the boulevard and beheld a giant Ferris wheel, the Eiffel tower, and high-rise resorts.

Dayo pointed at a distant space needle, "By night, Vegas puts on one helluva show. I don't know of any other city has more neon lights and more digital signage."

Desiree stroked Molly's head, "Yeah, Vegas is one of a kind, but we're headed to the South Point Equine Center. And I bet things will be less showy, and more like a horsey stockyard."

The commander had to hand it to her. Desiree always kept a positive outlook, and he should copy her enthusiasm and prepare for his event.

A man can't look at the trophy or even Cobb's bucket dream. He had to focus on Shepherd Cat and become one with this amazing show horse.

It was one step at a time for five minutes. And he had to impress the judges and win this contest.

The fearless warrior tugged on his Stetson and drove into the stockyards. There were paddocks of expensive horses stationed in steel pens. And above the livestock was a digital sign, which announced the Grandest RCH in the world.

Adrenalin coursed through his veins, and it was showtime. He had to put up or shut up, and the commander planned to give this one his all.

His cowboy boots hit the ground and he surveyed his surroundings.

Directly ahead was the indoor equestrian center, and he felt compelled to meet the enemy, and get his bearings.

After he parked the fifth wheel, his unit piled out of another RV. They were dressed in their Western attire, but there was a pronounced military bearing to their movements.

Trick narrowed his piercing eyes. "Captain let's take a look at the indoor arena. We can gauge the layout and determine where the hostiles might hide."

"This is freakin' Vegas and home to the syndicate, horse betting, and every evil known to mankind."

Dayo trotted up the steps, "And here I thought you held Vegas in high esteem?"

Heavy Duty flexed his biceps, "Captain, we're entering the lion's den. And I don't want you to have any illusions. The moment you trim your beard and break cover, the game is on."

"Gonzalez will come after you, and we plan to answer with force. We'll terminate the bastard. So, pardon me, if I don't get all mushy about Sheperd Cat's performance."

Whip slapped HD's shoulder, "Hey loosen up. This RCH event means the world to Cobb. And we're living on his property, and it's a great way to repay a favor."

The Commander glanced toward Thoroughgood, hoping to find comic relief. Whip did his best and flashed a friendly smile.

"Dayo, I have to level with ya. From a military standpoint, this RCH event serves as nothing more than bait. The moment Antonio discovers you; he'll tip his hand."

"Wild Man will detect his movements and determine his next move. And once we know his position, we execute."

The easy-going cowboy didn't lighten the mood. And the thing about this op was the fact Dayo had to lay military plans and immerse himself in Caribbean charm.

When the showmanship was over, he had to snap his warrior's helmet on, and that wasn't going to be easy.

The men stood at the top of the amphitheater. There were fourteen rows of velvet red chairs leading down to an immaculate dirt arena.

Hanging lights illuminated the giant rectangular space and the moment Dayo entered this horse shrine, he felt his hair stand on edge. Glancing into the future, there was the possibility for monumental success, and it came at a huge cost.

Desiree slid next to him. "Wow! This is one impressive arena. I still can't believe how Wild Man got us here."

"Pettigrew called in a ton of favors, and Eugene manipulated the system. But the important thing is, we're here."

"That's right, sweetheart. And you're going to ride Hunter Cat right down there. They'll shorten the arena, and there will be three zones."

"And knowing how you're a feisty horse woman, you'll take the little dogie to the outer zone. And that way, Hunter can show off his amazing cow work."

Desi giggled, "Hunter has done it in open range, and he's done it in Cobb's sanctuary. So, this will be a piece of cake." She dusted her hands, "Captain, we got this!"

On the one hand, he wanted Desi to enjoy this experience. But no sooner did they finish, it was time for battle. And he needed his combat pilot in top mental shape.

Dayo removed his black Stetson and hand-combed his dense hair. "All right, everyone, we've seen the arena. Memorize the layout and figure out where the enemy might take refuge."

"In the meantime, let's meet back at the command center and discuss the logistics. We have a split itinerary, and I'm counting on everyone to do their part."

There was a strong conviction among his men, and even Desi had a look of fierce resolve. Molly didn't need verbal commands; the Malinois heeled like a warrior dog.

This was precision horsemanship and shrewd military planning at its best. And it was the strangest op he'd ever been on. He just hoped he could pull it off.

The team approached Eugene's tricked out RV. The shiny horse trailer spanned forty feet, and was covered with satellite dishes, air conditioners, and generators.

Dayo pushed open the aluminum door and entered the living room. Can lights beamed from a diamond mirrored ceiling, and plush sofas lined the walls. Hardwood lined the walkways, and Eugene emerged from the far end.

Eugene stood inside his command center. "Hey Captain, I wondered when you guys would make it?"

"Tanya and I have been hard at it. We hired a professional driver, so we could monitor everything under the sun. I'm tracking Gonzalez, eavesdropping on the judges, and staging the AFB helos."

Declan felt reassured. Intel was on their side, and if they could stay two steps ahead of Gonzalez, they had a fighting chance.

The fearless Marine slid his hand to Desiree's backside, "Shall we enter the command center and discuss our agenda?"

His lady added a bit of levity, "Dayo, I love the intensity, but you gotta lighten up. If you want the judges to like you, you've got to be charming, and well spoken, and very polite."

The commander chuckled, "I hate those things, I truly do. And nothing could be more undercover than playing the part of a Caribbean charmer."

The unit gathered inside the command center. A bank of computer screens filled one wall, and there was an eerie blue glow about the place.

It was a surreal environment, but this was where it happened. On many late nights, Eugene flew from one laptop to the next, tracking the enemy. Dayo owed a lot to this little man, and by the looks of it, he had a new partner.

The streetwise cowgirl was parked in a swivel chair. Tanya flipped her auburn ringlets, "Howdy everyone, welcome to our command center."

Eugene jumped into an adjacent chair, "Ever since I started dressing normal, this hot chick can't keep her hands off me."

Tanya giggled, "It's true. I always liked you, but the Wild Man schtick got to be too much. Ever since Pine Whisper, you've changed, and I like the new you."

Declan was glad to see their budding romance, but he had more pressing matters. "If you'll increase the illumination, I'd like to start the meeting."

"Aye, Aye, Captain." Eugene worked the dimmer switch, and the headquarters turned into a buttery yellow. It was far less surreal, and easier to think.

The Commander started in. "In a half hour, I'll shave my beard, remove my shades, and don a white cowboy hat."

"My goal is to immerse myself in Belafonte charm and stay in the zone for the next three days. I won't be able to tackle military strategies."

"So, Trick will assume command, and make the final decisions. You're not experiencing anything new."

"Lt. Johnson planned the hits along the Sierras as well as the California coast. While Desiree and I are competing in the RCH, your job is to get ready for retaliation."

He gestured to the hacker extraordinaire, "Eugene and Tanya will monitor Antonio's position, and eavesdrop on transmissions, and determine the exact moment Gonzalez knows I'm alive."

"His two options are to attack Vegas or go after the Pettigrew Ranch. Either way, we've got to commandeer two black hawks and turn the tables."

Eugene adjusted his bolo, "Captain, let me jump in real quick. Antonio just arrived in L.A. He and his lady landed in a corporate jet, and they've returned from Mexico."

"The kingpin met with cartel members, and he's planning a whole new shipment of illegal arms, fentanyl, and human trafficking."

"From his transmissions, he's tired and it appears he'll remain in Malibu. Therefore, I've tracked his location, and I've got thermal images."

Tanya wheeled across the room, "And I've got the mansion blueprints."

The auburn cutie flipped through the front, back, and side views, and hovered over the white polyester rubber roof.

"There's enough room for two helos, and Antonio's luxury home is located right on the beach. When our combat helos come off the ocean, we'll be flying under the radar, and his stinkin' home is barely above the bluffs."

Dayo lowered his brows, "It seems easy, but it never works out that way. I want to consider this op from every angle, and anticipate what might go wrong, and prepare for an alternate strike."

Trick leveled an intense gaze, "When do you think Dayo's identity will actually be discovered?"

The happy hacker flew to another a laptop and drew up the itinerary. "I've been considering when they'll go live."

"Based on the elevated cameras, I don't anticipate an easy identification. When the Cowboy Channel airs a view of the arena, and the judges boxes, and the release of the steer, it's long-distance photography."

"They won't be able to see Dayo's features well enough to match him with Declan Cazador."

Desiree arched an S-curved brow, "Then why are we worrying about Dayo blowing his cover?"

Tanya flashed an interview over a wide screen. There was no sound, but clearly, the interviewer and the horseman were easy to identify.

The auburn cutie pointed, "God willing, Desiree and Dayo will make it to the finals. And going into the final competition, the Vegas tradition is to interview the top competitors."

"And once Dayo becomes the Caribbean Kid, and goes live on national television, the cat will be out of the bag."

Heavy Duty leaned against the wall, "Gonzalez could discover Dayo's true identity on the last day. After Declan competes, how much time do we have?"

Eugene wheeled his chair to another screen. "Based on Antonio's movements, he's not a sports fan. He fills his hours with business calls, swimming outdoors, and high-class hookers."

"So, in all probability, if one of the bodyguards spotted Dayo, there would be several hours before Gonzalez got the word."

"And in the meantime, the commander goes to the award

ceremony, and he can meet with Pettigrew. After that, I'll have a fully armed hawk, and a wicked-ass Longbow ready to go."

Declan listened to his unit. Undoubtedly, Trick and Eugene went through the logistics, and this was merely a review.

"Wild Man, I realize there's a Vegas AFB nearby, where exactly will we board the helos?"

Eugene broke into a glorious smile, "I've already enlisted Vance Killian to fly the hawk, and there's a temporary pilot who will station the Longbow."

"The rendezvous point is a short distance from here, located on the edge of the Mohave Desert. It's an old maneuvering sight, and we'll go unnoticed."

Desiree piped in, "What do you mean, there's a temporary Longbow pilot?"

Tanya chimed in, "Isn't it obvious, girl? You're going to fly the Apache combat helo, and if anything goes off course, you've got the missile power to light up a city block."

She clutched Molly's nape, "Wow! You guys aren't messing around, are you?"

Declan held her hand, "Sorry, you're debut experience will be overshadowed by such serious matters. But we're taking a huge risk."

He lowered his voice, "Personally, I feel it's the right thing to do."

"I want to pay Cobb for his hospitality. And to do so, we have to overcome prejudice, and I have to play the part of Jackie Robinson."

"Five years back, Cobb should have won this event. But he's far from a poster child. I feel the judges slighted him based on his appearance. But this time, it's gonna be different."

The unit pumped their fists in unison, "Ooh-rah! Ooh-rah! Let's do it!"

The meeting adjourned on an upbeat note. Their RCH event looked more like mission impossible than a pleasant horse show.

But they were all in, and he couldn't have asked for a better woman or a better group of friends.

Three days had passed since Dayo broke his cover. Eugene and Tanya were seated in the blue command center, and Wild Man wheeled over to the Gonzalez computer.

He searched the transmissions, and even intercepted Antonio's surveillance cameras. The bodyguards busied themselves by making the rounds, eating chip dip, and watching sports.

From the camera audio, the hacker realized the international hostiles enjoyed soccer, and the American insurgents loved baseball. There were channel-changing battles, but other than that, not much was going on.

Tanya hacked Antonio's media man. The enemy investigator traced credit cards, and random news reports, but he had uncovered nothing regarding Desi and Declan.

She even overheard a conversation that the media researcher thought it was a waste of time. Antonio conceded it had been three months. But he wasn't convinced that DeNiro died in that safe house fire.

Tanya watched the media investigator put on a bathing suit.

She twirled an auburn ringlet, "Eugene, our enemy hacker has taken a swim. How is your camera crashing going?"

"The hostile thugs aren't doing much, and no one has turned to the Cowboy Channel. European soccer and American baseball dominate the sports channels."

The auburn cutie giggled, "Since Dayo and Desiree are going into the third day of competition, let's crash the judges booth and see what's going on."

Eugene gave her a high five, "Girl, I love your devious mind."

"I've got the judge's booth over here. Let me angle the surveillance camera and turn up the volume."

"Oh, look, there's only two judges present. But they're old timers, and their assessment may be crucial."

Wild Man turned up the volume and sipped his energy drink. He knew the older judges by heart. Marcus Reinhold wore a black Stetson, a striped button-down, and a grey circle beard. The man spoke with good old boy enthusiasm, but he took his job seriously.

The second man, Abraham Dodge, peered through his reading

glasses. He wore a Western blue blazer, but he wasn't flashy, the man simply wanted to look sharp.

Abe finished the document and looked up. "Marcus, the final vote may come down to us."

He gestured through the glass window. "See that young man who looks like Harry Belafonte?"

"Dwayne Corazon is riding Shepherd Cat. And I'm tellin' ya, Sheppie is the best Quarter Horse out there."

"I've never seen such poise from a rider, and such an easy rein, and yet the Big Cat has put in an amazing performance."

"The sorrel is sensitive to imperceptible signals, and when it came to the cow work, the roan stud was all over it."

"From the fence work to the cow work, Shepherd was flawless. And I'd give Dwayne my full vote."

Marcus rose to his feet and pulled up his belt buckle. "Dammit, Abe, we're back in the hot seat. This is the same thing that happened five years ago."

"Cobb Pettigrew rode that same stud, and his performance was perfect. If the leathery old horseman wasn't so ... basic, I would have given him first place."

"But he wasn't the fitting image for our advertisements."

Abe removed his glasses and pointed the band toward Dwayne Corazon.

"Well, my friend, this time, you don't have that excuse. Cobb may have looked like Satchel Page, but his understudy is an all-American competitor, well spoken, and extremely polite."

"He has a great smile, an engaging manner, and the public loves him. Dwayne is definitely a poster child for the Big Time."

Marcus paced the booth. "Between you and me, our votes will decide the winner. And I happen to agree with everything you've said."

"Unofficially, Adeline did an interview, and she said the guy was likable, handsome, and charismatic."

"And for what it's worth, I'm leaning toward him, but I'm still teetering on the bubble."

Abe wagged his head. "We screwed Cobb five years ago, and we can't let it happen again. Between you and me, the RCH is all about that superlative animal down there. So, what in god's name are you looking for?"

Marcus popped his eyes wide, "I'm looking for a sign that the public will adore him. And after we make that decision, we won't regret it."

Eugene turned off the transmission, "Well, there it is. Dayo clearly has the talents, and it all comes down to politics."

Tanya added, "I imagine the same thing is true of Desiree."

"Yeah, I totally agree."

Wild Man leaped from his chair and glanced across the equestrian stockyard. Off in the distance was an advertisement for the Dumb Friends League.

Eugene clapped his hands, "That's it! Dayo and Desiree have to play the angle, and what works better than promoting a charity?"

Tanya pulled up a screen of western charities.

She stabbed a pretty finger at the screen, "Dayo should endorse retiring performance horses, and Desi should promote the injured cowboy charity. Everyone is sympathetic to the high risks of rodeo, and it will give her more credibility."

Eugene seized the communicator. "When Dayo meets with the interviewer, we'll have him announce the charities."

Tanya added, "Let's give thirty percent to each charity."

Wild Man chuckled, "Judge Marcus, this better push you over the edge, or so help me...."

The commander waited patiently for his interview. This was the moment of decision, and he had to make it good. It was imperative he win over the audience, but more importantly the judges had to believe in him.

It was the third day of competition, and Dayo vied for first place. The fearless warrior was poised, relaxed, and totally one with

Shepherd. The veteran Quarter Horse and the intuitive horseman were an unbeatable team.

The rein work went perfect, and later Sheppie showed off his cow sense. The cow work was so controlled, the run was a thing of pure beauty.

It left the judges open-jawed, and the fans gave him a standing ovation. Dayo didn't ham it up, but he walked a fine line between showmanship and humility.

The Caribbean cowboy removed his Silver Belly and pointed upward, and he waved a hand before the Big Cat. His meaning was implicit.

He owed his life to the Almighty, and he gave credit to his amazing horse. The fans went crazy, and they stomped their feet. And lastly, Dayo touched his heart and waved to the audience.

After three days, Declan wasn't pretending, he became a charming, bronze horseman. When he rode down horse alley, three days ago, he overhead comments about his resemblance to Bellefonte.

One and all got behind him. His polite manner appealed to all people, regardless of color.

Dayo knew a personal interview was about to begin, and this was the crucial moment. He stood beside Desiree, better known as Rae Corazon.

His ginger red beauty wore a white cowgirl hat and traditional Western apparel. Her red ringlets fell past her shoulders, and her peach glow makeup was so vibrant, people went out of their way to congratulate her.

Tanya assisted with her makeup, and they dialed back the flamboyance. Instead of the peach-colored nails, Desiree wore clear polish.

And instead of spiky flared lashes, she sported her natural lashes with a touch of mascara. Declan glanced at his beloved, but this time he wasn't thinking about eating her up. He was so darn proud of her; he could hug her to pieces.

The bronze warrior leaned over. "We're really close, and it won't come down to points, the call is going to be political. I'm thinking about what we should do."

Just then, he received a call from his communicator. "Dayo, we just eavesdropped on the top judges. And you'll get Abe and Marcus' vote if you endorse a local charity."

Dayo whispered, "Which one do you suggest?"

"We think a charity for retired performance horses is a sure bet. Give thirty percent of your winnings, and Cobb will get his first-place trophy."

"Thirty percent?"

"Yeah, it sounds like a generous amount, but we've got to put the judges on the hot seat. If your ride is immaculate, then the charity angle will work."

"And furthermore, it means that you support the RCH program, and you're not after the money."

Dayo lowered her brows, "You got it, Eugene. What about Desiree? What charity should Desi endorse?"

"Tanya feels that Western riding is sympathetic to rodeo. So, she advised the charity for injured rodeo cowboys."

"Hey, that sounds perfect. Too bad we can't run this past Cobb, but I'm gonna run with it."

Eugene clicked off, and Adeline McAlister called his name.

"Lady and Gentlemen, this is Dwayne Corazon, the leader of the RCH competition. Would you care to join us, Dwayne?"

Dayo tipped his ivory white hat, "Yes, ma'am, I'd love to have a word."

Adeline wore a platinum blonde shell, and her features were laced with a keen wit. She adjusted her off-the-shoulder blouse and started in.

"Dwayne, you're riding a famous stud named Shepherd Cat. Can you tell us something about this eighteen-year-old veteran?"

"Why, yes, ma'am, it would be an honor. I've worked with Sheppie all summer, and I've never ridden a more amazing competitor."

"He's pure Quarter Horse, and he's registered to the Pettigrew Ranch. And this old boy has sired hundreds of colts, and in next year's futurity, it would be a joy to ride one of his offspring."

"When you mentioned the Pettigrew Ranch, are you talking about Cobb Pettigrew?"

"Yes, ma'am. Mr. Pettigrew breeds horses, and he has a lifelong fascination for Reined Cow Horse competitions. A few years back, he took second place."

Adeline inquired, "What would you attribute your success to?"

Dayo removed his ivory felt hat, so he could speak from the heart. "Adeline, there are several things that have led to my success."

"First off, Shepherd Cat is a tremendous champion, and no horseman would fail to credit his riding partner. Afterall, it's Sheppie's cow sense that has led us to number one."

"And second, Mr. Pettigrew is a master horseman, and he's taught me everything I know. I'll say his lessons have been a little unorthodox, but he gets results."

Adeline was behind him, "And earlier you pointed heavenward, so you do acknowledge the hand of the Almighty."

"Yes, ma'am. The good lord has protected me all my life, and any success is certainly due to him."

The commentator paused, "Before we leave, is there anything else our fans should know?"

"I'm glad you asked that question. I want my fans to know that thirty percent of the prize money will go to a special charity."

"And I've decided to make a donation for retired performance horses."

"They've given their lives to this sport, but when they get up in years, these former champions need a little help. It's a worthy cause, and I hope others will join with me."

There was another standing ovation as Dayo left the stage.

Dayo whispered on the way down. "Honey, I suggest you endorse the charity for injured rodeo cowboys."

Desiree swept her ginger mane to the side. "You got it, big guy. I'll see you after the cutting event."

Desiree shook hands with Adeline McAlister. The platinum blonde eyed her carefully and didn't know what to make of her.

Addie leaped into a hard-hitting question. "How does it feel to be the first black woman to compete in the cutting event?"

The peach-glow beauty remained calm. "Adeline, I'm not on a campaign for a particular cause. But I feel that Hunter Cat deserves full recognition."

"In the qualifier, he exhibited timing, agility, and a deft awareness. He knew what that cow was going to do, even before the Charolais knew it."

"So, I just want the world to see what an amazing cutting horse Hunter is. Afterall, it's all about the horse, and the rider is really secondary."

Adeline regarded the answer. "I noticed that your husband, Dwayne Corazon is fond of making charitable donations. Do you have a favorite charity?"

"Why, yes, ma'am. I plan to donate thirty percent to the injured rodeo cowboys."

"I know how many folks have relatives in pro rodeo. And unfortunately, accidents do happen. And we should never forget those who have been injured."

"So, I hope others will join with me, and give to this fine organization."

Desiree hoped her natural sincerity would come through. The charity was an excellent suggestion, and she was glad that Eugene thought of it.

Adeline extended a hand, "Rae Corazon, I wish you the best of luck. You've been an admirable competitor, and I hope to see you in the winner's circle."

"Thank you, Adeline."

Desiree trotted down the steps and waved to her adoring fans. She won them over, and all she had to do now was win the cutting event.

Two hours later, Declan and Desiree entered Cobb's Airstream. Hallie May guided them to the trophy room. It was a smaller office than the horse stable, but the resemblance was uncanny.

There was a leather sofa, a coffee table, and a red colonial trophy case. The Old Man opened a glass cabinet and seated the trophies with reverence. He had tears in his eyes, and he was so incredibly grateful.

Cobb tilted his head and savored the moment. He waited a lifetime to experience this victory.

"At long last, Shepherd and Hunter received their due."

"The world acknowledged them as true champions, and I can check off this bucket dream. And I owe it all to these two young people standing in front of me."

Dayo shook his hand, "I'm glad I shared in your victory. But it should have been you out there. And this first-place trophy should have been given five years ago."

Mr. Pettigrew cocked his head and tried to speak. His mouth was dry, and he was all choked up. "There simply aren't words to describe my gratitude, and the fulfillment of a lifelong dream."

Cobb patted Dayo's shoulder, "It should have been me, but I can live with it. The Caribbean Kid won it for me. You're the Jackie Robinson the fans can adore, and I don't regret a thing."

The Old Man smiled through his circle beard. "Thanks to you, son. Hunter and Shepherd's net worth has tripled, and my futurity colts are worth a fortune."

Pettigrew waved a leathery hand. "Awww, it was never about the money."

"But I am glad to see the monetary value, it's another way of saying how good my breeding program was. And at this age, I'll take compliments any way I can them."

Desiree crossed the floor, and she was overcome with emotion. She tiptoed to Cobb's face and gave him a big kiss and hugged him.

This man was responsible for giving her a home, for giving her respect, and allowing her to raise a family. It was a small price to win a cutting contest.

She stammered, "I'm sorry I had to give away thirty percent. If we could have taken first place any other way, I would have done it."

"But the judges were looking for a sign, and I think we persuaded them."

Cobb gazed down at her, "Little lady, it was a brilliant strategy and a smooth move. It put the judges on the hot seat, and it pushed us over the hump."

"Public sentiment swung in our direction, and finally, those old farts did the right thing."

Dayo echoed her apology, "Yes, sir. It was the right decision, and I'll make good on it."

"The charity for retired performance horses will receive a large donation. And maybe, next year, we can win the RCH straight out."

Cobb chuckled in a dry voice. "At this stage, the pot of gold means little. But the fact that Sheppie and Hunter finally received their due means the world to me."

"It's like a crown of approval for my life's work. Even though the judges may not understand my breeding program, they endorsed the results."

Pettigrew heaved a deep sigh. "I'm exhausted. It's been a long day, and for the first time, I held hands with Hallie, and we prayed during the entire run."

"I sat in those velvet chairs and prayed for every maneuver. And the good lord answered our prayers, and you two were incredible."

He touched Desiree and Dayo, "Folks, I'll see you in the morning."

Just then, Eugene and Tanya burst into the trophy room.

Wild Man stammered, "Gonzalez got wind of your victory. He saw the award ceremony, and he recognized you."

He sent a hit team to the DeNiro Ranch. They haven't arrived yet, but I've got two combat helos waiting. Boss, we gotta go!"

In the darkness, they heard the sound of two helos. The choppers landed next to the stockyards.

Dayo called out, "Cobb, we gotta go!"

Chapter Nineteen

Declan raced through the darkness and stripped on the run. The cargo bay was open, and his men were already dressed in night camos.

He ducked beneath the stub-wing artillery and scrambled to a cargo seat.

Trick threw him his combat uniform, "Dayo, we don't have much time. The syndicate hostiles have a head start, and they'll arrive any minute."

"I realize you had to make a public appearance. But damn it all, you gave away our position, and you broke our cover."

Dayo transferred into his camos, and the moment Whip slammed the assault rifle into his hand, seven years of Marine training came sailing back.

His long barreled tactical weapon featured a mounted Trijicon scope, and for medium-range marksmanship, it was a badass automatic.

He wasn't orchestrating this mission, and three days ago, he relieved himself of command. It was so odd taking orders from Trick Johnson, but his second did what was necessary.

Good lord, he hoped it was all worth it. Cobb fulfilled a bucket dream, but at what price?

The armed Black Hawk airlifted right as Dayo belted himself into the wall harness.

"I don't expect to be coddled, but Trick is calling the shots. Whatever you and Wild Man decided, I'll go with it."

"Thank you, Captain. Since you're out of the loop, here's the situation."

Trick produced an electronic planning screen, and the DeNiro ranch came into view.

The Lieutenant stabbed the screen, "This timber-log ranch is the main homestead, and here's a blueprint of the floor plan."

Declan studied the architecture. "Easy layout, right-loaded garage, dead center foyer, and left elevation bedrooms."

Trick summoned an aerial satellite view. "The log homestead is located off a service road and the cattle ranch features a feedlot, cattle chutes, and six outbuildings."

"Vance Killian will sweep wide of the ranch and maintain audio silence. We'll deploy behind this hill, and we've got a one-mile trek to the back elevation."

"Shit! We're cutting this close, aren't we?"

Heavy Duty jumped in. "Trick and Wild Man have got this. We've got body heat readouts, and we know the exact locations of the hostiles."

"It's a standard headhunting op. We use the grenade launcher, go through the back wall, and hurl a flashbang. When the hostiles are blind and deaf, we take 'em out."

Declan set his M16 against the floor. "Why am I carrying a precision scope on a field weapon?"

Trick eyed him, "Captain, no disrespect, but we've been training for this. We've got to take the homestead, and it requires close-range combat."

"When we enter the back elevation, you and HD will set up sniper nests. Each of you will be positioned at a strategic angle. If the leaders try to take hostages, you'll have the shot."

Dayo encountered hostage situations before. Since the Marines weren't limited to negotiations, they were free to shoot and kill.

All the sniper needed was a clear shot, and the hostile was dead meat. The Commander exhaled and focused. He visualized the calibration procedure and how to establish a sniper cell.

From thirty yards, if the captor poked his head too high, he was an easy target. All the Commander had to do was wait.

Back at the stockyards, Desiree shot past the horse pens and rounded the auditorium. She spotted two combat helos sitting on the helipad. Her heart leaped with joy.

The Longbow was a flying weapon, and the perfect instrument for mass destruction. Antonio's hitmen were going down.

Her eyes adjusted to the dim light, and she spotted a combat pilot. The cockpit was tipped open, and a familiar face stared at her.

If memory served, it was Lieutenant Blake Scott. The man positioned himself in the tandem seat. Desiree had the honor of flying in the attack module. And she loved the way Longbows handled.

The combat girl trotted up the staircase and lifted Molly into the seat. Desi took the forward seat and settled Molly into a bumper chair.

Blake extended his hand, "Good to see ya, Lieutenant DeNiro. The enemy has a head start, and we're headed for an intercept point."

Blake unclipped his belt and handed a bullet proof vest to each of them. Desi ripped off her cowgirl clothes and donned the flight suit.

Desiree slipped the jacket around Molly's mid-section and fastened the breast collar.

"Molls, I want you to be a good girl, sit in the bumper seat, and keep an eye out." Her pupper licked her face as Desiree tossed her wig aside.

Blake spoke into the communicator. "The coordinates for the DeNiro Ranch are set. We're flying back-up to an armed hawk. And we must take the rear position, beyond hearing range. It will give Killian sufficient time to deploy the Marines.

Good lord, she was back in the Middle East. There were no flashbacks because this time it was personal. Her parents, Mariah and Austin DeNiro, were under attack. And her brothers and sisters could be held hostage.

Desiree performed the triple checks and inventoried the weaponry. "Blake, it appears the stub-wings are armed with Hellfire missiles and Hydra pods."

"Double check, and the undercarriage has an M230 chain gun, which is fully loaded."

She winced at the thought of drilling three-inch projectiles through her parent's log home. But if push came to shove, Desi would do whatever it takes.

She airlifted and activated the nose sensors for target acquisition. The monitors came alive, and Desi was ready to engage. The combat girl flicked a switch, and the night system was in gear.

Blake came over the communicator, "Lieutenant Johnson and Eugene have orchestrated this op. Wild Man has your ranch on thermal readouts, so we'll know where every family member is."

Desiree blasted over the Mohave Desert and saw the Sierras rapidly approaching. The attack helo hit top speed, one-hundred-eighty-miles per hour.

She spotted the ass end of the black hawk. Judging from her nose sensors and readouts, the fully armed hawk carried air-to-ground missiles, not to mention a complete arsenal of 50 caliber guns and minis.

The combat girl asked, "Where will we hide while the Marine unit is deployed?"

Blake answered, "Our Longbow will hang back, behind the foothills. Once Trick gives the command, we'll blast across the prairie and be there within seconds."

She chewed her lip nervously, "Geezus! I hate hovering and not knowing what's going on."

Blake squeezed her shoulder. "It's all part of the drill. We don't want to tip our hand until we have the hostiles where we want 'em."

"Roger that! As soon as Dayo and his men secure the building, then any transport units will be toast." She hated Antonio with a passion, and now the mother effer was going after her family.

Her Longbow cleared the high peaks and within seconds, the California lowlands came into view. She watched the Black Hawk streak forward, and they pulled north along the range.

Biding her time required patience, and a successful assault was all about timing. She knew the strategy, but when the indigenous were actually her relatives, this made it a hundred times harder.

Blake praised her, "Desiree, you're doing fine. Just cut the engine speed and cruise back and forth along the front range."

It seemed odd that Lieutenant Johnson planned the op. Cazador was the superior officer, and an experienced field commander.

But moments ago, her beloved participated in a reined cow horse event. She sure hoped Dayo had his game face on. Switching from a Western cowboy to a Marine headhunter wasn't an easy task. But if anyone could do it, it was her fearless Captain.

Declan glanced out the stern windows and watched the terrain change. The armed hawk hit top speed, and the Mohave Desert gave way to the high Sierras, and they were almost there. The Sikorsky helo shot over the high peaks and descended like a bird of prey.

Pilot Killian called out, "Estimated time of arrival is in five minutes. It's showtime!"

The hawk swung ten miles wide of the DeNiro's ranch and came up from the south. The combat helo cut its engine and all auditory indicators reached dead silence.

Killian hovered behind a high knoll and landed beyond a wind break. The helo gently touched the ground, and the cargo door was thrown open.

Trick leaped to the ground and touched each man's shoulder. "Go, go, go!"

They assumed a tight formation and shot into the darkness. Each man secured his night goggles. The Marines raced through the leafy wind break and worked their way from cluster to cluster. The unit kept a low profile and covered the distance in ten minutes.

The unit moved in a low-profile run, moving from outbuilding to outbuilding, until they came to the equipment shed. The were no hostiles posted at the back elevation. Dayo stood next to Trick and listened.

Johnson called in, "Wild Man, we're in position and ready to storm the homestead. Where are the hostiles?"

Eugene, "You're ten minutes too late. The hitmen went through the front doors, and hostages have been taken. There are two groups of heat clusters."

"There's one cluster in the family room, and another waiting by the front door. You better move fast; the hitmen are headed for the getaway vehicle."

Trick and Whip raced across the backyard and huddled against the outside wall. The Lieutenant gave a hand gesture, and Dayo and Heavy Duty ran around the side.

Heavy Duty kept a low profile and paused at the garage corner. He scanned for point guards, but there none were stationed.

HD whispered, "The hostiles figured this was a quick in-and-out. They're all inside, so let's get moving."

Heavy Duty stationed himself in an ornamental rock field, near the driveway. Since the Big Man had the West elevation covered, it was Dayo's job to cover the East.

Declan rounded the garage corner and stayed to the shadows. He ran in a low crouch, passed through an aspen grove, and raced to the far corner.

His boots padded over a green lawn, and he reached his destination.

There was a rounded knoll with granite boulders. The commander dropped to his belly, extended the tripod, and sighted every inch of the escape route.

The front porch was covered in a sloped shingle roof, and there were timber posts, and an entry dormer. If the captor took the hostage through the front walkway, the hostile had to descend two times.

At each interval, the captor would be higher than the hostage, and Declan had a clean shot.

Declan considered an alternative route, which would be a low-mounted bedroom window. He had a clear shot down the timber-chink walls, and the minute the captor stepped into view, it was over.

Heavy Duty spoke, "I've got the garage door, and the west porch covered, are you in position?"

Dayo finished calibrating his scope. Using his night vision, the commander calibrated altitude, wind, earth movement, and clear visibility.

"HD, I've got this."

Just then, Declan heard the grenade launcher blow out the back wall. He saw a blinding light flash through the living room, and seconds later, there were the telltale sounds of rifle fire.

He heard people scream, and the front door flew open. The first captor dragged Mariah DeNiro across the front porch.

She was dressed in blue overalls and a long-sleeved sweatshirt. Her brown hair was disheveled, and Desi's mother had an angry look about her.

Mariah craned her head, "You asshole, you haven't got a chance. Let me go, and you can make a run for it."

Her captor stuck the 9 mm to her throat, "Shut up, and keep moving. The SUV is by the garage, so pick up your feet and get going."

Dayo let the first captor make it to the end of the wraparound. There was a significant height difference, so HD had an easy headshot.

All they needed was the second hostage. Eugene whispered, "Captain, your man is on the way, hold tight."

Just then, a second captor dragged Austin DeNiro across the front foyer. Desi's dad wore a double XL shirt, and a pair of Wranglers. There was a pistol wound across his forehead, and the cattle rancher bled profusely.

Dayo kept his head and focused. All he had to do was wait for a change in elevation.

Heavy Duty whispered, "I'll take Mariah's captor first, and you take Austin's."

Mariah's captor spotted the SUV, and he hauled his hostage down the steps. The minute there was separation, HD squeezed the trigger, and he executed a clean headshot. Austin heard the gunfire and dropped into a low stance.

Dayo had separation, and in a split second, he drilled the captor. His hostile's head snapped back, and he was dead before he hit the ground.

No sooner did the man fall, then four black sedans hurled into the driveway. The doors flew open, and men burst from the doors.

Dayo used his night vision, scoped the hostiles, and pinned them inside the wings. His automatic sprayed the engine block, the windshields, and the passenger doors. The hostiles couldn't get outside.

Declan and Heavy Duty had them pinned, but he needed a better angle. Dayo rushed from behind the ornamental boulders and dashed to an elevated flower bed.

Just then, he saw Desiree angle the Longbow into a steep dive. She was traveling one-hundred-seventy mph, and she squeezed the trigger, and a Hydra rocket pod whipped beneath the caravan, and she blew four cars sky high. A fireball bloomed in the driveway and smoke billowed from the wreckage.

The bronze beauty pumped her fist in exaltation. He could imagine what his bad girl was saying. "You son of bitches, that one was for Tinder Williams. And no one, but no one, messes with my parents."

The Longbow careened into a steep banking curve and hovered above the property.

Wild Man came over the communicator, "Trick secured the interior, and the incoming have been neutralized. I'm not getting a heat readout from any hostiles. Double check the perimeter and secure the ranch."

Declan contacted each member. "Trick, have you gone through the entire house?"

"Yes, sir. Whip and I moved from room to room, main floor and basement. All the hostiles were eliminated, and the family has been liberated."

"Roger that."

Dayo spoke to Heavy Duty, "What's the status?"

"The sedan insurgents have been neutralized, and there are no survivors."

Declan spoke to his combat girl, "Desiree, it's safe down here. You can make a quick landing and speak with your folks."

The Longbow landed in the front yard, and Declan rushed to her parents. He removed a first response kit and tended to Austin's facial wounds.

"Mr. DeNiro, I wish we could have made it sooner, but you seem to be in one piece."

The middle-aged, bronze cowboy eyed him carefully. "With that blow to the head, I'm a bit rattled. But you look like Declan Cazador, the kid who Desiree used to date."

Declan daubed his forehead and handed him a cold pack. "Place this to your head, it will quell the bleeding, sir."

Dayo stood back and replied, "For what it's worth, I am Declan Cazador, and it just so happens, I married your daughter."

Austin couldn't believe it. "If that's the case, then my little girl must still be alive."

"That's right, and in a few seconds, you'll get to meet her."

Mariah exclaimed, "Thank god, she made it. We attended Desiree's funeral, and your parents told me that you were dead."

"According to Sanchez, you and Desi died in the safe house fire."

The Commander felt for them, "It was a cover-up, and the kingpin tried to flush us out."

Declan added, "And I want you to know how sorry I am. No one should mourn the loss of such a beautiful person."

Desiree tracked her scanners and searched the skies for enemy aircraft. It was a quiet night in central California, and there were no incoming.

She landed the Longbow in the front lawn. "Blake, can you take over? My parents thought I died in a safe house fire, so I've got to reassure them."

Desiree threw open the cockpit, stepped onto the running board, and dropped to the lawn.

She patted her thighs, "Hier." Molly leaped out of her tiny seat and bounded to the ground. Desi spoke to her Malinois, "We're going to meet Mom and Dad, and I want you to be a good girl."

The combat girl raced across the lawn. She saw Mariah and she threw her arms around her mom. The two women hugged and cried, and it felt so good to be in her mother's arms.

She felt awful for the pain she caused. No parent should grieve the loss of their child, and that's exactly what Desiree put her through.

Mariah said, "Let me look at you, girl. We thought you were dead."

Desi wiped away the tears, "It was a fake funeral and Gonzalez tried to draw us out. I'm so sorry you grieved my death, but there was no way we could contact you."

Her thick-chested father hauled her into a loving hug. "You little dickens, you survived and that's what's important."

Desi glanced at her mountain of father. "Dad, you're bleeding."

"Aw, it was nothin'. A hitman pistol-whipped me, but I've suffered worse."

The big man paused, "So, I hear you ran off and got married."

Declan slipped his arms around her. "Yes, sir, this is my beautiful wife. And she's a package deal. Desiree comes with Kay Bear, Molly, and house full of teddy bears."

Desi lifted her wrist cuff, "Kay Bear thinks this is a joyous occasion, and if we had more time, we could tell you so much more."

"But any minute, we'll get a fix on the enemy leader, and we'll have to run."

Dayo shook Austin's hand, "Sir, we plan to have a real wedding, and your whole family will be invited. I'm a ranch foreman for the Pettigrews, and we've got a big spread."

"We can have the ceremony in the shade of our timber log manor, and we'll even erect a flower trellis."

Mariah touched her eye, "It sounds wonderful."

She inspected Dayo's face, "You were on the Cowboy Channel

today. You went by the name of Dwayne Corazon, but we knew that couldn't be right."

Austin squeezed his meaty hands, "Son, you did some fair riding, today. Shepherd Cat was my favorite, and I'm glad you won."

Her man slid a hand behind her back, "And I wasn't the only one with honors. Your daughter took first place in the cutting event. She rode Hunter and even took the steer deep in the zone."

Desiree giggled, "It increased the level of difficulty, and I had a better chance of winning."

Mariah gave her a hug, "And honey, you won it all."

Her mom pulled back a pile of hair. "I apologize for not recognizing my own flesh and blood. But those ginger ringlets and peachy makeup threw me for a loop."

"Yeah, it's my disguise. We didn't want Gonzalez to know I was alive. But when they recognized Dayo, they came after you."

Desi wrung her hands, "I'm so sorry, but we'll make it right."

Right then, Eugene made an announcement. "Desiree, I have a fix on Antonio. He's in Malibu, and he just returned from a party. Girl, now's the time to finish him off."

The bronze beauty bit her lip, "Sorry, you guys. We'll have to socialize later. Duty calls, and we've got to finish the mission."

Declan escorted her to the Longbow, and he lifted her to the running board. Molly leaped to the ledge and jumped inside. Desi leaned down and kissed the man she loved.

"Commander, we've got to take down Gonzalez. So, let's get a move on it." She couldn't wait to get this thing over. She was less than a half hour from freedom.

Her commander winked, "Just stick to Trick's plan, and follow Eugene's intel, and Antonio is a goner."

Desiree knew that special ops were never routine, and there were bound to be problems. But she closed the shield, blew him a kiss, and gave her hubby a thumb's up.

It was showtime, and Gonzalez was going down.

Chapter Twenty

Declan ducked beneath the stub-wings and climbed into the cargo bay. He was greeted by Trick Johnson who delivered a fist bump.

"Captain, phase one is complete, and now we're hunting big game. I'll lay out the mission, and if you feel up to it, I'll reinstate your command."

Dayo lowered his heavy brows and flashed a charming Caribbean smile. "Dude, that sounds good to me. Let's hear about the op, and don't spare any details."

Vance Killian airlifted, and the hawk rose into the sky. The Sikorsky battleship shot Westward, and within ten minutes the California interior gave way to a starlit ocean.

Points of starlight danced on the waves, and they shot over the rugged coastline at more than two-hundred-twenty mph. It was attack speed, and they didn't have a moment to waste. Wild Man finally nailed Antonio's position, and they didn't want to lose the son of a bitch.

Dayo clicked his communicator, "Eugene, we're headed down the California coast. And by the looks of it, we're flying under the radar."

"Do you have a fix on Gonzalez?"

"Yes, sir. He's either in the East or West Wing. Using the heat imaging system, I can't tell for sure."

Declan removed his combat helmet and hand-combed his thick hair. "Eugene, did any of the DeNiro hostiles radio back to Gonzalez?"

"Boss, I'm checking the transmissions, but nothing has turned up."

Tanya chimed in, "You guys took out the insurgents, and even the messengers were eliminated."

The Commander wrapped a wooden board, "Honey, I hope you're right. The best way to fly is by total surprise."

Eugene growled, "It won't be a surprise if you don't get there quickly. Antonio sent his hitmen to take the DeNiros hostage."

"And radio silence means something went haywire. The longer it takes to get there the more suspicious he'll get."

The Commander turned his attention to his men. Heavy Duty, Whip, and Trick reloaded, and instinctively, he jammed another clip into this M16.

He unloaded a full magazine into four sedans, and if Antonio's mansion was heavily armed, he'd need a full arsenal.

The bronze warrior turned to his second. "All right, what have you got?"

Trick pulled up his screen, and a photo of a Malibu mid-century appeared.

It was a real estate photo taken at night, and the Gonzalez manor stood high on a hill. Huge vista windows glowed with an amber light, and a brilliant reflection created a watery image.

"Since his mansion runs parallel the beach, there's an East and West Wing. Looking at the oceanside elevation, do you have a best guess?"

"No, Captain, I don't. The wings are practically mirror images of each other, and if you look at the blueprints, the master suites are situated in the back."

"The rubber roof features large soffit overhangs, and the back elevation has a plate glass balcony that wraps around the entire building."

"All right, I've seen the master suites, and the connecting hallways. What do you suggest?"

"It's a weak theory, but Wild Man wants to hit the East Wing. He thinks the West encounters too much high wind. Gonzalez likes his sleep and howling winds might keep him awake."

"That is weak, but at least, we have a theory. Let's land the hawk on the East roof. While we're blasting through the ceiling and combing the suites, we need the Longbow to cover our ass."

"You got it, boss. Vance already contacted Desiree, and she'll hover close by. If anything goes sideways, we've got the fire power."

Declan placed his hand in the center, "Oorah! Let's do this."

The Black Hawk flew way out into the ocean. The combat helo shot beneath the radar, and they were untraceable. As the Sikorsky accelerated down the coast, Vance suddenly veered inland. They passed the point, and the Malibu beach stretched before them.

Dayo glanced out the window as the helo swooped up the beach, crossed the Olympic pool, and landed. The cargo doors flew open, and the men went into formation.

Heavy Duty angled the grenade launcher and blasted a hole through the roof. A gaping hole revealed a tongue-and-groove ceiling and a vault with stained beams.

Whip and Trick were stationed around the hole. And immediately, Johnson whipped a flash bang into the dark suite.

Dayo and HD grabbed a rappelling rope and slung into position. By the glaring white light, Declan dropped all three insurgents. He raced to three corpses and rolled them over.

"Dammit! Gonzalez isn't in this wing."

Immediately, they heard the thunder of footsteps. Trick demolished the French doors, and the men leaped into position. From the vantage point of a solid pony wall, Whip peered over the cap rail, and gunned down the hostiles.

Within seconds, there were bodies piled along the staircase, and the upper balcony was laden with dead guards. Trick and Whip rushed back into the suite. It was an in-and-out mission, and they didn't have time to waste.

Heavy Duty blasted a hole through two adjoining rooms. They had to fight their way to the West Wing. The headhunters moved swiftly through the debris.

Dayo whispered to Eugene. "How many men are there in the West suite?"

"Four men. It's got to be Gonzalez and three bodyguards."

The Marine unit came to the last room on the second floor. They overheard a man shouting orders in Spanish. Dayo wasn't sure, but the one word he caught was about the outdoor balcony.

He whispered, "Desiree, Antonio may be headed your way. We're going in."

HD fired the grenade launcher, and it blew a hole through a thick stucco wall. Whip tossed the flash bang, and it created a blinding light. The three insurgents dove over a Spanish Colonial bed, and the fourth rushed out the French doors.

Desiree heard the transmission, and she floated into position. Her eyes were peeled for any outdoor movements. Using her magnifying lens, she scanned the plate glass balconies, waiting for any hostiles to emerge.

Suddenly, she caught sight of the West Wing. The French doors flew open, and a heavy-set Latino rushed to the balcony.

Desi would have recognized that arrogant face anywhere. It was Gonzalez in the flesh. She hovered the Longbow into position and Antonio looked up.

She turned on the cockpit light, so the man would know it was her. He threw one leg over the plate glass and stopped cold. Gonzalez looked at her with absolute horror.

Desi turned to Kay Bear, "K-Man, you better avert your button eyes. This won't be pretty."

Desiree squeezed the M 230 chain gun and drilled the shit out of the bastard. Antonio's body shook like a leaf, and the bullet fire ripped him to pieces. He fell over the balcony and landed in the blue pool.

It was finished. She raised one fist in triumph, "Take that you piece of shit. Tinder Williams life has been avenged, and that's for attacking my parents."

She spoke into her communicator. "Gonzalez is dead. We got him, and it's time to go home."

Dayo heard the transmission as his men burst into the Spanish suite. His team eliminated the three guards, and now it was time to retreat.

They leaped through the stucco wall and raced back to the East Wing. One by one, they ascended the rappelling ropes and crawled onto the roof.

Desiree had to make sure everyone made it. When she spotted a hostile carrying a ground-to-air missile launcher, she rifled a Hellfire missile into the West Wing. A huge fireball billowed into the sky.

"You sons of bitches, you don't know when to give up, do you?"

The Apache Longbow hovered out of range, but she covered the Black Hawk. She watched the team climb out of the hole, and they scurried into the cargo bay.

Dayo was the third man in line. But when he heard gunshots, he dropped to one knee and covered Trick's escape.

Her warrior cut down three insurgents, but out of nowhere, a sniper drilled him in the chest. Dayo took a direct hit and flew backward.

Trick and Heavy Duty seized him by the arms and dragged his limp body inside.

Desiree screamed in horror, "No, no, not Dayo! That wasn't supposed to happen."

She spotted the sniper and turned her chain gun on him. The guy fluttered like a rag doll and dropped to the balcony. She was livid and scared out of her mind.

The combat girl rose high in the sky and blasted a Hellfire missile into the East Wing. A fireball consumed the mansion and billows of smoke appeared. Off in the distance, she heard sirens wail, and it was time to get the hell outta there.

She watched the Black Hawk shoot over the beach and out over the coastal waters. It was a starlit night, and the Hawk and Longbow flew in a tight formation.

Desiree fought back the tears. She called over her shoulder, "Blake, did you see what happened?"

"I sure did, but Desi it's going to be all right. Dayo was wearing his Kevlar vest. It's standard procedure. When the Marines go into battle, they come fully prepared."

"Oh god, oh god, I hope you're right. Trick wouldn't let him go into battle without it. Would he?"

"Here, I'll contact Vance and get Johnson on the line."

Desiree heard the Lieutenant's voice. "Trick, is Dayo all right?"

"We've stripped away his camos and removed the body armor. He's out cold and totally unconscious. Hey, I've got to go. When he comes to, I'll let you know."

The line went dead, and Desiree nearly lost it. This should have been a victorious return, but it had turned into a nightmare.

Gonzalez reached out with his stone-cold fingers and tried to snatch Declan's life. Would that freakin' bastard ever stop haunting her?

The combat girl panted for air. It was like the world was closing in. Suddenly, Molly leaped to her chest, and deluged her with a ton of doggie kisses.

Her Malinois gave her a good facial bath and didn't relent. Finally, Desi pushed her doggo's chest. "Hey girl, I'm fully grounded."

The Longbow shot over the waves, and she watched white crests spill into the swales. It was eerie and beautiful.

"Oh Blake, I can't lose him. Dayo and I just got married, and he means everything."

"In fact, we're going to have a baby."

She heaved her bosom as huge tears rolled across her cheeks. "Lieutenant, can you pray for me?"

"Hey, Desiree, I'm not the right guy. Maybe, you can get a prayer warrior on the horn, and call in an intercessor. I'm not really good at this stuff."

She wiped her tears and gazed at Kay Bear. "That's it! Blake, you're a genius."

Desiree contacted Eugene, "Wild Man, patch me through to Hallie May. I need help, and I need it fast."

The hacker shot across the floor, and she heard the wheels screech. "Hang on, I'll call the landline and wake up the Pettigrews."

"Hello, this is Hallie, is something wrong?"

Desi stammered, "Oh, Mrs. Pettigrew, it's horrible. Dayo finished the mission, and just as they were about to board, a hostile drilled Declan in the chest."

"He took three bullets to the midsection, and he's been knocked unconscious. It's horrible, I think he might not make it."

"One of those projectiles could have gone high or it could have gone low. Can you pray for him? He means the world to me."

By this time, tears trickled down her cheeks, and her throat closed up. Desiree could barely breathe. There was a remote possibility Declan could die.

Hallie replied, "Honey, you've got to have faith. He was wearing body armor, wasn't he?"

"Yes, he was. But depending on the length of the projectile, a bullet may have wounded him."

She whimpered, "A Kevlar vest does have a breaking point, and I just hope it held fast."

Mrs. Pettigrew spoke calmly. "This is in the hands of the Almighty. I'll get off the phone and drop to my knees."

"I won't stop praying until you're in Dayo's loving arms."

The phone clicked off, and Desiree couldn't have called a better person.

She brushed back the tears. "Blake, where are we?"

"We've flown the length of California, and we've entered Oregon's airspace. Vance Killian is about to head inland, and we'll follow his lead."

Desiree forced herself to concentrate. Everything would be all right. It had to be. After all they had been through, it would be so unfair if Dayo didn't make it.

Within minutes, she crossed over the Cascades, and the town of Pine Whisper appeared. The sunrise broke over the ridge and cast the valley in a golden glow.

It was so flippin' beautiful she wanted to cry. But no sunrise would be perfect without her stud warrior.

She clenched her delicate hands, Dayo had to make it. He was the best, and her valiant Marine always did the right thing. He'd been at her side since this whole nightmare began.

Desiree brushed back the tears and spotted the Pettigrew Ranch. The pale-yellow clapboard and the buff grey roof never looked more appealing. And there she was, her personal prayer warrior was on the front porch.

The combat girl allowed the Black Hawk to land first. Vance headed into a slight breeze, nosed upward, and alighted in a soft landing. She didn't want anything to jolt Declan, and the Sikorsky pilot did a great job.

She copied the landing and touched down in Cobb's helipad. She cut the engine and threw open the cockpit. Desiree fumbled with the seatbelt, but finally got the dang thing to work.

The bronze beauty unbuckled her Malinois, "Molls, you've got to do me a favor. If Dayo doesn't come to, I want you to lick his face off."

Her pupper seemed to understand, and her therapy dog leaped out of the cockpit, hit the running board, and dropped to the green lawn. She was right on Molly's heels as she pumped her arms and ran toward the hawk.

The cargo bay was thrown open, and the men piled out. Trick caught her by the arm.

"He took three direct hits, and his chest is badly bruised. He's been on oxygen, but he's come to several times. Your man loves you, so take it easy."

How could she take it easy? Desiree pushed Johnson aside and ducked beneath the stub-wings. Dayo lay on a wall stretcher, and his camos were ripped open. His Kevlar vest was cut with scissors, and his handsome chest was covered in massive bruises.

Desi straddled his waist and removed the oxygen mask. "Declan, it's me." Her stud warrior opened his brown eyes, and she seized his shoulders.

"Don't you dare die on me. I love you so much, it hurts. And the thought of losing you would be the worst blow of all."

"We're gonna a have a baby, and you will never die, and you'll always be by my side." She shook him extra hard, "Do you hear me?"

Dayo rose to sitting position, "Yes, ma'am, I hear you loud and clear."

"And babe, I'm not going anywhere. I plan to be around when the baby is born, and every day after that."

He glanced around, "Did we get him? Is Gonzalez dead?"

The bronze beauty felt herself breakdown. "Yes, we avenged Tinder's death, and it's all over. We won't have Antonio hanging over us. He's dead and gone and I blew his mansion to shit."

Declan chuckled, "That's my girl. You don't take crap from anyone, and you come out fighting."

He chucked her cute chin, "Babe, I couldn't have married a better woman, and for your information, I'll never die on you."

Desiree straddled his waist and buried him in a kiss of eternal gratitude. Time stood still, and she had everything she ever wanted.

Her man was alive, and she had a muffin in the oven, and her worst enemy was gone. She had a whole life to look forward to, and at the center of it all, was one amazing Marine.

Chapter Twenty-One

3 Years later

Not a day went by that Desiree didn't thank God. To think that she almost lost her amazing Marine. Bad memories still haunted her, but she brushed aside that fateful day and pursued the present.

Today was her son's birthday, and her stud cowboy was training Sheppie's colt. Life had come full circle, and her life was absolutely incredible.

She held the reins to a retired rodeo horse named Danger. Cobb's rodeo horse served him well, but in the Palomino's retirement, he was ginger-footed.

Danger could only bear the weight of a child, and that precious little boy happened to be her pride and joy, Jayden Cazador.

His brown eyes were enormous, and the cute bug sported an Afro of ringlets. Her tyke had the cutest little face you've ever seen. Desi tiptoed above Danger's saddle and gave Jayden a big kiss.

Her youngster loved attention, but he was too smart for his own good. Jayden pointed to the koala toy wrapped around the saddle horn.

"Mommy, Kay Bear needs a kiss too. He thinks Daddy is gonna win the next horse show, but he wants to be sure." She chucked her boy's adorable chin, "You think so, do you?"

Desiree kissed her son's Kay-Bear, but she still had one of her own. K-Man peered from her wrist cuff, and his button brown eyes were filled with perpetual happiness.

Desi didn't need her koala to talk her down, but it was reassuring that her good luck talisman was always present.

The bronze beauty reached above the pipe rails and pet her faithful Malinois. Molly was perched on an elevated platform.

It was constructed during her post-traumatic years, but her pupper loved an aerial view. And Molls could keep an eye on her, as well as her new charge, little Jayden.

The morning light streaked through the open-air arena. A translucent roof allowed sunshine to bathe the horse sanctuary in a golden glow.

Kissed by sunshine, the indoor arena transformed into a spiritual oasis. A million diamonds danced over the glittering sand, and the place was pure paradise.

She loved the sanctuary and the anointed feel. Simply gazing over the arena and watching Dayo train a new colt brought back roping memories.

Three years ago, this was where it all began. And who would have thought one roping session would have led to such a miraculous gift?

The hourglass beauty had become a proud momma, and her peach bronze complexion glowed with pride. She had it all, a loving husband, her first born, and a thriving horse ranch.

She curled her lips, and her dimples formed, and she glowed with contentment. Of course, nothing remains the same, and Dayo didn't know it yet, but she had plans for a little girl.

Jayden bounced on Danger's saddle and pointed across the arena. "Daddy is riding Shepherd Boy, and he's going to win the next rodeo."

Her bundle of joy broke into a cute smile, and he glanced sideways as though he knew a secret.

"Actually, honey, Shepherd Boy is a futurity colt, and Daddy is getting him ready for an RCH contest. Sheppie Jr. has his father's cow sense, but he's not ready for the big time."

"We'll take him to a small event, and he'll get use to the audience."

"What do you mean, Mommy? Sheppie Jr. is super-duper. He's ready for the Big Time, I can feel it." Her adorable tyke repeated everything he heard.

The bronzed beauty leaned against Danger's skirt, "Actually, Sheppie Boy needs to get accustomed to loud noises."

"When the fans start talkin', and stompin' their feet, it may scare him. He's a youngster, and one minute he's brilliant and the next minute, he's skittish."

"Oh, I understand. I'll make a lot of noise and help Sheppie Boy win." Jayden cupped his cute hands to his face, and yelled, "Way to go, Sheppie Junior, you can do it!"

Declan finished his last splash stop, and Junior hunkered into a low skid. The young sorrel had complete body control, and he was a push-button rein.

Dayo trotted Junior backward ten steps, and the horse complied willingly.

When the colt reached the end of the maneuver, the youngster perked his ears, and glanced at Jayden. Dayo held the reins aloft and gave up. Her astute husband trotted over to the pipe rail.

"Hey, little man, what's going on?"

Jayden beamed with happiness, "Mommy said that Junior needs to hear more noise. We've got to get him ready for the RCH."

"And when he goes into the arena, folks will be hootin' and hollerin' and it might scare Sheppie. So, I'm helping him by yelling encouragement."

Dayo broke into his Caribbean smile, "I appreciate the positive horse talk, but audience enthusiasm is scheduled for tomorrow."

"And son, you did catch Sheppie's attention, but he almost blew the backward trot."

"I'm sorry Daddy, I didn't mean it. But I want to help!"

Dayo patted his son's Afro ringlets, "I appreciate your help, but let's wait until tomorrow. For right now, I want the colt to get his footwork down and master cow control."

Jayden asked innocently, "How long will it take? I want Mommy to get my birthday ready. And this horse stuff is taking way too long."

"I hear ya, son. But it will take five more minutes."

Jayden rolled his cute eyes, "Sounds like an eternity." Declan chuckled as he turned to his beautiful wife, "Where does he get this stuff?"

Desiree dropped a hand to her flared hip, "What do you mean? Where does he get this stuff?"

"This horse ranch is loaded with stimuli. The Pettigrews dote on him, and they carry him everywhere. And the unit launches one project after another. This remote place is bustling with activity, and everyone speaks their mind."

Dayo wagged his finger, "There's the problem. We have to be subtle and say what's appropriate."

She burst into a huge smile, "That a fine thing, coming from you."

"You, Declan Cazador are the least subtle person I know. And when you get carried away, you expand Jayden's vocabulary a hundred-fold."

The Caribbean Kid grinned, "Be that as it may, I'm doing my very best."

Desi tiptoed toward Declan, and her loving man leaned down for a beautiful kiss. He cupped her cheek and held her sweetly, and kissed her in a wonderful, tantalizing flourish.

Good lord, her man still had it. He could make her tingle, and he could make lady dew pool low and sweet.

"All right, you big stud! Get out there and finish the run." The fearless cowboy trotted Sheppie Junior to the far side.

David T. opened the gate and a brown-eyed Charolais rushed forward. Declan reined Junior ever so slightly, and the colt cut off the steer's advance.

The horse and cow maneuvered back and forth until the newbie found his cow sense. Dayo had the steer completely figured out, but the goal was to show off the colt's abilities. And in the mind of young horses, anything could happen.

When Dayo allowed the Charolais to run down the longwall, he lifted the rein, and Sheppie took off like a shot. The young colt accelerated past the runaway, got two strides ahead, and then cut off the little escapee.

The youngster had excellent cow sense, and he loved every minute. Dayo performed the fence work, and then he was ready for the open arena.

The fearless horseman guided Sheppie to the steer's left flank and the colt took charge and ran the little runaway in a full circle.

The young stud exhibited total control as horse and steer ran shoulder-to-shoulder. It was a thing of beauty, and after Dayo completed the circle, he patted the colt's shoulder.

"Good work, little guy. That was a fair piece of cow work."

Dayo trotted over to the stands. By that time, Cobb and Hallie were seated in the bleachers, alongside Desiree and Jayden.

Pettigrew clapped his hands, "In the snaffle futurity, you would have taken first place."

Dayo tipped his Stetson, "In our hallowed arena with peace and quiet and beautiful sunshine, our little guy performs well. But as Jayden pointed out, we've got to put Sheppie Boy into a noisier environment."

Cobb spoke slowly, "I agree, but the first thing is to learn fence work in a quiet place. Later, we can throw a party, and simulate an RCH auditorium."

Jayden waved his little hands, "Grandpa Cobb, today's my birthday, and I was wondering?"

Pettigrew eyed the youngster with affection, "And son, what were you wondering?"

His first born rolled his adorable eyes, "I was wonderin' how many presents you're going to give me?"

Hallie flashed a birdwing smile, "Little Man, you're not supposed to ask that type of question. But I'll make an exception, and I'll let you know, we have three beautiful gifts."

"Oh, boy, do you hear that Mommy, Grandma Hallie is giving me three presents."

Desiree curled her lips, and she booped his little nose. "Little Man, it's best to be thankful, and it's impolite to ask for things."

Cobb placed a leathery hand on Jayden's shoulder. "Son, I gave you my rodeo horse, Danger. That seems like a mighty big gift."

"Oh, it is, and I love Danger. He's the fastest horse in the whole world. Yesterday, we rode the round pen, and we were going faster than ninety miles an hour."

Pettigrew curled his lips, "Kids and their wild imaginations."

Desiree scooped Jayden off Danger's saddle. "We're going inside. My little man needs a break. Tanya is headed over with Galileo, and the boys can play with my teddys."

She flashed her pretty eyes. "So, hold your thoughts, and I'll be right back."

Dayo watched the love of his life race out of the open-air arena. Through the iron uprights, he watched her trot up the pine steps to their timber log home.

It filled him with so much pride to look at their new home. This was where he planned to raise a family and excel at horsemanship. And he owed it all to the man standing next to him.

Somehow, Jayden's birthday triggered a trip down memory lane. And what's more, he took full stock of his loved ones.

It was his responsibility to see to the Pettigrews' bucket list. If they were happy, then the ranch could flourish, and all debts had been paid.

Just then, the military unit strolled into the arena. Trick, Whip, and Heavy Duty were all dressed in Western wear.

Dayo fought by their side for seven years. They even joined forces and took down Gonzalez. They were instrumental to the ranch's success, and he was damn proud of them.

The precision cowboys integrated into Western society, and they succeeded. And finally, they were courting pretty cowgirls, who wanted to settle down. Just looking at them caused his chest to burn.

Trick relaxed his piercing eyes, "Captain, we'll be over at the kid's playground, setting up a miniature obstacle course."

Heavy Duty folded his massive forearms, "That's right, boss. I broke down and assembled a tiny course for kids."

He raised a big hand, "No need to thank me. It will come in handy when I manage the civilian boot camp. While the parents are dying on the course, the little ones can play."

Whip broke into his party-going smile, "Hey, Captain, we're all bringing cowgirls to this shin dig. But don't tell Hallie, I may have found a keeper. If she finds out, she'll make me marry the girl."

Trick stroked his stubble, "Dayo, it's been three years since we knocked off Gonzalez. And when we returned, I had no idea if we'd fit in."

"But I want to thank you."

"Whip and I are hitting the rodeo, and I'm finishing horses, and my life couldn't be better. And Captain, we owe it all to your generosity and straight forward decency."

Declan lowered his brows, "Gentlemen, it's been a pleasure. Seeing you integrate and find your life's calling has been a rare privilege. Just knowing, everyone has a productive career has made my life truly fulfilling."

Trick groaned, "There's just too much sentiment here, I've got to get going."

"But Captain, I just wanted to say it one more time, Thank you."

All three of his men gave him a thumb's up, and he'd remember that to his dying day. They were first rate, every darn one of them.

Just then, Eugene and Tanya strolled into the open-air arena. Wild Man wore casual Western wear, and long gone were the days of eccentricity. His lovin' woman wore cowgirl chic, and she looked like a sassy little momma.

Simply seeing his intel man caused him to choke up. From the time they heard the Vegas betting line, three years ago, his life took a huge turn.

Dayo extended a hand, "Eugene, I want you to know how much

our relationship means. If it weren't for you, I would never have busted Desi out of that safe house."

Wild Man smiled, "Hey, boss, it was my pleasure. And if you hadn't been so insane, I would never have teamed up with Tanya."

The sassy cowgirl fingered her ringlets, "It's true. From the moment, you guys hit the high Sierras, I was all aboard."

"I helped the headhunters cover your ass, and I spent endless hours with this wonderful guy."

It was evident, the intel man and the sassy cowgirl were deeply in love. And that's all Dayo had to know.

Declan hauled Tanya into a hug, "Girl, I want to thank you for everything. Those long hours in the command center led to our freedom. And I can never completely thank, either one of you."

Eugene chimed in, "Boss, quit squeezing my woman. Don't you have a ranch to run?"

The Commander stepped back, "Wild Man, you're right. I've got a meeting on Cobb's front porch, and I better get to it."

Declan felt a huge amount of closure, but he still had to set the record straight.

Dayo arrived at Cobb's front porch. He pulled three rocking chairs into a circle.

"If you don't mind, I'd like to get an update on your bucket dreams. I want to make sure your golden years are fulfilling, and you're experiencing everything you ever wanted."

Hallie May touched his face. "Dayo, why the sudden interest? You know how happy we are, and other than more grandbabies, I don't want for anything."

Declan laughed, "I realize that you have your bucket list. And Desiree and I are thinking about number two. More than anything, Desi wants a cute little girl."

Just then, his bronze beauty rounded the corner, and raced up the steps.

Desiree piped in, "Sorry to interrupt, but I just got Jayden and

Galileo settled in. The boys are playing with teddys and dinos, and they're having a blast."

Hallie jumped up, "Who's looking after them?"

Desi touched her arm reassuringly, "Not to worry, Halls. Tanya is keeping an eye on them, but I sensed Dayo was going to say something important, and I wanted to be present."

The commander cupped her face, "Honey, I'm glad you're here, but I'd like to get a few things off my chest. So, if you could lend quiet support, I'd appreciate it."

Desiree knew him pretty well, and it wasn't easy for him to share. And when he got rolling, he didn't like being interrupted. Desi zipped her lips shut and gave him the floor.

Hallie pushed off the floorboards and rocked back and forth. "If you each have four children apiece, I'll be happier than a pumpkin."

"I'll kiss my grandbabies and the ranch will be alive with the pitter-patter of little feet. A grandmother couldn't be happier, nor could I ask for anything more."

Cobb could see where this conversation was headed. "Don't mind Hallie, she's living vicariously, and making up for lost time. We never had children, but as a grandmother, she'll accept a kindergarten full of grandbabies."

Declan said, "I hear ya, Old Man." He paused, "As an explanation for why we waited, Desi wanted to devote herself to Jayden, and I had to figure out how to run this place."

Cobb jumped in, "And son, you're doing an amazing job. In the last three years, you've increased every revenue stream I ever had. The cattle ranching is booming, the rodeo victories are comin' in, and you've become a celebrity horseman."

"You and Shepherd Cat won two Western riding finals, and this year we're headed for a third. If you're askin' about my bucket list, we're there."

Dayo gazed into their eyes. "I owe you folks the world, and if I haven't said it enough, I just want to thank you for this opportunity, and the life you've given me."

"You took a wandering Marine, and gave him a home, and a career. You taught me how to run a ranch, and you shared your wisdom. I've inherited your legacy and your life's work. In reality, I can never thank you enough for your generosity."

Declan addressed the man with deep respect. "Cobb, none of this could have happened without you. Your wisdom and compassion has set me free."

"Before I met you, I didn't have a calling, and I had no idea what I was doing. But you gave me a once in a life opportunity, and I just want to say how deeply grateful I am."

"Sir, you've become my father, my mentor, and my guiding light. So, I want to make sure you're completely satisfied. I want your golden years to be full, and I'd like to see every bucket dream come true."

Cobb held Dayo's hand, and both men were deeply moved.

Desiree chimed in, "And I want to second that motion. You took a post-traumatic girl, helped me find a therapy pupper, and gave me the tools to pursue my dream."

"Without you folks, there wouldn't be a timber log home, a LifeNet job, or a champion cutting horse. You gave me the world, and I owe you all my happiness."

She squeezed Hallie's hands, "Halls, you're the mother I never had, and you're my best friend. And best of all, you've become a grandma to my son."

Tears streamed down her cheeks. Desiree brushed them away as she hauled Mrs. Pettigrew into a grateful hug.

She held the old prayer warrior tight, and she cherished every minute. Desi didn't know how long her mentor would be around, but she hoped it would be forever.

Hallie squeezed her hands. "You two have added so much life around here. And it's we, who don't know how to thank you."

Mrs. Pettigrew announced, "We've come to the promised land, and Canaan is flowing with milk and honey. Just keep doing what you're doing, and it will bring joy to everyone."

Hallie touched their faces, "The day the Lord brought you into our lives, I will never forget it. I received a prophecy of good things to come. And I told Cobb, we'll be carrying in the sheaves."

"And lo and behold, down the road were a husband and wife headed our way. I didn't need to test your roping skills; I knew you were sent by the Lord."

Hallie's faith exceeded hers by a thousand to one. But Desiree was happy to be an answer to their prayers. The Pettigrews were an answer to hers.

Desiree bounced on her heels, "I have a plan for a baby girl. So, Halls, you're going to get your wish." She touched her eyes, "You guys make me so happy; I feel like I'm going to cry all day."

Instead of being Jayden's birthday, this was more like a day of thanksgiving. And taking inventory, she had a wonderful life, an amazing hubby, and a great little boy.

Desiree trotted down the wooden steps. "See ya at the party!"

She blew them a kiss and rushed beneath Dayo's arms. As they crossed the lawn to their timber log home, she peered up at her beloved.

"Dayo, what you did, was extremely thoughtful."

"Not only are you a good manager, but you've brought joy to all of us. And most of all, you've made me, the happiest woman in the whole world."

Declan dug her tummy, "Babe, you're truly amazing. And I couldn't ask for a better wifey bear."

Hallie, Desiree, and Tanya set up three tables. Their beautiful timber log home featured a large porch deck with enough room to accommodate all their guests. In the dappled light, Jayden was about to have a wonderful birthday.

Balloons hung from each table corner, and flower bouquets ran down the center. And the star of the show was Jayden's blue gingham table.

Desi erected a jungle backdrop with yellow balloons, a three-tiered cake, and stacks of birthday presents. When her little guy laid eyes on the cache, he was going to flip.

Across the front lawn, Declan built a kid's playground set. The men raced around, trying to catch their tykes, and they all had a ball. Dayo ran behind Jayden and faked a tackle.

The button-eyed youngster dodged his old man and made a run for the staircase. He was joined by a little boy wearing a crocodile shirt, blue sweatpants, and red tennis shoes.

Jayden called out, "How ya doin', Galileo? I bet I can beat you to the top."

Even though Galileo was Eugene's boy, the kid was far more athletic than his father. Thanks to Tanya's tomboy genes, the youngster loved sports and climbing trees.

The two boys dashed up the wooden staircase and raced to the landing.

Jayden came to a dead stop, "Whoa! It's a long way down. Just look how far it is. I can barely see my dad."

Heavy Duty folded his arms with pride. "If you're going to build something, I say, you should build it right. And boys, that's not a very big slide. When I was a boy, slides were a lot bigger."

Desiree listened from a safe distance. She enjoyed the men's boasting, and how much pride they took.

Whip called out, "Are you boys scaredy-cats?"

Jayden yelled back, "No I'm a fearless Marine like my dad." Galileo and Jayden sat down and wrapped their arms around one another. "Here we come!"

The boys slid to the bottom and Dayo caught Jayden, and Eugene caught Galileo.

Declan lifted his son high into the air and whirled him in an airplane spin.

"Buddy, you're a fearless Marine just like me. But I got to tell ya something."

"What's that daddy?"

"You don't have to join the military to be a great guy. There's a ton of things a man can excel at."

Jayden combed his adorable Afro. "You mean like riding horses and driving cattle?"

"Yes, those are two things that bring satisfaction, and no one has to get hurt."

Desiree listened to her bronze warrior. It had been three years since they terminated Gonzalez. When they returned, the news cast described the incident as a syndicate war.

They were off the hook and free to live their lives. And that's exactly what she planned to do.

The bronze beauty arranged birthday plates and noticed the arrival of more guests. Her parents crossed the lawn, and each carried an armload.

She raced over to Mariah, "Oh mom, you didn't need to buy all those things."

Her mother wore a cute pair of overalls, pretty long sleeves, and a pair of tall boots.

Mariah curled her lips, "Honey, what good is being a grandparent unless you can spoil your grandbabies?"

Her father, Austin, echoed the sentiments. "Yep, we don't get up this way too often, but when we come, we like to bring lots of goodies."

Her dad wore a summer Stetson, plaid button-down, and a denim Wranglers. He removed his sunglasses, "Girl, you just get prettier every time I see you."

Mariah arranged the presents. "Honey, are you in the family way?"

Desi giggled, "I don't think so, but later this evening, I plan to have a baby party. I've invited my stud cowboy, and he's got it all figured out."

Jayden raced over and held out his arms. "Howdy, Grampa Austin, what did you bring me?"

"It's a surprise, but I'm sure you'll like it. And since we're both cowboys, I happen to know what a kid likes."

The big man scooped up Jayden and held him in his arms.

Mariah leaned over and kissed Jayden's cheek, "Will you look at this little man. Every time I see him, he doubles in size."

Her button-eyed boy reached out, and her mother took him. "Boy, you're growing like a weed. Do you like new clothes?"

"Yes, I do, but I prefer toys instead."

She booped his little nose, "Son, you're in luck because we're giving you both."

Desiree clapped her hands. "It looks like we're all here. Let's gather around the cake and sing Happy Birthday."

Declan stood by her side as Jayden danced all over the place. The Marines, the Pettigrews, and the DeNiros sang in one accord, "Happy Birthday to you!"

Desi felt like such a doting, helicopter mom. Just like her helo background, she hovered near her little guy, and she loved him to pieces.

Molly stood next to Jayden, and she placed a paw to Jayden's black sweatpants.

"All right, Jayden, blow out the candles and make a wish."

Jayden blew out the candles, and he opened his adorable eyes. "Mommy, can I open all these presents?"

"No, baby, let's just open one gift from each person. And we'll save the rest for later."

Her little man burst into a cute smile, "Okay, Mommy, I'm still gonna have lots of toys."

Declan laughed, "Our son is goal oriented, and he gets it from you." Dayo dug her in the side, and Desi burst into a belly laugh.

"Me? You're the famous Commander, and you've got one goal after the next."

One by one, his unit presented gifts. Heavy Duty, Whip, and Trick were all there. And she knew how much Dayo loved them. And lastly, Eugene and Tanya brought up the rear.

They integrated and each had a promising future. Her stud Marine could rest at night, knowing his team had found their way.

Jayden ripped open the presents and marveled at each gift. And after every present, he announced, "This is the exact present I was hoping for."

Desiree curled her lips in motherly pride. And her dimples were so noticeable, it made her face hurt. She had been smiling all day, and she couldn't stop.

When her handsome boy finished the last present, Jayden looked exhausted. If she pushed him too far, he'd get cranky and start to cry.

Desiree scooped him up, "Jayden is ready for a nap, but you all can stay longer. I've made plans with Grandma Hallie, and she's having a sleep over."

Hallie took Jayden into her arms, "Care to visit our home? You and Galileo can sleep in the bunk beds. Does that sound fun?"

"It will be your very first sleepover."

"Oh, boy, a sleepover. This is the best birthday ever!"

Jayden waved goodbye, and finally, Desiree had her husband all to herself.

Like school kids, they rushed through the front door, dashed through the great room, and shot into the boudoir. Declan spun her in a big circle, and then her stud Marine heaved her onto the four poster.

Desiree giggled, "Before you pounce on me, I have a surprise." She leaped up and dashed into the bathroom.

The hourglass beauty skipped into the loo. She put on a corset and a pillowing red bustier. For the crowning touch, she slipped her ginger red ringlets into place.

Desiree applied her peach-glow makeup and popped her pearly pink lips. "Girl, you look hotter than hell, and when Dayo sees you, he's gonna feint."

The bronze beauty sashayed to the four poster. She traced a delicate finger between her breasts.

"Are you ready to join me? I have delicacies, body oils, and you can taste my peachy delights."

She surveyed the amber glow bedroom. Dayo had the fire burning, and the floor was covered with candles. Her ruby satin comforter was turned down, and the love chaise was ready and rarin' to go.

Molly leaped to her doggie bed, and an audience of teddy bears beamed their button brown eyes.

She reflected on how romantic Declan was. He was more than an action-packed Marine, the guy was her go-to person, and the glue that held her life together.

Years ago, he was her bodyguard, but he evolved into a loving husband, and she couldn't have been more thankful.

Dayo ripped off his shirt and dropped his drawers. "Are we going for a little girl?"

Desi giggled, "I just got my figure back, and now, we can do anything you want."

He removed his trunks with a grand flare. His manhood stood upright, and Desi knew her outfit had the desired effect. She was sexy as all hell, and her man couldn't wait to taste her lips.

"How about I throw your heels over your head, bury it deep, and treat you to swooshy long strokes?"

She rushed across the room and leaped into his arms. Her man lowered her into the saddle, and he threw her feet way above her head. Declan angled deep, buried his enthusiasm, and drew her ever so close.

His handsome mouth joined her awaiting lips, and they dissolved into a dreamy love session. They were joined in every way, and that was just the way she liked it. Life didn't get any better, and to think, she had this man for all eternity. It was a dream come true.

The End

About the Author

The cowboy watercolors of William Matthews, the cattle drives of Colorado, and professional rodeo events have inspired Mark E. Scott to write western romance, western fantasy, and sci-fi fantasy novels. A storyteller at heart, he lives in Denver.

Books by Mark E. Scott

Felinius Fantasy Series

The Felinius Healer

Tigerian Retribution

Salt Fork Western Romance

Cowboy Takes Flight

Obsessed With a Rodeo Cowboy

Lone Rock Cowboy

Stunt Action Cowboy

Montana Western Romance

Angel Dare Cowboy

Cowgirl Warrior

A Coeur d'Alene Romance

The Llama Cowboy

A Colorado Western Romance

Savant Cowgirl and Her Lumberjack

Old West Dragon Fantasy

Dragon Cowgirl

Victorian Cowgirl and Latent Dragon

Contemporary Dragon Fantasy

Dark Walker and Hidden Dragon

Hawaiian Warrior and the Sea Dragon

Fire Goddess & Dream Dragon

Virginia Shapeshifter Romance

Lady Warrior and the Billionaire

Arizona Western Romance

Arizona Cowgirl and the Badman

Grand Teton Romance

Enchanted Cowgirl

California Romance

Cowgirl Witness & Her Bodyguard

Made in the USA
Columbia, SC
15 January 2024

30498588R00217